Restoring Grace

Katie Fforde lives in Gloucestershire with her husband and some of her three children. Her hobbies are ironing and housework but, unfortunately, she has almost no time for them as she feels it her duty to keep a close eye on the afternoon chat shows. *Restoring Grace* is her tenth novel.

Praise for *Katie Fforde*

'A witty and generous romance . . . Katie Fforde is on sparkling form . . . Jilly Cooper for the grown-ups' *Independent*

'Old-fashioned romance of the best sort . . . funny, comforting' *Elle*

'Delicious – gorgeous humour and the lightest of touches' *Sunday Times*

'A heart-warming tale of female friendship, fizzing with Fforde's distinctive brand of humour' *Sunday Express*

'Joanna Trollope crossed with Tom Sharpe' *Mail on Sunday*

Further praise for *Katie Fforde*

'The innocent charm of Katie Fforde . . . belies a perceptive wit' *Sunday Express*

'A spirited summer read that's got to be Fforde's best yet' *Woman & Home*

'Acute and funny observations of the social scene' *The Times*

'Can be scoffed at one sitting . . . Tasty' *Cosmopolitan*

'Perfect holiday reading. Pack it with the swimsuit and suntan lotion' *Irish Independent*

'Fforde is blessed with a lightness of touch, careful observation and a sure sense of the funny side of life' *Ideal Home*

'Gaily paced and told with trade-mark chattiness and smooth dialogue' *Herald*

'Top drawer romantic escapism' *You Magazine*

KATIE FFORDE

Restoring Grace

arrow books

Published by Arrow Books in 2005

3 5 7 9 10 8 6 4

First published in the United Kingdom in 2004 by Century

Arrow Books
The Random House Group Limited
20 Vauxhall Bridge Road, London, SW1V 2SA

Random House Australia (Pty) Limited
20 Alfred Street, Milsons Point, Sydney,
New South Wales 2061, Australia

Random House New Zealand Limited
18 Poland Road, Glenfield,
Auckland 10, New Zealand

Random House (Pty) Limited
Endulini, 5a Jubilee Road, Parktown 2193, South Africa

Random House UK Group Limited Reg. No. 954009

www.randomhouse.co.uk

A CIP catalogue record for this book
is available from the British Library

Papers used by Random House UK Limited
are natural, recyclable products made from wood grown in
sustainable forests. The manufacturing processes conform to
the environmental regulations of the country of origin

ISBN 0 09 944663 4

Typeset by Palimpsest Book Production Ltd,
Polmont, Stirlingshire
Printed and bound in Great Britain by
Bookmarque Ltd, Croydon, Surrey

To D.S.F., *without whom all this would have been perfectly possible, but not nearly as much fun.*

Acknowledgements

Since I've run out of my own life to write about, I've had to fall back on research and I can't do this on my own. The following people have helped in many and diverse ways. I thank you all, deeply and fondly, and take all responsibility for the inevitable errors.

To Desmond Fforde who told me to look in the *Yellow Pages*, where I found Clare Herbert, picture conservator, who not only gave of her own time and expertise so generously, but who introduced me to Richard Watkiss, who made picture conservation even more fascinating and romantic than ever. To Mel Denne, who let me come to her wine evenings. To Geoffrey Brett and Tim Marshfield who both sorted out my computer when I was beside myself. To Jonathan Early and Louise Ratcliffe who advised me on various things. To Sophie Hannah and Debbie Evans, who advised me on pregnancy. To Duncan Broady, from Bristol Preservations, who confirmed how expensive dry rot is.

As always to everyone at Random House, in no particular order – Kate Elton, Georgina Hawtrey-Woore, Charlotte Bush, Kate Watkins, Justine Taylor, the wonderful sales team and everyone else who has been such fun and so supportive and so well deserving of the brownies.

To kind, conscientious Richenda Todd for continuing to copy-edit my books with such tact and sensitivity, and to Sarah Molloy for being a tigress, huge fun and a dear friend.

Chapter One

It's a lovely house, thought Ellie. Perfect proportions. Probably Georgian, Queen Anne, something like that.

There were five sets of small-paned sash windows in the house and a couple of dormers in the roof. The front door had a fanlight above it and a neat path led up to the jasmine-covered porch. Looks just like a doll's house, she thought, and then laughed at herself: doll's houses were built to look like real houses, not the other way round.

The high walls which enclosed the garden were of fine grey stone and, peering through the gate, she saw carefully pruned fruit trees interspersed with something less formal, possibly roses, growing up them. A large patch of fragile mauve crocuses broke up the green of the lawn and there were clumps of daffodils lining the path. It was a perfect time, and although the details of the flowers weren't really important from Ellie's point of view, the house looked utterly charming, despite the icy wind.

She put down her bag and inspected the gate. It looked sturdy enough and she put her foot in the gap between the posts, trusting it would take her weight, and hauled herself up for a better view.

Propped against a stone pillar, one of a pair that framed the gate, she could see the house in its entirety. It was what estate agents would call a gem. It looked empty, but there could easily be someone observing her from behind one of the windows which glinted so symmetrically back at her. Hoping fervently that there wasn't anybody looking – it would be so embarrassing, humiliating even – she jumped down. Then she remembered, and wondered whether, in the circumstances, she ought to have jumped.

Sighing, she fished her camera out of her bag and climbed back up to her vantage point. She adjusted the shutter speed and aperture, and fiddled with the focus, wishing she had more up-to-date equipment which would do these things for her. It wasn't as if she was a photographer, after all. She just wanted a picture of the house.

She took several shots, got back down to ground level and put the camera back in her bulging raffia bag. Then she took out her nose-stud, which was tiny and silver but could still appear threatening to certain sorts of people, removed two of her earrings (leaving only a single pair), and tweaked at her clothes and hair. It was important to appear respectable; owners of Georgian rectories tended to be on the conventional side.

As she tucked a strand of scarlet hair under her bandanna, she realised she had no real idea of the effect of her fiddling: she could be making herself look like a tepee-dwelling New-Age traveller, or the doorstep equivalent of a second-hand car salesman. However, she put her shoulders back, picked up her bag and opened the gate. This was the brave bit.

The owners of such a house must be affluent, she thought, determined to be positive. She just hoped they didn't have dogs.

'Not that I don't like dogs,' Ellie muttered, in case

they did have dogs and they were listening. 'I just don't want to be bounced on, not just now.'

But no dogs came bounding up, plunging their friendly but forceful paws into her stomach (as had happened in the last place), and she made it to the front door unmuddied and able to breathe normally. Then she took a deep breath and pulled hard at the knob which protruded from the stone door jamb, hoping it was attached to something. It jangled encouragingly, but waiting for the door to be opened was always the worst part. She ran her tongue round the inside of her mouth so it wasn't dry, and her lips wouldn't get caught on her teeth when she stopped smiling. Then she relaxed her mouth so she could smile sincerely the moment the door was opened.

She didn't have to wait long. A young woman wearing several layers of jumpers, cardigans and scarves over her jeans, sheepskin boots and an anxious expression, answered it quite quickly. Almost certainly not the owner, Ellie decided, more likely the daughter of the house. Probably a bit older than she was herself – late twenties, early thirties – she had an ethereal quality, enhanced by her draperies, as if she had been out of the world for a while. Her hair was light brown, recently washed and looked difficult to manage. Ellie thought she probably needed some sort of product to get it under control, but this woman didn't look as if she'd ever heard of styling wax or mousse. Her eyes were a sludgy green, reminding Ellie of a semi-precious stone someone had brought her back from India once, and a few freckles peppered her nose and cheekbones. Ellie liked freckles; she had them herself, and seeing them on this woman gave her confidence.

'Hello,' she said. 'I wonder if I can interest you in a

3

picture of your house . . . your parents' house?'

The young woman shook her head, making her shiny hair even more disarrayed. 'No, it's my house.'

This was a bit of a surprise, but Ellie tried not to show it. 'Well, I've just taken some photographs of it, and if you're interested, I could paint a watercolour from them. See?' Ellie produced her album from the bag. In it were photographs of houses, and next to them, photographs of the pictures she had painted. Then, deftly, she produced an actual painting, mounted but not framed. 'And here's one I did earlier!' She laughed, trying to lighten the atmosphere.

The young woman took the sample painting. 'It's lovely. The trouble is, I couldn't possibly afford—'

'I'm very reasonable. I could do you one for about fifty pounds. Unframed.'

'That is reasonable,' the woman agreed. 'But the thing is . . .' She paused, sighing. 'On the other hand, a painting would be lovely if . . .'

Ellie shifted her weight to her other foot. It would be fatal to rush this woman when she might be about to decide to have a painting, but on the other hand, her need to go to the loo, which had been faint but bearable up to now, was becoming more pressing. Jumping off the gate hadn't helped.

'I'm sorry I'm being so slow to make up my mind,' the woman went on, still gazing at the sample painting with her head on one side.

'You're not. People take ages.' Ellie regarded the woman more thoroughly. 'I'm sorry, I know it's an awful cheek, but would you mind terribly if I used your loo? Normally, I'd just hang on but I'm pregnant.' She blushed as she said it. She'd told almost no one, not

4

even her parents, and it was shocking to hear the word out loud.

'Oh! God! How lovely! Of course! Do come in. The place is in a bit of a state, I'm afraid.' The young woman opened the door.

Ellie paused on the doorstep. 'I'm Ellie, Ellie Summers.' She took hold of the woman's hand. 'It seems sort of rude to use your loo when you don't know my name.'

The woman laughed and instantly became pretty. 'I'm Grace – Ravenglass or Soudley.' She wrinkled her forehead in thought. 'I'm recently divorced and I can't decide if I should go back to my own name.'

As they shook hands Ellie wondered what it was about this young woman that made her feel all right about mentioning her pregnancy. Possibly it was because she appeared slightly vulnerable too.

'Come in,' said Grace. 'I'll show you where to go.'

Grace hadn't opened her front door to anyone except builders for a while, but there was something about the girl – Ellie – which she warmed to. It might be to do with her easy smile, bright clothes and even brighter hair escaping from under her scarf, but more likely it was because she was fairly near her own age and female. She hadn't had any contact with someone like that for aeons.

She probably wouldn't buy a picture – she could never justify the expense – but she felt OK about ushering the girl down the passage to the downstairs cloakroom, freshly cleaned for tonight.

She hovered in the kitchen nearby so she could hear when Ellie had finished and she could show her out. She rearranged the bottles on the table, scouring her memory for where she might find something else to sit on. Her few chairs were already in place round the table, but there were a couple of empty spaces which would have to be filled by something. There were probably some more tea chests in the attic. They were a bit high, but comfortable enough if she put cushions on them. Luckily she had plenty of cushions. A fan heater was valiantly gusting into the icy air, as yet making no impression on the cold.

She heard the old-fashioned flush and was ready when Ellie emerged.

'It's a lovely house,' Ellie said eagerly. 'Even the cloak-room has got period features. I love that cistern! And the washbasin! Just like an old washstand, only china!' Realising she'd run off at the mouth again, she bit her lip. 'Oh, sorry. I hope I didn't sound too like an estate agent.'

'It is a lovely house,' agreed Grace, pleased with Ellie's enthusiasm. If everyone reacted like that she need feel less worried about opening her house to strangers. 'If rather on the cold side.' On an impulse she added, 'Would you like a bit of a tour? I could do with the practice.'

'What do you mean? You're not opening the house to the public, are you?'

Grace laughed. 'Not exactly, but I have got lots of people I don't know from Adam coming this evening, and I haven't had anyone here for ages.' She frowned. 'Of course, I won't let them out of the kitchen except to go to the loo. But I wouldn't mind showing you round.'

'Well, if it would be useful, I'd *love* a tour.' Ellie didn't hide her excitement. 'I love houses. I suppose that's why I paint them.'

I must be mad, thought Grace as she led the way

down the passage, inviting people in off the street to look round my freezing cold house. No, she consoled herself, Ellie had shown interest; she wanted to see the house. It wasn't as if there was anything in it that would make it a target for burglars, after all. As they passed the kitchen, she said, 'Shall I put the kettle on? Would you like a cup of tea or coffee afterwards? I was just about to have one myself when you rang the doorbell.'

'That would be great, if you're making one. When I was looking for a loo earlier, I couldn't find anything that wasn't a pub or an antique shop, and they were both closed. Nothing like a coffee shop for miles.'

'No, we are very far away from everything here. How did you find me?'

'I drove past the other day, when I was delivering a picture and got lost. When I saw your house, I knew it would make a lovely painting.'

'I'm sure it would—' Grace became diffident again, and Ellie hurried on.

'No pressure, honestly. I do understand about being broke.' She paused, embarrassed by her frankness. 'You may not be broke, of course . . .' She shivered, although she tried not to, inadvertently drawing attention to the cold.

'Broke about covers it. I'll put the kettle on.'

'Well, then, this is the hall, obviously.' Grace stood in the square, panelled space from which a stone, uncarpeted, staircase led to a small gallery. She had always liked the way the shadows of the window bars patterned the bare stone flags, revealing their unevenness.

'And here's the drawing room,' she went on, when Ellie had had time to admire the perfect proportions, the fine panelling and the arched space under the stairs which now contained boxes of wine and glasses.

The drawing room was also panelled, but was brighter, holding on to the last hour of February light. As well as the two sash windows which went down to the floor, there was a curved window, also to the floor, at the end, which had French doors opening on to the garden at the side of the house.

'I don't know if that's original,' said Grace, flapping a hand at it almost apologetically, 'but it's lovely in summer. We get the sun almost all day.'

'What period is it?' asked Ellie. 'I would have said Georgian, but I know nothing about architecture. I ought to really, seeing what I do for a living.'

'It's been messed around with so much it's hard to tell, but my aunt always told me it was William and Mary. There's an inscription saying sixteen ninety-seven over an archway in the garden, but I think there's been a house on this plot for ever.'

'That's so old!' Ellie wandered round the room, absorbing its lovely proportions, wondering about its emptiness. 'This is a beautiful fireplace,' she said (it being the nearest thing the room had to furniture), admiring the delicate stone carving.

'And it draws really well too,' said Grace. 'We used to light it all the time, when we were together.' She hadn't had the heart to light the fire and sit in the big room by herself all winter, so she'd spent most of the winter evenings in bed, snuggled up with the radio, a pile of books, two hot-water bottles and her goose-down duvet. Perhaps it was time for her to start lighting the fire again, to stop being such a recluse. 'Come on, I'll show you the dining room.'

They went back into the hall and down a passage on the opposite side of the hall to the one they had entered. Grace opened the door. 'This part of the house is much older than the front. Even when Edward – my husband – was here we didn't use this room much. It's too far away from the kitchen, really, and it's not as light as the drawing room. It gets forgotten, rather.'

'If you didn't have the drawing room you'd love it,' said Ellie, thinking of her own small home, where the front door opened straight into the living room, and the staircase ran up the back wall to three, tiny bedrooms.

Grace blushed apologetically. 'Of course. I'm just so spoilt.' By way of apology she said, 'Those curtains have been up for ever – I don't dare draw them in case they fall apart. I could never afford new ones. The curtains in the drawing room are newer, just from my aunt's time.'

After an inspection of the study, a large, panelled room, they moved upstairs. After a more cursory tour of that, Ellie said, as they came back downstairs, 'I don't want to be rude, but I can't help noticing that you haven't very much furniture. You weren't burgled or anything, were you?'

The idea was horrifying. 'Oh no, it wasn't stolen! It went of its own accord.'

'What?'

Grace chuckled, realising how that must have sounded. 'Not by itself, of course. It was accompanied by an adult. It was my husband's.'

'Oh.'

Grace, aware of the kettle on the gas, said, 'Let's go back to the kitchen before the kettle boils dry. And it should be a bit warmer in there now.'

Together they went into the large, rather bleak room. It had a high ceiling and more stone flags on the floor.

'What this room needs,' said Ellie, 'is lots of copper pots and pans, a roasting spit, sugar grinders, stuff like that.'

Grace said, 'I'd rather have an Aga.'

Ellie giggled. 'I suppose I would, too.'

'Now, is it tea or coffee?' asked Grace, but she'd lost Ellie's attention. She was standing in front of the huge, built-in dresser, on which a few unmatched but ancient-looking plates tried valiantly to fill the space.

'That's wonderful! It would take whole dinner services at a time! I suppose your husband couldn't take that.'

'Oh no. He was very scrupulous.' Suddenly it seemed important to Grace that Ellie shouldn't think badly of Edward – she still loved him, after all. 'He didn't take anything that wasn't his, and he left me the bed and the duvet, which were his, too, really. Do sit down. So is it tea, or coffee?' Grace's hand hovered between a jar of coffee and a packet of tea bags, wishing she hadn't mentioned the duvet. It was so personal.

'I'm off coffee at the moment,' said Ellie. 'But tea would be great.' She pulled out a chair. 'I don't usually get hospitality before I do the picture, although I sometimes do when I deliver.'

Grace laughed. 'I'm not sure if you'd quite describe this as hospitality, although it's the nearest thing I've been to it in a while.' There was something very cheering about having Ellie sitting at her kitchen table. She was so up front and, if she was a little outspoken, she wasn't critical.

Now Ellie said, 'I know it's cold, but why are those bottles wearing socks?'

'It's to hide the labels,' Grace explained, laughing again. 'I'm having a wine tasting tonight. The first one in my own house, although I've done a couple of others.'

'Oh? Is it like an exam? Do people have to guess which wine is which?'

'Oh no, nothing like that. Not at this sort of wine tasting. This is much more low key and is more about finding out what people like. We're testing supermarket wine basically, seeing which one we like best. I'll write up the results for a few local papers I've got contracts with.' She frowned. 'I do it by hand and then take it into a place in town to get it typed. It's silly really, they won't pay me much and I spend most of it on secretarial services. But it's something and it's good publicity. And it means I can quote it if another paper or magazine wants a wine correspondent.'

'Imagine being a wine correspondent. It sounds very high-powered. I don't know a thing about wine.'

'You don't have to unless it's your job. You just have to know if you like it. You could stay for the wine tasting, if you like.'

Grace hadn't known she was going to say that, but once she had, she realised it was because she quite wanted the moral support of someone she could relate to. She'd lost touch with a lot of her girlfriends when she got married and moved away from home, and then she and Edward had mostly socialised with his contemporaries. That was the trouble with living in a large house away from other houses: it was hard to get to know your neighbours, especially if you were single. Meeting Ellie reminded her of how much she missed female companionship.

'That's really kind of you,' said Ellie, 'but I'm not

11

drinking at the moment. Because of being pregnant.'
Then, to Grace's horror and surprise, Ellie began to cry.
'Oh God, I'm so sorry. It's my hormones or something.
It's to do with telling – people.'

'Have you told many people? Has it happened every
time?' Grace instantly stopped feeling sorry for herself
and wished she wasn't too shy to put her arms round
Ellie.

Ellie sniffed, looked in her bag for a tissue, and
produced a bit of kitchen towel which had obviously
been used as a paint rag. 'No. Hardly anyone. In fact,
only my boyfriend, and now you.'

'Oh.' Grace felt tremendously flattered. 'Well, it's
often easier to tell people things when you're unlikely
to see them again. Like on trains.'

Ellie sniffed again and nodded.

'So you haven't told your parents, then?'

Ellie shook her head. 'It would be all right if I could
say Rick and me were going to get married. But we're
not.'

'I don't recommend marriage myself, having just got
divorced. You could just live together,' Grace suggested.

'We could, only Rick doesn't want a baby. He says
we're fine as we are, and he's right. Only I'm pregnant.
He thinks . . .' She sniffed some more. 'He thinks I
should – God, I can't even say it!'

'No, don't. You don't have to. I know what you mean.
He thinks you shouldn't go on being pregnant.' Grace
got up and found a box of tissues and put it in front of
Ellie. 'I'll make the tea.'

'So, why did you get divorced?' asked Ellie a couple
of minutes later, having taken a heartening sip. 'Did he
find someone else, or did you?' Realising she'd let her

curiosity get the better of her again, she bit her lip. 'Sorry! You don't have to tell me. It's none of my business. I'm terribly nosy.'

'Well, on the understanding we're unlikely to see each other again . . .' Grace frowned, suddenly sad at the thought that this cheerful-even-when-weeping person would soon go out of her life for ever. '. . . I may as well tell you.'

'Why did you marry him? Not because of his furniture, presumably.'

Grace chuckled. 'I didn't know about his furniture – although he had some wonderful antiques – when I fell in love with him.'

'So why did you?'

'He was – is – terribly attractive. He's older than me and I was very young when I met him. He was so witty and cultured, and for some reason he turned his attention to me. It was like the sun was shining on me alone. I couldn't resist him.'

'So how old is he now?'

'Forty-six. I'm thirty-one.'

'It is quite a large gap,' said Ellie cautiously.

'Yes, but I don't think that was the problem. Not really.'

'What was, then?'

Grace sighed. She had thought about it all so much she was almost numb to the pain. 'Well, the main thing was that I wanted a baby and he didn't. He's got children by his first wife. But really, I wasn't up to his speed intellectually. He found someone else who was more on his level. I can't blame him, actually.'

'That's generous of you! Don't you want to scratch her eyes out? I would.'

Grace shook her head. 'Not really. And in a way it

13

was sort of a relief when he went because the thing I had been dreading had actually happened. So I didn't need to dread it any more, and could just start to get over it. I'm not saying I wasn't devastated' – she paused to wonder how long the devastation could possibly last – 'but I always knew I couldn't keep him interested. I never believed he truly loved me – or if he did, that he would go on loving me. And I was right there,' she added ruefully. 'Although he has been very kind.'

She looked at Ellie, so calm and together in spite of being pregnant by a man who didn't want it. 'Why am I telling you all this?'

'We're on a virtual train,' Ellie reminded her. 'We're never going to see each other again. Unless you can afford a painting after all.' She paused. 'Did he give you the house?'

'Oh no. I inherited it from my aunt.'

'So did he give you money when he left?'

'Oh yes, he gave me a very generous settlement, but although I've got enough left to keep me going for a few months, I spent most of it.'

'I can't exactly see what on, from here,' Ellie smiled.

'Well, no,' Grace laughed, 'but if you went into the attic you would see that every joist and beam is new, and that every dodgy tile has been replaced by a reclaimed stone one. It cost a fortune. I bought a car with what was left after the roof.'

'That's awful. And he's left you with hardly any furniture at all?'

'Well, only what I inherited.'

Ellie was confused. 'But didn't your aunt have any furniture, either? It seems weird!'

'Oh yes, but it went to my older brother and sister.

14

They got the furniture, I got the house, because she was my godmother as well as my aunt. They were livid.'

'Why?' Ellie was staggered.

'They felt the house should have been sold and the money divided between us. But it just so happened that Edward and I were newly engaged when she died, so living here made perfect sense. Besides, it's what my aunt wanted, obviously, or she'd have made her will differently.'

'So from his – your ex-husband's – point of view, marrying a woman who had a really great house was a good idea, if he had lots of lovely antiques that needed a home.'

She shook her head. 'No. He didn't marry me for my house, I'm quite sure of it. He fell in love with me in a sort of obsessive way. When the obsession faded he realised we didn't really have that much in common, and then of course he fell in love with someone else.'

'So how long were you together?'

'We married when I was only twenty-two, and had five very happy – ecstatic really – years, one less happy, and one downright unhappy. It's taken nearly two years to get divorced.'

'He sounds a complete bastard.'

'He wasn't, really he wasn't. He was a sort of serial monogamist, and probably incapable of staying faithful to anyone for more than a couple of years, but not a bastard. He was very fair to me.'

Ellie shrugged. 'I think it's very grown up of you to feel like that.'

'I'm not saying he didn't make me suffer, but he didn't do it on purpose. And the baby thing is understandable. After all, he has got two perfectly good children already.

15

When he realised how I felt, particularly as I'm fairly sure he had someone else in mind, we decided to call it a day.'

'It is a bit ironic,' said Ellie, draining her mug. 'Here are you, wanting a baby, and here's me, pregnant, not wanting one.'

'I thought you did want one? I thought you said you couldn't – do anything about it.'

'That's slightly different. I didn't want a baby before I got pregnant. But now I am pregnant, I couldn't not have it.'

'And you don't think your parents will be supportive?'

'Well, yes, they will. But they'll tell me off terribly for not being more careful.' She gave a wry smile. 'I was on the pill, but I threw up. It must have been just at the wrong moment.'

'Or the right moment. From the baby's point of view.'

'It's a pity we're not the sort of people who could just swap lives. I could give you my baby and carry on, and you could have my baby and not worry about having to find someone else to give you one. But we couldn't, could we.' This was a statement, not a question.

'Nothing's ever that straightforward. Would you like another cup of tea?'

'No, thank you, but another trip to the loo would be very welcome.'

Grace stayed in the kitchen while Ellie visited the cloakroom again, then went with her to her car and waved until she was out of sight. Back in the house, it suddenly felt larger, lonelier, and possibly even a bit colder, than it had done before.

'I shall be looking forward to feeling lonely when the

house has been full of strangers for an evening,' she murmured, and turned her mind to finding seats for the wine tasting, and to giving her latest article a final polish. 'I must get a computer, or even a typewriter,' she went on. 'I must get back into the real world.'

Chapter Two

As Ellie drove away from the house beneath an evening sun colouring the sky, she thought about Grace and her story. It was kind of bizarre, her being alone in that big, freezing, empty house, her marriage over, preparing to have strangers in to taste wine.

On the other hand, her own existence was far from perfect: she and Rick, living together in a tiny cottage in Bath, less happily day by day.

She bit her lip to ward off the sadness she felt when she remembered how happy they had been when they first moved in together. It had been such fun finding the house to rent, waiting to hear if they'd got it, and then making it a home.

Of course, it had been Ellie who'd done most of it. Rick was an installation artist. He rented a corner of someone else's studio and spent most of his waking hours there. Not that there were so many of those, thought Ellie, irritated. Not getting up until midday was fine when you were a student, but when you were a working person, you had to put the hours in.

It was easier for Rick. He didn't have a day job, he devoted all his time to his art, and, at first, Ellie had thought this was perfectly right and proper. He'd been two years ahead of her at university, doing Fine Art, and had got a first. Of course his art was more important than hers.

Ellie, two years behind, had done Creative Art and had got a perfectly respectable two-one, but although she loved painting and drawing and had actually sold several paintings even before she finished the course, she knew she wasn't an artist like Rick was.

And so she'd been happy to work in a café during the day and a bar in the evenings, so he could concentrate on developing what everyone acknowledged was a special talent.

But now, eighteen months after moving in together, she'd started to resent his tunnel vision even before she got pregnant and he threw such a tantrum.

'Now breathe, Ellie,' she instructed herself as she got into the town and began negotiating her little car down the narrow lanes towards their cottage. 'Don't get in a state all over again. It was bad enough at the time, it's not good for the baby, and you can't afford any new plates.'

At the time she had wept bitterly: at his attitude, because she was so tired, because she felt more premenstrual than she had ever felt before she was pregnant, but mostly because it was the plate she had made at college that she had broken. She had loved that plate. It was oval, yellow and had clay fishes and other sea creatures stuck to it. It had a mate, but this one had been her favourite, the best one, and she had broken it.

'Be a grown-up, Ellie,' she said aloud now, putting her key into the lock, mentally preparing herself for the mess which would await her. 'Wash up or ship out!'

She paused to pick up the pile of letters on the mat, reflecting that in some ways she was in fact more grown up than Grace, in spite of her having been through a divorce. That's what getting pregnant by a boy you no longer love does for you: gives you a crash course in maturity.

'Hi, babes,' she called up the stairs as she stepped into the living room and put down her bag.

'In the bath!' Rick called back, and she went upstairs.

His long, elegant limbs could not be contained in the narrowness of the tub and he had draped them over the edges. Water threatened to spill every time he moved. A large sponge sat on his stomach, and patches of bubbles still lingered in the water. Part of Ellie thought how gorgeous he was, and remembered how passionate and excited he was about everything when they'd first met. The other part was aware that he would have used every drop of hot water but wouldn't have switched on the immersion heater, so that if she wanted a bath, she'd have to wait at least an hour. And he'd used the last of her lavender oil.

'Good day?' she asked, noticing the towel she had washed and dried only the day before lying on the floor, already in a puddle.

'Crap day. Why don't you get in with me? Make me feel better?'

Ellie shook her head. She didn't want water all over the floor, she didn't want to have sex when she had to work later, and she needed to pee again.

'Don't be too long, sweets. I need the loo.'

'Don't mind me,' said Rick.

Ellie shook her head. 'I'll hang on. Did you do anything for tea?'

'No time. When I finished at the studio I got straight in the bath. Needed to sort my head out.'

Ellie smiled, hoping he wouldn't spot that it was false, picked up the towel and draped it over the washbasin, and left the room. His fabulous body and irresistible smile had lost their charm somewhat these days.

Back in the kitchen, a small, often mildewed extension behind the living room, she filled the kettle so she could deal with the dishes. Considering he spent most of his time at the studio, and that he and his mate always went to the pub for lunch, it was amazing how much washing up he managed to generate.

He'd obviously had a fry-up, including fried bread and baked beans, for breakfast, and added a lot of tomato ketchup. In spite of presumably having his routine pie and chips and several pints at lunchtime, he'd had time and appetite to grab a handful of Bombay Mix and some crisps. The Bombay Mix packet had fallen over and tipped half of its contents on to the floor. Apart from the fact that the smell of curry sickened Ellie, she was annoyed. There wasn't much money for luxuries, so she didn't like sweeping them up off the floor.

While she washed mugs and scraped ketchup and egg yolk off the plate with her nail, and her boyfriend luxuriated in hot water, Ellie thought she could do with a little of the latter herself. What would it be like to be a pampered mistress, fêted and adored, every whim indulged? Even having a boyfriend she didn't actually live with would be better than this: only herself to clean up after; no disgusting socks and boxer shorts to wash.

However, that would be slightly hard to arrange now that she was pregnant – soon she'd be too fat to attract anyone. She stopped her scrubbing for a moment. If time was limited, perhaps she should just go for a fling, a quick, fabulous affaire, before her pregnancy showed?

After all, it was often the beginning of a relationship that was most fun. Why not just have the beginning, the wonderful, exhilarating passionate sex, and then call it quits?

The idea lifted her spirits quite a lot and she turned her thoughts to Grace. How was she doing with her wine tasting? By the time she'd finished the washing up, she'd decided she would do the painting of her house anyway, and give it to Grace as a present. She'd seemed so forlorn that Ellie wanted to do something to cheer her up.

'So,' said Rick, when, clean and nearly dry, he presented himself downstairs and sat on the sofa. 'How did you get on? Flog any daubs of mansions to the bloated plutocrats?'

Ellie shook her head. Grace had not been a bloated plutocrat, even if some of her ancestors had been. 'No, but I took some photos of a really lovely house.'

'Get a commission?'

'No. The owner couldn't afford it.'

'I think it's a waste of time, Ellie, spending all that petrol money trying to sell your paintings. You'd be better off with a job.'

She realised that this was Rick 'taking an interest', and she wished he wouldn't bother. 'I have two jobs already, Rick, and they both involve standing. I'm not supposed to stand too much now I'm pregnant.'

Rick scowled and it made him even more attractive. 'I thought we'd agreed you were going to do something about that.'

Ellie bit her lip. She didn't have the energy for a row, but how could he bring this all up again? All Rick's sensitivity seemed to go into his art; there wasn't any

22

left for his relationship. 'You agreed. I didn't,' she said.

'We talked about it and agreed it was the sensible thing to do.'

Don't cry, Ellie, just hang on and keep calm, she ordered herself. 'I agree it's sensible, I'm just not going to do it.'

'Susie had one. She was fine.'

'I'm sure she was. I'm happy for her, but I'm not doing it.'

'Sentimental fucking bitch,' he said without rancour.

Rancour or not, Ellie winced. He didn't mean to hurt her feelings, but he did it, all the same.

'Are you going to cook me some tea, then?'

'No. I'm going to work.' She would be early, but she didn't care. At least at work she was paid to clean up and people occasionally said 'thank you'.

After Ellie had gone, Grace had continued with her preparations for the wine tasting. It was a new project: her attempt to do something which would eventually be lucrative and get her back in contact with people again.

She was quite successful with her articles – a couple of the local papers had taken the ones she'd done so far and were keen for more – but she was mainly writing about special wine, which most people couldn't afford. The wine-tasting project was an effort to get ordinary people involved in tasting the wine that most people drank. It should be fun. She just hoped her social skills hadn't completely atrophied. It would be the first time she'd entertained since Edward left, and she'd never done it before she was married.

She fetched the glasses from under the stairs and took

them out of the boxes, checking for smears. Then, dissatisfied with their clarity, she put the kettle on and held each one in the steam before polishing it with a cloth.

Each place had six glasses placed over a sheet marked with numbered circles, so people knew which glass applied to which numbered bottle. She had lovingly drawn round the bottom of six glasses and photocopied them at the post office in the nearest town. While the man behind the counter had helped her when the machine broke down, she had discovered he was a wine buff; he and his wife were coming tonight.

Beneath the glasses was a score sheet, with numbers and letters down the side and columns for comments on the smell and taste of each wine. There were also places for scores. This sheet she'd made up from memory of a wine tasting she'd gone to when she still worked for the wine importers.

At the bottom of the sheet was a list of the wines, their origins, and their prices. It always made Grace smile when she remembered how people so often guessed wrong which was the most expensive and which the cheapest; they were always so indignant about it.

She was unnaturally nervous. It was, after all, only a very informal wine tasting – it was even free. She hoped people might make a contribution for the wine, but this was by way of an experiment. Would people drive out to the country and go into someone's house to taste supermarket plonk?

Her previous experience in the village hall for the WI had been hugely popular and enjoyable. Everyone had really got into the spirit of it, and although Grace had thought she might actually vomit from nerves, once she'd got into describing the wines, she'd discovered she liked sharing her interest with others. And meeting Ellie this afternoon made her feel a bit better about being social – she'd managed fine with her.

When the telephone rang, she assumed it was someone ringing up to cancel – probably on behalf of everyone – leaving her to drink all the wine and eat all the nibbles by herself. Unsure whether, in her current state, this was what she wanted or not, she picked up the telephone gingerly.

It was her sister. 'Hi, Grace, how are you?'

'Oh, hi, Allegra. Nice to hear from you.' In some ways it was nice, it would pass some time before her guests arrived and stop her getting so nervous she started on the wine and ended up a drunken wreck before anyone arrived.

'I was wondering if you'd thought any more about selling the house.'

Typical Allegra, straight to the point. 'Well, obviously I've thought about it, since you suggested it, but I'm certainly not doing it.'

'It just doesn't make sense, you living there on your own, now Edward's left.' Allegra was obviously convinced by the water-dripping-on-stone theory: if you went on at someone long enough, eventually they would agree, being unable to resist for ever.

'Edward left ages ago. Why should I sell now?'

'Because now you've had the roof fixed you'd get a proper price for it.'

If Allegra wasn't pulling her punches, then neither would Grace. 'You mean you'd get a larger chunk.'

'Don't be silly!' Allegra could be very sharp. 'Of

course the money you spent on the roof would be taken off before the money was divided. It was your divorce settlement, after all. But you know perfectly well it was very unfair of Aunt Lavinia to leave the house to you and not to all of us.'

'She left you and Nicholas the furniture! That was worth quite a bit.' Grace felt both bored and exasperated. It was not the first time they had had this conversation and she knew it wouldn't be the last.

'Nothing like the value of the house.'

'Well, she was my godmother.'

'Really, Grace, I wish you'd stop being so childish and stubborn about this! You must see that the house is far too large for you to live in. Aunt Lavinia never paid much attention to you when you were a child, so why did she leave you her house when she died? Obviously she was starting to go gaga. And if she wasn't in her right mind, it's only fair that you should do the decent thing and share the house.'

'Do say if you want to come and live here with me,' said Grace crossly, 'but I thought you were quite happy in Farnham with David and the boys.'

'Oh, don't be ridiculous!'

'Well, perhaps she felt guilty about never doing anything for me as a child. Anyway, gaga or not, she did leave it to me. And why bring it all up again now? I've had the house for nine years.'

'Yes, but when you had Edward it made a little more sense. And how can you live in a house without any furniture in it?'

'I've got a bit.' She looked round at the kitchen table, which she had bought from a junk shop in the local town. 'Tea chests are very versatile, and if my wine project takes off, I'll get lots of nice wooden crates. There was a girl I used to work with who built a whole kitchen out of wine crates.'

A sigh of irritation gusted down the telephone. 'Anyway, Nicholas asked me to ring you—'

'He could have rung me himself.' In spite of her indignation, Grace was quite glad that her brother had not done so; he was even more bossy than Allegra.

'He's very busy. He's got a very high-powered new job. Offices in Canary Wharf.'

'That sounds good,' Grace snapped. 'His ego will fit in nicely among the other skyscrapers.'

Accustomed to a much milder younger sister, Allegra was shocked. 'Grace! You never used to be so rude when you were a child! A complete idiot, but not rude.'

'No, well, I've grown up, I suppose. Divorce does that to you.'

There was a silence. Grace could tell that Allegra was debating whether she should say that she always knew her younger sister's marriage was doomed to failure, or whether she could keep her mouth shut on the subject. Edward's antique furniture had meant she and Nicholas could strip the house of everything that wasn't nailed down.

'I'm sorry, Grace, I suppose I am being a bit tactless, but I really do think it would be far better for you to sell the house. It must be worth a fortune.'

'Not necessarily. The property boom is over and I might well have death-watch beetle.'

'You haven't, have you?' Allegra sounded seriously alarmed. 'You've just had the roof redone.'

'There's lots more to the house than the roof,' said Grace, disconcertingly pleased at having rattled Allegra.

'Well, have you had it checked out?'

Death-watch beetle was obviously not to be made light of. 'Not yet.'

'You must! I insist on it. In fact, I'll do more than that, I'll send my friend's son along to do it.'

Grace held the telephone away from her ear. Her sister was getting very shrill.

'. . . he'll be very reasonable. In fact, I'll pay for it myself, then you can't possibly find any excuses for not having it done!'

'Er, no,' said Grace, acknowledging the truth of this. She would have found excuses, the most pressing one being that if the house were being slowly eaten by beetles she couldn't afford to do anything about it. Also, as long as there weren't too many beetles, the house would probably last as long as she would. It was very large.

'Let me know when would be convenient.' With Grace's acquiescence, Allegra became calmer.

'I'm here almost all the time, Legs.'

'I do wish you wouldn't call me that!'

'Sorry.'

Allegra sighed. 'No, well, it's a habit, I suppose. Bloody Nicholas, starting it. But really, Grace, I am a bit worried about you. You really should get out more.'

'But not now, I've got a lot of strange people coming for wine tasting in a minute, and I haven't put the bread out.'

Grace had found the telephone call from her sister strangely bracing. It reinforced all her thoughts and feelings about the house. She was determined not to sell it. She loved it; it was hers. Her brother and sister could go on envying her good fortune. After all, the furniture they had taken had been very valuable. They were both settled in successful careers, and had partners – a wealthy husband in Allegra's case, and a very glamorous, rather racy female investment banker in Nicholas's. And although investment banking wasn't the career it once had been, as a couple they were very well off.

On the other hand, the upkeep of such a house, even if she lived very simply, was a constant worry. At least, having made certain of the roof, she was fairly confident it wouldn't need anything spending on it for a while. There was the damp in the older part, at the back, but almost all old houses were damp somewhere or other, and as she didn't use the back, that wasn't a problem.

But in spite of her optimism about the house standing longer than she would, and her relaxed attitude to damp, she was aware that if the house wasn't kept warm, wasn't properly lived in, it would deteriorate. She either needed a way of earning a living which was sufficiently well paid that she could keep the house in good repair, or – and this was her present course of action – she could use the house itself to provide an income. Hence the wine tasting which, to her horror, she noticed was due to start in less than an hour.

'Oh God! Now I've got to disguise myself as someone who looks like she knows what the hell they're talking about!'

She *did* know what the hell she was talking about; she was just worried no one would believe her.

As she rushed upstairs to change, she realised how much depended on her making a success of the evening. It wasn't just the money, although that was important, it was that it would prove she needed to live in

Luckenham House, that it had value beyond what the bricks and mortar were worth, and beyond its beauty. Otherwise, the house, which was all she had in the world, would just be a very lovely, very uncomfortable place to live.

As she dug out her ancient make-up bag, she reflected that although she'd only visited her Aunt Lavinia once, when she was about seventeen, her aunt, who was a great-aunt really, must have sensed how Grace had fallen in love with the place. Her parents had commented on the cost of upkeep, and how difficult it was to get help in the house, but Grace had just said, unreservedly, that it was wonderful.

Looking at her make-up, most of which she'd bought before she was married, or even courting, she decided not to bother with foundation, and just breathed heavily on the mascara and hoped there was some left. As she scrubbed away with the dried-up wand she realised that was why she'd been left the house, and not the furniture. She'd seen what there was beyond the obvious.

To her enormous relief, the kindly couple from the shop-cum-post office were the first to arrive.

'I can't tell you how curious I've been to come to this house!' said Mrs Rose. 'My aunt used to clean here when I was a little girl and she used to tell me about all the wonderful things there were.'

Grace laughed. 'I'm afraid the wonderful things have all gone, but the house is still the same.'

'I'd love a look round sometime!'

It crossed Grace's mind that Mrs Rose might very well tell everyone what the inside of the house was like, but she decided she didn't mind. After all, honest poverty was nothing to be ashamed of and if the local burglars got to hear she had no furniture, it would make her safer.

'Well, I'd be happy to give you a tour afterwards. Not that there's much to see, really.'

'Thanks, pet, I'll look forward to it.'

As they were the first there, and she felt warm towards them, she steered Mr and Mrs Rose to the most comfortable chairs. The latecomers could have the tea chests.

The next couple, the Cavendishes, used to live in London. They were young, well dressed and overtly rich, but Grace warmed to them anyway. They seemed fun.

'Hi! I'm Sara and this is Will,' said Sara. She was dressed in a scarlet suit and draped with the most heavenly black scarf which probably cost as much as Grace's car. 'Will, darling, this is Grace, we chatted over the phone. Will's always spending a fortune on wine and I thought it was time I found out a bit about it. Oh, I know you!' she said to the Roses, who were sitting rather stiffly on their chairs, wondering if they'd made a mistake. 'You run the post office!' Sara put her hand out so Mr Rose had to take it. 'I love your little shop! It's like a treasure box! You never know what you're going to find in it!'

Mr Rose visibly softened, responding with satisfaction to Sara's compliments about his pride and joy, and Grace was pleased to know that they used the local shop. They could easily have been the sort of people who bought everything off the Internet from the huge hypermarket miles away.

'Can I sit on a tea chest?' asked Sara. 'Such fun!'

'You might ladder your tights!' said Grace, suddenly noticing the sheerness of Sara's leg wear.

'Oh, don't worry about that,' cried Sara.

'My wife has no idea of economy,' said Will.

Sara grinned. 'You spend your money on wine and fast cars, and I spend mine on clothes. Who else is coming?'

Grace had a list which she now pulled out of her trouser pocket. 'Um . . . one more couple. The' – she checked her list – 'Hamilton-Laceys. And there's someone called Margaret Jeffreys and a friend of the wine-shop owner, a Mr Cormack.'

'First name?' asked Sara.

'Flynn,' said Grace.

'Oh, Irish! How heavenly! I love Irishmen, they're always so good at flirting!'

Mr and Mrs Rose appeared a little uncomfortable and, as they had the chairs, Grace realised it was not the seating arrangements that were making them edgy.

Will frowned affectionately at his wife. 'Darling, do pipe down a bit. Wait until you've got the wine as an excuse for being outrageous.'

Sara shrugged apologetically. 'Sorree! What did he sound like on the phone?' she asked Grace in a stage whisper.

'I didn't speak to him. He came via the man at the wine merchants, in town.' In fact, Grace suspected him of being sent by the wine merchant to check if she knew her stuff. Which was fair enough, she supposed, because if she proved herself, he might send wine for her to taste.

The doorbell rang and Grace let in the other couple, who looked rather anxiously about them. 'Oh. Shabby chic,' said the wife, 'how lovely.' She was obviously wondering what on earth she was letting herself in for.

'Come into the kitchen,' said Grace, realising she'd forgotten their names again and couldn't check her list without seeming rude. Pointing them in the right direction, she took the coats the couple had rashly removed and draped them over the banisters.

'The kitchen? Oh.' The wife glanced longingly at the front door, wondering if it was too late to make a run for it.

The couple took their places and made token attempts at smiling. Sara Cavendish started chatting in a friendly way, and Grace, filling a jug with water, couldn't hear everything, but she did pick up on the words 'not quite what we expected from a wine tasting' issuing from the wife. When she put the jug on the table, she caught the woman giving her husband a very reproachful glance.

There were still two more people to come. Grace had put out slices of bread and glasses for water as well as the wine bottles, and she noticed people picking at the bread to fill the hiatus. If she'd been Allegra she would have made them play some sort of game, or asked leading questions about what people did, but as her guests didn't appear to have that much in common, Grace was at a loss. Particularly as the latest arrivals were refusing to join in the chat between the Cavendishes and the Roses.

'Well, I wonder if we should begin?' Grace ventured, hoping a few sips of wine would lighten the atmosphere. 'It's after eight.'

But that moment, to her enormous relief, the door bell jangled. Margaret Jeffreys and Flynn Cormack arrived together.

'Sorry we're late,' said Margaret to Grace as she held the door open. 'We got lost. Flynn kindly offered me a lift because I said I knew the way, and then I turned left at the crossroads instead of right, I'm so dyslexic. It's taken us hours!'

Grace smiled. Margaret and Sara Cavendish were obviously twins separated at birth, and would both take the edge off everyone's natural shyness. Flynn Cormack might well have been Irish, but he certainly didn't exude the bonhomie Sara was obviously expecting. In fact, he seemed distinctly irritable. He and the couple with the double-barrelled name that Grace still couldn't remember would get on fine.

Margaret talked her way into the kitchen and when she got there looked brightly around the table. She waved hello as she realised she knew Sara and Will, and faintly recognised Mr and Mrs Rose.

Grace relaxed. If they felt comfortable with each other, they wouldn't feel inhibited about expressing their feelings. In her opinion, lots of people took wine far too seriously. Her ex-husband certainly did.

'Well,' she began. 'As you know, because it said on the advertisement, we're here to discuss Cabernet Sauvignon bought from a supermarket.'

'We never buy wine from supermarkets,' said Mrs Double-Barrelled. 'We only ever buy from reputable wine merchants. Or from *caves* when we're in France.'

'If supermarkets didn't sell wine,' said Mr Rose, 'there'd be more call for it in a village shop.'

'Shut up, dear,' said Mrs Rose. 'You know you haven't got a licence.'

'Would it be worth your while getting one?' asked Sara. 'We'd buy wine from you if it was drinkable.'

'I think we should press on,' said Grace, aware that if she let her class get out of control before they'd even taken the first sip, she'd have no hope later on. She poured a small amount of the first wine into her glass. 'If you circulate the bottle, and each pour yourselves a little, I'll give you a bit of spiel about this grape. It's found in red Bordeaux wines, which we tend to call claret in England. It has a distinctive flavour, and once you've learnt to recognise it, and know you like it, you'll know which wine to pick when you're at the sup— wine shop,' she added for the benefit of the spy, who so far had said not a word.

'Right,' she went on, still in schoolmistress mode, once the bottle had done the rounds. 'Take a good hard sniff and tell me what you think.'

The spy caught her eye and regarded her with a strange, intent look. Grace wondered if her ancient make-up had done something funny to her face.

Eventually, it was over. Almost everyone had gone home except the spy – Grace was too tired to remember names – and Margaret Jeffreys. Margaret and Mrs Rose had had a guided tour of the drawing room and Margaret was still in there, having a cigarette.

The spy was helping Grace clear the table. 'Are you going to wash these up now?' He indicated the glasses which now seemed enough for a reasonable sized party.

'Not tonight, no,' said Grace. 'It's much better when it's sunny, don't you think? Washing up?'

'I have a dishwasher.'

Grace shrugged. How could you explain washing up to a man with a dishwasher?

'But if you have to do them by hand, I could help

you,' he offered. 'I could dry, anyway. It would be quicker with two.'

Grace shook her head. 'No hot water,' she explained with a smile, glad to have a proper reason for refusing his offer, when really the reason she didn't want him to help was that she found his presence in her kitchen, where she was used to being alone, oddly unsettling. 'I forgot to put the immersion on. I'll do it in the morning, and if I rinse in really hot water, I won't need to dry them.'

'Surely a house this size needs a better way of heating hot water than an immersion heater. It must be so expensive, for one thing.'

'Not really. There's only me.'

He frowned. 'That's strange, too.'

She bristled, waiting for the lecture about it being ridiculous her living in such a great big house etc. Although a second later she realised that was unfair. This man whose name she had forgotten was unlikely to lecture her like her sister did. 'What's strange? The fact that I live in this house all on my own?'

'No. The fact that you're single. You are single?'

Grace hovered between telling him it was none of his business and just answering the question. She decided a simple 'yes' would be quicker. Besides, she found being confrontational difficult. She nodded. 'Yes. But I like it that way.'

He nodded, as if in understanding, but then said, 'I was wondering if you might like to come out to dinner sometime.'

Grace, her head still a kaleidoscope of names, wines and the state of the hot water, stopped. 'Why would I want to do that?' she asked. Surely she'd just explained that she liked being on her own?

For the first time the spy smiled, and Grace wished she could remember his name. She'd be all right when she could refer to her list, but at the moment she was at a complete loss. Not knowing it added to the sense of confusion his presence gave her.

'Because you might get hungry, perhaps?'

Grace shook her head, on certain ground at last. Since her divorce, she hardly ever got hungry. And the thought of going out to dinner with a man whose name she couldn't remember was not appealing.

'I don't think so.' Then, aware she might have sounded abrupt, she added, 'But thank you very much for the invitation.'

The spy regarded her speculatively. He was about to say something else when Margaret appeared.

'Shall we go, darling? I've finished my fag. Lovely house,' she said to Grace.

Grace smiled. Margaret probably got hungry a lot. She could go out to dinner with the mysterious Irishman.

Chapter Three

Ellie got home at half past midnight. She was supposed to work until three, but she'd asked to go early. She hadn't had to say why she was so exhausted; she'd just said she felt sick. Which she did.

Rick was out, probably still at the pub, which was famous for its lock-ins. His dirty dishes filled the sink, accompanied by cold, greasy water. The water was Rick's idea of help, and it did help in that the food wasn't welded quite so solidly on to the plate, but Ellie found putting her hand through the layer of orange grease to the plug almost unbearable. She did it, because in the morning she'd feel even sicker. Then, having started the process, and because she'd put the immersion heater on earlier for a bath she'd never quite made time for, she washed up.

She would have to leave. She suddenly realised this had ceased to be a thought too dreadful even to form into words in her head and become an acknowledged truth without her processing the notion at all.

As Ellie rubbed in hand-cream, remembering too late that it would all wash off again when she got ready for bed, she wondered why she knew for certain now she must leave Rick when before she hadn't.

What had changed between them, apart from the pregnancy, which surely must be far too small yet to impinge on their relationship? In some ways, nothing; he was still the student she had fallen in love with. He got up late, he left beer cans, fag-ends and roaches all over the house. He wouldn't ever bother to wash up while there were still plates to eat off and he still wanted sex every night and every morning. That was evidently the same as ever.

But he used to be loving. He used to buy her little presents: chocolates, flowers, a little heart-shaped cheese. He'd decorate her pillow with flowers, and once, when she'd gone to bed much earlier than he had, he'd written 'I Love You' in sweeties on the table.

Without all that, clearing up after him was just a chore, not a home-making, nurturing thing to do. And even before he'd first been shown the thin blue line on Ellie's pregnancy test, he'd become less affectionate and more slob-like. If it had been a deliberate, thought-out attempt on his behalf to prove to her how hopeless he would be as a father, it would have worked. But Ellie absolved him of this – he wouldn't bother to change just to make her do what he wanted her to. Why should he? He'd always done exactly as he wanted, and now he was losing interest in Ellie as a person and just wanted her as an aid to his comfort and well-being. Well, he'd find another loving young art student soon enough. She refused to think of the time and energy she had invested in their relationship; she was too tired to cope with the emotions it would raise. She just decided: she was getting out.

The following morning at about eleven, before Rick was up, and before she had a chance to change her mind, Ellie took a deep breath and telephoned her mother at the shop, hoping she'd be there and not with a client.

Her mother was a highly successful interior designer

who had kept her career going more or less uninterrupted by Ellie's arrival. Her father worked in insurance and felt his contribution to child-rearing was not to interfere with the nanny, in any sense, and to take Ellie to McDonald's once every holiday. They both loved Ellie very dearly, she knew that, but they seemed to love their careers and foreign travel slightly more.

Ellie was their only child and she had always felt that both her initial arrival in the world and her subsequent existence were baffling to them. Her mother was artistic, but Ellie was 'arty'. Her mother loved good clothes, but Ellie loved weird, tie-dyed garments, things she bought from jumble sales and then adapted. To their enormous credit, something that Ellie was truly grateful for, her parents had allowed her to follow her dreams of studying art, hadn't visited her at university and made her alter her surroundings, and didn't comment on her friends as long as she kept them out of the sitting room.

'Hello, darling!' Her mother's voice greeted Ellie with that mixture of surprise and pleasure Ellie had become used to. It was always as if her mother had either forgotten her existence, or somehow never expected to hear from her again.

'Hi, Mum. How are you? Did you get that suit you were talking about?' This was partly to remind her mother that they had in fact spoken quite recently; Ellie had rung up to tell her parents she was pregnant, but bottled out.

'Yes. Frightfully expensive, but so lovely.' She paused. 'So, what news? Everything all right? Not short of money, or anything?'

Ellie sometimes had the impression that her parents protected themselves against her with money. But Ellie

40

was very independent, and since she had left university, had refused all offers of money unless they represented a birthday or Christmas present.

'I thought I might come and stay for a bit.' After she'd said it, she realised that at one time she would have said: 'come home for a bit'. Now it seemed more like paying a visit as a guest than going home as a daughter. Her bedroom had been redecorated and redesigned as a study for her father long since.

'That would be nice.' Her mother sounded flustered. 'Would you be staying for long? Only we're going away next weekend.'

Ellie sighed. Why did she expect her mother to cling, to beg her to stay for ever? She had never done so, and for most of her life, Ellie had been grateful – she knew some of her friends thought the distance in their relationship was odd, but it had always been like that. Not all mothers, after all, were that maternal. It was just that now she wanted her to be different.

'I thought I might stay a few days, if that's all right. I'm thinking of looking for somewhere else to live.'

'Oh.' A pause. 'Are you and Rick all right?'

'We're both fine. We just may not stay together, that's all.'

'Oh, darling!' Ellie heard genuine sympathy and warmed to it. Perhaps it would be OK telling her mother about the baby. Perhaps her mother might discover all those mothering instincts which had been a bit lacking when Ellie was a baby herself.

She left a note for Rick. He would read it when he got up, and probably be relieved that she wouldn't be there nagging him any more. He'd be annoyed about having to pay the rent on his own, but Ellie felt fairly sure he'd soon find someone else to look after him. He was a very good-looking boy and, consequently, rather spoilt. Although she would have been happy to have gone on looking after him herself, if he'd only been positive about the baby, and kinder to her.

Having stuffed the few possessions she felt attached to into a series of carrier bags and bin-liners and put them into her car, she took a deep breath and shut the front door on her home for the past eighteen months. 'Don't think about it, Ellie,' she said firmly. 'Just let go.' Then she set off out of the town into rural Gloucestershire, to the little market town where her parents lived.

Her parents' house was beautiful. They always described it as 'architect designed', the logic of which escaped Ellie, who thought that all houses must have had some sort of architect involved. It was modern, energy-efficient and elegant.

It would, however, never be cosy, Ellie realised a few hours later, after a pointless day of driving around waiting for her mother to get home from work. As she parked her 2CV in the driveway next to her mother's little MGTF, she thought of the cottage in Bath she had left, for which the word 'cosy' was almost too expansive. But it made the pages of the style magazines quite often.

Her mother's eye for design was evident everywhere. It had once appeared in a magazine in an article about the use of white paint, illustrating just how many shades of white there were.

Now, a scarlet amaryllis in a steel pot was the only colour evident, apart from her mother's suit, also scarlet. Even while they hugged, Ellie remembered how difficult it had been growing up in such a sterile space when she had been a teenager, and mostly in control of her limbs and possessions. It would be an impossible house for a baby. Fortunately the thought that she might bring up her baby in her parents' house had not dwelt for long in Ellie's imagination.

'Come in, darling. It's so good to see you! It's such a shame you have to leave that charming little cottage—'

'But it's Rick's name on the lease,' confirmed Ellie. 'And I could never get him to leave.'

'Drink, darling? Gin and tonic? I know you can't afford spirits.'

The thought made Ellie feel violently sick.

'No thanks, Mum. I'll make a cup of tea if I may. I've brought some peppermint tea bags with me.'

'So, you're still a dippy-hippy?' Affectionate amusement, with just a hint of disappointment, was Val's most frequent response to her daughter.

Ellie laughed. "Fraid so. Can I get you anything?'

'Oh no. I'll wait until your father gets home and have a drink with him. He won't be long now, I told him not to be late. We're going out for dinner. There's a new place we've been longing for an excuse to try.' Her voice faded as she looked rather pointedly at Ellie's many earrings. 'I don't suppose . . .'

Ellie removed the excess and the stud in her nose without a word.

'It's lovely that you've come and we can spoil you a little,' her mother went on.

As Ellie made tea in the stainless-steel kitchen, glad that she knew where everything was, otherwise she would never have known which silk-like door to open, she realised that her instincts for making a house into something special and beautiful were all inherited from her mother. It was just that their ideas of what constituted beauty in the home were diametrically opposed. Ellie liked colour, hand-thrown pots and gingham curtains. Her mother liked matt black, metal and the wrought-iron chandelier which hung over the kitchen table, narrowly missing its vocation as an extra in a Scottish costume drama.

Her mother followed her into the kitchen, a pristine dishcloth in her hand to wipe up the drips from the tea.

'Do you want me to help you find somewhere to live? Bath is so lovely, such super shops, but I suppose a bit pricey.'

'Very pricey. There are so many students there and not nearly enough accommodation.'

'But if we found somewhere nice, Daddy and I could probably help you out a bit. Pay your first month's rent, the deposit?'

'That's really kind but I might find it difficult to keep paying the rent on anywhere remotely "nice".'

'But you've managed all this time. And you'd share, presumably. Goodness, you work long enough hours! You hardly have any time to do any painting.'

'I know—'

'After all, that idea of yours, painting people's houses, is really good!'

'I know.' Ellie had painted a picture of her parents' house as a Christmas present. They had 'absolutely loved it', but it hung in the downstairs cloakroom. 'The thing is, Mum—'

'Oh! I think I hear your father!' Val rushed from the kitchen as fast as her pencil skirt would allow while Ellie reflected on the old saying that the children of lovers were orphans – and she was an only orphan.

* * *

44

Ellie started to feel restive after only a few days in her parents' immaculate dwelling. Up until then, in the mornings, she stayed in bed, telling them they didn't want to be bothered with her when they were rushing off to work. Really, it was so she could feel nauseous in private. And once they'd gone out she had rung her various employers and belatedly – guiltily – handed in her notice. She couldn't possibly drive all that way to work, even if she had the energy to work once she got there. They had been satisfyingly sorry to lose her – though not as sorry as she was to lose the income, now that she was homeless as well as pregnant.

When she had the house to herself she ate dry toast, drank peppermint tea and made sure she left no trace of her habitation. From time to time she wondered if coming from the background she did had indeed made her a neurotic neat-nik, as Rick had once suggested. It was possible, but she thought it unlikely. Her parents would have died of shock if they'd set foot in Rick and Ellie's little rented house. For one thing, the throws on the sofas and chairs didn't quite blend with the walls.

After she had watched enough daytime television to make herself feel better, she went for walks around the village, buying packets of flour and butter so she could make cheese straws, tiny olive-flavoured scones, or crostini for her parents to have with their drinks when they got in from work. It wasn't that they liked snacks, particularly, but it made her feel less useless.

When she'd done her little bit of baking, and tidied up behind herself, she painted. That too took a bit of tidying, and the idea that paint might land on some of the virgin whiteness of the sitting room terrified her. She was dicing with death painting in there, she knew, but the light in the kitchen was hopeless, and she did drape everything in newspaper before she started. It would be worth it when Grace saw the picture.

One morning she decided to go back to the beautiful house she was painting and have another look at it.

It took her just over an hour to get to the town nearest to the house, but she wasn't sure of her way from there. She found a parking spot and went on a hunt for a loo and some information, in that order. Having found a loo, she was on her way down the High Street when she saw Grace coming out of a shop further down the road. It was too far to shout, so Ellie sprinted. 'Grace! It is you. For a moment I thought I might have done something really embarrassing.'

It took Grace a minute to recognise Ellie, not because she'd changed, but because she was out of context. 'Oh, hello! How nice to see you. What are you doing here?'

Ellie didn't want to say anything about the picture, in case it didn't turn out well, so she said, 'I just thought I'd have a look around. I'm staying with my parents and am getting a bit bored.'

'Well, why don't we have some coffee or something?'

'That would be nice, as long as I don't have to drink it.'

Grace smiled, cheered by this chance meeting. 'The pub has got a cosy snug and there won't be anyone there at this time of day. They'll let us have what we like.

'So,' said Grace, sipping mineral water, when they had settled themselves by the log fire in the pub. 'How is it going with your parents?'

'I haven't told them I'm pregnant yet, if that's what you mean.' Ellie rubbed her hands and held them to the flames.

'Oh.' Grace regarded Ellie, wondering how she'd have told her parents if she'd got pregnant before she was married. It would have been very hard. She didn't blame Ellie for not having had the courage to do it yet.

'I'm staying for a few more days, so there's plenty of time. In the meantime, I've got to find somewhere else to live. The trouble is, Bath is terribly short of accommodation at the best of times, let alone accommodation I can afford. Although my parents have offered to help out,' she added, falsely bright – but not before Grace had glimpsed a look of extreme sadness.

It was ironic, Grace realised. Here was Ellie, pregnant when she didn't want to be, with no space to live in, and here was she, Grace, who so wanted a baby, with too much space.

'I'm sure you'll find something,' said Grace. 'I mean, you're very resourceful and your paintings are lovely. I'm sure you'll have no trouble selling them, and you could carry on doing it when you've got the baby.'

Ellie nodded. 'Yes, I know. And there are other things I could do, too.'

'So it will be all right.' Grace put her hand on Ellie's wrist. She was not accustomed to this sort of closeness, but she found it came very naturally. 'I'm sure it will. You're a great girl, Ellie.'

Ellie was touched. After Rick's casual attitude to the baby and her parents' fond indifference, it was nice to be with someone who had faith in her, and who cared.

'Thank you, Grace. You're a great girl, too.'

Grace laughed. 'More mineral water? The Ladies here is quite nice.'

Ellie drove home feeling much more positive. She would start ringing accommodation agencies: there must be people willing to share with a baby somewhere where she could afford. She was resourceful, she knew, but it was nice that Grace spotted it and reinforced it. She was definitely going to finish the picture now, even if she hadn't had time to go and look at the house again.

After supper, which was a meal you bought in kit form, and cooked in minutes in the wok, Ellie plucked up the courage to tell her parents she was pregnant. She had done the same last night, too, and the night before, when they had been at a restaurant. But tonight, as before, she failed to do it.

One evening a couple of days later, when Ellie had been there a little over a week, her mother said, 'Well, darling, it's been lovely having you, but don't you think it's about time you moved on?'

Ellie knew she couldn't stay any longer – didn't want to – but it was still a bit of a shock to hear her mother say it. 'Er . . . yes.'

'You've got somewhere to stay while you're flat-hunting?'

'Yeah!' There was sure to be a floor she could crash on somewhere.

'So you don't think we're throwing you out?'

'No, but, Mum . . . there's just—'

'And I know it's been proving difficult to find anything in your price bracket, but if you find somewhere a bit more expensive than you can afford, tell us, and we'll pay your deposit and your first month's rent for you, as I said. You may be quite old enough to stand on your own feet, but we're always here for you.'

Ellie regarded her mother, so elegant it was difficult to imagine she had ever been pregnant, or given birth, or even had sex. Her hair was blonde with the subtlest high-lights, cut every six weeks at a London salon. Her clothes were superb. 'It's important I look my best,' she had explained to Ellie years ago. 'Who would have their house made over by someone who couldn't dress properly?'

'That's really kind,' said Ellie. 'I'll let you know how I get on. I'll go tomorrow morning, if that's OK.'

'I'll take you to fill up your car,' said her mother, sounding relieved. 'I'm playing golf tomorrow after-noon. They don't usually let women play at the week-ends, but we've forced them to acknowledge that women work too!'

'Good for you, Mum,' said Ellie. 'Now, if you don't mind, I'll go to bed. I'm awfully tired, for some reason.'

In the morning, while her mother was plying her with orange juice, and other perfectly ordinary breakfast food that made Ellie sick, she finally managed to say what she'd been trying to say for days.

'Mum, Dad, I don't want to worry you, but I think I should tell you I'm pregnant.'

There was only the tiniest pause. 'Oh, darling!' said her mother. 'You can't possibly have it here! I don't want to seem unwelcoming, but you can see how impossible it is!' Her mother's speech seemed to come out very well prepared.

'Did you know I was having a baby, Mum?'

Val glanced across at her husband. 'We guessed, because of you not eating anything normal, and we thought about what the best thing to do would be, and what we decided was to support you in every way we can, but not to tell you to come and live with us. We just couldn't cope.'

Ellie stared at her mother's flawless face. 'Oh. Well, at least that's honest.' It was only what she'd been expecting, but she was surprised at the sudden hurt that lanced through her.

'You do want to keep it?' asked her father.

'Of course she wants to keep it!' snapped her mother. 'Otherwise she'd have done something about it by now.'

'Mum's right, I do want to keep it.'

'And what about Rick? Is he going to take any responsibility for his child?' asked her father.

Ellie shook her head. 'No. He rang me the other day and he doesn't want it and would be a crap – sorry – hopeless father anyway.' It had been a short, painful conversation which had underlined for Ellie the rightness of her decision to leave, but had made her wish that Rick was more mature, and a little less bound up in himself.

'It's not going to be easy, bringing up a child on your own,' said her mother. 'But I don't suppose there's time to find a suitable father for it now!' she added brightly, trying to make a joke about something she didn't find remotely amusing.

'No,' said Ellie, 'although I dare say I could fit in a short fling, if I acted quickly enough.'

Her mother laughed anxiously. 'Silly girl!'

Ellie smiled. The idea had lots to recommend it.

'Well, I've written you a cheque,' said her father, impatient with all this frivolity. 'For five hundred pounds. It's all we can lay our hands on at the moment – things are a little slack at the firm.'

'But we will send you some more money quite soon.'

Val put out her hand and took hold of Ellie's. 'I hope you don't think we're dreadfully unsupportive, but I was a hopeless mother and don't suppose I'll be much better at being a grandmother.'

Suddenly tearful – her mother *was* being pretty hopeless but she honestly wasn't any less helpful than Ellie had expected – Ellie got up and hugged her mother. 'You're a great mother. And you'll be a great granny, too.'

'Oh, darling, you won't let it call me Granny, will you? It's so ageing!'

So, with a cheque for five hundred pounds, a full tank of petrol and a painting, Ellie set off for Luckenham House. She planned to deliver the painting, and then look up an old college friend who'd stayed in the area. She was bound to have a bit of floor space, even if Ellie would have to share it with her artwork.

There was a van parked outside the house with 'Goscombe Woodworm and Pest Consultants' written on it in very smart gold lettering. Heavens, was the house infested? Ellie felt instantly protective of Grace, wondered why, and then put it down to gratitude to Grace for being so supportive the other day. She was looking forward to her seeing the painting; she herself was very pleased with how it had turned out. She parked her own little 2CV behind the van, picked up her bag, and marched down the path.

The front door was open, allowing the biting wind to knife through the house. 'Hello! Anyone at home! Grace?'

Grace heard Ellie's friendly shout, abandoned the young man in a boiler suit who was rapping at the wainscoting in a way almost guaranteed to make a hole, and ran to the gallery. 'Hi! How nice to *see* you! Come in.'

'Shall I come up?' said Ellie.

'No,' said Grace, grateful for an excuse to exchange lovely, cheerful Ellie for the young man who sucked his teeth in such a depressing way. 'I'll come down. I've got to make him coffee, anyway.'

'Who's he?' asked Ellie when Grace joined her and they set off together for the kitchen.

Grace sighed guiltily: guilty for letting her sister bully her, guilty for not being grateful to Allegra for sending him. 'Oh, it's a man my sister sent. He's perfectly nice. Young. I should be pleased, really.'

'Why? If you don't want him here, why do you have to be grateful?'

Grace sighed again and put the kettle on. 'Because I'm so pathetic! I let myself be bullied and then grumble about it. I should just accept I'm a doormat and quit moaning!'

'I think moaning's OK. I can be a bit of a doormat too,' Ellie added, thinking of how meekly she took out her earrings when her mother looked askance at them.

'Anyway, it's great to see you.' Grace sought for a way of asking Ellie why she was there without seeming rude. Her presence was so welcome.

'I brought you this,' said Ellie, producing a painting from her bag. 'I did it while I stayed at my parents'. It's a present,' she added hurriedly.

Grace took hold of it, incredibly touched and charmed by the vision of her house. 'It's lovely! But you can't just give it to me. I should pay you for it!'

Ellie shook her head. 'No. I knew you couldn't afford it when I painted it.'

'But you probably can't afford just to give it to me either.' Grace let herself admire her house, and the way Ellie had captured the warmth of the stone, the delicate

52

violet of the crocuses and the bright yellow jasmine, which wasn't actually out yet. She had added some large climbing plant, possibly a magnolia, which didn't exist, but it did look charming.

'Well, I am giving it to you, so there. How did the wine tasting go? I was so wrapped up in my own troubles, I forgot to ask about it the other day.'

Grace, aware that Ellie was not going to be argued with about payment for the picture, said, 'Well, thank you very much. I love it. It's so kind. I must get it framed. And the wine tasting – well, it was all right in the end, I suppose.'

'After people had got drunk, you mean?'

'You don't actually drink that much. You could do it and drink less than a whole glass.'

'Really? They didn't spit it out, did they?'

'No! It was really very informal. At least, most people were informal. There was a couple who were obviously expecting something very different and a man – can't remember his name – who wrote lots and lots on his sheet and didn't say much.' Grace frowned. 'I think he was a spy. He certainly knew his wine.'

'A spy! How do you know? Surely they're supposed to keep that sort of thing secret!'

'I don't mean that sort of spy!' Grace chuckled. It really was so nice to have Ellie here. 'What can I get you?'

'Nothing, thank you. Tell me about the spy?'

'Well, he said nothing all evening, but stayed and helped clear up at the end while his girlfriend had a cigarette in the drawing room. I didn't think I could make her go outside in the middle of winter.'

'But why is he a spy?' Ellie was obviously fascinated by the concept.

'I think he was sent by the man at the wine shop in town to see if I knew my stuff, but didn't say anything in case it made me nervous. And it would have done! Although I do know my stuff, I haven't had much practice at being public about it.' She frowned. 'It was funny at the end though – he asked me to have dinner with him.'

'And he came with a girlfriend?' Ellie was appropriately horrified.

'I said no, of course. But fancy asking me out when he was with another woman!' Grace frowned. That wasn't the reason she'd turned him down. 'Although, to be fair, he might not have really been *with* her. Actually, I just thought they'd shared transport until she came in and called him darling.'

'Maybe she calls everyone darling,' suggested Ellie.

Grace bit her lip. 'She *did*.'

'So would you have gone out with him if you hadn't thought he was attached?'

Grace was horrified. 'Oh, no. I couldn't possibly go on a date. It's far too soon after my divorce.' Though it wasn't really. It was just too soon for her.

Ellie decided not to mention her mad but cheering plan to have a quick affaire. Grace might be very shocked. 'Wine seems a weird thing for someone like you to do,' she said instead. 'If you don't mind my saying. I always thought of wine as something that blokes did.'

'Not for years, now. But I understand you thinking that.' Meditatively Grace stirred the mug of coffee she had just put two spoonfuls of sugar into. 'I'll just take this up.'

'I don't suppose you've got any biscuits, have you?' called Ellie as Grace left the room. 'I'm suddenly *starving*.'

Grace came back. 'I suppose he'll want biscuits too.' She got down an old cream enamel jar with 'Biscuits' written on it in green. 'Ginger nuts?'

Ellie nodded enthusiastically. 'Perfect.'

When Grace had reappeared, having taken the coffee and some of the biscuits to the young man who seemed intent on dismantling her house, plank by plank, she joined Ellie at the table and sipped her own tea.

'So, how did you get into wine?' Ellie suddenly sighed apologetically. 'God, I'm sorry. I am so nosy! And rude! Demanding biscuits, asking all these questions. What must you be thinking?'

'I think a few biscuits are the least I owe you. After all, you've just given me a painting.' Grace looked at it again, and then took it to the dresser, moved aside a couple of plates, and placed it in the centre of the middle shelf. 'It'll be safe until I get it framed, and can put it up somewhere proper. Although it does look nice there. Thank you so much.'

Ellie blushed, touched at how pleased Grace was with her present. 'I wanted to do it.'

'And I don't mind about the questions,' said Grace, returning to her seat. 'It's quite nice to be listened to, instead of lectured. Perhaps that's why I want to do wine tastings. People won't keep telling me what to do, and interrupting, which they seem to have done most of my life. At least, I hope they won't.' She hadn't kept the evening quite as under control as she would have liked.

'So? How did you get into it?'

'The getting into thing was straightforward enough. I didn't want to do A levels.' Grace frowned at the memory of her parents' horror that one of their children should be so unacademic as to want to go and get

55

a job rather than go to university. Grace, knowing she could never compete with her parents, or her brother and sister, had decided to go in quite another direction. 'And I got a job at a wine importer. I got quite interested in it, and while I was there I did the preliminary exams. It's funny, when I was at school I thought I never wanted to do an exam again, but the wine thing was different. I suppose that was because it was something no one else in my family had ever done, so they wouldn't keep looking over my shoulder and telling me how to do it better.'

'Are your parents still alive? Sorry, I'm one of those people who has to know everything.'

Grace laughed. 'They're still alive but they live in Portugal, surrounded by golf courses, other elderly people and about a million books. I was definitely an afterthought, which is why Allegra got to boss me about so much. They'd lost interest a bit by the time I came along.' She smiled to show this wasn't an issue, it was just how it was.

'And you met your husband at the wine place?'

Grace nodded. 'He was a customer. My family were beginning to nag me to go in for improving my wine skills, try for a Master of Wine, which is like a degree, you have to know so much. But Edward didn't want to change me. It was one of the reasons I married him, I suppose. He liked me as I was. And I needed to get further away from Allegra and co. I was beginning to get bored with being bullied.' Grace stopped, realising Ellie had gone rather quiet. 'Have you told your parents that you're pregnant yet?'

Ellie nodded.

'Were they horrified?'

'Sort of, but they'd guessed.'

'Oh my God! How?'

'Possibly because I went to stay with them for days and days for no apparent reason.'

'So what did they say?'

'They said I couldn't bring the baby up with them, and they're quite right, I couldn't possibly. Their house is like a show home. No place for a baby. It's hard enough being an adult in that space.' Ellie smiled, but it didn't reach her eyes. The hurt she'd felt at their reaction had been slow to dissipate.

Grace didn't quite know how to react. She knew that her own parents were woefully inadequate, or perhaps just inappropriate for her – they'd made a very good job of Allegra and Nicholas – but they were her parents, and only she could comment on them. She didn't want to offend Ellie by saying the wrong thing.

'They gave me a cheque, though,' said Ellie, 'for a deposit on another house.'

'Have you got anywhere in mind?'

'Yeah. There's a friend of mine from college who stayed in Bath and has got a studio attached to her flat. I'll be able to kip on her floor until I find something. I won't be able to afford to live anywhere on my own, so I'll have to find people to share with who don't mind babies.'

'I don't mind babies,' said Grace, aware she sounded wistful. She regarded Ellie, wishing there was something she could offer her that had the same bright lights, jobs and so on that Bath could offer.

'Yes, but you're not looking for a flatmate.'

'I could be looking for a person to share the house if I thought anyone else would want to live out here in the sticks.'

'But it's lovely here! I'm sure you could find someone . . . Grace?' Grace had a curious expression on her face.

'I was just thinking – I don't suppose for one minute you'd want to, but you could stay here until you found somewhere you could afford in Bath. I know it wouldn't be any good to you permanently, but . . . I have got a blow-up mattress.'

There was a moment's silence while Ellie took in what Grace had suggested.

Grace rushed on. 'I realise it's not a very attractive proposition. Freezing cold, miles from anywhere, but there's plenty of space. And I would love having the baby here.'

'And I would love to live here! I don't want to live in Bath at all. It's just the work thing.'

'You could do your painting. I've got a lovely attic you could have as a studio.'

'And I've got a bit of money to tide me over.' Ellie suddenly frowned. 'Oh, God, I do hope it didn't look as if I was dropping hints. I would so love to live here. It's such a beautiful house, and we could have so much fun doing things to it. But only if you want to do things to it, I mean.' She suddenly felt rather awkward. After all, they hardly knew each other.

Grace smiled. 'The reason I haven't done much is because I don't know if I can afford to go on living in it—'

'But if you had a lodger – me, for instance – that's another way of making money out of it. Apart from the wine tastings.'

'Oh, Ellie! It would be such fun! Facing all this alone is dreadfully daunting. Sometimes I even wish circumstances would force me into selling the house, so I wouldn't have to struggle any more.'

'That would be so sad! To give up this lovely house!'

'I know. But it does get terribly lonely.' There was a huge banging noise from above. 'And the poltergeists are dreadfully noisy!'

Ellie smiled at this little joke. 'So what do you think would be a fair rent? It's hard to relate this house to anywhere I've stayed before.'

'I really don't want to charge you rent—'

'I won't stay if you don't. You need the money.'

'But I have no idea what to charge you. I'm so out of touch. Couldn't we just pool our expenses? After all, unless your parents are going to keep on sending you money' – a look at Ellie's face told her this was probably not the case – 'you're going to need to save all you can.'

'Grace!' said Ellie firmly. 'I'll pay you rent or I won't stay.'

The thought of Ellie not staying was so dreadful, as if a treat she had been promised for a long time was now being taken away from her, that Grace capitulated. 'No! You must stay. But not too much rent. We don't have many facilities. Though I might buy a television licence and rent a television.'

Ellie got up and hugged Grace. 'Thank you so much! Instead of being a homeless single parent, because of you I'm living in a mansion. It's going to be such fun!'

Grace hugged her back. Meeting her was the best thing that had happened to Grace for a very long time.

Chapter Four

'Could I have another tour?' said Ellie.

'Of course. And I'll find the blow-up mattress. Oh, this is going to be such fun! Although I ought to warn you that the immersion heater is very small so we have to be careful about hot water.'

'What happened to all the beds that were here?' Ellie asked as they trooped upstairs. 'There must be at least five bedrooms. What would your brother and sister do with so many? And they couldn't have been worth anything.'

'Well, no, they didn't take the beds,' Grace explained, trying not to feel embarrassed. 'They were all burnt when Edward and I first moved in. My sister had the idea they had bed bugs – they were fairly old and smelly, with horse-hair mattresses.'

'Oh,' said Ellie. She stopped on the landing. 'The futon that Rick and I used to sleep on is actually mine. When I'm feeling a bit – stronger – I'll go and get it. In fact, I bought all the furniture. We could bring it here.' She paused. 'It's all tat, really. It won't fit in this house at all.'

'But it'll be better than nothing. I was going to have to trawl the junk shops for stuff, as and when.'

'At least they left you a bed.'

Grace chuckled. Ellie obviously thought she'd been attacked by a swarm of furniture-locusts. 'Of course. It's not as bad as that. Edward left me ours, the goose-down duvet and pillows and bed linen, the wardrobe and a chest of drawers, which was generous, because it had been his before we were married.' Ellie noticed a shadow of sadness pass across Grace's face and saw her try to shake it off. 'Mind you,' she went on, falsely bright, 'I might not have got the bed and the duvet if his new wife hadn't insisted that she wasn't sleeping in a bed that Edward had made love to his previous wife in.' She made a face designed to be comical, but didn't quite manage it. 'It must be rather expensive, having to buy a new bed every time you get married. At least for Edward, who's on his third wife now.'

'Serves him right,' said Ellie. 'Now, which is your room?'

'In here. You can have any of the others. But I suggest you use one in this section of the house. It's slightly less arctic than the rest of it.'

The young man in a boiler suit emerging from one of the rooms made them both jump.

'Right, Miss Ravenglass—' he began.

'It's Mrs, actually. Mrs Ravenglass or Miss Soudley.'

'Or Ms Ravenglass-Soudley,' added Ellie, for texture.

The man looked down at his clipboard. 'I was asked to come by a Mrs Statherton-Crawley. She told me to speak to a Miss Ravenglass.'

'Just tell me what you want.' Grace took pity on him. She knew only too well how bossy Allegra was.

'Well, she said I was to send the report to her, and just tell you when I've finished.' He frowned. 'Is that right? I mean, you live here?'

'I do, but that's fine. You do what Mrs Statherton-Crawley asked you.'

'You just sign here, then.'

When Grace had signed, she said, 'I'll come down and show you out.'

When she went upstairs again, Ellie had found the bedroom she liked best. It was double aspect with a fantastic view, and Ellie was kneeling on the built-in window seat admiring the distant hills when Grace came in.

'This is a nice room,' said Grace. 'Good choice. Pity about the wallpaper. Could you live with all those roses?'

'Of course. They may be a little bit – colourful, but I'm sure I'll get used to them.'

Grace frowned. 'They must be about a foot across! And day-glo pink. They'll give you nightmares.'

'So why did you leave them here, if you feel like that about them?'

'The decorator we always used left the country, and then Edward went, and I never got round to doing anything about it.'

Ellie, who had been peeling off a bit of loose wallpaper, turned round. 'You didn't fancy tackling the decoration yourself?'

Grace shook her head. 'There seemed no point, really. But now you're here perhaps . . . Would it be very difficult?'

'Of course not! Easy as pie to paint over that lot. We should strip the wallpaper really, but that would take ages.'

'And it needn't cost a lot?'

'No! And redoing it could be such fun! If you could see what I did in the cottage – I hardly spent a thing, but it looked wonderful in the end.'

'Oh. You must be sad to have to leave it,' said Grace.

'I mean, however you feel about Rick, it was your home.'

'Oh, I'll get over Rick soon enough. He was just a boy, really, and being a father is man's work. Leaving the house did cost a pang or two, because we were happy there in the beginning, but Rick . . .' She sighed. 'He was just an interlude, I guess.'

'That's how I feel about this house. Edward and I were happy here, too. Unfortunately he was a bit more than an interlude.'

That flicker of unhappiness passed across Grace's face again and Ellie, determined to cheer her up, chirped, 'But we're both going to survive! We're strong, modern women!'

'Yes!' Grace tried to punch the air to demonstrate her positive spirit, but even the air seemed too much of an opponent just then.

'Hey!' Ellie didn't comment on Grace's pathetic little gesture, but an idea had suddenly come to her. 'I must tell you! I wasn't going to, because I thought you'd be shocked—'

'And don't you think that now?'

Ellie shook her head and grinned. 'Don't think so. It's just that I thought I'd like to have an affaire! Why don't you have one, too?'

Grace couldn't help laughing. 'Ellie! That's so silly! I couldn't possibly have an affaire!'

'Couldn't you? Not ever?'

'Well, possibly sometime in the future, but not now. It's far too soon after Edward.'

'It's probably a bit soon after Rick, but I haven't time to wait!' Ellie explained. 'If I'm going to have a love life again, it's got to be soon and short, because let's face it, no man is going to want me when I'm the size of a house.'

'What about after the baby is born? When is it due, by the way?'

'I'm not quite sure, early autumn, maybe.'

Ellie seemed embarrassed by her vagueness, so Grace didn't press her.

'You could have an affaire when you've got a baby. Lots of people do.'

Ellie nodded. 'Eventually, possibly, but no man is going to take on a woman who's breastfeeding another man's child.'

Grace took the point. 'You could bottle-feed.'

'No, no. I'm just going to have a quick fling and then give up men until the baby's older.'

'You don't think you'll get hurt?'

'Well, I might, but if I know from the beginning it's only temporary, and so does he, I can't see any harm in it.' Ellie regarded Grace, who was being maddeningly inscrutable. 'I haven't shocked you, have I? You won't think I'm a slut? I'm not, really. I just want a bit of fun, a bit of glamour and cherishing. With me and Rick, I did all the cherishing. I'd like a little of it in return before it's too late.'

'No. No, of course I'm not shocked. It wouldn't do for me, but I perfectly understand how you feel.' Grace looked at her watch. 'I tell you what, let's whizz into town and get what we need to redecorate. We can sort the mattress out later, and if we go now we should just make it before everything shuts. I've got to go anyway, to deliver my article about the wine tasting to the secretarial place. I told you I write them by hand?'

'If you have, I'd forgotten, but you should certainly do something about that. How can you make money writing articles if you haven't even got a typewriter, let alone a computer?'

'I'm managing all right now, but you're right. I will try and get a second-hand computer organised sometime. If only I knew something about them.'

Ellie looked stern. 'I'll put "typewriter" on our shopping list.'

'Good idea. You make one while I just make sure my handwriting's legible.'

'Excuse me,' Ellie asked the man in the junk shop, who had been a bit taken aback by Grace and Ellie's appearance just as he was about to go home for the day. 'Is the paint in those tins likely to be usable?'

'Oh yes, and at fifty pence a can, you can't go wrong.' Once he had realised they were serious buyers, he viewed them much more favourably.

'Not if you can't get it out of the can,' said Ellie sharply, 'but we'll take it. If it's all dried up, we'll demand our money back.'

'Don't you want to see what colour it is?' asked Grace.

'No. It's a soft grey, you can see from where it's dripped over the edges of the tin. If it's nice we could do more than just my room with it. But we'd better get some white emulsion as well. You don't happen to have . . . ?'

'No,' said the man. 'Hardware, over the road.'

Ellie turned to Grace. 'Can you go and get that? A nice big tin? I'll carry on here.'

Grace wasn't long on her errand but when she returned she was impressed by the accumulation of furniture and bric-à-brac that Ellie had assembled in her absence. 'Are you sure we can afford all that?'

'Oh yes. He's doing us a deal. But there's just one more thing.' Ellie hunted out the proprietor who had retreated to his cubby hole at the back of the shop. 'You don't happen to have a typewriter for sale, do you? Anything would do.'

He shook his head. 'I'm afraid I haven't. There's really no call for typewriters these days. Everyone's got computers.'

'Except me,' said Grace. 'Come on, let's go home.'

'I'm sure you shouldn't be painting when you're pregnant,' said Grace to Ellie the next day. 'Especially not standing on a chair.'

'I'm having a baby. It's a perfectly normal condition. If I didn't stand on the chair I wouldn't be able to reach.'

'But that paint may be toxic!'

'Possibly, but it was very cheap, and I quite like the colour, don't you?'

The paint wasn't quite the same as it had been on the side of the tin, it was a little darker and not quite so soft. 'Sort of. It's quite dark.'

'It'll dry lighter.'

'I should be doing it really.'

'I thought you and Edward always got people in to do painting.'

'He did, but I'd like to give it a try. I've missed out on a lot of perfectly normal activities, getting married so young.'

'Like going clubbing?'

'Definitely.'

'We should go. It would be fun.'

'I think on balance I'd prefer painting. Can I have a go now?'

When they had changed places, and Grace, wearing a pair of Edward's old chinos belted in tightly, with one of his shirts over the top, had got the hang of wiping the brush on the side of the tin, Ellie said, 'It's like *Changing Rooms* on telly, isn't it?'

'What?'

'You know, when two couples swap keys and do up a room in each other's houses, helped by a designer and Handy Andy. Haven't you ever watched it?'

'No. Edward didn't like television much.'

Ellie opened her mouth to say that she thought Edward sounded really boring, but managed to shut it in time. 'Have you got any more furniture hidden away anywhere we could adapt? Or am I getting my programmes muddled up? As a student, you get to watch a lot of daytime telly,' she explained.

'I don't think there's anything anywhere. Not in the house, anyway. But we got quite a good haul yesterday. That little bookshelf, the nest of tables—'

'I'm going to sand those down and varnish them, possibly paint one. I thought I might nail some of those wine boxes together and make a little chest of drawers, with cardboard boxes for the drawers,' Ellie added. 'I made a really good occasional table out of a nappy box once. Where do you write your articles, by the way?'

Ellie had the look of a woman prepared to make a desk with drop-down lid, drawers and secret compartment out of Grace's tea chests, and Grace put up her hands defensively. 'Oh, I've got a little table which works fine. Doesn't need anything doing to it! You don't need to turn it into a wardrobe or a three-piece suite, really.'

Ellie laughed. 'I'm not making you worried, am I, Grace? I'm so sorry! You must tell me to stop if I'm doing anything you don't like. I know I do get over-excited about things.'

Grace chuckled – Ellie was a bit like a Labrador puppy, sometimes. 'If you really want to go to town, you can think of something nice to do with the bathroom. Edward liked that Spartan look, but without all his leather and silver bits and pieces, it just looks gloomy. I think I'd like something more feminine.'

Ellie followed Grace, carrying her paint and her brush, managing not to ask Grace why, if it was her house, she didn't get to choose what sort of bathroom they had, or at least have a bit more input.

'I think it needs a mural,' she said, after some thought. 'Something appropriate – like a Roman bathhouse scene.'

'But we've only got grey paint,' said Grace, not quite able to hide her relief.

'That's OK. I've got my oils with me, and the white emulsion. Although maybe a painting of the sea at dawn would be best. It could be very romantic, with a boat, the sea and sky almost the same colour—'

'Exactly the same colour, seeing as they'll both be grey . . .'

'It only needs a little touch of something on the waves – ooh! I've just remembered, I've got my silver and gold pens with me. Perfect.'

'Mm.' Grace tried not to wince.

'We could have a *trompe-l'œil* window frame. It could be really romantic.'

'I'm off romance,' said Grace. 'It's official. I'm a jaded ex-wife, remember?'

'I promise I'll paint over it if you don't like it,' went on Ellie, completely ignoring Grace.

'Oh all right! Do your worst. But stop soon, I'm starving.' As she said the words she remembered the man at the wine tasting, Cormack Flynn, or something, and telling him she never got hungry. How odd that she was ravenous now. Perhaps it was something to do with being busy – and Ellie's presence had certainly cheered her up. But why did he pop into her mind just then, when usually her mind was full of Edward?

In the end, however, it wasn't until half past nine that night, when they were both exhausted but the decorating was starting to look as if the end might be in sight, that they finally collapsed in the kitchen. Grace got out one of the left-over bottles of wine. 'Is alcohol forbidden for pregnant women?'

Ellie turned round from the stove, where she was making scrambled eggs. 'I think a little is OK, but to be honest, I've gone off it.'

'But you don't mind . . .'

'Good God, no! I think you need a drink, something to help you relax. Do you want Marmite on your buttered toast? And do you like the eggs actually on the toast, or just beside it?'

'I don't really mind. I didn't realise it could be so technical. Edward didn't eat scrambled eggs.'

'Rick did. I'm an expert.'

Ellie went for Marmite, Grace for plain, and they ate in companionable silence before wending their way to bed. Later, Ellie regretted her choice, because she woke up in the night incredibly thirsty. She went to the bathroom and scooped up handfuls of water and then, her thirst quenched, she realised she was hungry again, too. She spent several freezing moments trying to talk her stomach out of this idea but eventually gave in to it.

She was fairly sure there were still some ginger biscuits in the cream enamel jar.

She didn't put any lights on. There were no curtains in the hall and the moon was full and very bright. The house looked beautiful, and reminded Ellie of a poem she'd read at school, about moonlight. Silver something . . . When she reached the kitchen and opened the door, she was shocked to see a large shape apparently draped over the kitchen table. Some instinct stilled her hand on the light switch, and a second later she heard the sound of sobbing. It was Grace.

Grace looked up when she heard Ellie, gasped, and then sniffed loudly. 'Hi! Can I get you anything?' She wiped her nose on the sleeve of her nightie.

'Grace, why are you crying down here in the dark?'

For a couple of moments, Grace tried to bluff her way out of it. 'I'm not crying . . .'

'Yes, you are. If you're not, what else could you possibly be doing? I'll put the light on.'

'No! Please don't. I'll get a candle.'

Once the candle was lit, Ellie realised that Grace had her duvet with her, which was why she'd looked such an odd shape.

'What's going on, Grace? What are you doing here?'

'I could ask you the same question! Oh, I didn't wake you, did I?'

'No. I was hungry and I came down for a biscuit. What's your excuse? It's freezing down here.'

'I know. That's why I brought my duvet.'

'But why are you here?' Ellie wondered when persistence became plain rudeness.

Grace sniffed again and found a tissue up her sleeve. 'I woke in the night and – and I felt like crying, so I came down here, so as not to wake you.'

'Oh, love!' Ellie came over to Grace's side of the table and sat down next to her, so she could put her arm round her – and also sneak a bit of duvet, for warmth. 'Is it Edward?'

Grace nodded.

'Do you want to talk about it? It might help.'

'I don't know! There's been no one – I'm not in the habit—'

'Can't you talk to your sister about it?'

Grace shook her head. 'No! I pretend I'm perfectly all right in front of her.'

'Wouldn't she be sympathetic? After all, we've all been dumped.'

'Not Allegra. Besides, the words "I told you so" were practically written for her. She's been "telling me so" about Edward ever since he first took me out.'

'Tell me then. I'm sure it's good for you. Sort of . . . what is the word?'

'Cathartic? You may be right.'

'So give!'

'There's nothing that you don't know, it's just it's been nearly two years and I'm so bored of being so unhappy! When will I get over him?'

'Well, does it go in phases, or is it constant?'

'Fits and starts, really. I seem to be getting on quite well, don't think about him for quite long periods of time and then, *woomph*, something reminds me of him and it all comes flooding back and it's worse than ever. It's almost better if I do think about him all the time, then at least it doesn't take me by surprise.'

'Have you cried every night since he's been gone?'

'Oh no. Quite often I sleep straight through.'

71

'So what happened this time?'

'I don't know really. I think it's something to do with having had such a good time with you. Maybe I have to come down as much as I went up.'

'That seems very unfair.'

'Nothing's fair, Ellie. We all know that.'

'So do you think my being here will make things worse for you? If so, I could easily find somewhere else to live.'

'No! Please don't do that! It's been such fun, and I even think I'll get to like the mural in time. I just think having good times sort of points up how bleak I feel inside.'

'You won't be bleak inside for ever,' said Ellie, wondering what on earth she could say to make Grace less desolate.

'I have to believe that. I do believe it, because as I said, sometimes – a lot of the time – I'm fine. Then I go back to being heartbroken. I'm a recidivist.'

'Ooh, what's one of them?'

Grace had to smile at Ellie's attempt to make her laugh. 'It's someone who constantly reoffends. I keep getting heartbroken all over again, when I should have been over it ages ago.'

'I don't suppose you do it on purpose, but I do think a distraction would be a good idea. Are you sure we can't go on the pull together?'

'What?'

'Go out to pick up men. It would be fun, really—'

'No,' said Grace firmly. 'I am in no state – never have been actually – to go out and pick up men. And I don't expect you are either, seeing as you don't drink, and even I know that to "go on the pull" you have to be completely rat-arsed.'

'Ooh! Not quite as out of it all as you like to pretend. You know some of the language.'

'Only a smattering and I'll never be fluent,' said Grace firmly. 'But you have cheered me up, Ellie. Really.'

'Let me cheer us both up. I'll make you some hot chocolate and toast. Would you like that?'

'Yes, I think I would.' She watched as Ellie rummaged in a cupboard for a saucepan. 'You're mothering me, Ellie.'

Ellie looked up apologetically, pan in hand. 'I know. It's an awful habit of mine.'

'No, it's a good habit. Convenient, if you're going to actually be a mother.'

Ellie chuckled. 'God, I suppose I am.'

Both girls woke up late the following morning. Grace's eyes were distinctly puffy and Ellie's back was aching; the blow-up mattress was designed for women who didn't have curves. They were sitting at the kitchen table eating a late breakfast when the doorbell jangled.

'Oh God, who can that be?' muttered Grace, jumping to her feet and scraping her hair back from her face.

'You're not expecting anyone, are you?'

'No!' The bell jangled again. 'I'd better go and answer it.'

On the doorstep was a man whom Grace recognised perfectly well, although she still felt muddled about his name and unsettled at seeing him again. It was the Spy.

'Hello,' he said. 'I was here the other night. For the wine tasting?'

'Oh yes. Did you leave your coat or something?' She blushed as she remembered he had not removed his coat. She'd always been led to believe that Irishmen didn't feel the cold. Obviously just another myth, like them all being charming.

'No. I just wondered . . . it may not be appropriate, but I'm getting rid of an old Rayburn and I wondered if it might be of use to you.'

'Why would it be?' asked Grace, wondering why this man kept offering her things she didn't want. What was a Rayburn when it was at home?

'It's a solid-fuel range,' he explained. 'It would heat your kitchen, provide hot water, possibly run a few radiators. I'm offering it to you. For nothing,' he added.

'Oh, I don't think . . .' she began, embarrassed, wishing he wouldn't look at her with that sort of intenseness.

Ellie, who'd followed Grace to the door in case the mystery caller was a mad axe-murderer, realised Grace was going to send away an offer of warmth without even considering it. 'You definitely want it, Grace. Rayburns are great. My granny has one.'

'Oh. Well, perhaps you'd better come in.' Grace was aware she was being less than gracious and tried to smile. She never had been much good with men, her early marriage to Edward meant she'd never got any practice dealing with them, and this man in particular seemed to throw her off balance. She hoped Ellie, with her bouncy-puppy charm, would do the nodding and smiling for her. She stood back so the man – she wrestled for a moment with the order of his names – could get into the hall but then didn't know where to go.

'Perhaps we should all go to the kitchen?' suggested Ellie. 'Then we can see if there's room for a Rayburn.'

'Good idea,' said the man. 'I can have a look at the chimney.'

'I don't think there is a chimney,' said Grace, almost hoping there wasn't. She hadn't had much sleep and was aware that her eyes were very puffy and swollen. The Spy was too big and bulky and male: she didn't want him in her house when she was looking so awful. She hadn't quite forgiven him for asking her out like that. It had been so unsettling.

'Of course there's a chimney!' said the Spy irritably. 'They wouldn't have taken it out!'

'That's good,' said Ellie, wondering why Grace was being so offhand in the face of this very generous offer.

Grace led the way to the kitchen.

'It is a lovely house,' said the man. 'If a little fridge-like.'

'It's February,' snapped Grace. 'It's bound to be cold.'

'There's a draught through this house that would clean corn, and it's nothing to do with February,' he said. 'A Rayburn would help.'

'Well, there may not be a suitable chimney.' She was still sounding ungracious but couldn't help herself. A solid-fuel stove would involve workmen. She'd felt invaded enough with builders in her attic, and now that they'd gone, she was reluctant to have strangers in her kitchen, which, although cold and uncomfortable, had felt like the heart of the house since Edward had left.

To Grace's slight annoyance the site of the house's original range was obvious. She just hadn't really noticed it because it was behind the cooker and someone had put some pale green tiles over the brickwork. She'd thought it was just part of the wall.

'Perfect for a solid-fuel stove,' said the man. 'Do you mind if I pull out the electric cooker and have a look?'

75

Grace shrugged, and Ellie said, 'No, not at all. Shall I put the kettle on?'

'That would be nice,' said the man, looking at Grace. She was aware she should have introduced him by now, but still hadn't decided which name came first. Why couldn't he have a proper first name, like a normal person? She had a fifty-fifty chance of getting it right. 'This is – Cormack Flynn.'

'Flynn Cormack,' he said.

'Flynn Cormack,' went on Grace, trying not to care that she'd got it wrong. 'This is Ellie Summers.'

'It's really kind of you to offer us – er, to offer Grace – a Rayburn,' said Ellie. 'How much will it cost?'

'It's a present,' said Flynn. 'I'm replacing it. It's going spare.'

'Fantastic! That's *so* kind!' Ellie, delighted at the thought of a permanent heat source after a couple of days freezing to death, moved forward, as if to hug this stranger, but then held herself back. He would have been unnerved by a spontaneous hug, she could tell.

'So, if it's so fantastic, why don't you want it any more?' asked Grace who, in spite of trying quite hard, couldn't make herself behave in a normal way.

'Because I'm installing a gas-fired one,' he explained. 'But I imagine you have a good supply of wood, what with owning the spinney.'

'How do you know I own the spinney?' demanded Grace.

'It's in the curtilage of the property,' said Flynn, bringing his eyebrows together. 'Everyone locally knows that—'

'Shall I make some tea?' interrupted Ellie, afraid that

Grace was not only going to look this gift horse in the mouth but send him away with a flea in his ear.

'It would probably be very expensive to put in,' said Grace cautiously.

'I'll do it for you,' Flynn replied. 'All you need to do is buy a few metres of copper piping and possibly a new hot-water cylinder.'

'I couldn't put you to the trouble. I don't know you—'

'For God's sake, woman! I am offering you something you need! Could you not just say thank you?'

Grace confronted him. He had the very slightest Irish accent which was more to do with the order in which he used words than anything else. He was not as handsome as Edward, not anything like, but he had a certain energy which she found somehow challenging.

'Tea?' repeated Ellie, unaware until that moment how deep her middle-class roots went. 'It's a reflex action with me. I make it all the time.'

'What a good idea,' said Grace, trying to live up to her name just a little.

'What room is above the kitchen?' asked Flynn.

Grace had to think. 'The bathroom, I think.'

'Excellent. Would you mind if I had a look? Presumably your hot-water tank is up there somewhere, too?'

'I'll show you,' said Grace.

'No, don't bother. I'll find it myself.'

'I'm a bit fed up with all these men poking about in my house,' said Grace when he was out of earshot, wanting to explain to Ellie why she'd been so unenthusiastic.

'But you really want a Rayburn! You said you wanted

an Aga – Rayburns are just as good, if not better,' insisted Ellie. 'I know it's a pain having people hanging round, but a Rayburn would make a huge difference. They produce gallons of hot water. Or at least, my granny's does.' Ellie briefly thought about her grandmother, who lived in a certain amount of rural squalor, was despised by her daughter, but didn't care. She and Ellie had always got on and if her little cottage hadn't been so tiny and so unhygienic, Ellie was sure she would have let her have the baby there. 'It's a slightly different way of cooking, and of course you have to get used to dealing with the fuel – you mustn't put a great wet log on if you want to boil the kettle – but you get used to that too. Do you have a wood supply?'

'Actually, one of the old stables is full of it. A big tree came down when my aunt still lived here and there's still masses left, as she didn't bother with fires much.' Grace grinned suddenly. 'I remember after she died, when my brother and sister were clearing out the furniture, they looked long and hard at the wood. Fortunately my brother lives in London, in a smokeless zone, and my sister doesn't have fires either – too much mess. She was just about to suggest getting a log-dealer along to sell it, when Edward appeared. He gave her such a look, she shut up.'

Ellie put a sympathetic hand on Grace's arm. 'But Flynn's nice.'

Grace frowned, not misinterpreting the meaning behind this simple statement. 'I'll take your word for it, but even if I agreed with you, it's far too early for me. I told you. Why don't you have a crack at him?'

'Because it's you he's interested in. Quite obviously.'

'We'll have to manage without men,' said Grace

firmly. 'Oh!' She turned round, surprised, as Flynn re-appeared far too soon. 'Was the bathroom in the right place?'

'Perfect. You could have a radiator in there and another couple along the hallway, or in the bedrooms.'

'That would be like central heating. My aunt didn't approve of it. Said it was bad for the furniture, and my ex-husband was aesthetically opposed to radiators.'

Flynn raised a sceptical eyebrow. 'Doesn't seem to me that there is much furniture. And your aunt's dead, isn't she?'

'Yes!' Grace said defensively, aware that she sounded absurd. 'But that doesn't mean she can't haunt me from beyond the grave, if I do something to her house she doesn't like.'

'Don't talk bollocks,' he said firmly, and Grace was horrified to discover she found his robustness oddly attractive. She turned away to make the tea that Ellie had offered with such abandon.

'And it will be better for the baby if it's a bit warmer,' said Ellie.

'Oh!' said Flynn. 'Are you pregnant?'

Grace turned round. 'Are you talking to me? No, I'm not pregnant.'

'I am,' said Ellie, and realised she felt proud of her condition.

'Oh,' said Flynn again. 'It doesn't show.'

'It wouldn't,' said Ellie. 'It's approximately the size of a broad bean.'

Flynn grunted, probably to avoid saying 'oh' again.

'Here's the tea,' said Grace, putting mugs on the table. 'We're getting a little short of milk, I'm afraid.'

Flynn drank his tea rather fast, as if he hadn't really

wanted it but good manners compelled him to accept. Then he stood. 'Well, I'll be off then. Would it be convenient for me to bring the Rayburn round later this week? I've got a builder who could help me with it. They're extremely heavy.'

'Yes, that would be fine,' said Grace. 'Thank you.' She forced herself to get up so she could show him out, although she didn't want to be alone with him. Not because she was frightened he'd do anything: it was just the expression in the back of his eyes which she didn't understand but couldn't ignore.

'Well, I think he's gorgeous,' said Ellie, when Grace got back to the kitchen. 'Why were you so off with him?'

Grace sighed, feeling silly. 'I don't know really. I think it's partly because he asked me out, and then that woman, Margaret, came in and called him darling. Edward had his faults, but he didn't pick up women while I was actually there.' Although it wasn't that, really.

Ellie made a dismissive gesture. 'Well, you shouldn't worry about Margaret! She probably wasn't with him at all! Calling him darling doesn't mean a thing.'

'It does if I say it,' said Grace crisply. 'Now put the kettle on, and I'll wash the mugs.'

'When you've got a Rayburn you'll have plenty of hot water . . .'

'Oh, shut up!' Grace threw a tea towel at Ellie who, annoyingly, caught it.

Chapter Five

'Why don't we go to my house in Bath and get my stuff,' said Ellie later on, feeling the need to get up and do something.

'Do you feel up to it?' asked Grace. She was feeling flat for some reason too, but hadn't said anything in case Ellie linked it with Flynn.

'Yeah, I think I do. I think I'm a lot shallower than you are, Grace. My broken hearts don't last nearly so long as yours do.'

'It's not a competition! Anyway, it doesn't mean you're shallow, just that the relationship wasn't all that durable. Marginally less durable than mine with Edward was, anyway.'

Ellie laughed. 'Come on, let's get some stuff. I'm really looking forward to having some of my things around. I think you'll like them too.'

'You can't transport murals, can you?' Grace asked.

Ellie pushed Grace's arm affectionately and they went upstairs to get ready. They were back downstairs in the hall about to go when the doorbell rang.

'It can't be Flynn again,' said Grace, uncertain how she'd feel if it was, and opened the door.

Standing on the doorstep was a tall young woman wearing a rucksack. It was possible she had been on the doorstep, on the point of ringing, for some time: she looked very cold.

'Oh! Demi,' said Grace, who took a moment to recognise her stepdaughter. Aware that she had been about to add, 'What are you doing here?' she stopped herself. Whatever she was doing there, she did not look happy. 'Come in. How did you get here?'

Demi was Edward's daughter. Grace didn't know her well, but they had always got on all right when she came for visits. She had grown quite a lot since Grace had last seen her and was very thin now. She had a look of an orphan foal which Grace found quite touching. But why on earth was she here?

'This is Ellie,' introduced Grace, when Demi and her rucksack were through the door. 'She lives with me now.'

'Hi,' said Ellie, realising that this news was not entirely welcome; Demi was regarding her defensively. 'Shall we move out of the hall? Would you like a cup of coffee, or something?'

'Don't mind,' murmured Demi, gazing at the flagstone floor, stroking the edge of one of the stones with the toe of her trainer.

Grace didn't know what to do. She didn't know why Demi should have suddenly appeared, but felt she couldn't ask – at least, not immediately. And Demi didn't seem exactly communicative. She glanced at Ellie for help, but got none. Grace had led a solitary life for some time, now suddenly her house was a people magnet and she was expected to organise them.

'Well, let's dump your stuff here,' she said cautiously, wondering too why Demi should have so much stuff with her. 'Are you OK?'

Demi sniffed again. 'Can I crash here for a bit?' she asked nervously. 'Will there be room for me and . . .' Demi had obviously forgotten Ellie's name, and although she wanted to refer to her as 'her', her good manners went too deep.

Grace forced a laugh. 'Um, well, there's just a bit of a problem because we haven't actually got any beds.'

'I don't mind sleeping on the floor.' Demi sounded so pathetic, Grace's heart lurched; she must have noticed how cold the house was, yet she still wanted to stay. Why wasn't she at home?

'I've got to pee again,' said Ellie, sensing that Demi wanted Grace on her own. 'Why don't you guys go into the kitchen? You probably need to talk.'

Once there, Grace filled the kettle again. 'I'm practically waterlogged, so I won't join you,' she said to Demi, 'but it looks like you need a cup of something.'

'You haven't any vodka, have you?'

'No,' said Grace, hiding her shock at Edward's daughter asking for vodka in the middle of the day.

'It's just that life's been quite shit lately, and I don't want to cry,' Demi explained, looking intently at the table.

'It's probably better to cry than drink vodka at this time of day. In the long term, at least.'

'I'll have black coffee then, if that's all right,' she added, her rebelliousness fighting with years of conditioning.

Ellie came back from the loo and hovered in the doorway. 'Would you two like to be alone?'

'No,' said Grace, suspecting that whatever was up with Demi, she might need Ellie's help.

'I wasn't expecting anyone else to be here,' said Demi.

'Well, Ellie is here, and she's staying,' said Grace gently, but firmly. 'She's my friend, and I want her here.'

'But I have to stay too!' said Demi to Ellie. 'I'm Grace's stepdaughter! I'm family!'

'Are you?' said Grace. 'I'm not sure you still are, because Edward and I are divorced.'

Demi put her arms on the table and banged her head down on to them. 'Oh, that's so crap!'

'But it doesn't mean you can't visit me,' said Grace, putting an ineffectual hand on her shoulder. 'It's just that technically—'

'Fuck technically,' mumbled Demi into her folded arms.

'Demi's a really cool name,' said Ellie, trying to cheer things up.

Demi raised her head. 'It's short for fucking Demeter.' She lowered her head again.

'Oh,' said Ellie.

'Her father and mother won't call her Demi,' said Grace. 'They think it's common.'

'Oh,' said Ellie again. 'But you do?'

Grace nodded. 'I think it's mean when people won't call you what you want to be called.' Then she frowned, aware that she called her own sister 'Legs' when she wanted to annoy her. 'I don't mean so much when it's a nickname, but if you've been given quite a – a—'

'Crap,' put in Demi from the table.

'—difficult name,' Grace went on, 'I think you should be able to adapt it to something you like better.'

'So do I,' said Ellie. 'And Demi's really cool.' She looked at Grace. 'Apart from the bed problem, is there any reason why Demi couldn't visit?'

'No reason at all, if you're not missing college.' She

smiled at Demi, aware of the dark circles round the girl's eyes, and wondering if Edward had seen her lately.

'I don't want to visit,' said Demi. 'I want to live with you.'

'Why?' asked Ellie while Grace sat down, looking distinctly shocked.

'Because . . . it's crap where I live.'

'No, it's not. It's very fashionable, lovely shopping and there's a regular train service, not like here.' Grace contradicted gently. 'Have you fallen out with your best friend, or something?'

Demi looked as if she was going to cry again. 'That's part of it. Her bloody parents have taken her to New Zealand, of all places.'

'I hear it's lovely,' said Ellie, then realised she wasn't helping and shut up.

'But it is quite a long way away,' said Grace. 'Demi, that's awful. You've known each other for years, haven't you?'

'Primary school.'

'But you will find other friends. I know it seems like the end of the world but really—'

'Oh, I know all that!' said Demi, 'really I do. It's just . . .'

'What?' A spasm of anxiety shot through Grace like a spear. Supposing Demi was pregnant? How on earth would her family cope with that? 'You're not pregnant, are you?' The words came out as a whisper, her mouth was so dry.

'No!' Demi was clearly just as horrified as Grace at the thought.

'Well, what is it, then?' Grace took hold of Demi's hands across the table, partly in relief. 'You can tell me.'

'I just don't want to live at home any more,' Demi said in a slightly strangled voice, 'that's all. I want to live with you.'

'But, sweetheart, you can't!' said Grace. 'What would your parents say?'

'They wouldn't care,' Demi grunted, burying her head in her arms again.

'Yes, they would! They would go mad at the idea of their precious daughter living with me! Your mother despises me, and Edward, well, he wouldn't ever think of me as a fit person to have the care of his daughter.'

Demi raised her head. 'Yes, he would! I told Mum about Lorraine moving to New Zealand and she just said, "Never mind, she was common anyway."'

'That is a bit unsympathetic,' murmured Ellie.

'Now they've both got partners, they've forgotten all about me.' She sniffed and wiped her nose on the back of her hand.

'I'm sure they haven't.' Grace got up and found Demi a bit of kitchen towel. 'I know children always blame themselves when their parents get divorced—' she began, dragging out the party line.

'I didn't blame myself!' said Demi firmly. 'I know perfectly well why Dad left Mum – she's a cow! But for a while she was at least a mother. Now she's in "lurve" she doesn't give a toss!'

'Darling, of course she does!' insisted Grace. 'She loves you very much. She's your mother!'

'Oh, I expect she loves me! She's just got no time for me!'

'Well, what about Edward,' Grace continued. 'I know he thinks the world of you. Always has.'

'He may think the world of me, but that bitch he's

shacked up with doesn't! You were cool, you never tried to come between me and him, but she won't ever let us be alone together, and when I asked if I could live with them she . . .'

'Went mental?' suggested Ellie.

'And the rest! So that's why I've come here.'

'Well, you did the right thing,' said Ellie firmly.

'What?' demanded Grace. 'She did the right thing, running away from home? Oh, God, Demi, does anyone know where you are?'

'They won't have noticed I've gone, don't worry.'

'Yes, they will! They love you!'

'Not on a Saturday,' went on Demi. 'They think I'm out with my friends. They always think I'm out with my friends, but they've no idea where I am really.'

'And where are you?' asked Grace, horrified at what she might be about to hear.

'With my friends! But I could be doing anything. I went and stayed with mates up in London for two days, and no one said a thing.'

'But that's quite cool, isn't it?' suggested Ellie. 'Not being nagged for a timetable of who and where and what all the time?'

Demi bit her lip. 'It should be, but when you know it's just like that because they haven't noticed you're not there, and don't really give a shit what you do as long as you don't interfere with their lovey-dovey crap, it's not.'

Grace, who had been left in the care of her older sister and brother quite a lot as a child while her parents were busy working, had some sympathy with this. She remembered being posted into a cinema to see a film she didn't want to see so Allegra and the man who became her husband could be alone. And there had been many similar occasions.

'OK. What we'll do is ring your mother and ask her if you can stay for a while.'

'Are you at college or something?' asked Ellie.

Grace had forgotten about that for a moment. 'Oh, hell, they'll never let you stay if it means you'll miss college. Your mocks must be any minute! Love, you'll have to go back. A levels are important!'

'You haven't got any,' Demi reminded her bluntly.

Wishing she'd never confided this to an impressionable Demi when she was first trying to make friends with her, Grace said, 'No, well, it's do as I say, not as I did years ago and may live to regret.'

'She's right,' said Ellie. 'A levels are dire, but you do need them. Especially if you want to go to university, or anything. I've got them,' she added. 'It meant I could go to uni and do art. I had a great time.' She sighed, thinking of how she'd fallen in love with Rick and how joyous it had all been to begin with. What would it be like seeing him again, when they finally got to collect her furniture?

'But Grace hasn't got them. She's just got those wine qualifications,' persisted Demi.

'But she's got something!' said Ellie. 'Something that can earn her a living!'

'I wouldn't go as far as that,' murmured Grace.

'Anyway, it doesn't matter,' said Demi. 'I haven't been to college for weeks, and no one's noticed. They're not likely to make a fuss about it now.'

'What! They'll go . . . mental!' Grace borrowed from Ellie's vocabulary in her hunt for a word bad enough.

'Not if they don't know.'

'They will find out,' said Ellie. 'Although at college they reckon that if you're over eighteen—'

'Demi's not over eighteen,' said Grace.

'But I look older,' said Demi. 'Everyone says so.'

'Looking older is not the same as being older! Your parents know how old you are, and so will the college!'

'I don't know about anyone else,' said Ellie soothingly, 'but I'm starving – because I *am* pregnant. Shall I make us all something to eat? Sandwiches, something like that?'

'That's a good idea,' said Grace. 'Do you need me to do anything?'

Ellie turned to Demi. 'I don't know if you know this, but if Grace was left to her own devices, she would never cook and hardly ever eat, which is why I've taken over the cooking. Self-defence.'

This got a grudging smile out of Demi. 'I am quite hungry. I didn't have breakfast.'

'Demi,' asked Grace tentatively, sure she didn't want to hear the answer, 'how did you get here?'

'I hitched.'

Grace groaned and took up Demi's stance of arms on table, head on arms.

'It's all right!' said Demi. 'I got here safely!'

'You're to promise never, ever to hitch on your own again.'

'OK,' agreed Demi. 'The bloke who drove me here gave me a terrible telling off. He said it was dangerous, too.'

Ellie suppressed a smile, and went over to the table by the fridge. She observed Demi and Grace as they sat at the kitchen table. They were talking quietly, both slightly pleading, but Demi also a little defiant.

Grace seemed far too young to be a stepmother, but she could understand why Demi would choose to come and live with her. If only Demi could stop seeing Ellie as competition, it could work very well.

Ellie took care with the sandwiches, mostly to give Demi and Grace more time to talk, but also because she was an expert at making meals which cost virtually nothing. It had been such fun in the early days with Rick, before she lived with him. She would go round to his flat and find that he hadn't eaten all day, and there was practically nothing in the house. Making tasty (if not particularly nourishing) meals out of what was there felt so cosy and caring. She hoped Demi could stay with them, it would make them like a family, which would be fun.

Feeling very like an Earth Mother, and really quite proud of herself, she put a plate of sandwiches on the table between Grace and Demi, and they both looked up, startled.

'Oh, wow!' said Demi. 'I'm starving! Can I start?'

'So what have you guys agreed?' asked Ellie, biting into a ham and salad sandwich.

Grace sighed. 'After lunch we're going to ring Demi's mother and tell her Demi's here.'

'She won't care,' said Demi, her mouth full.

'Yes, she will! But if it's OK with her, and we can sort something out about college, she can stay here. Providing the parents agree.'

'Good,' said Ellie. 'So, who wants to come with me to get my furniture?'

'I do,' said Demi, who was looking a lot more cheerful now she was eating. 'This is going to be so cool.'

'It might not be,' warned Grace. 'Your mother may not allow you to stay with me.'

'I told you! She doesn't care! All she cares about is that new bloke of hers. It's so gross. They touch each other all the time – in front of me.'

'That is a bit gross,' said Ellie.

Grace said nothing. She was remembering how she and Edward couldn't keep their hands off each other when they were first in love. Demi would have found that gross, too.

'OK, let's ring her up, shall we? Do you want to or shall I?'

Ellie could hear that Grace was finding her new responsibilities taxing. 'How well do you get on with Demi's mother?' she asked, finding herself wanting to protect Grace, not for the first time.

'Not all that well. She thinks I'm an idiot,' said Grace. 'I suppose you can't blame her. I was responsible for Edward leaving her. She's bound to hate me.'

'Honestly!' said Demi. 'She won't care!'

'So you'll ring her?' asked Grace.

'Oh, OK.' Demi got out a mobile from a pocket and pressed a few keys. 'She's not in,' she said after a few moments.

'Leave a message,' said Grace firmly. 'Tell her it's very important that she rings you back as soon as possible. Now ring Edward.'

Demi tried to hand Grace the phone. 'You do it. I can't bear that cow of a wife of his.'

'Haven't you got his mobile number?' asked Grace.

'But I don't want to speak to him!' said Demi, rather unreasonably, Ellie thought. 'You do it.' After she had produced a ringing tone, she thrust the phone at Grace, who didn't want to speak to Edward either, for all sorts of reasons, mostly because the sound of his voice still affected her, but also because she'd never been any good at arguing with him. There was a tense silence.

'Hello?' said Grace eventually. 'Can I speak to Edward please, it's Grace.'

Demi and Ellie watched as Grace pushed bread crumbs into little piles, bracing herself, obviously waiting for Edward to be brought to the phone. 'Edward? It's me. I've got Demi here.'

There was a pause while Edward responded to this.

'She just arrived. She wants to stay for a bit.' Another pause. 'We've left a message for her to ring back, but she hasn't.' Then Grace sighed, and handed the phone to Demi. 'He wants to talk to you.'

'Dad!' Demi's voice had an edge of hysteria to it. 'I'm not going home! I hate it there! Mum hates me! Her bloke hates me! And as for those poxy children of his, why can't they stay with their own mother, where they're wanted?'

Ellie and Grace both looked at their plates. Ellie started following Grace's example and drew a palm tree in crumbs. They both felt they were intruding somewhat, hearing Demi and her father have an almighty row.

'I don't care about fucking A levels!' Demi shouted.

Grace winced. She knew Demi would not have used language like that if her father had been more than an electronic presence. But she was crying when she handed the phone back to Grace. 'He's such a bastard!'

'Listen, Edward,' Grace plunged in, not waiting to hear Edward's side of the story, which she knew anyway. 'Demi's quite upset about a lot of things. I know college is important, but she says she hasn't been going in anyway. At least she's safe here, and not sleeping in

92

some student squat. Do you know she's been spending time in London with no one having a clue where she is?'

While Edward responded to this, at length and with feeling, Grace mouthed 'Sorry!' at Demi for betraying her secret, but indicated by more mime and mouthing that she felt it would help Demi's case if Edward knew the whole story.

Grace didn't say anything for a long time. Eventually she just lowered the phone and pressed a button.

'Did you get cut off?' asked Demi.

'Well, we certainly weren't communicating,' said Grace, sounding tired.

'You mean you put the phone down on him?' asked Ellie. 'Respect, Grace!'

Grace was puzzled, realising Edward had failed for once to terrify her. Perhaps it was something to do with Ellie's supportive presence. Whatever the reason, it felt good, if a little strange. 'I would never have done that when I was married to him, but I just suddenly thought, I don't have to be shouted at or told off about things which aren't remotely my fault or my responsibility, any more.' She smiled at Demi. 'I'm really looking forward to you living here! Why don't we go and choose you a room?'

'Then we can go to my – old house' – Ellie found a lump in her throat and swallowed it away – 'and see how much stuff we can get in the back of my car.'

'We're going to steal furniture?' said Demi, obviously much cheered by the prospect.

'Not steal it,' said Ellie. 'Take it away. I paid for it. Not that we'll get much in the car.'

'We could go in my car,' said Grace. 'It's a bit bigger

than yours—' She stopped speaking as the phone rang. 'Oh no! That'll be your mother, Demi.'

'No, it won't. She doesn't know I'm here. I just left a message for her to ring me.'

'Edward knows you're here, and I put the phone down on him.' She picked up the receiver, preparing to be thoroughly told off. Flynn's deep tones, with their subtle Irish accent, were strangely soothing.

'I was wondering if I could bring the Rayburn round this afternoon instead. I've got someone who can help me now, but may not be available later on.'

Grace took a longing look at Ellie and Demi and realised she would not be able to join them. 'That would be fine.' She pulled herself together. 'I mean, thank you very much.'

When Ellie and Demi set off in her 2CV, having first put the back seat down, they both felt a sense of excitement.

'So, tell me about your friend. Was she a best best friend, or just a best friend?'

'Best best,' said Demi. 'We did everything together and, while she was around, living at home was just about bearable. We plan to go travelling together for our gap years, though.'

'Good idea. You could meet somewhere like Hong Kong and go back-packing.'

'That sounds great!'

'Having us around will be quite different for Grace, won't it? I mean she's led quite a quiet life up to now, hasn't she?'

Demi shrugged. 'Dad used to have friends to stay quite a bit. They had dinner parties, stuff like that.'

'Oh.' Ellie was surprised. 'Did Grace do the cooking?'

Demi shook her head. 'Nah – Dad did, or they got caterers in.'

'And did she enjoy them, do you think?'

'Dunno really.' Aware that she was being unhelpful and not meaning to be – after all, Ellie didn't seem to be the obstacle she'd appeared to be – Demi went on, 'She never complained. But she didn't seem to be having a brilliant time.' Demi frowned. 'She was always nice to me, though, took my side when Dad got heavy. That's why I wanted to stay with her.' She suddenly grinned. 'He didn't like being called "Dad". He preferred "Daddy" or even "Father". I remember once him having a go at me about it and Grace saying he couldn't expect me to use such an old-fashioned expression, and certainly not in public.'

'So, she wasn't bullied by him then?' A second after the words were out of her mouth Ellie realised she shouldn't have been talking to Demi about her father like that, but she decided she didn't care. She needed to know these things.

'Dad doesn't do bullying. He just expects his own way. Grace went along with him most of the time, but if she didn't agree, she just kind of ignored him. They didn't argue or anything. Not like when he lived with my mum.'

Ellie nodded. 'I see.'

'So tell me about us taking the furniture. Will your boyfriend be there?'

Ellie took advantage of a road junction to glance at her watch. 'I shouldn't think so, but you can't be sure.' She couldn't decide if she wanted to see him or not. Supposing she fell in love with him all over again? She pushed this scenario firmly to the back of her mind. She couldn't afford to think like that. 'The most important thing is to get the futon,' she said to Demi, 'but we should be able to get that in the back if we take the base apart. And there are some bits and pieces in the kitchen I'd quite like. My mum bought me a food processor for Christmas; I'm not leaving that behind.'

'But supposing your boyfriend is there? Will there be trouble?'

Ellie could hear the mixture of anxiety and excitement in Demi's voice. 'Well, I hope it doesn't turn into a scene from *EastEnders*,' she said, trying to sound reassuring. 'I don't think Rick will mind my leaving him because he doesn't want the baby and he knows he can get someone else to cook and clean up for him. But he might be a bit pissed off about the bed.'

'Right. I can't decide if I want him to be there or not. When did you last see him?'

'I don't know. Early last week? Listen, if you're nervous, you can stay in the car.'

'No, no. I'll come in. I'm sure you shouldn't move furniture if you're pregnant.'

Ellie sighed. 'And I'm sure you're right. I just hope the baby doesn't know what I was doing before I knew I was pregnant!' She frowned suddenly. 'You don't think I'm taking advantage of Grace, do you? I mean, I can see how you might think that. We haven't known each other long.'

Demi shook her head. 'I think it's nice for Grace to have a mate, someone like you who's more her own age. Dad's friends are all ancient, and some of the women were dead patronising.'

Ellie was silent, imagining Grace in that huge house,

being patronised by Edward's smart, sophisticated friends. Edward must have been some man for her to put up with that.

'She never says anything bad about Dad, though,' said Demi. 'Not like Mum. She's very loyal.'

Ellie shuddered. 'We must look after her!'

Demi giggled. 'I expect she's thinking the same about you and me. We're both homeless and you're pregnant. She probably thinks she's looking after us.'

'We'll be a team. We'll look out for each other.' She frowned suddenly. 'I hope you're allowed to stay. You're fun!'

Demi felt herself blushing. She hadn't felt fun for ages.

Rick's van was parked outside the house when they arrived and there was nowhere else near where Ellie could park.

'Bugger!' she said, not sure if she was annoyed because Rick was there, or because she couldn't park outside. 'Now we'll have to carry the futon for miles.'

'But will there be a row?' demanded Demi, still undecided if she wanted one or not.

'I don't know. Let's find somewhere to park and we can find out.'

'I suppose it's better if we can sneak up on him,' said Demi after Ellie had found a spot in the next street. 'And then, while he's not looking, we can drag the futon down the stairs and run off down the street with it.'

Ellie couldn't help laughing but gave her a stern look. 'You can't run with a futon, you know. They're very solid. We'll have to get Rick to move the van so we can park outside.'

'Will he do that?'

'I have no idea! Come on, I've got my key.'

'Rick?' Ellie called as she opened the front door. 'Are you home?'

The most gorgeous man Demi had ever seen appeared at the door of what seemed to be the kitchen. 'Hi. Oh, hello,' he said to Demi, looking at her hard. 'Who are you?'

'Hi, Rick, this is Demi. We've come to get my things.'

'So you're leaving for ever, then?'

'Yes. You don't want the baby and I do.' It seemed very straightforward now.

'You got somewhere to live?'

'Yes. Now, do you mind if I take the futon? I paid for it and I need it.'

Rick scowled, an expression which diminished his good looks not one jot. Demi was finding it difficult to breathe. 'What am I going to sleep on?'

'I have no idea, but I'm sure you'll manage to scrounge a bed from somewhere.'

'That's not fair—'

'Not fair! What do you mean, not fair? I'm the one who's leaving my home!' God, he was so insensitive!

'It's my home. My name is on the lease!'

'And my name is on the futon! At least, it is now!' Aware of the affect Rick was having on Demi, she took her by the arm. 'Come on, Dems. Let's go and get it.'

Demi, more than a little reluctant to be dragged away from the smoulderingly delicious Rick, followed Ellie up the stairs to the bedroom. Ellie opened the wardrobe and produced some carrier bags. 'The bedside light is mine: I made it at college. I've already got most of my clothes and my portfolio so we can just fill the car up with furniture. Can you take that little table, and the vase – Rick won't want that.' She stopped. 'God, it feels so sad, dismantling everything.'

'What about the wardrobe?' said Demi, once she'd allowed Ellie a few moments to get herself together.

'It won't fit in, or if it does, nothing else will,' said Ellie, feeling much more matter-of-fact now. 'I'll just go and ask Rick to move the van so I can park outside.'

'I can't imagine Grace asking my dad to move his car so she could take stuff.'

'No? Well, I'm not Grace and Rick isn't your dad. Do you want to check the bathroom for stuff that's likely to be mine?'

'No, I'm coming with you.'

Rick was sitting in the kitchen smoking a joint.

'Could you move the van so I can park my car there and load my stuff?' asked Ellie.

'I don't see why I should help you to move out,' said Rick, unhelpful, but not aggressive. 'After all, you're taking my bed.'

'*My* bed. And you may as well cooperate because if I'm out of the way, it'll be easier for you to move someone else in.'

'You're very hard all of a sudden, Ellie.'

'No, I'm not, I'm practical. You may as well be, too.'

Acknowledging this point, Rick carefully rested his roll-up on the side of an ashtray, got up, and felt in his pocket for his keys.

'You do it,' he said to Ellie, passing them to her.

Ellie sighed. 'I just wonder how your bum is going to get wiped when I'm gone, before you find another silly cow to do it for you.'

Rick shrugged.

'Come on, Demi,' said Ellie.

99

When they were in Rick's van, trying to find another space big enough for it, Demi said, 'You didn't really wipe his bum for him, did you?'

Ellie glared at her. 'Of course not! It's just an expression. I did everything else for him. Do you think we'll get in there, behind that skip?'

Demi shrugged. 'Dunno. Do you think it will take Rick long to get a new girlfriend?'

'About five minutes, if he hasn't done it already. Bastard!' Ellie shouted at a red Mercedes. 'This is my space! Don't even think about taking it. Thank you!' She smiled and waved as the man moved on. 'This van always was a bitch to park.'

Chapter Six

❦❧

Disappointed that she was not able to be part of the raiding party, Grace washed up the mugs and plates from lunch while wondering what she could do to make the house more homely. She and Ellie had done a certain amount upstairs, but downstairs was still fairly austere.

It was starting to get dark; soon she would go round the house and put the lights on – her strategy for living alone had included putting lights on early, so she didn't have to go upstairs into the dark. She had learnt those strategies the hard way, and now wondered if having Demi and Ellie living with her would cause her to lose her skills; if, when they eventually left, as they inevitably would, she would have to learn them all over again.

She was about to do her rounds of the house when the telephone rang. It was Demi's mother. So much for her using Demi's mobile.

'Can I help you?'

'I cannot believe you've been so irresponsible!'

Usually, Grace would do anything to avoid a conversation with Hermia; Edward's first wife terrified her. But today, for some reason, she felt brave enough to speak her mind. 'If you want to speak to Demi, why don't you try her on her mobile?'

'Her name is not Demi! It's Demeter! And you're to bring her home immediately.'

'She's not here.'

'What do you mean, she's not there? Where the hell is she?' Hermia's anger was so incandescent Grace wondered if the energy from it could somehow be garnered and stored. She could probably provide enough to heat the hot water and run a couple of radiators, and then Grace wouldn't have to have the stove Cormack Flynn – or was it Flynn Cormack – was so intent on giving her.

'She's gone with a friend to pick up some furniture. Anyway, how did you know she was here?'

'Edward told me. Bloody useless man! He won't go and get her! Expects me to go down there and bring her home!'

'And you want me to do it.' Grace tried to remember that Hermia would be worried, and make allowances.

'I can't just drop everything for that stupid girl! I've got people coming for dinner, this couldn't have happened at a more inconvenient time!'

Grace was shocked, but stayed calm. 'Well, I suppose it's never a good time for your daughter to run away from home.' Demi's statement that her mother no longer had time for her was obviously true.

'What?' Hermia had obviously not put this interpretation on Demi's absence. 'Demeter has not run away from home! What are you talking about?'

Grace couldn't unsay her words, but now tried to be a bit more soothing. 'If she hasn't run away, why are you getting so worked up?' Too late, she realised she should have said 'upset'.

'I'm not worked up! Or if I am, it's with perfectly good reason. I grounded her the other day and she just went out anyway! I've stopped her allowance, of course, but what can you do? Edward still gives her money. He's got no sense of how to discipline children.'

'Well, she's not here just now. Shall I ask her to ring you when she gets back?'

'No! You will *tell* her to ring me! And you'll make sure she gets on the first bus home in the morning.'

Annoyed as she was, Grace began to feel sorry for Hermia. There she was at the end of the phone, giving orders, with absolutely no ability to make sure they were carried out. 'I don't think I can do that.'

'Why on earth not? I know you've never been a mother, but surely you must have *some* understanding about how I feel?'

Grace took a calming breath. 'Of course. I'd be very upset if my daughter found it necessary to run away, but I can't put her on a bus.'

'Why not? God, I find you incomprehensible!'

'For one thing, there are no buses at the weekend and a very infrequent service at other times. She hitchhiked here. And for a second thing, I can't make her do anything she doesn't want to do. She's quite a lot taller than I am. And thirdly, I'm very fond of Demi and think she *should* stay here for a bit.' She hadn't realised she was going to say that because, in principle, she felt children should live with their parents. But Hermia was so appalling, Grace not only felt she shouldn't be allowed to have custody of Demi, but that she probably shouldn't be allowed to keep pets, either.

'Out of the question!' Never mind a couple of radiators, the woman's wrath could run an entire central-heating system. 'She's to come home and finish her education. What a suggestion! Stay with you? I wouldn't trust you to look after a hamster!'

'That's funny, I was just thinking the very same thing about you,' said Grace.

'Grace! I know Edward married a child when he left me, but I didn't realise it was one who was educationally subnormal!'

Grace thought about putting the phone down but decided that listening to Hermia rave was actually quite entertaining. How could she ever have been frightened of someone so inhuman? It was like being frightened of a cartoon monster.

'You're to tell that young woman, when she gets in,' went on Hermia, unaware she'd been downgraded to a minor character out of *Scooby-Doo*, 'that she's to stop being so disobedient and come home! And you're to bring her! I can't and I know you got a very good car out of Edward!'

'My car is my business, and your daughter is your responsibility, not mine, you know,' said Grace gently, aware that Hermia would prefer her to get angry back. 'You and Edward have to sort it out between you. I'm very happy to have Demi here. I think she's a lovely girl, and with a little understanding might even be persuaded to go back and do her A levels.'

Then Grace did put the phone down.

She decided it would be nice for the others if they came back to a house with lights shining from all the windows and not just the ones Grace usually put on. The house deserved it too; it was too lovely to be lived in only by an anti-social ex-wife. She went first to the drawing room and switched on the wall lights. She was never quite sure about wall lights, but they had always been there, so she'd never seriously considered changing them.

Then she went into the dining room. From here she could see the spinney, her potential wood supply, its leafless trees silhouetted against the pale sky edged with pink. She gazed at the view for a few moments, admiring the tracery of the branches against the duck-egg-blue backdrop, and then, because beauty always made her think of Edward and it was a habit she was trying very hard to break, she reached out and pulled the curtain.

'Oh, bugger!' she said as the curtain collapsed into a pool of tattered silk on the floor. 'Why did I do that?'

Then she gave a little scream of shock. There was a figure, pale and spectral, behind where the curtain had been. Sweat formed instantly and the hair on her neck stood up; it took her a heart-thumping moment to realise that she hadn't seen a ghost. The figure was a painting, almost life-size, on the panel of the shutter.

Her fingers continued to perspire and her heart to pound, however hard her brain told them it was no longer necessary. The house wasn't haunted; it wasn't the wraith of a long-lost soul behind the curtain; it was only a picture.

How could she not have known it was there? she asked herself as she crossed the room to the door, to turn on the light, hoping that would banish her fright. To think it had been lurking behind the curtain all these years, and she'd never known. She felt quite guilty as she flicked the switch.

But the only illumination in the dining room came from a central bulb, covered by a heavy shade which conspired to keep all the light to itself. It didn't so much add light as emphasise how dark the room was.

In spite of this, Grace went back to the window, determined to have a good look at what had given her such a shock. It was almost impossible to see properly, but it looked like something out of one of Edward's art books. She peered closer, but realised that didn't help and decided to get a torch. There was one in the tea chest in the hall.

She had just removed the cloth (which gave the impression that the tea chest was actually a table) and found the torch when the doorbell rang. She jumped at the noise, her nerves already jangled, then took a breath, ordered herself to calm down, and looked out of the window to see if it was a Headless Horseman. It was Flynn. She opened the door reluctantly.

'Why is it I always get the impression that you're not pleased to see me?' he asked, with a slightly crooked grin.

'Possibly because I'm not?'

The fact that she'd answered so acerbically shocked Grace almost as much as thinking she'd seen a ghost. It was so out of character for her. The conversation with Hermia must have somehow disconnected her good-manners gene. She tried to smile, but it didn't feel very convincing.

It obviously didn't look convincing, either. 'I hope you're not planning to hit me on the head with that blunt instrument.' He indicated the torch. 'I have come to give you something, you know.'

'Fear the Greeks, even when they come bearing gifts,' she said, trying to lighten the atmosphere. She tried to put down the torch but it missed the cloth and fell through into the chest with a crash, making Grace give a little moan of fright. Her nerves were all over the place.

'Are you always this agitated? You're like a two-year-old going into its first race. That would be a horse, by the way.'

'I'm not remotely agitated! I just had a bit of a shock, that's all. You came at a bad time.'

'I'm sorry.'

'It's all right. I know you didn't do it on purpose.' It was just that every time he turned up he unsettled her, and she was unsettled enough already.

He stood there as if expecting some sort of explanation. Well, she had no intention of telling him about the painting; she had to get used to the idea of it being there herself.

'I thought I saw something move on the stairs and it made me jump.'

'I see. The house isn't haunted or anything, is it?'

'No, of course not! And even if it were, I don't believe in ghosts.'

'That's all right, they won't appear to you then.' He paused. 'Is there somewhere we can put the Rayburn for now? An outhouse or something?'

'Yes, of course.' She felt on home ground now. The supernatural was beyond her, but she knew her stable yard well. 'Where are you parked?'

'We came in via the back drive.'

'There's a stable you could use. I'll come.'

He put a hand on her arm. 'No, don't. We'll find it. You're in no state to go wandering about in the dark. You may not believe in ghosts, but you still look a little pale.'

She smiled, mildly relieved. 'Don't you want a hand?'

He shook his head. 'We have a special trolley and moving Rayburns is men's work.'

'Or strong women's work?'

He shook his head. 'No woman is that strong, and you certainly aren't.' He glanced down at her slender form.

'I'm thin, but I'm tough,' said Grace, wondering why on earth she was trying to convince him that she wanted to help hump a cast-iron stove about.

'No, you're not. Why don't you put the kettle on? Or do something else that'll make you feel useful and keep you out of our way?'

'That's not very polite!' Honestly, this man was beyond the pale, or whatever it was they said in Ireland.

'I'm sure the hot water will come in useful.'

He was definitely teasing her, but she refused to respond. 'That's hardly the point!'

'You're very argumentative,' he said, amused.

'No, I'm not!' Grace scowled at him, determined not to let him have the last word, and then realised what she'd said and tried not to laugh.

Flynn didn't try quite hard enough and she could see the corner of his mouth twitching. 'Go and busy your-self in the kitchen and let the men get on with the hard work.'

This time she had to respond to his ironic twinkle and as she had no real desire to heft a cast-iron cooker around in the dark and cold she said, 'OK,' and fled towards the kitchen, biting her lip, half wanting to hit him and half to indulge in her suppressed laughter.

As she found the switch for the outside lights at the back of the house she realised that while she had been with Flynn, she hadn't thought of Edward once, although Edward had been the background of all her thoughts for so long. It was a step forward. It was nothing to do with Flynn, of course, but it was a sign of her recovery.

For want of something better to do, Grace did indeed put the kettle on, and then inspected the wooden crate that was her wine rack. It was nearly six o'clock and maybe Flynn's mate might like a glass of wine when he came in. She would certainly appreciate one herself – she was still shaken up by the quasi-ghost she had discovered behind the curtain. She pulled out a bottle, examined it for a few moments and then extracted the cork.

How soon was it reasonable to expect Ellie and Demi back? It was ridiculous, a week ago she'd been living in this house on her own – if not happily, at least serenely – and now she was feeling lonely because her new housemates had gone out for a couple of hours.

There was a knock at the back door and Grace went down the passage to open it, determined to be polite and sociable and not to let Flynn Cormack make her do or say anything out of character. She smiled determinedly.

'This is Pete,' said Flynn. 'This is Grace, who doesn't live up to her name.'

Grace ignored this and directed her smile entirely towards Pete.

Pete was wearing a boiler suit. Flynn was wearing very dirty jeans and a fisherman's sweater which was fraying at the cuffs. Grace tried hard to think what Edward would wear if he were moving a stove about but couldn't. He would either have some specialist garments, or not do it, just direct operations from a distance.

'I boiled the kettle,' she said, 'as instructed.' She glared at Flynn. 'And there are some biscuits. But I wondered if Pete' – she smiled at him again, to point up the fact that she was not smiling at Flynn – 'would like a glass of wine?'

'What about me?' asked Flynn indignantly.

'You're driving!'

'No, I'm not. Pete is. I'd love a glass of wine.'

'What about you, Pete?'

'I'm more of a tea man, myself. And I'd love a biscuit.'

She made the tea, and poured a glass of wine for herself and Flynn.

'Not exactly *chambré*, if I may say so,' he said, having held his glass up to the light and taken a sip.

'People don't realise that "room temperature" was the room temperature of the eighteenth century, not of the centrally heated house of today,' she said, aware she was sounding incredibly pompous.

'Ooh! Get you!' Flynn directed his glass towards her in a toast.

Grace bit her lip, determined not to smile. 'Have a biscuit, Pete,' she said and he extracted a biscuit from the bottom of the packet.

Flynn was looking at her in a way she found unnerving. There was nothing improper in it, but feeling his eyes upon her in that quizzical, speculative fashion was unsettling. She wondered what on earth she could say to make him stop doing it.

To her enormous relief, the bell's attention-seeking jangle indicated that the girls were back. The relief! She rushed to open the door.

'How did you get on?' she asked as she opened the door.

'Really well! Come and help us!' said Demi, who seemed excited and looked particularly pretty. 'We've got loads of stuff!'

110

'Flynn's here. And Pete. They're in the kitchen.'

'Who's Pete?' asked Demi. Ellie had filled her in on Flynn.

'Friend of Flynn's, I think,' said Grace.

'I must say, I'm dying of thirst,' said Ellie, sensing that Grace wanted company in the kitchen. 'I could murder a cup of peppermint.'

'We must buy peppermint tea bags,' said Grace. 'In fact, now that Demi's come, we'll probably have to get lots of things. We must make a list so we can go shopping.' As they walked down the corridor to the kitchen, she added, 'Once we've got these bloody men out of the way.'

Ellie, anxious lest Grace should banish the men before she'd taken advantage of them, said, 'Would you mind if I asked them to help with the futon? It's not really heavy, but it's awkward.'

'Of course. Have your tea and we'll set them to work. You shouldn't be carrying things if you're pregnant.'

'Great. I'll go and ask them,' said Ellie, going ahead into the kitchen.

She found Flynn and Pete regarding the fireplace behind the cooker as if it contained the answer to all life's most taxing questions.

'Hi, Flynn! I'm Ellie,' she said to Pete. 'Would you mind giving us a hand with some furniture? It's just that I'm pregnant and I shouldn't really lift things.'

'What is it you need shifting?' asked Flynn.

'A futon.'

'Should be able to manage that all right,' said Pete, rising to his feet. As their big feet pounded along the flags behind her, Ellie reflected that she liked men like Pete and Flynn. They had an honesty about them which

Rick, who was so good-looking he was practically a danger to traffic, would never have.

Grace and Demi had got lots of the smaller items out of the car: black plastic sacks; cardboard boxes; and a pile of saucepans. Ellie regarded the saucepans a little guiltily.

'Perhaps I shouldn't have taken them,' she said, to no one in particular. 'I think they may have been given to Rick by his mother.'

'We can always take them back if Grace doesn't need them,' said Demi eagerly.

Ellie glanced at Demi but then Flynn said, 'Where's this futon, then?'

'On the roof of the car,' said Ellie. 'I'll show you.'

'Don't worry,' said Grace to Ellie. 'We'll get it. You move the blow-up mattress out of the way. That's for you, Demi,' she said, and went out into the dark, followed by Pete and Flynn.

Demi and Ellie loaded themselves with plastic bags and boxes and went upstairs together. 'Where are you going to sleep?' Ellie asked.

'I used to sleep in a little room by the bathroom. It's really pretty in a chintzy sort of way. Dad was going to have it decorated for me but I liked it as it was.'

They reached the landing. 'Put the light on, there's a love. I can't let go of anything.'

'I don't know where the light switch is.'

'Oh, hell. We'll have to do it by feel. Let's dump the stuff.' The landing light at last on, Ellie said, 'So, which way to your room?'

'Along here,' said Demi, leading the way.

The room revealed itself to have very pretty Victorian wallpaper, possibly original, very much nicer than the ghastly overblown roses Ellie had covered with grey paint. There was a little fireplace, too.

'I always wanted to have a fire here,' said Demi, 'but Dad said the chimney probably needed sweeping.'

'He was probably right.' Ellie dumped her load of bags on to the floor. 'I'm glad we got the chest of drawers in. It's very small, but it's better than nothing. Would you like it in here?'

'Oh, that's really kind. I could use the top as a dressing table, for my make-up and stuff. But don't you want it?'

'I haven't got all that many clothes, I'll be fine with those boxes you were practically sitting on.'

'We got quite a lot, really.' Demi frowned. 'Will Rick be all right without furniture? I don't know how you can leave him. He's so gorgeous.'

'Not that gorgeous to live with,' Ellie said wryly. 'And he didn't want me to keep the baby.'

'Oh,' said Demi, and Ellie realised she didn't quite understand.

'I think we'd grown apart, really,' she went on, 'but he was the best-looking bloke in college.' She shook herself, there was no benefit to reminiscing. 'Let's go and get your mattress.'

'I don't think Grace likes Flynn,' said Demi as they carried the mattress along the passage.

'I don't know why not. He's a nice bloke.' Ellie sighed. 'She was very upset when your dad left her.'

'Being dumped is always crap,' said Demi, as if she knew from personal experience. 'And she was potty about him. You could see it.' They lowered the mattress on to the floor in the corner of the room. 'Although she was always so nice to me,' Demi went on. 'His new wife is potty about him, too, but I don't think she realises I exist.'

'Oh, dear. Doesn't she make an effort at all?'

Demi shook her head. 'Nope. And Mum only cares about her new bloke – that and having beauty treatments so she can keep him. He's a bit younger than she is.'

'Oh. My mum's very keen on therapies too,' said Ellie. 'Her house is like a show home. I feel like an old sack tied up with string when I'm next to her.'

'My mum's like that too! She only ever speaks to me to tell me to do something to my skin, or to do my college work.'

They smiled at each other, a moment of mutual understanding, then turned as they heard a crash from the landing.

The futon was coming up the stairs on the shoulders of Pete and Flynn, and Grace trotted behind them, carrying an armful of bedding.

'Where do you want it?' asked Flynn.

'In here,' said Ellie. 'We've moved the mattress.'

Flynn and Pete deposited the futon on the floor in Ellie's room. 'Is the base still in the car?' asked Flynn.

'No, we brought it in,' said Ellie.

'Right. I'll go and fetch it.'

'I'd better come with you,' said Grace, sounding reluctant as she followed the two men.

'I don't know why she doesn't like him,' said Ellie *sotto voce* to Demi.

Demi shrugged again. 'He's not good-looking like Dad.'

'No, but he's OK-looking, in a rugged sort of way.'

Demi giggled. 'If Grace liked rugged men she would never have married my dad.'

114

'Oh. That might explain it.'

'Anyway, it's a bit soon, isn't it?'

'I don't know. After all, your dad's got someone new.' The more she thought about it, the more she thought an affaire with someone like Flynn might be just what Grace needed. But as the futon base was announcing its imminent arrival by the grunts and stifled expletives of its bearers, they were forced to abandon their conversation.

'Now,' said Pete, when all the various bits of pine, fixings and Allen keys were assembled on the floor. 'Do you want a hand putting this thing together?'

'Oh no!' said Grace. 'It's been very kind of you to help, but we'll be fine now.'

Ellie shook her head and frowned at Grace. 'No, we won't! It was hard enough taking the damn thing apart! It would be brilliant if you'd help us get it set up.'

'Yeah,' said Demi. 'Ellie must be really tired. She'll need to sleep on it quite soon.'

Grace glanced at Demi, wondering at this sudden flash of consideration and realised that Ellie and Demi didn't seem to understand about her wanting Flynn and Pete out of the house. She didn't really understand it herself, she just knew she'd feel more comfortable when they'd gone.

'I'll go and get the wine,' she said, feeling it would be better if she offered hospitality now, while everyone was doing something.

By the time she got upstairs with the wine and glasses, the futon was nearly complete. Demi was wrestling with a duvet cover and Ellie was putting pillows into cases.

'They've been marvellous,' she said as Grace appeared,

wine bottle tucked under her arm, glasses hanging from between her fingers. 'Got it together in no time.'

'How kind,' said Grace. 'Would you like a glass of claret – as you didn't seem to like the other wine all that much? It's nothing special. It's from a case I and my husband bought in France a few years ago.'

'But he's not your husband any more,' said Ellie.

'No, but the wine's still wine,' said Grace, wondering why Ellie was being so pedantic.

'Dad's latest wife doesn't drink,' announced Demi.

'You make him sound like Bluebeard,' Grace protested.

Demi shrugged. 'Well, it is wife number three he's on now, you know.'

'Yes, but is that so many?' asked Ellie.

'Yes,' said Flynn. 'More than one is "so many".'

Grace looked at him. 'Which one are you on, then?'

'Oh, I'm Bluebeard too,' he said solemnly. 'My wife couldn't stand always living in a building site and walked out. I'm a property developer.'

Grace's shudder of distaste was nearly visible. Sensing it, Ellie said, 'But what about your present wife?'

'Oh, I haven't found her yet.'

'So you're not Bluebeard yet?' said Demi. 'Just sort of gearing up to be?'

'Oh, for goodness' sake!' said Grace, hating this conversation for lots of reasons. 'Let's just have a drink. Pete, did you ever get time to finish your tea?'

'Yes, thank you. And a fine cup of tea it was. And I ate all the biscuits.'

'That's fine, we've got a good supply for Ellie.'

'Perhaps Ellie, or Demi, or whoever's bedroom we're in, might not like us drinking wine in it,' said Flynn.

'Oh no, it's fine. I've only just stopped being a student,' said Ellie.

'And you're pregnant! You don't want to drink alcohol!' Grace was mortified with herself for forgetting and grateful for an excuse to escape. 'I'll run down and get you something soft.'

She was out of the room before anyone could speak, but was caught up with by Flynn in the kitchen.

'Actually, Pete and I really must be going. Thank you for the wine.'

'You didn't have time to drink it.' Now that he was actually going, she wanted him to stay. 'And I should be thanking you for helping Demi and Ellie with the bed and everything.'

'It was no trouble. And I would just like to say something.'

'What?' If he had something to say, why didn't he just say it, and not announce that he was going to in that ominous way?

'I'm not the sort of property developer you thought I was when I said it.'

'I don't know—'

'You thought I was the kind that puts up nesting boxes on greenfield sites. I don't. I buy houses, do them up and move on.'

'Oh.'

'I couldn't help seeing your expression.'

'I didn't mean to be rude.'

'You weren't rude, you just winced.'

'The thing is, my family have suggested that I sell off part of the land, for building, but I won't – can't.'

'You shouldn't. Besides, nowhere round here would ever get planning permission.'

She smiled. 'That's a relief!'

'So you can tell your family that.'

'Yes. I will, next time they mention it.'

'I'll be off now. I'll ring you when we can come round and install the Rayburn. It will make a big difference to this kitchen, you know.'

'I'm sure it will. It's very kind—'

'No, it's not. It's surplus to my requirements.'

Then he walked out, leaving Grace rather confused.

As she went to join the girls she noticed the dining-room light on and suddenly remembered. She ran up the stairs. 'Hey! You'll never guess what happened while you were out!'

Chapter Seven

❦

'What happened?' Ellie and Demi had been patting pillows into place, and now they looked up at Grace.

'I thought I saw a ghost, but it turned out to be a painting!' said Grace. 'Come and look! Bring your glasses and the bottle. Oh, Ellie! I never got you anything.'

'Never mind that! Let's go and look at this painting!'

Demi, who'd drunk her glass of wine rather fast, said, 'Ooh, this is so exciting!'

'It might not be,' said Grace. 'It might be just a daub. I was getting a torch to look at it better when Flynn arrived.'

'He's really nice, isn't he?' said Ellie, distracted from Grace's news for a moment. 'Very kind.' She nudged Grace in the elbow.

'Yes,' said Grace.

'Really quite attractive in a rugged, rough-hewn sort of way.'

'You should definitely go for it, Ellie,' said Grace, deliberately misunderstanding. 'And I'm sure he'd love a ready-made family. He didn't mention any children. I'm sure you'd be just what he needs.'

'Not for me, idiot! For you!'

'He's not nearly as good-looking as Dad,' said Demi, glancing crossly at Ellie. 'Besides' – she suddenly sounded tired and potentially weepy – 'please don't fall in love! I'm so pissed off with watching people being in love with each other.'

Grace stopped halfway down the stairs and turned to confront Demi. 'I promise you, there's absolutely no chance that I am going to fall in love with anyone ever again. So don't worry about that. I'll always be here for you.'

'Even though I'm not really your stepdaughter?'

'It doesn't matter who you are. I'm off men for life.' She shot a sly glance at Ellie, who was, as she'd expected, looking disappointed. 'So no matchmaking, Miss Summers!'

Ellie shrugged. 'OK. I don't want you falling in love either, or you might throw me out so you can share your love nest.'

'Oh, for goodness' sake!' But Grace laughed, despite herself. 'Come and look at this picture, although we'd do better to wait until morning.'

'We can't do that,' said Ellie, 'not now you've told us about it. But we must eat as well. I'm starving.'

'Yeah,' said Demi brightly. 'We bought a Chinese take-away. It'll only need heating up.'

'Lovely! Takeaway – so decadent.' Aware that Demi and Ellie were looking at her strangely, she explained. 'Edward—'

'Didn't approve of takeaways,' Ellie finished for her. 'Come on, let's see the painting and then we can hit the food. I have an awful craving for prawn crackers.'

Grace collected the torch and then led the way to the dining room. 'It may not be anything, really, but I was just in here drawing the curtains—'

'I thought you said you never drew the curtains in

here,' said Ellie. 'The material was too fragile.'

Grace made a face. 'We never used to, but I forgot and it all came to pieces. Then I thought I saw a ghost.'

'Why?' asked Demi, thrilled and horrified.

'Because of that,' said Grace, shining the torch at the window shutter.

Demi gave a little scream, suppressed it and then there was silence. The moon shone in through the window and the single bulb glowed dimly. The torch highlighted the painted figure.

'Wow,' said Ellie after a few moments. 'I can see why you thought it was a ghost. It looks really old.' She went closer. 'I think it's Eve, or something.' She frowned. 'I can't quite see if the panel has been painted, or if it's on a board stuck on top.'

'Oh my God,' said Grace softly.

'What?' said Demi, obviously still spooked.

'Nothing. I've just thought of something. I—' She changed the subject. 'Listen, why don't we go and eat and have a proper look in daylight? We don't want the Chinese to be ruined.'

'What's the matter, Grace?' asked Ellie.

'Nothing. It's just—'

'Come on, Grace! Don't leave us in suspense! You find what could be a wonderful painting and you're not jumping up and down with excitement. I did a bit of History of Art on my course. It could be really valuable!'

'That's the problem,' explained Grace. 'What will my bloody sister do when she finds out about it?'

'You mean she'll try and claim it as hers?'

Grace nodded. 'She could. She and Nicholas. They could do just that.'

'I'm really hungry,' said Demi, who had been staring

121

at the painting and not really concentrating on what Ellie and Grace had been saying.

'Let's go and eat,' Ellie agreed, hungry herself and aware that Grace was distressed.

Grace stood by the light switch and waited until Ellie and a slightly tipsy Demi left the room. Then she shut the door on the moonlight-flooded painting, wondering what on earth she'd discovered. If it was nothing but someone's home-painted mural, all would be well. If it was as old and interesting as Ellie seemed to think, it could create all kinds of problems. Or, possibly, solutions.

'Well,' said Grace the next morning, watching Demi spread butter on a piece of toast she had previously cut into tiny squares. 'What first?'

Demi yawned. 'I might go back to bed for a bit.'

Grace, suspecting that Demi had got up at roughly the same time as her and Ellie only out of politeness, felt that bed might be the best place for her, if she did have a hangover. She'd certainly had more wine with the Chinese last night than Grace had wanted her to have.

'Headache, Demi?' she asked.

'No, no. Just tired.'

'Well,' said Ellie, 'I really want to have another look at the painting.'

There was a moment's silence. 'Oh, yes,' said Grace. 'Of course. The painting.'

Grace hadn't exactly forgotten about the painting, but she had filed it in the section of her mind where she kept things she didn't want to think about. She kept trying to stuff Edward in there, but he was too big for the space available.

'Us looking at it won't cause a problem, and the more we know the better. "Information is armour", or something.'

'You're right. Let's go and see it. Are you coming, Demi, or are you going back to bed?'

'Oh no. I'll come if there's something good going on.'

'Come on then,' said Grace, but she lacked what Ellie felt was the appropriate enthusiasm.

Ellie carefully removed the remnants of curtain still hanging and bundled them up with the rest of the fabric on the floor. Then she allowed herself to look at the painting.

The figure which had given Grace such a fright was a naked woman, that much was clear, but a lot of the detail was obscured.

Ellie came close. 'She's awfully mouldy, poor thing! I wonder how long she'd been hiding behind the curtains.'

Demi giggled. 'Perhaps she was playing sardines and no one came to look for her.'

'She's in a really bad state,' said Grace. 'Look, there's a hole. I wonder what did that?'

'A mouse, possibly,' said Ellie.

'As long as it's not a rat,' said Demi.

'But look at the details! Those wonderful flowers and animals. Look at this little rabbit!' Ellie was ecstatic.

'She's not wearing a lot,' said Demi. 'I thought they always kept their hands over their rude bits.'

'You're thinking of Botticelli,' said Ellie. 'But you're right. This is quite . . . explicit.'

'And hugely damaged,' said Grace. 'I don't think she can be remotely valuable, do you, Ellie?'

Ellie glared at her. 'You've got to be kidding! I think this could be an old master!'

'Looks more like a mistress to me,' said Demi helpfully.

Grace regarded her ex-stepdaughter. 'You never would have said anything like that when you stayed with us before.'

'Sorry.'

'No! It's great. Jokes are good. Aren't they, Ellie?'

'Do stop wittering, you two. I think there's probably a matching painting on the other side. I don't think this lady has been alone all these years.'

'She definitely looks on the pull,' said Demi, getting into the spirit of things.

Grace suppressed a sigh. Ellie ignored it. 'She is lovely. And look at the way this fern leads the eye up to her ...'

'Pussy?'

Grace shuddered at Demi's choice of word. 'What would Edward say?' It was a rhetorical question and was duly ignored.

'Can I look behind the other curtain?' asked Ellie. 'I think this might be Eve. See? There's the serpent. You can hardly see him. The varnish has bloomed horribly. Gone milky,' she added, seeing her companions' confusion. 'I bet you Adam is behind that curtain.'

'Eating the apple, probably,' said Demi.

'I'll get a chair and take the curtains down,' said Grace. 'It would be nice to save the silk if possible.'

Ellie didn't comment, but going on what had happened to the curtains covering Eve she suspected there was no chance of saving the silk. She watched as Grace slowly detached the fabric. When it was all safely in Grace's arms, and she had got down from her perch, Ellie saw what she was hoping to see.

'It's covered in dust and grime,' she said, gently stroking it with her finger. 'But he's there. Look.'

Adam was even more salacious-looking than Eve. His member stood proud and upright with not a fig leaf in sight. He was leering, there was no doubt about it, and a couple of extra nymphs – certainly not present in the traditional Bible story – cavorted behind him, their hands flirtatiously over their faces.

'Wow,' said Demi. 'I didn't realise old paintings had stuff like that in them.'

'It's antique pornography,' declared Grace.

'If it's old, it's considered art,' said Ellie. 'They must have been here for centuries. Did your aunt know about them?'

'If she did, she never said anything. Perhaps she didn't like them much.'

'Have you got something we could dust them with? A really soft cloth? I'd like to have a better look.'

Wishing that she could say no, Grace sighed. 'I'll go and have a rummage in the rag bag.' She didn't move.

'What is it, Grace?' Ellie asked, concerned. 'You should be thrilled. These are beautiful paintings, possibly painted by some really important artist.'

Grace sighed deeply. 'Yes, but you don't understand. If they're old and by someone important, they'll be valuable. And if they're valuable, my sister and brother will want some of their value.'

'I didn't think you were serious last night. Do you really mean they'd want you to take them down and sell them?' Ellie was outraged.

Grace nodded. 'Everything that wasn't tied down, they inherited. I got the house, so obviously my inheritance was much more valuable than theirs was. They can't get past that. If they knew I had a valuable old painting—'

'Two,' Demi interrupted.

'Two valuable old paintings on my walls, they would go—'

'Ballistic?' suggested Demi, interrupting again.

'That would probably describe it,' Grace agreed.

'Well, let's have a good look at them,' said Ellie. 'There's no reason your brother and sister would find out about them, is there? How often do they visit?'

Grace sighed again. 'Not all that often, but my sister is on my case at the moment. She thinks that now Edward has left and the roof's been repaired, I should sell the house. She can't believe I'm happy to live here on my own.'

'But you're not on your own,' said Demi. 'You've got us.'

'Yes,' said Grace, 'and that's not going to please her either.'

'Please let me look at the paintings!' Ellie was beginning to be really frustrated by Grace's lack of enthusiasm. 'We can sort out the other stuff about your brother and sister later. After all, they may not be good. They may be just daubs.'

'Even I can see they're not just daubs,' said Demi.

'So can I,' said Grace. 'But they are extremely damaged.'

'You'd be damaged if you'd been hidden behind a curtain for three hundred years! Now let's get a cloth and get rid of some of this dust! We'll have to go carefully, though, and not scrape the surface.'

'I know you think I'm mad not to be pleased about these,' said Grace, when she'd finally located a clean

126

duster in a cupboard in the scullery. 'It's just that they're going to make things so much more complicated.'

'Not if no one knows about them,' said Ellie.

'But how can you keep something like this secret?'

Ellie had lost interest in Grace's desire for secrecy. Very gently, she stroked the cloth downwards over Adam's delicately painted pectorals. 'I'm not sure I should be doing this.'

'Then don't. Let's go and do the washing up,' suggested Grace.

'I think you should get an expert in. These might be really important.'

'I can't do that,' Grace stated.

'It would cost loads,' agreed Demi, and yawned. 'Where's the telly, Grace?'

'There isn't one. Sorry. The big wide-screen was Edward's, and I didn't get another one.'

Ellie frowned. 'Why not? Don't you like telly?'

Grace shrugged. 'It made me feel lonely. But we can get one,' she added, not wanting to expand on the subject of her loneliness.

'Now?'

'Well, no. Now now. It's Sunday, and although I'm sure there are places where we could rent a telly on Sunday, I have no idea where they are.'

'Rent one?' said Demi, to whom renting was obviously a novel concept.

'I'm sure my parents have got a spare one. I had one in my room at home,' said Ellie, 'but it never got a very good picture.'

'I just don't understand how you managed without one,' said Demi.

Grace bit her lip. 'When your father left me, I had

to manage without a lot of things.'

Demi regarded the toe of her trainer. 'Yeah, sorry. I didn't think.'

'Oh, I wasn't trying to make you feel bad! You're not responsible for his actions. I was just trying to explain.'

'It's OK,' said Demi. 'But if he had asked me how I felt about it, I would never have let him leave you for that cow.' She turned to Ellie. 'What about you? You must have had a telly? Could we go over and get it?'

'Babes, I am not going to take Rick's telly from him. I've taken the bed, the duvet, most of the saucepans and a lot of other useful stuff. I'm not going to take away his means to watch the footie!'

Feeling that this question was now settled, Ellie changed the subject back to her own most pressing concern. 'So, what shall we do about the paintings?'

'Nothing,' said Grace firmly. 'Yet,' she added, seeing Ellie's expression. 'Let's just think about what to do, and go and do the washing up!'

'They will need to have *something* done to them,' said Ellie, 'just to stop them deteriorating further. I mean, you may not want them, because of all the trouble they're going to cause, but for art's sake, you have to make sure they don't crumble away.'

'I'll get some new curtains for them to hide behind,' said Grace, opening the dining-room door in a way which suggested the others went through it. 'And I'll have a think. But there's no way I'd let a picture restorer in here. If they need attention that badly, you'll have to do it, Ellie.'

Ellie squeaked. 'I'm just an ex-art student! What do I know about picture restoration?'

'More than I do,' said Grace.

'You could learn,' said Demi. 'There must be something about it on the Internet.'

'Oh hell! Then we'll have to buy a computer as well as a telly. Unless we could get yours from home, Dem?'

'I'm not going back there!' Demi was outraged. 'She'd never let me out again!'

'You're both in a very negative mood,' said Ellie. 'We've just been looking at a great work of art.'

'Very rude art,' said Demi.

'And it may not be great,' said Grace.

'And all you can do is think about material possessions,' Ellie finished.

'Talking of which, what about a trip to the supermarket?' said Grace. 'I know it's not exactly entertainment, Demi, but we do need to go.'

The following morning Grace abandoned Demi and Ellie to their own devices and went into town. She needed a bit of time on her own and in spite of apparently buying everything in sight at the supermarket the previous day, there were several vital items they had managed to forget. Also, she wanted to buy the local paper, which should have run her article by now – their very welcome cheque had arrived that morning.

She was also worrying; Demi's education could not be ignored for very much longer and while the little market town where her aunt had shopped for thirty years had previously seemed perfect, the fact that it lacked a sixth-form college and a bus service meant that it had now lost some of its charm for her. But then her aunt had never had a difficult teenager; Grace and her brother and sister had been extremely conformist and well behaved, and only visited briefly.

To cheer herself up, she called in at the local wine shop.

The wine-shop man was pleased to see her. 'Grace! How nice to see you! Very nice little article in the paper, well done! And I've had very good reports of how your wine tasting went!'

Grace, feeling disadvantaged because she didn't know this man's first name, and had been unaware that he knew hers, said, 'Oh, so you did send a spy.' She thought of Flynn, whom Ellie was so keen for her to pair up with.

The man made a gesture which was only nearly apologetic. 'Well, he's very knowledgeable and I had to check you out if I was going to tell other wine merchants about you, and encourage them to send you stock for tasting.'

'Oh, are you going to do that? In which case, I'll forgive you for the spy.'

'Flynn was very impressed by *your* knowledge.'

Grace suppressed a sigh. It was maddening: even though women had been prominent in the wine trade for decades, men in general still didn't accept that sensitive taste buds were not gender specific.

'What are you going to do next time?' asked the wine merchant, whose name Grace realised she must discover in record time. 'What about English whites? Some very good English whites about, you know.'

'I'm not prejudiced against English wine,' said Grace, not entirely truthfully, 'but they do tend to be a bit expensive. I'll do them when my columns are more established. Although one of the magazines might want a special feature. If they show interest, I'll get back to you.'

'I have contacts with a vineyard,' said the man.

'Why don't you give me your card?' Grace felt this was a master stroke. 'Then I can get in touch by phone if anyone wants an article on English wine.'

When the card was handed over, and Grace had glanced at it, she went on, 'I'm thinking of doing New World whites. Could you let me have a discount – Graham?'

'Tell you what, I'll supply the wine for nothing, as long as you give me a good plug.'

Grace wandered over to a shelf of New World reds. 'I could say how helpful you'd been, and what a marvellous range of wine you supply, but I absolutely cannot recommend your wines above other people's unless they really are better.'

Graham grinned. 'I'd better give you a really good selection then.'

'Don't forget, most people buy wine by price,' said Grace. 'And you have to be very good value to be able to compete with the supermarkets.'

Graham came out from behind the counter and picked up a machine for sticking on prices. 'We're in a wealthy part of the world, Grace. Lots of the weekenders like a really decent bottle to offer their friends.'

'Yes, but they don't read the local paper!'

'They may not, but I've got a friend who writes articles on food for one of those glossies full of pictures of people's houses. He said their wine columnist had packed it in. Want me to put in a word for you?'

'Graham! That would be great! That's just what I need. I'm so grateful for your support.'

'It's a pleasure, Grace. It's hard for all of us making a living these days. We should all help each other.'

131

Grace left the shop feeling distinctly guilty about the fact that, for the local paper, she was still going to talk about wines you could buy in the supermarket. Graham was being so kind! So to celebrate the fact that she might get a column in an up-market magazine, she decided to go to the nearest big town and either buy or hire a television. It really was time she joined the rest of the world and she wasn't sure how long Demi could manage without one.

While Grace was out, and Demi was rearranging her room, Ellie cleared up the breakfast things and then, having had permission from Grace to do it, arranged the crockery she had liberated from Rick and her old house on the dresser. It was extremely satisfying. Then she rearranged the cupboards so everything was to hand, and cleaned the cooker. Only when the kitchen was looking as pretty as possible, with a few fronds of forsythia, the yellow buds still completely closed, in a jug on the table, did she allow herself to go and look at the paintings again.

They were so beautiful in the morning light that there was no doubt they were by an extremely accomplished and possibly famous artist. But their condition was worrying. The varnish had darkened considerably over the years and had a bloom on it which Ellie suspected might have been caused by damp. In parts the varnish had come off and the paint beneath it flaked away. There was a lot of mould, and there was mouse damage on both paintings, although only Eve had a neat hole chewed through the flowery sward at her feet.

Grace might want them just to stay out of sight behind their tattered silk robes but Ellie felt that was almost a sin. Even if they were never on show, they really ought to be restored.

Of course, having them restored would be extremely expensive, but surely there must be some sort of grant that Grace could apply for? The National Trust? English Heritage? Would they help? Or would they want the whole house, plus a huge endowment, before they cared even remotely?

Grace's words – 'you'll have to do it' – still lingered in Ellie's mind. She shook her head and muttered, 'Oh Grace, honey, have you any idea how complicated and delicate such work is?' An amateur picture restorer could ruin something that's been beautiful for centuries. Her History-of-Art tutor's strictures about the restoration of the Sistine Chapel still rung in her ears. He had been apoplectic about what he described as 'almost criminal over-restoration'.

As Ellie's course didn't run to a weekend trip to Rome to see for themselves, the words hadn't meant as much to her and her fellow students as they should have; but remembering her tutor gave her the idea that he might know of a picture restorer, or know someone who did.

Ellie made a decision. She would have a quick drive round the immediate countryside looking for likely houses to paint – there was a very sweet little village not far away that could be a source of several commissions, especially if she started with the pub – and then she would go back to her own college and track down Mr McFadden.

Grace got back from town a couple of hours after Ellie had left. She went in through the back door, and called, 'Hi! Anyone in? I've got milk and some more bread.'

When there was no response she experienced a moment of desertion, then she saw the note on the table. *I've gone out to take some photos and to track down my History-of-Art tutor. Oh, and your sister rang. Can you ring her straight back? It's urgent.*

Demi ambled in. She was wearing a dressing gown and her head was wrapped in a towel.

'Hi, Grace. I've just been putting some streaks in my hair.'

'Oh. Right.' Grace tried to appear positive. 'I look forward to seeing it when it's dry. Now I've got to ring my sister.'

'Oh pooh,' said Demi sympathetically. 'I'll leave you to it.'

'Thanks,' said Grace with a laugh, and then pulled a chair, now decorated with one of Ellie's bright crocheted cushions, near to the telephone and settled down for a long harangue.

Chapter Eight

Ellie had set off in the direction of Bath, to see if she could track down her old History-of-Art tutor. She had a feeling that he'd left the college but she was sure someone there would have an address or a telephone number for him. She felt her mission to be urgent. If the paintings stayed in their current condition for much longer, they would deteriorate even more, and now they had been exposed to the light, there might be a risk of further fading.

It took her a tiresomely long time to track down the university secretary who, after a lot of pleading, gave Ellie an email address for her ex-tutor.

'I'm sorry,' the woman explained. 'It's more than my job's worth to give out a tutor's home address to a student.'

'I'm not a student here any more. I left a while ago.'

'Even worse.' Then the woman softened. 'You can use one of these computers, seeing as it's lunchtime. Goodness knows how often he signs on. And that email address may be old.'

After Ellie had finally managed to send her email, 'What do you want him for?' asked the secretary.

'I need a picture restorer. I thought he might know one.'

'Well, have you tried the *Yellow Pages*?' The woman

produced a ragged copy. 'It's always worth a look. And if there's nothing in there, you could try the art galleries or antique shops. They're bound to know of picture restorers.'

'You're a genius,' said Ellie. 'Why didn't I think of that! I forgive you for not giving me Mr McFadden's telephone number.'

Once Ellie had found the right section, she discovered several picture restorers. She glanced at the woman, toying with the idea of asking if she could use the phone, but as she had her mobile with her, she decided not to push her luck.

When she had eventually found somewhere in the college that was both quiet and had good reception, she looked at the list of numbers she had made. It was sort of embarrassing, ringing someone to ask advice. It would have been fine if she'd just been researching the best person for the highly skilled and delicate job of restoring Adam and Eve to their former glorious salaciousness, but it was more difficult asking to pick the brains of someone who'd probably trained and practised for years, just so she could try her amateur hand at what they did for a living.

And she couldn't even say why she was doing it. If she had been allowed to, she would have appealed to them on the artistic version of humanitarian grounds – 'Please tell me how to save these fantastic works of art' – but Grace's neurotic insistence on secrecy forbade that. She'd just have to think of something else. Seeing a group of students walk by and hearing a snatch of their conversation gave her the answer.

'Hello,' she said to the very up-market-sounding person who answered the telephone at the first number.

'I'm an art student and I need to study a few basic techniques about picture restoration. Would it be—'

'We don't have time to talk to students. Sorry.'

When the next two numbers produced similarly negative results, Ellie changed her tack.

'Hi, I'm an art student looking for a work placement. You don't have to pay me and I'll work for nothing for two weeks. I'll do anything.'

There was a long silence, then a sigh. 'Well, my studio needs clearing out. Will you do that?'

'Yes, as long as I get the opportunity to get some idea of how to restore pictures.'

'Why? Are you thinking of going into the business?'

'It's an option,' said Ellie, who'd had lots of opportunity to think of the reply to this obvious question. 'After all, it's very difficult to make a living in Fine Art.'

'Hmph. I don't think of what I do as second fiddle to pickling sheep.' God! The man did sound hostile! 'What I do is an art and a science in itself.'

'I'm sure it is,' went on Ellie. 'Which is why I want to study it.' She crossed her fingers. 'I was sorry to give up science at school, and want to do something more scientific.'

There was another grunt. 'Well, you'd better come over and I'll have a look at you. But I haven't got time to babysit you. You'll have to be able to work on your own.'

'Clearing out your studio?'

'Not the studio I'm working in at the moment, obviously.'

Ellie mouthed an obscenity into her mobile phone.

'Do you want to come, or not?' demanded the man, who perhaps had picked up the four-letter word.

'Oh, yes. Please,' said Ellie, abandoning her plan to try some galleries to see if she could find someone a bit more forthcoming. It would be better to be actually in the same place as the work, especially as it was possible she would have to give up two weeks to studying it.

'You'd better come now, then. I'm busy later.'

This wasn't quite what Ellie wanted to hear but as she might not get a better offer, she had to go with it.

'Oh, good. Where are you?'

There followed a stressful few moments, during which Ellie had to run back to the helpful secretary for a piece of paper on which to write down the myriad directions how to get to the unhelpful man's house. But at last Ellie said, 'I'll be there in an hour, then.'

'An hour! It's only twenty minutes away, for God's sake!' And he put the phone down.

As she walked back to the car park, having thanked the helpful secretary (whom she might very well need again) and checked the address, Ellie seriously considered abandoning the hostile picture restorer who lived at such a complicated location and looking for someone more willing to share their secrets. After all, he didn't have any information about her, like her name or, more importantly, her telephone number. But by the time she reached her 2CV she had decided against this softer option. The world of picture restoration was bound to be small and cliquey. If Mr Nasty was remotely put out by Ellie's non-appearance, it was almost bound to get around that she was unreliable. She'd better pitch up, even if it was a waste of time.

She got there in thirty-five minutes, which she felt was pretty good, considering the complications of Bath's one-way system and the narrowness of the streets. Even more extraordinary was the fact she managed to find somewhere to park really nearby.

She knocked on the door of one of Bath's huge Georgian houses, most of which had been divided into flats. This was no exception, but as it was definitely the address she had been given she just assumed that he worked from home and that picture restoration didn't take up much space.

The man who opened the door was surprisingly clean. For some reason Ellie had thought he would look like an artist: streaked with paint. He was tall and thin with black hair streaked with grey, and he still appeared hostile; it might have taken Ellie thirty-five minutes to get there, but that hadn't been long enough for him to become welcoming and pleasant. 'You've come to do work experience?'

'No!' Ellie put her hand in his, determined to turn his mood around. She smiled, making sure she captured his attention with her eyes. 'I'm Ellie Summers. I'm offering my services to you as unpaid labour for two weeks. Work experience is what you do at school.'

Her silent insistence that she was offering something no sane man would refuse made him smile, obviously against his will. It was, Ellie was forced to acknowledge, a very attractive smile.

He shook her hand. 'Randolph Frazier. Sorry, you look about seventeen. You'd better come in. Coffee?'

'I'd rather have tea.'

'Come through, then.'

It was a huge, loft-like space, which was surprising after such a traditional exterior. Natural light flooded in through the many, tall windows and she realised that he must have knocked out every wall in the place, and possibly had extended into next door. Beyond the windows, which still retained their original dimensions, Ellie glimpsed a wonderful view.

Ellie was accustomed to being in artists' studios: cluttered, often untidy spaces, their floors, walls and doors covered in paint. The space he led her through to where a small kitchen lurked under a window was more like a laboratory than a studio. It was immaculately clean and tidy. A couple of easels stood with paintings on them, one obviously halfway through being cleaned, and another which looked perfect. There were two huge tables as well, and on one was another painting, lying on its back.

'Wow,' said Ellie, drawn to one of the easels. It was a picture of a St Bernard dog, and could have been an old master, it was so vivid, so fresh. She went close up to it and peered at the beautifully painted fur, the softness and nobility of expression in the huge dog's eyes, the brightness of the brass ring in the collar. 'That's really lovely.'

'A touch sentimental for my personal taste,' said the man, who had presumably restored it. 'It was quite badly torn and some of the paint was flaking. The frame was in a bad condition too.'

Ellie peered closer. 'Where was the tear?'

'Can't you see?'

'No.'

'Try these.' He handed her a pair of magnifying glasses with lights in them. 'Right. Look over there.'

'I can just see something,' said Ellie after a few moments' staring. 'But hardly.'

She straightened up and handed him the glasses back. He wasn't good-looking in the way that Rick was, but he had an arresting quality that she acknowledged many women would find attractive. If he weren't so utterly terrifying, she'd consider having her affaire with him – he certainly wouldn't be clingy and sentimental when she told him it was only temporary.

'So why did you want to get involved with picture restoration?' he asked, continuing the journey to the kitchen.

'The usual reasons. I got my degree and wanted to use it, but I also want to earn money.'

'You don't need a Fine Arts background to be a picture restorer. A degree in chemistry would be more useful.'

This was a rather dampening statement. 'Oh.'

'I mean,' Randolph Frazier went on, 'if you're going to do it remotely seriously you'd have to do a course at somewhere like Newcastle. It's for two years and they won't let you in without a science A level.'

Ellie didn't need her GCSE in Maths to work out that it would take her a minimum of four years to get any sort of qualification in picture restoration and, fond as she was of Grace, and important as she believed the paintings were, it was too great a sacrifice.

'There aren't any shorter courses, which you could do without the A level?'

He didn't deign to answer this. 'If you're going to do it, do it properly. How do you like your tea?'

Ellie sighed. This whole idea was probably a complete waste of time, but perhaps if she could get him chatting over the tea mugs he might inadvertently give her a few hints. 'Just a drop of milk, no sugar, thank you. So how did you get into picture restoration, then?'

'It was different for me. I left school at sixteen and

wanted to work in the summer holidays before going to college. I applied for a job – someone wanting just what I was, a completely untrained school-leaver – and got it. I wasn't allowed near a painting for months, but by that time I'd given up the notion of university and knew what I wanted to do with my life.'

'Wow!'

'I did take A levels, at evening classes, to pacify my parents, and they were quite useful. But it's not something you can learn in five minutes, you know.'

Ellie looked into her mug to hide her disappointment. 'Well, of course, I didn't think you could. So how do you start on a painting? Dust it?'

His horror made her blush. 'Certainly not! Supposing there was some loose paint?'

Ellie blushed harder. There definitely was loose paint on those panels. 'You mean dusting it would damage it in some way?'

'Of course! You'd lose paint for ever.' He frowned. 'Why are you looking so guilty? You've gone bright red.'

'I'm not! I mean, I haven't!' If only she could tell him about the panels, but she supposed he was the very last person who should know. He was bound to tell some higher authority. 'I'm pregnant,' she added as a diversion. It seemed to work.

'Oh, I see. I suppose that does explain your somewhat shifty manner. Not married, I assume?'

'I don't know how you can possibly tell that!' she protested indignantly.

'You're not wearing a ring, and even if you're not seventeen, you're far too young and you wouldn't be doing work experience if you had a husband to help support you. Are you really an art student?'

The bloody man could obviously read her like a book! 'I graduated nearly four years ago, actually. I got a two-one.'

His eyebrows went up. 'So you're older than you look. Why the interest in what I do?'

'I told you!' It had seemed a perfectly good explanation before, why was he questioning it? 'I want to make money out of art.'

'Well, this isn't the way to do it. No picture conservators are rich.'

'I don't need to be rich! Just earn a living!'

'Even that's questionable. But still, you're welcome to work for me for nothing, for a fortnight.'

'But it won't really be just cleaning out your studio, will it? What I'm really after is some sort of training. Like an apprenticeship.'

'Apprenticeships last approximately seven years. And there's something you're not telling me.'

Ellie sighed. 'There is. Unfortunately, it's not my secret, so I can't tell you.'

He stared at her for what seemed like for ever. Then he slowly nodded. 'Very well, then. You clean out my studio, and I'll tell you about what I do. It is a fascinating subject.'

He smiled again, just very slightly, and Ellie suppressed a sigh. He's far too old to think about having an affaire with, she told herself as she went down the steps to the pavement. Now concentrate!

While Ellie was hunting out someone to help her with the picture restoration, Grace was biting her own particular bullet and telephoning her sister.

'Oh,' said Allegra, 'I'm glad you've rung back. The

143

thing is, I think I should come round and see you.'

'It would be lovely to see you.' Grace crossed her fingers superstitiously against the lie. 'But why don't you all come, as a family?'

'It wouldn't be social, really. I've got this report. From the man who came round and inspected the house?'

'I remember.' Grace wondered if there was anything significant in the fact that Allegra had said 'the house' instead of 'your house'.

'Yes. It's awfully bad news, I'm afraid.'

Grace was determined not to let Allegra hear her heart sink. 'Well, couldn't you just send me a copy of the report? I'm sure I'll be able to understand it if I concentrate hard.'

'I don't trust you to read it at all!' Allegra went on, oblivious to Grace's sliver of sarcasm. 'You know what you're like about that wretched house. You refuse to see its faults.'

'I don't think that's true. I'm aware how cold it is. Did I tell you someone's given us a Rayburn? It should make a vast difference to the kitchen.'

A moment's silence while Allegra considered. 'I think that's probably quite a good idea. A range always adds a homely touch and some people might be put off if the house seems too chilly.'

'Sorry?'

'Love, I know you're not going to like it, but when you read this report, and find out how much money it's going to take to put it all right, you'll realise you're going to have to sell. But don't worry,' Allegra added, clearly feeling she might have piled on the agony a trifle too much. 'There will be plenty for you to buy something really sweet with your share of what's left.'

Grace examined her nails for a moment to give Allegra the impression she was considering what she'd said. Then she suppressed a sigh. 'Allegra, what makes you think I'm going to want to sell the house this time? I haven't before when you've asked me.'

'Because you won't be able to afford to pay for the dry-rot treatment.'

Dry rot. Those words did create a bit of a sense of doom. 'Oh. So how much is it?'

'I don't want to discuss it now. I want to come over and talk you through my plan. The thing is, you're never going to be able to raise the cash to have it done. So I can pay, and then you can pay me back when you've sold the house.'

Grace nearly said: 'If you've got the money to lend me, couldn't I just borrow it and pay you back as and when I can?' But she didn't, because she knew Allegra wouldn't lend her the money on those terms. 'Well, just tell me how much it is and then I can decide how to pay for it. I could probably get out a loan. The house isn't mortgaged, after all.'

'If you do that, you'll be paying the loan back for the rest of your life!' Allegra sounded irritated that Grace had found a solution which didn't involve her so quickly.

'But as I'll also be living in my house for the rest of my life, that wouldn't matter,' said Grace sweetly, but actually not happy at the prospect of being in debt for ever.

'Don't be silly. I can come over now, or tomorrow night.'

Grace needed time to think. 'I've got to go and do something with Demi now.' She crossed her fingers in the hope that it would prevent Allegra asking her what.

It worked. Her question was more *who*. 'Demi? Your ex-stepdaughter? Why?'

'Oh, didn't I mention it?' Grace knew very well she hadn't mentioned it, because she knew Allegra would make the most awful fuss. 'Demi's come to live with me for a bit.'

'For God's sake, why? You're hardly—'

'A fit person to be in charge of a teenager? That's just what Hermia said, but Demi's miserable at home.'

'That's ridiculous! You can't look after a teenager on your own!'

'I'm not on my own. I've got Ellie to help me.'

'Who's Ellie?' Allegra's sharp tone made Grace wince.

'Oh, didn't I tell you about her? She's another lodger.'

'It sounds as if you're turning the place into a doss house! Do the council know?'

'No! What business is it of theirs?'

'Your Council Tax! You're only paying for single occupancy.'

'OK then, I'll tell them. Honestly, Allegra, why you should object to me having a couple of people to live with me – women, both of them – when you've been saying ever since Edward left that it is ridiculous me living in the great big house all on my own . . .'

'It's not the same! Having lodgers—'

'They are not lodgers, exactly!' She crossed her fingers again, this time against the lie. 'Demi is my step-daughter—'

'Not any more.'

'And Ellie is my friend. Now I do wish you'd keep your nose out of my business!' Allegra obviously had far too much time on her hands.

'The dry rot is my business, especially if I have to pay to have it fixed.'

'But you don't *have* to pay! You can tell me how much it'll cost and I'll pay!'

'You won't be able to!'

Schadenfreude travelled well over telephone lines, Grace discovered. Allegra was barely able to stop herself sounding smug.

'Not if you don't tell me how much, no.' Grace spoke calmly, as if to the slightly slow of understanding. She knew it would madden Allegra and it did.

'Very well then, thirty thousand pounds!'

'Oh my God,' breathed Grace, unable to feign indifference to mere money any more. 'How much? How can it possibly cost all that?'

Allegra's anger turned to sympathy. 'That's why I wanted to come and tell you in person. I knew it would be a shock. These things just are horrifically expensive, and you can't not get it dealt with, the house will crumble away.'

'Surely not!'

'Well, eventually it will. It's serious, Gracie. This is a problem you can't just ignore and hope it will go away.'

Grace gave in. 'I suppose you'd better come over then – come tomorrow evening, for supper at about eight.'

It was only after she'd put the phone down and was rubbing her ear, having pressed the receiver to it too hard in her anxiety, that she took in the fact that she'd invited her sister for a meal with no Edward to protect her. It would be the first time since he'd left. Before her renewed interest in Grace's house, Allegra had always been too busy to come so far just for a meal and always expected Grace to make the journey to Surrey. What had she been thinking of?

When Ellie returned, she was very tired but bubbling with excitement.

'I've had such a good day! I went to Bath to try and get in touch with my old History-of-Art tutor—'

'Did you do it?' asked Demi, who was bored.

'I sent him an email – God knows if he'll get it – but I did get in touch with this ace picture restorer.'

'You didn't tell him about the paintings?' asked Grace, who had not had a good day and was inclined to panic.

'No! I just got him to agree to have me on a work placement.'

'What does that mean?' asked Demi. 'Is it like work experience?'

'Just, only when you're at university, it's called a work placement.'

'What's it called when you're not at university?' asked Grace.

'Working for nothing,' Ellie said, sinking on to a chair.

'Poor you. And you're doing it for my paintings. You're a star,' said Grace.

'Grace's sister is coming for dinner tomorrow,' said Demi. 'I've met her. She's really scary.'

'Is she? Oh, Grace! Did she invite herself?'

'No, I invited her, but she'd said she had to see me. I didn't have much choice.'

'And what are you going to give her to eat?' Ellie asked, knowing Grace didn't really do cooking.

'I don't know. A joint, perhaps?'

Demi giggled. 'You're going to give your sister marijuana for dinner? Wicked!'

Grace made a cross face at Demi. 'Which is easier, do you think? Beef, lamb or pork?'

'Quite honestly, they're all about the same and I don't recommend doing a joint,' said Ellie. 'I used to do them for Rick, and they're lovely, but it's really difficult getting the roast potatoes brown and the veg all cooked at the same time, and then there's the gravy.'

'Oh God. What should I cook then? She's terribly gourmet. It was all right when Edward was here, because he was terribly gourmet, too, and we'd either get someone in to do it, or Edward would cook himself.' Grace found herself overwhelmed by a pang of wistfulness when she thought about Edward cooking. He did it with such attention to detail. In the early days of their marriage he would come home from the office and cook her delicious little morsels.

She shrugged off the pang with a shake of her head. She had been getting so much better lately, only thinking about Edward about seventy per cent of the time. She must not allow herself to backslide. 'On the other hand,' she went on briskly, 'although I did invite her she forced me into it. She can just have what we're having. We'll get a takeaway and Allegra can eat chicken korma like most of the rest of the country.'

'What?' asked Demi, confused.

'It's the nation's favourite dish,' explained Grace.

'Would you like me to do it?' suggested Ellie, ignoring this diversion. 'I mean, I don't want to take over if you were looking forward to doing it, but if—'

'Oh, Ellie!' Grace hugged her. 'That would be brilliant!'

'But you'll have to go shopping tomorrow. I want to

149

read some art books, so I don't look a complete idiot when I go back to the picture restorer's the day after tomorrow.'

'Of course! And you're quite sure you didn't tell the picture restorer about the paintings?' Now she had stopped worrying about the cooking Grace found herself free to worry about Allegra discovering her hidden treasure, and it seemed entirely possible that there would be some complicated code of practice which compelled art experts to report important discoveries to some higher authority, so they could be saved for posterity or something. 'I'll have to get some curtains, too,' she added, thinking aloud.

'Why would having curtains stop Ellie's picture restorer finding out about the paintings?' asked Demi.

'Oh, I wasn't talking about him, it's Allegra. She's got this report that young man did on the house and she wants to discuss it. She might want to look round everywhere.'

'Then we'd better pin the old ones up again,' said Ellie. 'She's bound to notice new ones. Especially if you buy them off the peg.'

'I was thinking of the charity shops, junk shops, places like that,' said Grace.

'Those windows are bloody enormous, Grace,' said Ellie.

'Well, we'll see if we can get the old ones up. Oh, bloody Allegra!'

'Tut, tut, language,' said Demi.

Chapter Nine

❧

The tune of 'Jingle Bells' issuing from her shopping bag made Grace jump. Then she remembered that she'd borrowed Ellie's mobile and it was probably her, adding to the shopping list which Grace was now working her way through. She retrieved it and found an area in the supermarket which was less busy.

'Hello?'

'Hello.'

It was Flynn. It was so strange hearing his voice in the supermarket that Grace felt herself blush.

'Demi gave me your mobile number. I've got a case of wine here for you, and she thought you might like to collect it on the way back from the shops.'

'Oh. Why have you got it?'

'It's from Graham. He sent it to the wrong address.'

'Who's Graham?'

'From the wine shop? Also, I wondered if I could come round and make a start on putting in the Rayburn soon. Possibly tonight? I'm going away and want to get it done before I go because I'm going to be really busy when I get back and otherwise the thing won't be operating until the summer.'

With part of her mind Grace was studying a packet of shiitake mushrooms, wondering how they could ever taste of anything except bits of stick, but the other part was wondering if having Flynn in the house would be a good distraction for Allegra.

'Um. I've got my sister coming for dinner.'

'You have a sister, have you? Is she anything like you?'

'Not at all! She's very spiky and demanding.'

'Just like you, then.'

'I am not demanding,' said Grace, acknowledging that spiky did describe her when she was near Flynn. She had certainly never allowed herself spikes when she was with Edward.

'Well then, shall I come over tonight or not? I couldn't get it plumbed in so it won't heat the hot water, but it would heat the kitchen and you could cook on it. It might be your last opportunity for heat this side of next Christmas.'

'I haven't got the pipe and bits and pieces that you said you needed.' She felt strangely flustered. It was so out of context, talking to him while she was in such a crowded place.

'I knew you wouldn't have. I'll bring what I need, and as I said, I won't have time to do the plumbing. I'll come about six.'

'Six. Fine. My sister's coming at eight.'

'I might well be out of the way by then.' He laughed. 'We don't want your snotty-nosed sister catching you with an Irishman in the kitchen.'

Because this was a fair estimate of how Allegra might react to Flynn's presence, she said, 'No, no. I was just thinking it would be nice if you could stay for supper. Ellie's got a lovely meal planned.'

'Oh.'

'Well, make up your mind!' She didn't want to appear

152

too keen. 'I'm in town now and if Ellie needs more ingredients, I'll have to get them!'

'You do have a way of making a man feel wanted.'

'I'm sorry! I'm just in a bit of a state. The supermarket is not where I usually arrange my social life.'

'Social life, is it?' She could hear him smiling. 'I see I've been promoted.'

'Oh, for God's sake!' She felt herself blushing. 'Are you coming or not?'

'I'll be there at six and I'll bring the wine Graham sent by mistake. Though it doesn't look as if there's anything drinkable in it. I'd better bring something decent myself.'

'I have plenty of wine, thank you!' said Grace and disconnected. What was it about that man? She was as meek as milk with every other human on the planet, but with Flynn Cormack – or Cormack Flynn, whatever his bloody name was – she was a cow.

As she slipped the phone back into her bag she absolved herself of 'cow' and realised that it wasn't only Flynn she'd been more assertive with lately. Allegra and Hermia, even Edward to some extent, had all heard the rough side of her tongue recently. Perhaps she was growing up at last, pushing past the stunting influence of a pair of bossy siblings and a dynamic husband. Then she fished the phone back out of her bag. She'd better tell Ellie she'd invited Flynn to dinner; she was bound to want more pork fillets.

Grace's first thought when she turned back into the drive was that Ellie's little 2CV had been turned into two, much larger, newer cars. Then she realised that the inevitable visit from Hermia and Edward had finally happened and that Ellie was out. Grace hoped that Demi was with her, or it would be difficult to fight off a kidnap attempt if that's what Hermia and Edward wanted. Although part of her didn't think they did want Demi back, or they'd have been here before now.

They were waiting beside their cars, their arms folded, watching each other with hostility. When Grace parked, they both looked round and the hostility was turned on her. Grace tried hard not to let her heart sink as she looked at them through her rear-view mirror, but it was obviously weighted with lead because, without permission from her, it plummeted.

She turned round to the back seat, ostensibly to gather up the carrier bags, in fact giving herself time to collect herself. She reminded herself that she was actually doing them both a huge favour, and soon they would realise it. And it was high time she stopped being frightened of Hermia and daunted in a different way by Edward.

By the time she finally emerged from the car she was feeling positively belligerent.

'Hello, you two.' They would hate being lumped together like that. 'I won't be a moment. I'll just get this shopping. Have you been here long?'

'Fifteen minutes,' snapped Hermia. 'Where have you been?'

Tempted to answer 'the opera', Grace ignored this and carried her bags to the front door, dropped them, then fished about in her bag for the key.

'Where's Demeter?' asked Edward, more pertinently, and impossible to ignore.

'I'm not sure,' said Grace, opening the door. 'I expect she's with Ellie – my friend – and they will have left a note. If you could just give me a hand with the bags?'

Reluctantly, Hermia and Edward helped Grace get the bags into the house and then followed her to the kitchen.

'Ah, yes. Here's the note,' said Grace, heartily relieved that there was one. *Ellie and I have gone shopping for hair stuff, back soon,* she read.

Don't get back too soon, thought Grace, putting the perishables in the fridge, if you don't want your parents to see what you've done to your hair already.

She ignored the rest of the shopping – one advantage to having a cold house – and put the kettle on.

'I'm just going to make you comfortable in the drawing room,' she said, aware she couldn't possibly make coffee – or anything – with them standing about like animated marble statues that hated each other.

She had chivvied them as far as the hall when the doorbell rang. It was Ellie and Demi. Ellie had a key, but had obviously seen the cars and decided not to use it. As Grace opened the door, she wondered how much persuasion, or indeed force, it had taken Ellie to get Demi out of the car; she must have freaked when she saw not just one parent's car, but two.

'Demeter!' shrieked Hermia. 'What have you done to your hair?'

'Hello, Mummy,' said Demi.

'Hello, darling,' said Edward, embracing his daughter.

When Grace had last heard him say those words it had been to her, a very long time ago. She must be a lot better, she thought, because it hardly hurt at all.

'Tell me, Grace,' asked Hermia, while this was going on between Demi and her father, 'how did you get

155

Edward to buy you such a good car? He was far more generous to you than he ever was to me, and I had two children to keep!'

Grace knew at least part of the reason Edward had been so generous was because she had behaved so well when he said he'd found someone else, putting as few difficulties in his path as possible. At the time she had done it in the very faint hope that if she was terribly civilised and reasonable, he might come back. That and the fact that Edward hated scenes, and she just thought they would make the whole agonising experience even more painful.

Fortunately, she didn't have to answer as Hermia realised she should have hugged her daughter before shouting at her, and made up for lost time.

'This is Ellie,' said Grace to Edward. 'She's living with me now. This is Edward.'

'Hello,' said Ellie. 'Would you like me to go and make some coffee?' she said to Grace.

'That would be terribly kind,' said Grace, who seemed to Ellie to be coping quite well.

'I'll help!' said Demi.

Grace was about to forbid this when Ellie said, 'You'll need more chairs. Demi can help me bring them.'

'We don't want coffee!' snapped Hermia. 'I just want my daughter back!'

'Let's have coffee while we discuss it,' said Grace, opening the door of the drawing room, pleased to see how much early spring sunshine filled it, although it was still very cold.

'If you think I'm going to discuss my daughter with you' – Hermia almost spat out the words – 'you are very much mistaken!'

156

'No need to be rude,' said Edward. 'Grace has made a very sensible suggestion.'

He always did stick up for me, thought Grace, as he opened the door and ushered in his ex-wives.

Hermia shivered loudly as they entered.

Ignoring it, Grace said, 'I'll just go and tell Ellie there are biscuits among the shopping and fetch something to sit on,' she said.

'Where did you find Ellie?' asked Edward.

'I told you, she's a friend of mine,' said Grace, refusing to be intimidated by his steely tone and raised eyebrow. 'She's staying with me for a bit and helping with expenses.'

'Oh, she's a friend of yours, is she? I wondered if you'd started taking in lodgers,' said Hermia, earning herself a reproving glare from her ex-husband.

'Would you both like coffee?' persisted Grace, trying to keep the atmosphere polite. 'Or would either of you prefer tea?'

'Coffee, please,' snapped Hermia.

'Me too,' said Edward. 'Hermia, shall we go into the window embrasure? There's a wonderful view of the garden from there.'

Grace escaped, feeling very ambivalent about her ex-husband showing his ex-wife her garden. She hoped they appreciated the hundreds of Wordsworth daffodils she had planted in the grass, their tiny heads nodding in the wind.

'I daren't leave them in there alone for long,' said Grace in the kitchen. 'Come with me, Demi, and bring a chair.'

'No, I've got to help Ellie!' Demi said in fright. 'She's going to help me put a bandeau on.'

'Honey, they've already seen your tiger stripes, and they can't do much about it. Come on!'

'No! Please, Grace! I'll bring the coffee and as many chairs as you want, but please don't make me go in there a minute before I have to!'

Looking at Demi's worried face, Grace took pity on her and returned to the drawing room alone, a chair in each hand, just in time to hear Hermia say, 'God, it's a heavenly house! Freezing bloody cold, of course. Wasted on her! A half-decent developer and it would be worth an absolute fortune.'

Horribly reminded of her sister, Grace wondered if Hermia and Allegra knew each other, and remembered that they did, slightly.

'The coffee will be along in just a moment. Ellie and Demi will bring it. Do sit down.'

Edward held a chair for Hermia and tried to do the same for Grace, but she resisted. She didn't want to confront Edward and Hermia perched on a kitchen chair.

'And how did you meet your friend Ellie?' said Edward. 'You've never mentioned her.'

'No, I met her since you left. She's an artist. I met her through her work. She's perfectly respectable.'

Hermia snorted. 'Respectable or not, Demeter's got to come home. She has her education to think of.'

'I certainly agree with you there, but I think the trouble is, she feels a bit neglected,' said Grace boldly. 'You both have new partners and Demi feels you don't have time for her.'

'Typical self-centred teenager!' snapped Hermia. 'I've always had to work – since you left, anyway,' she added, shooting a resentful glance at Edward. 'And I have to nurture my relationship—'

There was a sound from Edward.

'I do!' went on Hermia. 'And I have to have a little time for myself. Demi gets every second that's left over.'

'Not many seconds, obviously,' said Edward. 'What do you do with the "little time for yourself"?'

'Go to the gym, have the occasional massage or facial. I know you' – she indicated she meant Grace with a sort of grimace – 'never bothered with any personal maintenance, but it is important, you know. Edward did leave you, even if you are young enough to be his daughter.'

Aware that Hermia was still very bitter about her own divorce from Edward, Grace managed to ignore this dig and, seeing the door handle move, she said quickly, 'Please don't mention Demi's hair again. She knows she made a horrible mistake.'

Demi and Ellie came in. Demi, looking rather pale, was carrying a tea chest and Ellie mugs. While Demi turned the tea chest over so that it became a table, Grace muttered to Ellie, 'Only four mugs! Where's yours?'

'I'm going to unpack the shopping,' said Ellie. 'You don't need me, this is a family thing.'

'Quite right,' agreed Hermia. 'You don't need to be here either, Grace.'

'Yes, she does,' said Edward with the sort of authority not even Hermia would care to argue with. 'Demi! Where are you going?'

'To get a chair, Dad! If that's all right with you?' she said defensively.

'You're to come straight back,' he ordered, and Grace realised why she had never argued with him. He was very commanding.

'Right,' he said when Demi had joined the circle and

was sitting looking down at her hands. 'Let's talk this over reasonably. Hermia, is it true you have no time for Demi?'

'She gets every spare penny and every spare moment—' Hermia began.

'Except there aren't any,' interjected Demi. 'You and Tod are always chewing each other's faces off.'

Grace winced, wondering how someone who had called her children Perseus and Demeter could possibly live with someone who had a name like a character off *Neighbours*. Hermia opened her mouth to protest. Edward raised a hand and no one said anything.

'Well, would you like to come and live with Caroline and me?'

Hermia gave a mirthless laugh. 'That bitch! She hasn't a motherly hormone in her body, however many of them she has pumped in! She won't want a teenager cluttering up the place, making her feel old!'

'Hermia!' began Edward.

Grace felt obliged to mediate. 'I think, Edward, that Demi feels that you and Caroline haven't been together long and that she wouldn't really appreciate having Demi there.' Demi had actually described Caroline as a selfish bitch, but Grace didn't think it would be helpful to tell Edward this.

Edward exhaled. 'It's true that Caroline does find Demeter difficult, because you don't behave well when you're with us.' He frowned at his daughter.

'I can't think why. It's not as if she wasn't properly brought up,' said Hermia. 'Even if I did have to do it single-handed.'

'Possibly her role model wasn't all it might have been,' bit out Edward from between clenched teeth.

'Her role model was fine! It was her absent father running off with schoolgirls that made life difficult for us! Perseus left the country to avoid watching you make a fool of yourself all over again.'

'That and the place at Harvard,' murmured Edward. 'Or possibly it was his mother he didn't want to see with a man only a few years older than himself! No wonder Demeter has gone off the rails.'

'For goodness' sake!' Grace exploded, really angry now. 'Will you two listen to yourselves? You're talking about Demi as if she wasn't here! You're supposed to be discussing what's best for her, but all you can do is score cheap points off each other! You should both be ashamed of yourselves.'

Only when she'd finished did she register how silent the room had gone and realise how loudly and vehemently she must have spoken to create such an effect. She must be getting stronger.

Demi, who had been sitting inspecting her nails, wincing slightly as each salvo was exchanged, sat up. 'Yeah! That's right, Grace. Thank you.'

At this moment, the door opened and Ellie came in with a tray. Grace realised she must have been waiting outside for a good moment to bring it in.

Ellie put the tray down carefully on the cloth-covered tea chest. She had made proper coffee in the cafetière she had extracted from Rick, and heated some milk which she put in a charming little jug she had found harbouring a spider in the larder. She and Grace exchanged glances.

'Are you going to join us, Ellie?' asked Grace, a little desperately.

'I won't if you don't mind.' She looked up at Edward

161

and Hermia and explained, 'I'm pregnant and the smell of coffee makes me nauseous.'

Hermia yawned slightly and looked out of the window. 'So it's a home for unmarried mothers you're operating then,' she said, loud enough for Ellie to hear.

'Hermia!' Grace glared at her. 'We are here to think what's best to do for Demi!'

'Yes,' said Edward. 'Do try and stick to the point, Hermia.'

'And stop dissing Grace's friends!' said Demi. 'Ellie's cool.' She glared at her mother. 'She can cook.'

Hermia made a derisive noise which eloquently expressed her opinion of anyone who did anything so trivial.

'It's your education I'm concerned about, Demeter,' said Edward, more kindly now. 'How will you continue it here?'

'She can't stay here,' stated Hermia.

'Well, she won't go back to you,' snapped Edward.

'Of course she will. Demeter dear, you've made your statement, now go and pack your things and wait for me in the car.'

'No! I'm not going back with either of you!' shouted Demi, and she ran from the room. Grace thought she was crying.

'Now look what you've done,' said Edward dryly.

'What you've both done!' said Grace. 'Please just stop this childish bickering and think about what's best for your daughter!'

Neither Hermia nor Edward cared very much for being called childish, especially by Grace, who was so much younger than they were. They regarded her sourly.

'Now, it's quite obvious that even if you dragged

162

Demi home by her hair, she wouldn't stay there,' Grace said to Hermia. 'And I don't think Caroline really wants a troubled teenager thrust on her when she's just got married. Demi has made it quite clear she feels neglected by both her parents.'

Edward raised an eyebrow in a way which once would have had Grace lowering her eyes and murmuring apologies. No longer. At one time Edward could do no wrong in her eyes, now she saw that with regard to his daughter, he was definitely not perfect. Perhaps it was just as well they hadn't had children together.

'What I suggest,' she went on, 'is that Demi stays here. I will undertake to get her to and from her sixth-form college, but it is quite a trek.'

'Couldn't you find somewhere nearer to take her?' suggested Hermia.

'No,' said Grace firmly. 'I couldn't. I know perfectly well what would happen. If it all went wrong and Demi left without an exam to her name, you'd both blame me. And she is your daughter, not mine.'

There was a long silence as both parents realised what Grace had offered; that she had agreed to take on the child that they both found so difficult.

'That is a very generous offer,' said Edward. 'But are you in a position to get Demeter to and from college?'

'I don't see why on earth not,' snapped Hermia, less inclined to be grateful than her ex-husband. 'She's got a very nice car to do it in.'

'Actually I was thinking of selling the car and buying something cheaper,' said Grace. 'But I will have some sort of vehicle.'

'Won't you need to get a job?' demanded Hermia. 'Or

did Edward leave you so well provided for you can be a lady of leisure?'

'You should be glad I don't have to go out to work in the normal way,' said Grace. 'Because that way I can look after your daughter!'

'What do you mean, "in the normal way"?' asked Edward. 'What are you doing to keep yourself?'

'Not that it's any business of either of you, but I hold wine tastings and write articles for magazines about them. I've a column in the local paper and I've been approached about writing for a glossy magazine as well.'

'Huh! That won't put bread on the table!' said Hermia.

'No, not enough, which is why I'll need to ask for money for Demi's keep. And petrol money to get her to and from college.'

'Well, I can't afford to pay you anything! She's got a perfectly good home with me!' Hermia got up and wandered over to the fireplace. 'This really is a very pretty room. Have you thought of selling this place, Grace?'

Grace wanted to say, 'What's it to you? You obviously couldn't afford it,' but decided it was beneath her dignity.

Edward cleared his throat. 'Very well. I will make you an allowance to keep Demeter here on the understanding that she attends college, every day, and works for her exams.'

'I didn't realise you had funds to spare,' said Hermia. 'I thought Caroline was high maintenance.'

'Oh, she is,' said Edward, 'which is why I'll pay what I'm paying you now for Demeter's keep to Grace.'

'I so wish I'd been there to see Mum's face when Dad said that!' said Demi, half an hour after Grace's unwelcome guests finally left.

'I wish you'd been there, too, but you bailed out on me and left me all alone with a virago,' said Grace a little grimly. 'Although I must say, it will make a difference to our finances, getting your keep from Edward.'

Demi frowned. 'What's a virago?'

'A woman who's really, really angry. Which hardly describes her, actually. She went completely . . .'

'Mental?' suggested Ellie.

'That's it. But Edward coped, as usual. He's very good with her.'

'It's all right for him,' said Demi. 'He doesn't have to live with her.'

'And nor do you, now, thanks to Grace,' said Ellie.

'I know.' She looked up at Grace and smiled awkwardly. 'Thank you so much, Grace, you're the best. Really.'

She looked very vulnerable for a moment, and Grace suddenly remembered how young she was. 'It's a pleasure, Demi. It's good to have you here. Now come on, let's wash up the coffee things, so that Ellie can start cooking.'

'We could buy a dishwasher,' suggested Demi brightly. 'If we've got all this money.'

'We've hardly got any money at all just now, Dems,' Ellie explained.

'No. I spent a fortune at the supermarket on my bloody sister,' said Grace.

'Have I really got to go to college tomorrow?' asked Demi.

'I'm afraid so, or they'll drag you back, kicking and screaming.'

'Then there's an essay I should be doing. Can I borrow your desk, Grace?'

'Yes, but don't muddle anything up. I've got half an article written.'

'Don't worry. Shit!' said Demi with her hands in the air. 'I should have asked Mum if I could have my computer here!'

Grace frowned. 'It might be better to let your father handle that one.'

Chapter Ten

❧❧❧

In between banging pork fillets into next week and taking the filling out of sausages and trying to read up as much about History of Art as she could in the loo, which seemed to be the only place she didn't have to be doing anything else, Ellie helped Grace in the dining room. Grace had been surprised that Ellie had felt so strongly about being present at what seemed to her to be quite a simple task.

'If we put this curtain in that gap, we can drape the originals over it, and the missing bit won't show,' said Grace optimistically, clambering on to one of the stouter kitchen chairs. 'Hand me the hammer, Dem.'

'You will be careful, won't you?' pleaded Ellie. 'The panels are already damaged enough. I'd never forgive myself if you banged a nail into them.'

'I'll be careful! Anyway, apart from it being sad, it wouldn't really matter. "Don't cry over anything that can't cry over you," my old auntie used to say. Mind you,' she added, a couple of tacks between her lips. 'I think my sister thinks that Sèvres china can cry.'

Demi, who had used Grace's half-finished article as an excuse not to do her essay, said, 'My mother definitely cried when she broke a crystal decanter once. She said it was because it was a wedding present, but I think it was because she rang John Lewis and they told her it would be five hundred pounds to replace.'

'Good Lord! I hope no one gave us anything as expensive as a present,' Grace mumbled.

'Did you get wedding presents?' asked Ellie. 'If so, where are they?'

'In the attic. In boxes mostly. I didn't unpack a lot of them because Edward had so much stuff.'

'So get them out now then!'

Grace shook her head and released a tin tack from her mouth. 'I might need to sell them. Now hand me that curtain, Dem, the plain gold silky one. I think that's the best match, don't you, Ellie?'

'The curtain is fine, just don't bang nails into the panels! Can't you drag the original one along a bit? Then you won't be too near the painting when you start?'

'I'll do my best.' Grace tugged at the tattered silk which tore a little more as she did so. 'What does that look like?'

'The painting is covered,' said Ellie, not entirely truthfully. 'More or less. Just put the other curtain up next to it. No one will notice if there's a little gap.'

A few bangs, a bit of falling plaster, and the two paintings were more or less concealed. Ellie, satisfied that the paintings were not significantly more damaged than they had been before, rushed back to the kitchen, leaving Grace and Demi to finish.

'That should do it,' said Grace. 'As long as she doesn't come in here.'

'There's no point in doing all this if she doesn't come in here,' said Demi.

'I know, this is just in case. I'm sure if I light the fire in the drawing room and make it as cosy as possible, she won't be keen to come out into the cold of the rest of the house.'

'I thought she was coming to discuss some report she had. She's bound to want to see the rest of the house.'

'Demi, your logic is faultless, your tact is not! I'm in denial here. Please don't make me come out of it.'

Demi laughed. 'You are funny, Grace. You never used to make me laugh before, when you were with Dad.'

'Didn't I? I'm not sure I mean to be funny now. Oh, well, I'm going to see if I can help Ellie with the supper. Flynn will be here soon, spreading himself all over the kitchen, so the desk is all yours, Dem. You'd better get started on that essay.'

Demi sighed. 'Oh, pooh! I wish I'd never told you about it.'

'Come on, Dems. You know if you did a really good job on it and got a good mark, Edward would be pleased and perhaps bring your computer over.'

'I can't do it at all without the computer!'

'Nonsense. You can make a plan, write notes and then type it up at school – college, I mean. I tell you what, if you make a good start, I'll ring Edward and tell him you need the computer urgently. And the television. At least, I won't say you need that urgently, but I'll say you deserve it because you're working so hard. Deal?'

'Suppose so. Can I do it in the kitchen? It's freezing everywhere else.'

'Oh, all right! But don't get in Ellie's way, poor girl! Apart from cooking dinner, she's fretting about going to see her picture restorer tomorrow.'

Demi was impressed by Grace's perception. 'How do you know that? She hasn't said anything.'

'Art books in the loo. She spends so much time in there anyway, she's obviously decided not to waste it.'

Flynn arrived just as Grace had finished arranging

things in the drawing room. She opened the door to him and suddenly felt shy, remembering how sharp she'd been on the phone to him when he'd rung her at the supermarket. 'Hi.'

'Hi yourself,' he replied, regarding her quizzically. 'You've lost your spikes.'

'No, I haven't!' she replied, determined to prove him wrong but smiling despite herself. 'Do you want to bring your stuff in this way? Or shall I unlock the back door?'

'The back door is traditionally the servants' entrance,' he replied.

'Oh, pooh,' said Grace, aware that living with Demi had had an effect on her language.

He leant forward and brushed her cheek with his lips. 'Go on then, Lady Chatterley, unlock the back door.'

She blushed all the way to the kitchen, glad that he was driving his van round the back and wasn't there to see her. She managed to avoid the kitchen for a good half-hour.

'Hello, Allegra. How lovely to see you,' said Grace, kissing her sister on the cheek. She realised, rather to her surprise, that she *was* quite pleased to see her and only wished Allegra wasn't carrying a briefcase and wearing her office clothes; it made her look like a VAT inspector about to make a raid. 'Let me take your coat. No, I expect you'd like to keep it on.'

'It is only February,' said Allegra, returning the kiss.

'Well, come into the drawing room. It's quite warm in there. I've lit the fire.'

In fact, Grace was quite proud of the drawing room. Ellie, with her artist's eye and talent for home-making, had put branches of newly-unfurling leaves in a bucket disguised by an old chimney pot in the window embrasure. She had up-lit it with her bedside lamp and it cast decorative shadows on the wall. The stone mantelpiece was lit with a row of candles on a pile of odd saucers found in a box in the old tack room, and the most comfortable kitchen chairs had been drawn up next to the blazing fire, made inviting by well-plumped cushions.

Given that it had very little furniture in it, and only a very threadbare rug, it looked beautiful, if rather minimalist.

Allegra allowed herself to be ushered into it. 'But darling!' she cried. 'Where's all the furniture?'

'You know where all the furniture is, you and Nicholas took it,' Grace replied a little stiffly.

'But only what the aunt left. Where's all yours?'

'It was Edward's. He's got it.'

'But he didn't leave you with *nothing*, surely?'

'His furniture was all terribly valuable. It was only right he should take it. And, as you keep reminding me, he made me a generous settlement; I had the roof fixed and bought a car, and have got enough left to keep me going for a little while.'

Allegra put her briefcase down on the floor and sat as near to the fire as she could get without singeing herself. 'I had no idea,' she muttered. 'I suppose you come and visit me, mostly, and that time I came just after he'd gone, we sat in the kitchen.'

Thinking of the chaos in the kitchen now, Grace was relieved that Allegra wouldn't be near it until it was a little more organised. Still, it would be a lot warmer than it was usually. That should please her sister.

'Let me get you a glass of wine, then you must meet Ellie, who's living with me, and Demi, who should have finished her essay by now. Oh, and Flynn,' she added as if somehow she'd forgotten he was there. In fact, she was just trying to avoid the explanations.

'Who's Flynn?' demanded Allegra.

'Wine first, Legs, then you can meet everyone. Ellie is very kindly cooking the dinner for us, as you know I can't cook.' Grace frowned, hoping fervently that she hadn't let Allegra think that Ellie was staff. 'She's been such a good friend to me,' she said, hoping to make the situation clear.

'How long have you known her?' asked Allegra, perfectly reasonably, Grace realised.

'Not long, but we got very close very quickly. I'll get the wine.'

Once in the kitchen, which was warm and full of bustle and delicious cooking smells, Grace said, 'Pass me the wine and some glasses. You lot have got to come out of here and meet my sister.'

'I can't leave the sauce just at the moment,' said Ellie, stirring madly.

'My essay! I do have to do it, you know!' said Demi, who in fact had closed her file ages ago.

'What's your excuse?' Grace demanded of Flynn, who was observing the scene with quiet amusement.

'I need to wash my hands and take off my boiler suit,' he said gravely.

'Oh, yes,' Grace acknowledged. 'But you're to come in as soon as you can, you and Ellie. Demi, you can come now.' She picked up one of the bottles of wine sitting on the back of the Rayburn and a couple of the better glasses. She was nearly out of the door before she turned and said, 'The Rayburn is going to be great, Flynn. Thank you so much.'

'Oh God, I'm so nervous!' said Demi as they hurried across the hall.

'There's no need. She won't bully you, she's not your sister. Now be a love and open the door.

'Come in, Demi. Allegra, I don't think you've met my stepdaughter, Demi, have you?'

'We met at the wedding,' said Allegra, acknowledging Demi with a small smile. 'But I don't know, strictly speaking, if you're still Grace's stepdaughter, now your parents are divorced.'

'Well, never mind, we can just be good friends,' said Grace. She put the wine and glasses down on a tea chest covered with one of the leftover curtains she had bought to hide the paintings. 'Have a glass of this. I think you'll like it.' She spent a few moments describing the wine to Allegra before she remembered that she wasn't really that interested, and stopped.

'Can I have some wine?' asked Demi.

As Grace knew she'd already had some, and would probably have reached the giggly stage had she not been so nervous about Allegra, she wanted to refuse. But as she wanted Ellie and Flynn prised out of the kitchen, she said, 'Of course. Go and fetch a glass and could you see what Ellie and Flynn are up to? Ellie might not be able to leave her sauce, but Flynn should have washed his hands and cleared up his tools by now.'

'So remind me who Flynn is again?' asked Allegra when Demi had gone. 'Some sort of artisan?'

'He's a friend,' said Grace, deliberately not enlightening her sister, and wondering if 'artisan' was the politically correct term for workman. 'What do you think of the wine?'

'Very nice,' said Allegra.

'I'm glad I haven't got you as a wine taster,' Grace laughed. 'You have to be much more explicit than just "very nice".'

'Well, you know I think it's nonsense, but at least it's respectable. Now stop playing with the candles and let me tell you about this report while we're alone. Oh, too late.'

Ellie came in first. She was slightly flushed and Grace thought she looked extremely pretty although unmistakably an ex-art student. She was wearing an apron over her jeans and her hair was wrapped up in a bandanna. A brooch consisting of a bunch of bananas made of Fimo decorated her sweater, and there were matching bunches dangling from her ears. Grace couldn't decide if she was pleased that Ellie would look so Bohemian in Allegra's eyes, or sorry.

'Allegra, this is Ellie Summers, my friend, who's kindly agreed to live here for a bit.'

Ellie offered her hand. 'It's so kind of Grace to let me stay.'

Allegra gave a reserved but polite smile and waited for Flynn to be introduced. 'This is Flynn Cormack. My sister, Allegra Statherton-Crawley.'

'How do you do,' said Flynn, taking Allegra's barely offered hand.

Allegra's formal smile didn't move; she was confused as to Flynn's status. She'd assumed he was the plumber who, for some wild, loony-left reason, Grace had invited to eat with them. But although he wasn't wearing a suit, he obviously wasn't a workman, either.

'Demi's just finishing her essay,' said Ellie. 'And keeping an eye on the potatoes. I won't be able to stay long, either. We don't want overcooked vegetables, do we?'

Ellie had thoughtfully brought more glasses with her and Flynn, to Grace's gratitude, poured more wine for Allegra and Grace and some elderflower pressé for Ellie. When he had given himself a glass of wine, Allegra turned to him.

'So what is it you do, exactly?'

'Oh, you'll approve of him,' said Grace, aware that she was on her third glass, hadn't eaten much, and was already a bit unstable because of nerves. 'He's a property developer.'

Allegra turned to her sister. 'Grace, darling! Have you seen sense at last?'

'Oh no,' said Flynn. 'We're just friends. We have an interest in wine in common.'

'Pity. There are probably millions tied up in the property. There's a lot of land, you know,' said Allegra.

'I do know,' said Flynn. 'But you'd never get planning permission for anything out here. It's hard enough to get planning permission for a barn conversion in this area.'

'So, Allegra,' asked Grace, grateful to Flynn for slipping in this useful information. 'Tell me about the report, then.'

'I'd rather wait until we're alone, Grace. In fact, I had no idea you intended to have a dinner party as such. I thought we were going to have a working supper.'

'It is a working supper,' said Grace. 'Flynn's been working.'

'And so have I,' said Ellie. 'Well, cooking anyway.'

'And there's nothing you can't say in front of my friends,' said Grace.

She caught Flynn's eye and realised he was amused at being referred to as her friend. She gave him a quick furtive smile and realised that for the first time she did think of him as a friend. It was probably because she missed Edward. He had been so good at social situations. He could chat amusingly and eruditely about almost everything, which meant all Grace had to do was nod and smile. Without him, she had to do the chatting bit.

Ellie, glad of an excuse to retreat to the cosy disorder of the kitchen, got to her feet. 'Well, I must go and see to my sauce and set the table.'

'Don't go!' Grace pleaded. She knew Allegra had bad news for her and she didn't want to hear it without moral support.

'I have to. I can't trust Demi not to let the broccoli turn to mush.'

'I don't understand why that child isn't living with one of her parents,' said Allegra before Ellie was out of the room. 'And isn't her name Demeter?'

Grace regarded her sister. 'Tell me about the report, Allegra, please.' Allegra glanced at Flynn who immediately got to his feet. 'You don't have to go, really,' said Grace, feeling more abandoned by the moment.

'I do,' said Flynn. 'I still haven't cleared up all my tools. We don't want Ellie tripping over them.'

'Alone at last!' said Allegra. 'Honestly, Grace, where did you find those people? Don't you know any normal couples?'

'Seeing as I'm no longer part of one myself, the normal couples seem to have slipped out of my acquaintance.'

'And I don't know if you and Edward were ever quite normal,' said Allegra slightly acidly. 'Now, about this report. It's dry rot and it's very bad. It'll cost at least thirty grand to fix it. Tell me, have you got that amount left from your settlement?'

Grace shook her head slowly, silenced by the huge amount.

'Then you really have no choice. You'll have to sell. I'll lend you the money to fix the dry rot and you can pay me back when you sell. As well as giving me and Nick our share, of course.'

'Are you willing to *sue* me for what you describe as your share?' asked Grace softly.

Allegra nodded, but so slightly that Grace wondered if Nicholas had put her up to saying this, and suspected that Allegra was less keen on the notion. 'Of course we would absolutely hate it to come to that, but Nick and I feel that it's perfectly possible that the courts would agree with us, that the aunt was not in her sound mind when she made her will in such an unfair way.'

Grace sighed. 'Have some more wine, Allegra,' she said. She felt infinitely tired, and infinitely depressed.

In the kitchen, Ellie felt as if she were directing an opera. Getting the table and floor clear of Flynn's tools and Demi's work and made to look as if it was capable of being sat round as the setting for a dinner party took some doing. The knife and fork situation was dire, too. It was impossible to make Grace's collection of old silver forks, bone-handled knives with loose handles and suspicious holes in them and a selection of spoons with peculiar stains look co-ordinated. They were probably what was left after Grace's brother and sister had done their trawl of possessions. Ellie wondered if there was a nice set of good quality stainless steel in a smart box hidden in the attic. Or, and it seemed just as likely, a beautiful set of knives, forks and spoons wrapped in green baize and residing somewhere in the Home Counties, which had once come from here.

That sister really was the limit, thought Ellie, stirring her sauce and willing it to thicken. She was probably on a diet, too. With any luck it was the Atkins diet, where cream was perfectly all right as long as there wasn't a sniff of anything resembling a vegetable.

'I'm going back in,' said Flynn when he'd packed up the last of his tools and washed his hands in Ellie's clean sink yet again. 'I don't like to leave Grace with that woman.'

Ellie sighed. Did Grace appreciate what a nice man Flynn was? she wondered. Probably not, mostly because he seemed to make her nervous, and partly because she was clearly still in love with Edward. She wasn't normal in some ways. Any sensible woman would hate her ex-husband; it was the healthy way to feel. But Grace wouldn't hear a word against him, even taking in his daughter to make his new marriage easier. Not that Demi wasn't a lovely girl. Ellie glanced at her now, writing furiously at the end of the kitchen table Ellie had allowed her to keep.

'Nearly finished, Dem?'

'Yup. That should do it. I'll read it over tomorrow on the way to college.' Demi put her biro into her pink fluffy pencil case. 'It's odd, I've never thought about it before, but history really is quite interesting.'

'Good! Could you be a love and call them in to eat now? I'll just lay a place where your stuff is. If you do your work and get good marks it will really make life easier for Grace. If either of your parents think she's being soft and not making you do your work, they won't let you stay.'

'I know!' she rolled her eyes. 'As if Grace could make anyone do anything!'

In the few moments it took Ellie to finish setting the table she fervently hoped Grace wasn't the pushover Demi thought she was.

'Well, this is very nice,' said Allegra, seated at the head of the table with Flynn on her right-hand side. 'Although as you know I was hoping to get an opportunity to talk to Grace on her own.'

'There's nothing private about dry rot,' said Grace.

'No,' agreed Ellie, suspecting that Grace, like her, was thinking about what *was* private.

'It is a terrible nuisance,' said Flynn. 'It can get everywhere. Even into stone.'

'Does the report say whereabouts in the house it is?' asked Grace.

'Of course! It's mostly upstairs, on the west side.'

'Oh,' said Grace after a moment and glanced at Ellie, confirming what Ellie had just worked out: that the dining room was on the west side.

'What would happen if you didn't do anything about it?' asked Ellie, knowing Grace couldn't ask but might want to know.

'You couldn't do that. It could spread everywhere,' said Flynn, 'and in a house like this, that would be a tragedy.'

Grace suddenly began to feel sick. It was one thing Allegra banging on about dry rot, but to hear Flynn, a disinterested party, say that was frightening.

'Just what I was saying to Grace,' said Allegra whose

battle with *schadenfreude* was obviously not going well.

'I expect there are grants and things you could apply for,' said Ellie.

'Unlikely, for a private house,' said Flynn. 'Unless it was open to the public or something like that.'

'I have said I'll lend Grace the money,' said Allegra, swooping a piece of pork round her plate to catch the last of the creamy sauce.

'But under rather stringent conditions. I would have to sell the house,' said Grace, who at that moment felt that selling it would be like tearing out her heart. Childless and partnerless, it really was the only thing in the world that was hers.

'Grace! This is not something we should be discussing in front of strangers!' Allegra was indignant, either because she really was concerned about confidentiality, or because she didn't want her demands made public: it was difficult to tell.

'You can't sell this house!' said Demi. 'It's yours! You love it!'

'I'm sure she does, dear,' said Allegra, possibly forgetting how much young people disliked being patronised. 'But it is very expensive to keep up, and quite impractical for one person.'

'But we live here, too!' said Demi, who had had her glass topped up a couple of times already by Flynn.

'That is not the point!' said Allegra. 'Grace inherited it from our aunt. She was aunt to me and my brother just as much as she was to Grace.'

'She was also my godmother,' said Grace.

'That doesn't make any difference! She never paid you any attention when she was alive; it makes no sense that she left you her house when she died!'

'But she did! And you did get the furniture, some of which was very valuable. And I'm sure it didn't have dry rot!' Grace had had a fair bit to drink, too: Dutch courage in industrial quantities.

'There was some nasty woodworm in that little Davenport I had to have treated,' insisted Allegra.

'Would anyone like any more?' said Ellie, who wanted to go to bed more than anything else in the whole world. 'Or shall we move on to apple crumble. And cream,' she added.

'You cook awfully well for an art student,' said Allegra.

'I've graduated, actually,' said Ellie. 'But I learnt to cook during my gap year, when I had a job in France as an au pair. The madame thought it was her duty to teach me to cook, as I was English and would never learn otherwise.'

'We tried to encourage Grace to do a cookery course when she refused to do A levels, but she would insist on doing that wine thing.' Allegra drained her glass and Ellie resolved that, however drunk she was, Allegra was not having her bed. 'If you hadn't done that, you wouldn't have met Edward, which would have saved everyone a great deal of trouble.'

A whimper broke from Demi. Grace scowled at her sister. 'I wouldn't not have met Edward for the world. I loved him very much and even though our marriage didn't last – perhaps it couldn't have lasted – I wouldn't have missed a minute of it!' She drew a deep breath. 'Apart from anything else I wouldn't have met Demi.'

While Allegra and Grace faced each other across the table, Ellie whispered to Demi, 'Just to prove that Grace is right about you, would you like to gather the plates?'

'Would anyone like some water, to clear the palate?' asked Flynn, proving to Ellie that he could be tactful as well as kind.

'Actually, I think that would be a good idea,' said Allegra.

It turned out that Allegra had booked herself into a hotel in the town. Flynn offered to take her home, and as Ellie had been thinking that she should offer to do this herself, she mentally hugged him. When Grace nodded her head in the direction of the door, and Ellie took it that she'd been sent to bed, she was so grateful she could have cried. She had to get up and go to Bath in the morning; she was surprisingly nervous about it, and she was so tired it was all she could do to summon up the energy to brush her teeth. And even that made her gag these days.

Grace returned to the kitchen, determined that Ellie wouldn't find a single dirty glass or plate when she came down in the morning. Grace knew that Ellie was still nervous and trying very hard not to show it. She should be able to leave the house with a clear mind and a clear kitchen.

She was waiting for the kettle to boil for the third time, thinking about Allegra's 'sell or else' speech, when she heard the bell give a single jangle. It was one o'clock in the morning and she was cautious, but not frightened to open it. It was Flynn.

'You haven't brought Allegra back?' she said anxiously as she saw his figure outlined by moonlight. 'Or did you forget something?' A second too late, she smiled, remembering his many kindnesses.

'In a manner of speaking. Can I come in for a

moment? I won't keep you long. I know how tired you must be.'

Grace stood back to let him into the house. 'We'll go into the kitchen, I don't want to disturb Ellie.' She smiled again, genuinely this time. 'Demi has been asleep for ages and wouldn't wake for an earthquake.'

'Can I make you a cup of tea, or anything?' she said, when they had reached the kitchen.

'That would be nice,' said Flynn. 'I realised that I hadn't had the opportunity to show you how to keep the Rayburn going.'

'I'm sure I could work it out,' said Grace, wondering for the millionth time why her good manners always deserted her when she was with Flynn.

Flynn ignored her. 'This silver wheel is the draught. When you come down in the morning, open that right up, or even open that door, and put on some dry sticks, dried orange peel, a bit of a cardboard box, stuff like that, which you'll have handy, if you're wise. When the fire is going really well, or the kettle's boiled, you can put on some bigger logs and turn the draught down a bit. OK?'

'Fine. It's really kind of you to give it to us,' said Grace, valiantly fighting for the social skills which served her so well with everyone else she encountered. 'We're extremely grateful.'

He smiled in a way which made her feel that he didn't believe her gratitude, which was mean of him because she was trying so hard. She sighed deeply and looked at him, her head on one side.

'If you're really that grateful,' he said, 'there's a favour you could do for me.'

'Oh, what? I mean, anything, I'd be only too pleased.'

He laughed again. When she'd first met him he'd

hardly laughed at all, ever; now he seemed to think every little thing she said hilarious.

'You may not be when you hear what it is. I need you to feed my cat.'

Grace frowned. 'You have a cat?'

'I do indeed. A Siamese. And, as I told you, I'm going away and for the first time ever, there won't be anyone in the house to feed her and there isn't anyone else I feel I can ask. I was wondering if you'd be very kind and do it. My house is on the way back from town to here, so if you're ferrying Demi to college—'

'Of course I'll do it. Can I come over and see what I have to do tomorrow? Oh, no, not tomorrow, I'll have Allegra. What about the day after? If you give me directions to your house . . .'

'I'm going away tomorrow afternoon. Not sure how long for, I'm afraid. Could you come over at lunchtime? Or will you still have Allegra with you?'

'I don't know!' Grace was too tired to keep the desperation out of her voice. She wasn't looking forward to seeing Allegra again tomorrow; she would find it much easier to bully Grace if they were alone together.

'I'm going at two. I'd better give you instructions about the burglar alarm now.'

'What about keys? If you have a burglar alarm, presumably you don't leave the house unlocked?'

'I went home and got them.' He raised his eyebrows and almost smiled. 'I presumed on your good nature.'

She laughed. 'Rash, considering how my good nature seems to keep itself to itself when you're around.'

'I know. But you have been kind to Ellie and Demi so I knew you had it in you.'

The tension between them eased but not entirely.

Grace couldn't quite relax with him, couldn't have the easy, friendly relationship that Ellie and Demi achieved with no effort at all. She couldn't help remembering the way he'd stared at her that first night and how it had disconcerted her.

'Tell me about your alarm system then, and what your cat eats.'

'I'd better write it down.'

'Oh! Is it on a diet, then? I'm not cooking for it.'

'Not the cat, eejit, the alarm system.'

'Is "eejit" Irish for "idiot"?'

'No, it's a special word for when people are being particularly tick.'

'Don't you mean "thick"?'

'I know what I mean, and so do you. Find me something to write on.'

Grace found a piece of paper and he wrote a long list of instructions on how to get into the house. The cat feeding bit was just a line at the end of what could have been the plan for a major military operation.

'It seems terribly complicated,' she said, looking at his straight black writing and thinking that she liked it.

'But you must have a burglar alarm here. They're all much the same.'

She shook her head. 'Nothing to steal here. That anyone knows about, anyway,' she added, remembering the pictures.

'What do you mean?'

Covering up quickly, she said, 'I have a few wedding presents stashed away in the attic.'

'But when you were married, when you had furniture, didn't you need a burglar alarm then?'

'No. Edward could never find one that he could live with on the front of the house.'

'I can't believe you've managed with so little furniture since your divorce.'

'I've got a perfectly good bed,' she countered, and then wished she hadn't. He was unlikely to think she was being suggestive, but there was something about beds that made people think the wrong thing.

His mouth twitched in a way that was somehow more amused than a full-blown grin. 'I'm glad to hear it. I wouldn't like to think of you sleeping on bare boards.'

'Goose down,' she said reassuringly, reluctantly smiling back. 'And percale sheets. Edward had very good taste.'

'I'd realised that.'

'About this burglar alarm,' she went on, partly to make him stop looking at her with a smile in the back of his eyes that seemed to mean more than it should do.

'Try and come to my house before two,' he said after a moment. 'It would be easier if I could actually show you what to do.'

'And your house is . . . ?'

Flynn turned back to the piece of paper and drew a map on it for her and explained again about which key went where in what order.

'You'd better give me the number of the alarm, too. Or do I just press a switch?'

'Good God, no. I'll tell you. Do you want me to write it down? It's very simple. I expect you'll remember it.'

'I'd rather not take the chance.'

'Then don't lose this bit of paper. It's got instructions on how to get to my house and how to disable the alarm when you get there.'

'Not to mention which flavour of Kittikins your cat likes. Highly explosive information,' she teased.

'In the wrong hands, it could be,' he said, his voice not quite as serious as his expression.

'I won't let it get into the wrong hands,' said Grace, trying to match his sober manner.

When Grace finally shut the door behind him and pulled the bolt she was aware of a sense of loss. It must be because he was large and left an equally large space behind him.

Chapter Eleven

❧❧❧

Ellie set off in her car to Randolph Frazier's wondering how on earth she and Grace would find thirty thousand pounds before the house fell down or, in her opinion more importantly, the pictures fell apart.

Everyone had got up far too early that morning, in spite of going to bed so late: they were all so worried about oversleeping, they hardly slept at all. Grace had to get Demi to college, and Ellie had to get herself to Bath for ten o'clock.

Several money-making projects had been discussed and most of them dismissed.

'I could sell the car,' Grace had said. 'It wouldn't raise all of it, but it would be a start. On the other hand, I don't know if I'd be very good at buying a cheap second-hand car. I wouldn't be able to kick the tyres and say rude things about it.'

The thought of Grace trying to pull off a deal from a possibly crooked car salesman had made Ellie smile, in spite of herself. 'We'll buy a local paper and look in it, and when Demi gets her computer we'll be able to research how much yours is worth.'

Demi, who was using her spare time to sort out her pencil case – and trying hard to disguise the fact that she was actually quite pleased about going back to college, a life of leisure being less attractive than it had once been – had said, 'When I had my computer they were always emailing great loan deals to me. When we get it from Mum, we could go for one of them!'

Grace had been firm. 'Definitely not. Their rates of interest would mean I had to sell the house anyway, and if I'm going to do that, I might as well sell it to Allegra.' Then she'd frowned and wrinkled her nose. 'Mind you, if all else fails, we might have to look into it.'

'I do think you should think more about beefing up the wine tastings, and having food with them?' Ellie had suggested. 'I love fancy cooking. It would be fun.'

Grace wrinkled her nose again, a process which apparently aided thought. 'Would it be cost-effective, though?'

'Well, you could charge! "An Evening of Wine and Food". Thirty or forty pounds a head. You'll get the wine for nothing and if you have six different bits of food, some of them could be really cheap.'

'What wine goes best with baked beans, you mean?' said Demi.

Ellie nodded. 'What do you think, Grace?'

'It could work.'

'But you couldn't have them in the kitchen,' Demi pointed out.

'Why not? Shabby chic and all that,' said Grace hopefully.

'It would be rather nice to light the fire in the drawing room, like you did last night for your sister, and rig up some sort of table in there. It would still be shabby chic. Demi could put on a short black dress, black stockings and a frilly pinny and serve. A French maid to go with the French wine.'

Demi squeaked.

'That's a good idea!' said Grace.

'What!' Demi's indignation was possibly audible in the next village.

'Not the French maid thing,' said Grace dismissively, 'the drawing-room idea. We could make it lovely and if we got enough people, word would get round and my name would become better known and I might get more columns to write. I'll ask Graham from the wine shop. He knows someone on a magazine who might get me a column. We could ask him, too, perhaps.'

'You're hardly going to make thirty grand doing that,' said Demi, still smarting from the maid idea. 'At least, not for years.'

'But it could be an added regular income. Let's make a list of all the things we can do and sell to make money. We'll feel much more positive if we have a list we can cross things off from.'

'And the first thing on it is for you to register with a doctor,' said Grace.

Ellie ignored her. 'We've decided you need the car. What about the wedding presents?'

Grace nodded agreement. 'I've done without them all this time and they're not from people I knew, really, or who cared about me. Oh.'

'What?'

'One of them is a canteen of cutlery from Allegra. I'd better not sell that.'

'Let's get it down here then. I'm surprised she didn't mention it last night. Your knives and forks are worthy of student accommodation, Grace.'

'She gave us a cheque and that's what we bought, and although I did tell her, she's probably forgotten. Which means we can sell it!' she added brightly.

Ellie, who liked things to match because it saved so much decision-making, sighed and went back to the list. 'What else?'

'I should get a job,' said Grace. 'What could I do? Manage a wine shop?'

'Have you got retail experience? Ever worked in a shop? A filling station? Anything?'

Grace shook her head. 'I know about wine but not about buying and all that stuff. We'd better stick to wine tastings with food, and I'll get some more columns. I've had some quite good feedback from the local paper. I could always see if other areas would like to run the articles, and I can nag the wine merchant about his friend on the glossy mag, see if he really wants me to write for it.' She frowned. 'But is any of this going to earn us thirty grand before the dry rot gets to the paintings?'

'Oh, shit!' said Ellie. 'You don't think it might already have got there, do you?'

As one, they rose from the table and dashed along the corridor and across the hall to the dining room. 'Get the chair,' said Ellie, 'I must look.'

'No! Supposing you fall off! You'll lose the baby.'

'I won't fall off! I'm not drunk. I've been climbing on chairs all my life and never fallen off any of them.'

Grace held the chair, ready to catch Ellie. 'Can you see anything?'

'The trouble is, I don't really know what I'm looking for.'

'Come down and let me look.'

They swapped places. After a while Grace said, 'I'm not sure, but I think there might be, just a bit. We could go upstairs and you could look and see if I'm right.'

Ellie shook her head. 'I'd rather not, if you don't

mind. Let's go back and work on our list.' She felt that, in the scheme of things, having dry rot in the house was probably not as serious as having dry rot in the paintings. After all, there were lots of houses. The paintings were probably unique.

'I was thinking,' said Grace, when they were back in the warmth of the kitchen, 'that I could just sell the paintings. Would they fetch thirty grand, do you think?'

Ellie squeaked. 'Grace, they could be worth an absolute fortune! If they were restored and discovered to be by someone people have heard of, they'd be worth much, much more than thirty grand. They've got to be restored, and then an expert must come in and value them. And although it would be an awful shame to sell them, at least then you'd get a proper return for them.'

Grace sighed. 'But I need the money now!'

Ellie was desperate. 'We'll raise the thirty grand somehow, I promise you, but we must – *you* must not sell them until they're back to their full glory.'

'And you're going to do that? Restore them?'

'I'll have to if we can't afford to have them done properly. That would probably cost about thirty grand, too!'

'Oh, bugger.'

'Grace! I didn't know you knew that word!'

'I knew it all right, I just never use it much. It's rather liberating. Perhaps I could say "fuck", too . . . No,' she added a second later. 'It's too soon for the F word.'

'I think it's sweet that you're so refined,' said Ellie.

'It's pathetic, but it's the way I am. The trouble with me is I got married too young, but now I need a career. I can't spend the rest of my life being an ex-wife. We'll have to sell the paintings. There's no other solution.'

'But not in their present condition,' pleaded Ellie.

192

'Imagine if you sold them and a couple of years later heard they were worth millions, not the few thousands you'd sold them for.'

Grace was very unworldly, but after a moment or two's thought, even she saw the point of this. 'And Allegra and Nicholas would never let me forget it. It would make the house thing seem trivial. But we're back to money again. Restoration costs!'

'Apply for a grant or something. Surely that's what all this lottery money is for,' said Ellie, who was suddenly wondering if it would be silly to make sand-wiches to take with her.

'But if anyone got to hear about the paintings, and they were actually valuable—'

'They are,' said Ellie. 'Trust me on this.'

'The grant would have to go on insurance. I'd have to have a burglar alarm, like Flynn.' She smiled at the recollection of his late-night visit. 'He called round last night after he'd driven Allegra to her hotel. Asked me if I could feed his cat for a bit. Usually there's some builder or other who can do it, but there's no one there now. Presumably because the house is finished.'

'Hasn't he got any friends he could ask?' said Demi.

'I am a friend,' said Grace.

'I think he just wants to keep in touch,' said Ellie teasingly.

Grace laughed at the notion; it was about as funny as the thought of the virtually empty Luckenham House having a security system similar to the one which Flynn had explained to her in such detail.

'But going back to the grant thing, even if I didn't have to install burglar alarms and things like that; it's just sod's law that someone would say they can't be taken out of the place where they were painted and I'll be left with a million-pound insurance bill and still have dry rot.'

Ellie had decided against making sandwiches. It would make her look a bit unsophisticated, as if she were a child taking her lunch box to school. 'Well, let me get some tips and wrinkles from this picture restorer and I'll see what I can do. But it's a huge responsibility, Grace. Those paintings are probably a National Treasure or something.'

'Oh come on! They're just the eighteenth-century equivalent of that girl in tennis gear scratching her bum that was so popular in the eighties,' said Demi.

Shocked, both the other two looked at her. 'How on earth do you know about that?' asked Ellie.

'Media Studies,' said Demi, unbearably smug. 'It's the only bit of it I can remember.'

It was after that they had realised if they didn't leave the house immediately, they'd all be late.

The fact that Ellie managed to find a parking space relatively nearby was a good omen, and the fact that Randolph Frazier had remembered to expect her was another.

But as he ushered her down into a cellar which had obviously never been used for anything more artistic than storing bottles of chemicals and a few bits of timber, she realised that extracting the 'tips and wrinkles' might be harder than she had anticipated. She'd have to get him talking in her coffee break, if he let her have one.

Hard physical work in very unpleasant surroundings took the edge off Ellie's shyness.

'You're getting a lot of work out of me for nothing,

Randolph,' she said a couple of hours later, when she was filthy and tired, but the cellar was clear apart from about twenty black sacks of rubbish.

'Call me Ran,' he said.

Ellie was tempted to call him something much less polite, but she needed him more than he needed her. She also needed lunch.

'Ran, then. I mean, I'm supposed to be getting work experience – in picture restoration,' she added hurriedly, before he could say that she *was* getting work experience. 'But I could go out for sandwiches first, if you like.'

'Oh, yes, that would be a good idea. There's a little shop at the bottom of the hill. I'll have egg mayonnaise. Here's some money. I don't expect you to pay for your own lunch,' he added.

Grateful for small mercies, Ellie took the note he handed her, wondering if pregnant women were allowed egg mayonnaise. Probably not. Being pregnant made you give up most of the pleasures of life: soft cheese, soft-boiled eggs, strong drink.

When she got back a little later she found him upstairs in the studio. There was a picture of a battle scene – men wearing antiquated military uniforms – on an easel and as she came in he licked the end of what looked like a kebab skewer and dipped it into a roll of cotton wool. Then he took up a wisp and rolled it round, producing what looked like a doll's-house-sized stick of candyfloss.

'Home-made cotton bud,' he explained. Then he licked it again. 'Spit is always the first thing you try. It's got enzymes in it.'

He rubbed at a tiny corner of the painting, about one

centimetre square, changing the cotton wool several times, inspecting what was on the cotton wool intently. 'We start on the weakest chemical we can get away with.'

'Couldn't you just reproduce the enzymes and save yourself all that spitting?'

He shook his head. 'I was working at a major picture gallery, years ago, when an American came over. He thought the same as you. Got a chemist to work out what was in spit, had it reproduced, and put a tiny bit in the corner of the painting. Before he went home he checked that it was working. In the morning, what was fixing the paint to the painting had completely disappeared.'

'My God!'

'Which is why I like spit and not a fake version of it. Do you want to put the kettle on? We'll eat lunch over by the kitchen.'

'I do realise it would be dreadful to eat or drink anything in the studio.'

He frowned at her. 'No. It's just that the view's better from the kitchen.' Then he relented. 'But you're right, you shouldn't really bring food or drinks into a studio.'

Ellie sighed as she filled the kettle. Picture restoration was obviously an extremely painstaking, time-consuming business. She could probably work with this man for several years and still not have a clue what to do about the panels. She'd have to ask leading questions.

'So,' she said when they were both sitting on stools at a counter, their food and mugs well away from the work in progress. 'When do I get some hands-on experience?'

'You don't. It's all highly technical, you can't let amateurs do it.'

'So why did you take me on, if you're not prepared to let me have some real work experience?' She bit into her ham and salad baguette and a bit of tomato dropped on the floor.

He shrugged. 'You saw how badly the cellar needed clearing out. I'm going to turn it into a dark room.'

At the same time as she wondered how on earth she could get the information she needed from him, she marvelled that he was managing to eat an egg mayonnaise roll without making any mess at all. 'Well, now I've done that for you, and you took me on for two weeks, could we do something to do with pictures?'

Ran looked at her rather warily. 'You've got to be extremely careful. You shouldn't go near anything if you haven't got the right qualifications.'

'But getting them would be a huge commitment of time and money,' Ellie pointed out as politely as possible.

He frowned. 'If you're not willing to commit your time, picture restoration is not for you. You saw me with the cotton bud. I will go over the entire painting with cotton buds, possibly with several different chemicals. It's not something you can rush.'

'No, I see that, and I am a careful and patient person, normally. It's just . . .'

'What?'

She was very tempted to tell him. It would make life so much simpler. Had she promised Grace she wouldn't? She didn't think so. Randolph Frazier was not going to tell anyone Grace knew, and it was unlikely he would report her to the National Trust, despite Grace's fears. In essence, Ellie knew she had promised, but it was a promise she might allow herself to break.

'Hmm?' he prompted, his mouth full.

'It takes ages to apply for things. What with the baby and everything, I need to sort my life out.'

He regarded her sceptically, as if he wasn't quite convinced. 'I can see that, but it's still not something you can just rush into on a whim.'

'I know it must seem like that to you, but really, it's not a whim.'

'No?'

'No. I'd be really interested to know – for example – how you'd deal with some really old wooden panels.'

'Would you now?'

'Yeah. Just as an example, you understand.'

He sighed, a much beleaguered man. 'OK. After lunch, when you've washed your hands, I'll show you a bit more. But you must promise not to touch anything in the studio, but nothing! If you do, you're out on your ear and I'll tell every picture restorer in the country not to let you near them.'

'That would be very unkind, after I cleared out your cellar.' She tried a winning smile.

'I'm not paid to be kind.'

Ellie retreated into her baguette. When they had both finished, Ran stood up and walked over to the door. 'OK, come into the studio, don't touch anything, and I'll show you a few techniques. Why are you so interested in wooden panels? Have you got one you want to restore yourself? It's not amateur work, you know, unless it's just some bit of junk you picked up in a car-boot sale.'

Because she was still annoyed and very tired after clearing out the cellar, Ellie didn't give her brain quite long enough before she let her mouth engage. 'I did not buy them at a car-boot sale!' she snapped as she followed him back to the studio.

'So there's more than one of them? You picked them up in a junk shop, then. Or did your dear old Auntie Ethel leave them to you?'

'No! In fact, they're not even mine.'

Ran frowned. 'Are they interesting? Have a seat. Over there, out of the way.' He settled Ellie in a stylish but not very comfortable chair. Out of the window was a fantastic view of hills and meadows. She stared at it moodily, wondering if it was her hormones that were making her so irritable, or Ran. It was probably both.

'Tell me about these paintings. They're probably rubbish, you know, not worth restoring.'

Ellie sighed. 'I think the owner probably wishes they were rubbish, except that she needs the money.'

'What are they of?'

Ellie frowned. 'Why? What's the subject matter got to do with anything?'

He sipped his coffee. 'It'll give me some idea about them. They could be scenes from nursery rhymes, or something. If you don't know anything about painting, I can't really ask you much about that, can I?'

'I have a degree in Creative Arts, you know. I do know something about it!'

'It doesn't follow. I wish you'd stop prevaricating and tell me about these pictures.'

Not sure if she knew what prevaricating was, Ellie decided that the truth was the least exhausting option. 'You've got to promise not to tell a living soul – I have already promised and broken it, but I think it's best.'

He sighed, obviously bored and unimpressed by her dramatic statement.

'I think they're probably by someone really important.'

Ran raised an eyebrow which was the epitome of scepticism. 'So do most people who own paintings. They're almost always wrong.'

'Well, I'm not! They've been hidden in an absolutely ancient house for ever, and the painting is superb. They are not daubs!'

'What sort of condition are they in?'

'Bad. Which is why I wanted to work with you. There's a mouse hole for one thing, plus some of the paint has flaked off and there might be dry rot any minute.'

'What do you mean, any minute?'

'There's dry rot in the room above and we think it might have got down into the paintings. Which is why this is all so urgent. My friend needs to get the dry rot in the house seen to, and probably the only way to raise the money is to sell the paintings. Well, they won't get anything like what they might be worth in their present condition.' She scowled at him. 'Even I, a mere Creative Arts graduate, know that.'

'What's the subject matter?'

'Adam and Eve in the Garden of Eden, I think. But they're quite – explicit. No fig leaves. Adam . . . well, he has . . .' Her voice trailed off.

'Spit it out, woman. Do you mean he has an erection?'

'Yes.' Ellie, who'd lived with artists, who'd even modelled naked herself, found herself blushing. It was because of Ran, she knew it. She was sexually attracted to him. Which was a shame, because the chances that he should feel similarly were nil. She was scruffy, grubby after cleaning out his cellar, and pregnant, none of which attributes were exactly attractive. Besides, she had to concentrate, she mustn't let her mind wander from the reason she was here.

'I'd really have to see them to make any sort of judgement. They do sound interesting though, if they're as old as you think they are.'

Ellie considered. How would Grace feel if Ellie took this man to see the paintings, the paintings that were supposed to be a deadly secret? Not good. And Ellie's protective instincts for Grace were at least equal to her feelings for the paintings. 'I don't think that's possible,' she said cautiously.

'Well, there's nothing I can do to help then, is there?'

'I could tell you about them.'

'My dear girl,' he said in a way that Ellie found patronising and alarmingly erotic at the same time, 'you could tell me about every flower and baby animal and I still wouldn't have a clue as to their age, their condition or anything that would help me to help you restore them. That was why you came here, wasn't it? To learn from me so you could restore them yourself?'

He made it seem like stealing. 'I'm sorry. It's Grace, she doesn't want anyone to know about the paintings. If it was up to her she'd just sell them as they are—'

'Why don't you let her do that?'

'Because she needs the money! They won't fetch anything like their proper value as they are now. And even if she was willing to have them properly restored she couldn't afford to pay for it – not until she'd sold the pictures, anyway.'

Ran was silent for a moment. 'If they are really interesting I'd be willing to do them on those terms. But I do have to see the bloody things.'

Ellie thought hard. 'There is a way. My friend is a wine expert and she's going to do tastings, with food, as a way of earning money. You could come to one and I could slip you in to see the paintings.'

'What, between the claret and the Sancerre?'

'Something like that. It's not ideal, I know, but if she'd already met you, she might feel better about you seeing the paintings once we tell her – if you're interested in restoring them.'

'So I'd have to pay for the privilege of helping you with these things?'

'I'm afraid so. If I told Grace who you were before she'd met you she might not let you across the threshold! I love her, I really do, but I don't know her all that well. I can't take chances.'

'She sounds highly neurotic.'

'She's not. She's just had a tough time lately. Her husband left her, her brother and sister took all her furniture and she was living in a very old, very large, very lovely house, all on her own, before I met her. Now there's me and her ex-stepdaughter living there as well.'

'You've obviously taken her under your wing. Maternal type, are you?'

'I'd better be. Now, will you come? I'll get on to Grace to organise a wine tasting quite quickly.'

'I suppose so. But if these paintings are rubbish, I will be extremely cross and extract a hideous revenge from you.'

These unpromising words had a disturbing effect on Ellie's stomach. 'What would that be? Cleaning out your cellars for the rest of my life?'

'I've only got one cellar and you've cleaned that out already. I'll think of something else.'

Ellie looked at the floor, aware that she was blushing and hoping that he wouldn't notice. 'Well, let me know. But I assure you the paintings aren't rubbish.' She looked up. 'I may have given you the best commission of your entire life.'

'In which case you want a reward?'

Ellie nodded, a smile which refused to be suppressed twitching at the corner of her mouth. 'I'll think of something.'

She already knew what she wanted. A lovely, uncomplicated, entirely physical affaire; no falling in love, no heartbreak, no pain on either side. And Ran would be ideal. Pity he didn't seem to fancy her at all.

Then she considered for a minute. Right now she must look like a grubby art student, but she didn't always look like that. In fact, it could be said that she scrubbed up nicely. If she got him to Luckenham House, and she was properly dressed and made up, he might not be nearly so resistant to her charms. And he really was the perfect choice for her last fling. She was very thoughtful as she cleared up the lunch things.

While Ellie was cleaning out Randolph Frazier's cellar, Grace was having an action replay with her sister, who had hired a taxi to the house to pick up her car and to talk seriously to Grace about the dry rot.

She insisted on showing it to Grace. Not, she explained, out of sadism, but so Grace would thoroughly understand the extent and urgency of the problem. Grace had been hoping that Allegra would just get into her car and drive away, a hope increased when she refused refreshment.

'No, darling, I've just had some excellent coffee, so I

203

won't have your instant. Let's just have a look at the problem and then I must go. I was planning to leave my hotel immediately after breakfast, but I thought I would have had a look at it by then.' Allegra gave Grace a glance of gentle but definite reproof which meant she blamed Grace, most unfairly, for her hangover.

'But it is better in daylight,' said Grace. 'Let's go up.'

At the top of the stairs Allegra referred to her notes. 'It's mostly in the west bedroom. Along here, isn't it?'

Before she knew it, Grace had followed Allegra into the room that Edward had used as his study. She had managed not to go into it since he'd left because even the thought of it had made her too sad. He had had the walls lined with bookshelves and had had a huge partners' desk in the middle. The shelves were still there, empty now, and the heart of the room had gone. What had also gone, Grace noted with some surprise, was the sense of desolation the thought of the room had given her before.

'Ah, here it is,' said Allegra.

The wood-treatment man had taken away the skirting board and revealed a substance with the look of grubby cotton wool branching across the wall like coral.

'And here's the fruiting body he mentioned,' she went on.

Together they surveyed the rust-coloured fungus, which stuck out into the room like a badly cooked pancake.

'It's very bad,' Allegra emphasised. 'He says so here. It's spread a long way.'

'I can see it has,' said Grace, thinking of the paintings underneath. 'Does it spread rapidly?'

'It can do, the report says. It also says that treating it is not for amateurs.'

'Well, it would, wouldn't it? They want the work.'

'Grace, they wouldn't be able to charge people this much money for doing something which people could do for themselves if they had the right chemicals. And before you say it, these people are not cowboys. They came very highly recommended.'

'I'm sure.'

'What's the room underneath here?' asked Allegra.

'The dining room,' said Grace. 'But I'm sure it hasn't got that far, or I would have noticed.'

'And I expect the report would have mentioned it if it had. This stuff does smell, doesn't it?' she wrinkled her nose disapprovingly.

'So is it a report you've got there, or an estimate?'

'Both, really.'

'Don't you think we ought to have a second opinion? I mean, it's in these people's interest to find dry rot and then charge a fortune for curing it.' Too late Grace realised that the word 'we' in that context had linked her with her sister, which would look as if she'd accepted her verdict and was willing to go along with her plans.

Allegra shrugged. 'Well, we've seen it for ourselves, haven't we? But by all means get a second opinion. Just don't expect me to pay for it.'

'I can pay for it.' Grace did still have some pride. 'I'm not destitute, you know, Allegra.'

'I should think not. You own a house that's probably worth nearly a million pounds.'

Grace blushed. 'There is such a thing as land rich and cash poor. Think of Africa.'

Her sister at last out of her house, and soon to be out of the county, Grace picked up the telephone to ring

Edward about Demi's computer. While she was waiting to be connected she realised she had dialled his number without a trace of nervousness, something she had never quite achieved when they were married.

'I really think she should have a few of her own things, especially her computer,' Grace said firmly, after the preliminaries.

'Oh?'

'She didn't know she was going to college today until yesterday, but she put in a lot of time and effort making an essay plan and loads of notes last night.'

Edward wasn't impressed. 'I expect she knew she'd get into trouble if she didn't do it; it had probably been set weeks ago.'

'It would have taken a lot of courage to go back after three weeks off. The fact that she even remembered about the essay, let alone tried to write it, means she's taking it seriously this time. I read through what she'd done and was very impressed.'

'Hmph. I wonder when her mother last read any of her college work through,' Edward muttered.

Grace didn't answer. It was a rhetorical question, although, according to Demi, Hermia never had time to read through or take an interest in Demi's work.

'I'll bring the stuff over at the weekend. It might take me until then to prise the things out of Hermia,' said Edward.

Grace swallowed. 'And the money, Edward? I love having Demi, but I can't afford—'

'I'll set up a standing order. Let me have your bank details.'

'I think you know them, Edward. They haven't changed.'

'Of course. I'm sorry. I'll sort it out today.'

After Grace had put the phone down, she glanced at her watch and decided she just had time to get to Flynn's house before he left. It seemed important that she should do so. But fate did not share her priorities and decided it was time she got some fuel, forcing her to confront the fact that she'd been running out for a couple of days. The car didn't actually stop, but as she headed for the petrol station, she had only one eye on the road. The other was firmly on the petrol gauge.

Thus, when she reached Flynn's house it was two-thirty, and there was no car in the drive; she'd missed him.

It was a lovely house, she was forced to recognise. He might have been a property speculator, but he did it in a very high-class way. It was even bigger than Luckenham House and was probably a couple of centuries younger. There was a circular drive in front and from the outside the house looked immaculate – only some piles of sand, a cement mixer, a wheelbarrow and a neat pile of dressed stone to one side indicated this might not be the case.

She examined the jail-sized bunch of keys in her hand and went through the order in her head. The scary bit would be when she had to rush into the house and unset the alarm before it went off. She had about three minutes and as the house was strange to her, it might not be enough.

At least it was a cat she was feeding, not a Rottweiler, and while she knew Siamese could be eccentric, it was unlikely it would attack, especially as Flynn had only just gone.

The three locks in the front door worked well but as

she was rushing through the hall in the general direction of the kitchen to find the alarm, she realised she should have had the bit of paper with the number on it out ready. She thought she would remember it, it was only four digits, after all, but when she arrived in front of the box she knew she'd forgotten them.

She searched in her bag for the bit of paper for an agonisingly long time before she remembered it was on the dashboard of her car.

A string of words, including the one she hadn't been able to say this morning, tumbled out of her mouth as she rushed to the front door, grateful for the small mercy that had made her leave it open. She kept it open with her handbag and flew back to the car.

She was as quick as she could be but still the alarm burst into hideous song before she could get to it. Her brain fighting for calmness through the cacophony, she punched out the numbers, hoping against hope that this would be sufficient to stop the noise that was threatening, if not to deafen her, to give her tinnitus for the rest of her life.

The ringing in her ears went on for seconds which seemed like minutes after the noise had stopped. She was sweating and praying the alarm wasn't connected automatically to the police station. Her mouth had gone so dry she couldn't swallow and her heart was pounding as if she'd been fleeing for her life.

Grace was not the sort of person who, when given someone's keys and a cat to feed, would then go round the house, or help herself to the drinks cabinet, but after the shock of the alarm a glass of water seemed essential.

The kitchen was like something out of a magazine, or a catalogue for very expensive fitted kitchens. It had shiny stone worktops, dozens of cupboards, and a stone floor which felt suspiciously warm beneath her feet. He probably had under-floor heating. 'What a namby pamby thing to have,' she said aloud, wondering where on earth she might find a glass.

Then she found a note.

Dear Grace,

I'm sorry I couldn't be here to welcome you, but I had to rush off. I hope you find everything OK. Perhaps when I get back I could feed you in payment for you feeding my cat?

Best, Flynn

PS It's not crucial what time you feed her: there are always dry biscuits down so she won't starve; but she likes her sachets freshly opened or the floor cooks it.

She chuckled and then went back to her search for a glass. Although there were two sinks, there was no drainer with a mug or glass conveniently in view so she was forced to open a cupboard. And then several more cupboards, until at last she found something she could drink out of.

After the water had made it possible for her tongue to move about in her mouth again, and her breathing had steadied to something approaching normal, she set about finding the cat food and the cat.

She was just wondering whether finding the cat would involve a search of the whole house, a by-product of which would be a thorough inspection of it, when a loud yowl from behind her made her jump more guiltily than any burglar.

'Oh, there you are,' she said, as casually as she could,

in case the cat could somehow guess her thoughts and later relate them to Flynn. 'Now all I have to do is find your stash of food and give you some. OK?'

The cat rubbed itself against her legs, implying no one had spoken to her or fed her for days. As she knew this was not true, Grace regarded the cat sceptically while she scratched under its chin. 'It's all very well being affectionate, but could you be useful too and lead me to the pantry? Where your food is?' she added helpfully.

The cat flung itself on to the floor and clawed at the air round Grace's legs, as if catching invisible butterflies. Grace moved away, left the luxurious kitchen and found the pantry.

'This is a fabulous house,' she told the cat as she squeezed jelly-covered chunks of meat into a dish marked 'Cat'. 'Allegra would love it.'

It was only after she had completed the ceremony of the alarm and the keys and had driven away, leaving the cat twitching the tip of its tail, did she acknowledge that she quite liked it too. Luckenham House was beautiful, but after Flynn's mansion, it did seem a little Spartan. And, apparently, about to be demolished by dry rot.

Chapter Twelve

❦

'We must get on and organise a wine tasting,' said Ellie when she got back from Bath, allowing Grace to make beans on toast for supper. Totally exhausted, she was still bubbling over with enthusiasm, although she'd spent most of the day humping rubbish about and sweeping floors.

'What's the huge hurry?' Grace shared the beans between three pieces of toast, wondering if there'd be enough. 'I want to get Graham to come and bring his magazine friend. I don't suppose I could arrange that without a bit of notice.'

'I think we should do something immediately, almost a dummy run to see how it goes, and then ask the posh people.'

'I wouldn't quite describe Graham as posh.'

Ellie suppressed her irritation, annoyed that she couldn't tell Grace why they needed to do something immediately rather than wait until all the people she considered important could come. As far as Ellie was concerned, as long as Ran Frazier came, no one else mattered, and all this secret-keeping was very wearing.

'I've got an idea!' she said, giving a good impression of someone in a comic with a lightbulb over their head. 'If we made a poster tonight, I could take it down to Bath tomorrow. It's not too far for people to come, I don't think.'

'You're very keen about this, Ellie. Considering all the cooking you'll have to do,' said Grace, looking suspicious.

'But it'll be fun!' Ellie was so relieved about not having to covertly acquire picture-restoration skills and then apply them to precious old masters, she was feeling a bit giddy.

'Dem,' said Grace. 'Can you come and eat, now? And will you want more toast?'

'And I really want to know how you got on at college,' said Ellie, feeling she couldn't nag Grace any more just now.

'It was OK,' said Demi, coming to the table. 'And I saw Rick at lunchtime. We had a chat. He was riding his motorbike. Very cool!'

Ellie laughed. 'It is very cool on the back of it, I can tell you. You definitely need leathers. I used to borrow one of Rick's mate's girlfriend's. So it was OK, going back?'

'Yeah, quite good actually. It was nice seeing everyone again.'

'So, Grace, do you know what wines you'll have?' Ellie tugged the conversation back to what was uppermost in her mind. 'Or shall we set a date first?'

'I haven't really thought about it,' said Grace. 'I've hardly had a minute to myself what with running round after Demi and Flynn's cat.'

'What's it called?' said Demi.

'Cleopatra, I think.'

'I wish we could have an animal,' said Demi. 'We've got lots of room.'

'I'll think about it,' said Grace. 'An animal would make the house more homely.'

'So would furniture,' said Ellie. 'Did you say you had a table we could put people round?'

'You'd think after a day of clearing out cellars you wouldn't want to think about inviting umpteen people for a six-course dinner,' said Grace, sliding the kettle across to the hot part of the Rayburn as if she'd been doing it all her life.

'It was only one cellar, and we can't afford to hang around.'

'Well, can we at least wait until Edward's money comes through? I spoke to him about your computer today, Dem, and he's going to set up a standing order as soon as possible.'

The lightbulb went on again. 'I tell you what,' said Ellie. 'I'll pay for all the food for the first one, and you can pay me back later. After all, if we charge enough, we'll get the money back straightaway.'

'No, I can't let you do that. I have got some money, after all. You'll just have to be a bit economical when you plan the menus.'

'I'm used to that! I could write a book called *A Million Ways with Mince*.'

Grace frowned in mock reproof. 'I don't think we need go quite as downmarket as that. But thinking how much to charge is important. How much will people spend on an evening out?' Grace crinkled her forehead. 'I don't even know how much a cinema ticket is these days. What would be a reasonable amount to ask people to pay?'

'Well,' said Ellie, 'my parents go out to restaurants for meals and they spend sixty quid easily, and you're offering "education".' She emphasised the word. 'People love that.'

'But I'm not offering food cooked by a professional chef! With health and safety regulations, in fact, the whole idea is probably illegal.'

Ellie was not going to be defeated by a few rules. 'I know! We won't charge people, we'll invite them and suggest they make contributions, then you're not actually selling anything. It would just be like having your friends round for dinner.' So anxious was she to get Ran into the house she'd have invited him for a dinner *à deux* with Allegra if she thought she'd get away with it.

'What?' said Demi. 'Instead of bringing a bottle they bring a twenty-pound note instead?'

'No,' said Ellie, trying to keep calm, 'we have a basket on the table which says "Contributions Please". They do it in art galleries all the time, for the wine.'

'I think I'd feel a bit awkward about doing that. It's like charging for hospitality.'

Ellie patted her shoulder. 'You're forgetting the education aspect. And the fact they get to eat in a beautiful William and Mary house. And don't worry about the money. We'll ask people if they enjoyed themselves, would they like to recommend it to their friends or come again, and if they'd mind making a contribution – next time – the first time being free.'

'A loss leader,' said Demi, smearing the butter with baked-bean juice as she cut off the corner. 'Like they have in supermarkets. Media Studies,' she added in explanation. 'We had it today.'

'OK,' said Grace, feeling slightly bulldozed. 'Who shall we have? I could get in touch with the people who came to my ordinary wine tasting, I suppose.'

'Let's set a date first. Have you got a diary?' asked Ellie, determined to get the day nailed down good and hard, so that nothing could prevent it happening.

'Until you lot came to live with me, I didn't have any appointments,' said Grace. 'No social life. Things like the dentist, I just remember.'

'That's all right then! Next week?'

'Isn't that a bit soon? Who will be able to come at such short notice?'

Ellie realised she should have asked when Ran was available. 'All right, the week after, then. It's only a dummy run. We can book the proper one well in advance.' She decided if the date they agreed on didn't suit Ran, she would find an excuse to change it.

'Are you going to ask Flynn?' said Demi.

'Yes, have Flynn, definitely,' said Ellie.

'Yeah. He's cool,' agreed Demi.

'He is?' Grace was surprised at this. She wouldn't have thought he qualified as cool.

'For an older man. He's definitely attractive.'

'He may not be able to come. I'm not sure how long he's away for,' Grace stalled.

'Oh, well, never mind,' said Ellie. 'Perhaps I could invite the picture restorer? Ran? He's interested in wine.' Aware that she was blushing, for all sorts of reasons, Ellie started gathering plates.

'Is he attractive, too?' asked Demi.

'Definitely. Sexy, anyway.'

'Isn't it the same thing?' asked Grace, feeling terribly naïve.

Demi shook her head. 'Not necessarily. Quite ugly men can be sexy. And quite good-looking ones.' Demi lowered her head, alerting Ellie to the fact that there was someone in Demi's life she liked.

'Do you want to invite anyone, Dem?' Ellie asked.

'God no!' Demi tucked her hair behind her ears and Grace noticed a new earring halfway up her ear, where she hadn't been able to wear one before. She clearly hadn't spent her lunch hour in the canteen. But Grace didn't comment. Let Hermia or Edward worry about new piercings. Her role as ex-stepmother did not include discussions about when decoration became mutilation. She had enough to do.

'What about inviting your sister?' said Ellie. 'She'd add a bit of class.'

'No!' said Grace. 'We'd have to invite her to stay the night and where would she sleep?

'You can't say you haven't got room, Grace,' said Ellie reproachfully.

'No beds. No en-suite bathrooms. No central heating. And talking of beds, could you have a word with Edward about yours, Demi? I think I forgot to mention it when I was on the phone today and I don't want to look like I'm nagging.'

'Mum never cared about nagging. She did it quite happily.'

'No, well, Edward and I are trying to keep our relationship civilised.' At least Grace was, probably from habit, as much as anything.

'So two weeks today, then?' said Ellie aware that the others had begun to get distracted. 'I want to start thinking up menus. You tell me what sort of food you want, Grace, and I'll plan it.'

Grace thought for a moment. 'Shouldn't we wait until you've finished your work experience; you'll be far too tired to cook. Won't that be around the end of your fortnight?'

'No, please! I really want to—' Ellie realised she was

sounding much too desperate, and stopped for a breath. 'I just really want us to start making some money.'

Grace sighed resignedly, and decided not to comment on the fact that so far, the wine and food idea looked like costing money rather than earning it.

Demi's mobile phone, which was lying on the kitchen table, growled, squirmed and then burst into song. She picked it up, checked the name and said, 'Oh, shit! Mum! Do I have to answer it?'

'Yes!' said the others in unison.

Demi sighed, got up from the table and wandered over so she could lean on the Rayburn. 'Hi, Mum,' she said sweetly.

'So when's Flynn coming back?' asked Ellie. 'Do you think that Wednesday will be too soon for him?'

'Oh, don't worry about that,' Grace answered as airily as possible. 'It may not be his thing anyway.' She was aware that Ellie was inspecting her closely, and while she was not averse to confiding in her, she knew perfectly well that Ellie was trying to match-make between her and Flynn. And as she had no idea how she felt about him, she didn't want to raise Ellie's hopes. Time for a distraction. 'Listen, I'm just popping out to the garden. There's a shrub I planted years ago, and I want to see if it's flowered at last. Want to come?'

'Yes,' said Ellie. 'I'd love some fresh air. I've been breathing dust all day.'

The two women wandered out of the back door, up the garden to where a flight of steps in a low wall led to a circular lawn surrounded by shrubs. In the middle was an ancient sundial. Even on a cold spring evening, it was a pleasant spot.

'Here it is,' said Grace, looking at what seemed to

Ellie to be some dry sticks protruding from the ground. 'Still not flowered. How long do I have to wait? Still, gardening is all about being patient.' She glanced at Ellie, who was inspecting a patch of crocuses under a tree clearly wondering if she had this necessary quality.

Ellie wandered back over and peered at the sticks. 'So, why don't you think this dinner party would be Flynn's thing? He's interested in wine, he's sure to be interested in food. And he's definitely interested in you.'

Grace laughed rather uncomfortably. 'I'm sure you're wrong. We bicker all the time.'

'It's a sure sign, believe me. So how do you feel about him?'

Grace paused. She honestly wasn't completely sure. 'He is kind and funny and everything, but he's not Edward. And it's still too soon.'

'It can't be! It's been ages! I'm so over Rick I can hardly remember what he looks like!' A slight exaggeration, but she could certainly never imagine going back.

Grace, who had been inspecting a twisted willow for signs of new growth, glanced at her. 'Is that possibly because you've met a handsome picture restorer?'

'Oh, I don't think you'd describe him as handsome, exactly, and he's quite a bit older than me.'

'But?' Ellie's smile told her there had to be more.

'He would be perfect for me to have my last fling with!'

Grace chuckled. 'Is that why you're so keen to have this wine-tasting thing so soon, then? So you can work on Ran?'

'Yes.' It wasn't the only reason but it was certainly one of them. 'He's only seen me in my working clothes. If he saw me all dolled up he might fancy me more.'

218

'He probably fancies you already,' said Grace, moving on to a winter-flowering viburnum which was filling the air with sweet, peppery scent.

'No, he doesn't! It's so annoying! Still, I'm going to work on him.'

Grace looked back at Ellie, concerned now. 'Don't fall in love and get hurt, Ellie. It's so awful. Not worth it, really.'

'Oh no, I won't do that,' Ellie promised. 'I'm far too down to earth. But Ran is the perfect choice, partly because I haven't got much time to find anyone else. And . . . and I spent so long running around after Rick that I really do want something that's simple, and fun, and . . . and that's just for *me* before the baby's born.' She suddenly looked rather forlorn. 'Do you think that's silly?'

'Oh no, Ellie. I don't. And I'm sorry! You don't have to spend all your time worrying about my money problems and restoring the pictures. Go out! Have a good time!'

'I am having a good time. I love restoring things.' She patted her friend's arm. 'Especially people.'

Grace smiled, touched. 'Do you want to go in now? It's getting cold. I just want to go up to the end, and see what's going on there.'

Ellie, who had started to shiver, said, 'No, I'll come with you. When did you say you thought Flynn was coming back?'

'Judging by the amount of cat food he's left, he should be away a couple of weeks. Cleopatra is awfully sweet. Perhaps we should have a cat or something. Demi would love it.' Grace smiled, pleased with her elegant segue into safer topics.

'Pregnant women can't change litter trays,' said Ellie. 'Even I know that.'

'You must sign up with a doctor,' said Grace firmly. 'You need to look after yourself. Eat a balanced diet, get plenty of rest.'

Ellie laughed. 'The diet bit's OK as long as it includes chocolate. The rest part is a joke!'

'Really, Ellie, I just said, you don't have to do the work experience if it's too much for you. We could find some other way of restoring the paintings.'

'Oh no, it's fine! I like it.' Ellie smiled hard, hoping that Grace would be convinced that it was the picture restoration she liked so much.

'Getting the house ready for this food and wine shenanigans will be an awful lot of work.'

'Shenanigans?' said Ellie. 'That's the sort of word Flynn would use.'

'Is it? Whatever, it's still a lot of housework.'

'But housework is the new sex!' Ellie insisted. 'Didn't you see that series last year? No, sorry, you wouldn't have done.'

Grace grimaced. 'The new sex? I think on the whole I prefer the old kind. On the other hand, we may just have to settle for housework.'

'Maybe you will. I have plans of my own.' Ellie chuckled wickedly. 'It would be best to use the drawing room,' she went on, getting on with the matter in hand, 'rather than the dining room, because you've used it more recently.'

'And decorated it. Getting the dining room up to scratch would be real erotica, verging on the porno-graphic – if housework really is the new sex,' she explained to a confused Ellie.

Demi appeared. 'There you are! What are you doing out here? It's freezing!'

'We're just coming in. How did you get on with your mother?' said Grace.

'She wants to take me out for a meal after college. Have a chat about how things are going.' Demi broke off a stalk of lavender and fiddled with it irritably.

'That's OK. Go somewhere nice, have some nice food. What's the problem?' asked Ellie.

Demi sighed. 'I dunno! She seems to be happier now I'm not there to mess things up, but she obviously feels guilty. She'll nag me about college work.'

'But you've made a really good start with that, since you've been back,' said Grace, 'haven't you?'

'Yeah, but Mum says Media Studies isn't a proper subject and I've got to change to something like English.'

'But you're doing History. That's proper!' said Grace indignantly, remembering how disparaging her academic family had been about her subject choices.

'Anyway, she wants to meet me after college tomorrow, take me for something to eat and then bring me home later. Is that OK?'

'She's your mother, Dem, of course it's OK!'

Ellie was feeling a bit guilty as she set off for Bath the next day. Ran didn't need her, didn't want her hanging around, and after she had delivered the invitation for a date a fortnight hence, she really had no business being there.

But there was Grace; as far as she was concerned, Ellie was learning all she could about picture restoration. Ellie couldn't admit it wasn't possible to learn anything in a fortnight, far less enough actually to benefit the paintings. She had more chance of ruining them – that much she had learnt. Even their first, tentative dust with a soft cloth had probably done irreparable damage; Ellie hadn't had the nerve to confess to Ran that they had actually done that.

And there was Ran. How did one go about seducing a man who appeared not to fancy one at all? It wouldn't be easy, but Ellie liked a challenge and refused to be put off by a lack of appreciative glances. She had dressed carefully; she'd had to be careful to achieve a look which combined understated sexiness with practicality. It would be awful if he noticed that she'd dressed to attract more than just dust and stubborn limescale. She'd have to be subtle.

To this end, with her soft jersey trousers, she put on an old, tight-fitting cardigan, which she wore as a jumper with a bright silk scarf around her neck. And so as not to clash with the scarf, and to make herself generally more acceptable to someone over thirty, she had, the previous evening, dyed her hair to the nearest colour akin to brown as she could, given that it had been red before. Ellie hoped that appearing to be more conventional, but sexier, might be the key to opening his eyes to her as a woman.

Later, when she was squashing her 2CV into a space slightly smaller than her futon, she wondered about her chances. She really did want a final affaire – though she must be careful that she didn't get in too deep. Ran would be lovely to have an affaire with. And she was just not ready to settle for housework instead of sex.

Housework definitely came first, though, as it turned out. When he opened the door to her, he said, 'So you're

222

back, are you? Well, I've got a nice little job sorting cupboards for you.'

'And I've got a nice invitation to a very interesting evening with wine and food for you.' She smiled. No response. 'You'll love it.'

'I thought the point was that I was going to get to see the paintings during it, not indulge myself in Bacchanalian delights.'

'You spend too much time in History-of-Art books. It's affected your language.'

He smiled, just enough to tweak Ellie's libido, although she knew he wasn't doing it on purpose. 'Come and sort cupboards.'

Ellie sighed. It was probably the best offer she was likely to get. For now.

Later, when she gave him his coffee and sandwiches, she laid everything out in a way that involved quite a lot of bending over, revealing enough cleavage to tell Ran that she had one, in case he'd overlooked it. He gave her no encouragement, no hint that he'd noticed. She sighed, retreated to the other side of the table, and bit into her cheese and pickle.

'There's really no point in you coming here each day if I'm going to look at the pictures for you,' said Ran.

Ellie was ready for this. 'But I've told Grace I'm doing it. If I don't come, she'll wonder why and suspect I've told you her secret. You don't mind me coming, do you? I mean, there are things I can do for you?' She smiled in a way that would have had the punters at her old bar job buying her drinks, asking for her mobile number and offering to walk her to her car.

He smiled back, but there was no suggestion in it, no

hint that he was responding to her in the way that she wanted.

I must be too young and studenty, she decided, and resolved to find a little black dress that would be enhanced by a very small tummy for the dinner party.

Apart from needing to in order to keep up the myth for Grace, she had no reason to drive back down to Bath the next day except to be with Ran. Who was she fooling? Grace, or herself?

Hermia delivered Demi home at nine o'clock that evening. Demi was not happy. Apparently a white van would arrive at Luckenham House the next day full of Demi's bed, her bedding, in fact everything that currently filled her bedroom, including her computer.

'That's good, isn't it?' said Ellie, who was feeling chirpier because Ran had touched her arm that afternoon when he was explaining something.

'Well, yes!' said Demi, 'sort of! But she's going to turn my room into a gym!'

'Must have been a big room,' said Ellie.

'She's going to put in all sorts of equipment so she and her bloke can sweat it out together. It's disgusting!' She looked both furious and on the verge of tears.

'What is? Keeping fit? Surely not,' said Ellie, trying to lighten things.

'No, the thought of her and him . . . you know. Doing stuff. Yuk!'

Grace looked at Demi, feeling it was possible it wasn't so much the thought of her mother 'doing stuff' than the fact that her mother had eradicated her daughter's presence from her house. What would happen if Demi wanted to go home?

'It's probably just a phase,' said Grace reassuringly. 'People are always buying expensive subscriptions to gyms and never going. They get bored. I read about it in the Sunday papers.'

'But you don't get the Sunday papers,' said Ellie.

'We did when Edward was here. But I do understand how you feel, Dem,' Grace said awkwardly. 'We must decorate you a room, get it just how you like it. Put all your things in it, and then you won't feel you've been replaced by a cross-trainer-stepper combination.'

Demi turned to Grace, and Grace saw that the tears were now really threatening to overflow; she was far more upset that she'd wanted to let on. 'Thanks, Grace,' she said in a very small voice.

'And I dare say Hermia will get bored with her toyboy, too,' said Ellie. 'What would they talk about when they're not . . . you know.'

Demi obviously didn't want to think about it. 'Is there any hot water? I really need a bath.'

'Poor love,' said Ellie when she and Grace were alone. 'It was bad enough my mother turning my room into a study when I went to university, but at least she hadn't replaced my dad with a younger model.'

Grace nodded. 'My parents were very relieved when I got married, too, although I was so young. I think they'd got bored with being parents by then, me being younger than the other two.'

'Well, my baby can stay with me until he or she's thirty, no question,' said Ellie.

Grace grinned. 'I'll remind you that you said that, one day.'

Both women subsided into a warm glow, imagining the little bundle of cells in Ellie's stomach becoming first a baby, then a toddler, a child, teenager, and then an adult. It didn't seem possible.

'You must get a doctor, Ellie,' said Grace.

'You must get a man,' said Ellie. 'Oops. Sorry, I didn't mean to say that, I was just thinking . . .'

'Well, if I want a baby I'll have to,' said Grace briskly. 'Even if I don't keep him long. Do you think Flynn would father a child for me if I asked him? You're always saying how kind he is.'

'Grace! You are not to ask him! It wouldn't be fair! He'd want to be a proper father, in a proper family, not a sperm donor!'

'I was only joking, you know,' chided Grace.

'Oh. I'm sorry. My hormones have gone mental. I don't know what I'm thinking or saying at the moment.'

She must watch that, she thought. She mustn't let her mouth run away with her with Ran, or she might find herself suggesting they go to bed. That would never do.

'Flynn's not going to be back for a week, or probably more,' said Grace. 'He rang and left a message.'

'Oh, that's a shame!' said Ellie. 'It's funny, but I'll sort of miss him. Won't you?'

'Sort of.' Grace paused, thoughtfully. Ellie observed her, optimism creeping in.

'Yes,' Grace went on. 'It's a bit of a bore having to keep driving over to feed Cleopatra.'

'Oh! You!' Ellie threw a ball of kitchen towel at her.

'Only joking. Now, shall we talk about food? We'll have six wines, which means six different courses. Does that sound far too much work? I want to do at least one pudding wine.'

'I'll get some paper and make a list. What will people eat all this food off?'

Grace bit her lip. 'I'll ask Flynn to lend us stuff. He's got loads.'

'How do you know? Have you been through his cupboards?'

'Not on purpose, but it sort of happened,' she murmured, rather embarrassed.

'So what's his house like, then?'

'I've got to feed Cleopatra tomorrow morning, you could come with me. Oh, you're going to Bath, I forgot. How did it go by the way? Have you learnt anything so far?'

Ellie made a face. 'That we should never have dusted the pictures, especially when the paint was flaking because we'll have lost paint. And we should probably consolidate what we've got before doing much else. Then we use a lot of spit. For the enzymes.'

'Oh.' Then Grace said, 'Do you think Demi's going to be all right? She seems terribly upset.'

'I'm sure she will be. After all, she's not the only victim of a broken home.'

'Oh, Ellie! It's my fault her home is broken! If Edward hadn't met me, he might have gone back to Hermia!'

Ellie snorted her disagreement. 'For God's sake, Grace! He's a serial monogamist. He didn't make a go of it with you, either.'

'He didn't have the incentive. We didn't have children.'

'But didn't you tell me that he didn't want them?'

'Yes.'

'Well then. It's his fault you didn't have them, and his fault he left Hermia and his fault he left you. He probably gets bored easily.'

Grace nodded. 'He *does* get bored easily.' She brightened. 'That's probably it! Perhaps it wasn't all my fault that my marriage broke down.'

'Of course it wasn't. It was all his fault.'

'Oh no.' Grace was scrupulously fair. 'Some of it must have been. But it's nice to think the responsibility wasn't entirely mine.'

Ellie laughed. 'You are a chump, sometimes.'

Chapter Thirteen

When Ellie rang the bell to Ran's house the following morning she felt both nervous and excited: nervous because she was a bit late and excited by the thought of seeing him again.

He opened the door. 'Good morning. And how are you today?' he asked as they went up the stairs.

'I'm fine. Could I just . . . ?' She indicated the bathroom.

'Oh, yes. Frequency of micturition.'

Ellie halted in horror. 'What?'

'It's a symptom of pregnancy. Means you go to the loo a lot.'

'For God's sake!' said Ellie, running. 'As if I didn't know that!'

While she was drying her hands she realised she had completely blown her plans for seduction. She really should have found a Ladies on the way and not had to rush to his loo like that, but she had been late and there wasn't anywhere, and she would never have found a parking space if there had been. She flicked at her hair, pulled back her shoulders and practised her sexy smile. Just as well she did, she thought, not smiling any more. For sexy read scary – not a good look! She sniffed at his bottle of aftershave, wondering if he would notice if she came out smelling of it, and then tidied the towel and generally made the place look respectable. She might well have to clean it properly, later.

How did he know that constant peeing was a symptom of pregnancy? Did he have children of his own? Perhaps he was married! There were definitely some important questions to be asked before she embarked on her seduction.

'Sorry about that,' she said as she joined Ran in the kitchen. 'But you didn't seem surprised I needed to go. Does that mean you're a father yourself?' Then she wondered if she'd been a bit blunt. Perhaps she should have worked round to a question like that, and not just jumped in.

He shook his head, unfazed. 'Nieces and nephews, but my sisters didn't spare me a single symptom from the moment they got pregnant to the moment they held the baby in their arms. Would you like me to relate how long they were each in labour for?'

'No, thank you!' Ellie was horrified at the notion, but enormously relieved that his knowledge was not even second-hand. However, she didn't want details; she didn't want to connect Ran with pain and suffering, but with romance, sex, and good hotels. Or even just his double bed. 'What would you like me to do today?'

'I thought I ought to show you what I do.'

'Brilliant! Some real work experience! I know you're going to look at the pictures and do all that for me, but I am really interested in picture conservation, so if I could actually do something . . .' Her words tailed away as she saw him shaking his head. Oh well, he had warned her he wouldn't let her touch anything – ever, probably.

'I meant, I'd like to show you some work I've already

done. There's an antiques fair not far from here, and there's a picture for sale in it that I restored. I'd quite like to see it. I thought we'd go along.'

'Lovely!' A day out with her beloved. What could be nicer? Then she mentally scrubbed out the word 'beloved'; she must not, under any circumstances, fall in love with him. He was strictly for sex only.

'Come on then. Have you got your coat?'

'I'm wearing it.' She indicated her gilet, which was lined with fake fur and very warm.

'Sorry. I didn't recognise that thing as a coat. In my day coats had sleeves. Let's go.'

Ellie preceded him down the stairs and stood aside while he opened the front door. What was wrong with her gilet? She opened her mouth to ask him, but shut it again. She'd got away with being blunt when she asked him if he had children, she didn't want to push her luck.

He unlocked a sturdy-looking Volvo estate and opened the passenger door for her. 'Heave yourself in.'

'I do not need to heave myself!' she declared indignantly. 'My pregnancy hardly shows!'

'It doesn't show at all. I was just preparing you for what's ahead.'

'Thank you, but please don't bother,' she said primly.

'"Sufficient unto the day is the evil thereof"?' he quoted questioningly.

'Probably,' she snapped, and looked firmly out of the window, which mostly involved studying the gutter and was not a lot of fun.

Neither of them spoke until they were climbing up out of the town into the countryside. Now the view from the window was well worth looking at. Spring was just beginning to assert herself, decorating the trees with enough green fuzz to make one believe the rest would follow, and one day the world would be green again. The sun was shining, and although it was still extremely cold the air sparkled. Ellie felt a burst of optimism go through her. Perhaps they would get enough money to pay for the dry rot in Luckenham. Perhaps Grace would see what a nice man Flynn was. And perhaps, although it was a very long shot, she and Ran would end up having a glorious affaire.

'That is a fantastic view – across the valley,' she said.

'It is indeed. What's the countryside like round Luckenham House?'

'Oh, that's lovely too. Lots of trees, but it's a bit flatter.'

'Tell me about the house.'

As it was a safe subject and would stop her making any huge social gaffes which could mess up her chances with him for ever, Ellie obliged. 'William and Mary, I think. It has a sort of Sleeping Beauty quality to it. Most of the rooms are empty, and it does have this dry rot, but it's lovely. Perfect proportions. Which is why I wanted to paint a picture of it.'

He changed gear, giving her a questioning look.

'Oh, that's how I met Grace,' Ellie explained. 'I take photographs of people's houses, paint them as watercolours, and then sell them to the owner of the house. Grace couldn't afford a painting so I gave it to her. You'll see it when you come.' Then she subsided. That might not be a good thing. It might shoot her credibility down in flames.

'So do you paint the houses in an abstract way?'

'Oh no! That would never do. What people want is a nice conventional watercolour. Rick, my ex-partner, despised me terribly, but I need the money. It's just not practical for me to do installations that no one could ever buy, even if they did have enough money and actually wanted the contents of a skip strewn across the floor.'

She was referring to Rick's degree show which had impressed everyone so much they asked him to do an MA. At the time, Ellie had been impressed, too, but felt now that perhaps you had to be slightly in love with Rick really to appreciate his art.

'So are you genuinely interested in picture conservation, or was that just a ploy to help you sort out these panels?'

'I must confess that originally it was just a ploy, but since I saw what you do, I have become really interested. It's a fascinating thing to do, I think.' This was true, and she didn't think it would exactly lose her brownie points telling him so.

'Well, now you're going to see the end results. I've got slides of what the painting was like before.'

'Brilliant!' said Ellie, wondering whether his increased friendliness and the treat of a day out together meant she was getting somewhere.

They drove through South Gloucestershire to where a stately home had become a very smart girls' school. It was a magnificent building, late Victorian, thought Ellie, although she wasn't sure, and didn't want to betray her lack of knowledge to Ran. There was a long drive up to it, and elegant horses, wrapped up well against the cold, grazed in the sunshine in the fields that surrounded the drive.

'They have some wonderful trees here,' said Ran. 'It's at its most beautiful in autumn, though I think I prefer the more subtle tones of spring.'

'I'd love to paint it,' said Ellie, suddenly yearning to have a brush in her hand again. 'But I don't think I'd have a hope of getting it all into a photograph to copy. With my camera, I'd have to stand about a mile away.'

'Don't you think you should set up your easel and paint it from life?' Ran turned the car into a field designated for parking. 'I'm sure it's not ethical to paint from photographs.'

Ellie was tempted to be rude. 'Ethical? Who cares about that? I just want to paint houses that their owners are likely to want to buy. If I had to spend three days sitting in the freezing cold, doing it from life, I'd have to charge thousands for each one.'

Ran chuckled. 'You know your own business best, I suppose.'

'Yes, I do, as it happens!'

As they walked through the field to the entrance to the house, she admired the pillars, the pediments and general air of prosperity the house proclaimed. It was mainly red brick with marble columns, and although as a rule she didn't like brick buildings, she admitted to herself that it worked quite well in this particular case.

'It's about three times the size, but not nearly as lovely as Luckenham House,' she said. 'Although it is rather splendid.'

'I think that sums it up adequately,' said Ran. Then he regarded her through slightly narrowed eyes. 'I don't suppose I could get you in for half-price, could I?' he continued as they tagged on to the end of the queue. 'You don't look more than sixteen.'

Ellie was incensed. 'If you're too tight to pay the proper, full price for a pregnant woman, I'll buy my own ticket!'

'In my day we called it "mean".'

'Whichever,' she said dismissively, trying not to laugh: he was obviously teasing her. 'I think you're probably both.'

'Oh no, for my generation, tight meant—'

'Oh shut up, I don't want to hear it.' She paused. 'I expect you could get a reduced rate, though, for being a senior citizen,' she added sweetly.

'The cheek of it! I'm not a day over thirty-five, I'll have you know!'

'Sorree!' she said blithely, quite glad they were in a queue of several dozen people; it was satisfying to get a reaction, but she wouldn't have dared to be so provocative in private. Then she sighed. She'd have to change the way they were with each other somehow. How would she ever seduce him if he treated her like a child and she treated him like an old-age pensioner?

Once inside the antiques fair, Ellie did feel quite child-like, dazzled as she was by the wonderful things on display. She ran to where a doll's house was set up, with lights, tiny, apparently antique furniture, and carved wooden inhabitants. There were teddy bears, too, with enormous price tags on them because of the metal tags in their ears. She was just wondering why a very worn old teddy bear could be valuable to anyone who hadn't personally loved off all its fur, when Ran took her arm.

'Come on. We're not here to look at the toys. Although if you're good, I'll buy you an ice cream later.'

She flounced, mostly because he wanted her to.

After briefly consulting the leaflet, which had a guide to where everything was, he led her through several rooms, past furniture, ancient garden tools and ornaments, including antique (and therefore acceptable) garden gnomes, to where there was a stand selling pictures. There, in the middle, was a portrait of a young woman. Ran and the proprietor greeted each other.

'Ted, how are you?' said Ran. 'I've brought an apprentice along with me, so she can see the work of a master.'

The man laughed. 'You're good, Ran, but maybe not that good.'

'Come on, you know you wouldn't use me if I wasn't. This is Ellie . . . what's your other name?'

'Summers,' said Ellie, suddenly shy.

'This is Ted Matthews, who makes his living fleecing innocent victims of their pension money.'

'My paintings are as good as a pension. Pure investment, and at least you get to look at them while they increase in value.'

Ellie moved away from where the men laughed and joked, fascinated by the figure in the painting. She couldn't decide how old the girl was, such was her composure. She could have been nineteen, made old for her years by her responsibilities. Or she could have been in her mid-twenties, Ellie's age. She had clear brown eyes and was dressed in a simple pale grey gown. The ruffle of one elbow was held back with a string of four pearls which could have been real, they were so glowing and opalescent. Although her name was written in fine gold print on the portrait, stating that she was the wife of the Governor of Madras, she was not wearing a ring in the picture. Her long, white fingers were entwined with some white flowers with pointed foliage; she'd need Grace to tell her what sort they were. It was possible, thought Ellie, that the portrait was painted before she left for India, for her parents, who might

236

never see her again. The thought made tears spring to her eyes. Wretched hormones, making her sentimental about someone who'd died centuries ago.

'She's wonderful!' she said, genuinely impressed as Ran came up and stood behind her shoulder. 'What did you do to her?'

'Look closely, and see if you can tell.'

'I can't see anything wrong with it.'

'That is rather the point. But concentrate. There was a tear right across it. Can you see the mark?'

'No. Not a thing.'

'You need a magnifying glass,' said Ted. 'Ran thinks he's the best conservator around, and to be honest, he's not far wrong. Should be, the prices he charges.'

'If you want museum-quality conserving, you or your clients must pay for it. But she is lovely, I have to admit. Had much interest?'

'A bit from a couple of dealers, but I'll wait before I start accepting much below the asking price.'

'Do you come to antiques fairs often?' asked Ellie.

'Only the ones that are reasonably near. We always do well here. This one during half-term is always popular because people who don't go skiing at this time of year have days out instead. "Antiquing" is the hobby of the affluent middle classes these days.'

'I see,' said Ellie, who could indeed see a lot of them, milling about, pointing and exclaiming.

'So.' Ted turned his attention to her. 'Ellie, was it? What do you do?'

He might as well have asked outright what she was doing with Ran, and fortunately, while the men were chatting, she had prepared an explanation.

'I'm a Creative Arts graduate and I'm interested in

studying picture conservation. As the training's quite long and hard, I thought I'd better do some work experience first, to make sure it was really what I wanted to do.'

She stopped for breath and smiled, pleased with how all that came out, but she was relieved when a woman with white hair and a determined expression came up to the stand, getting Ellie out of any further interrogation.

'Shall we have a look around?' said Ran. 'And then I know a nice pub where we could have lunch. We'll probably have to sit in the garden though.'

'Why? It's freezing!'

'I'm not sure you'll pass as being over eighteen.'

Ellie grimaced. 'It's all right. You're allowed into pubs when you're sixteen if you're with a parent.'

He growled and she grinned, pleased to have got the last word. But then, as they strolled through the house, looking at lovely things, she realised that being so quick had worked against her – she had just emphasised the difference in their ages again.

'Shouldn't you – we – be working?' asked Ellie, trying to sound especially adult. 'Should we go out to lunch?'

'I think "you – we" can have days off sometimes. After all, you don't really need to do work experience now.'

'No, but I would like to have some. Really. When all this business with the panels is over, I'd really like to study picture conservation.'

'You'll have a baby to look after.'

'I know, but I'm young, my child won't stay a baby for ever, and I'll have to earn a living somehow. Do you get plenty of work?'

'I do, but I've got a reputation. That takes time to build up.'

'Then the sooner I start the better!' she said, bright but firm.

'So come on, let's go and look at the toys and then find the pub.'

'I'll just find the Ladies, first.'

The pub had a log fire, and because it was still quite early, they were able to get seats next to it. 'This is lovely,' said Ellie, looking at the menu that Ran had handed to her.

'What do you feel like eating? Have you developed any strange tastes or violent antipathies?'

'Not really, I just get very hungry.'

'That's rather nice. I get fed up with women who are on diets, and can't eat anything except steak without the chips or salad without the dressing.'

'Well, I'll have the steak and the chips and the salad and the dressing.' She smiled at him and he smiled back. God, he was attractive, she thought. 'Excuse me, I'll just—'

'Go to the Ladies – again. Tell me what you want to drink first?'

'Mineral water. Fizzy, please,' she said, and left. For once in her pregnant life it wasn't her bladder that led her to the lavatory, but an urgent need to make herself look a bit more grown-up. She'd given as good as she got – or even better – in their bantering about age, but there was no benefit in winning if he just thought she was too young to have sex with.

She was back in her seat by the fire, looking much the same as before, when Ran returned with the drinks. She had decided there was nothing she could do to her appearance, lacking grey hair powder or a pencil suitable for drawing in some laughter lines. She

239

would have to depend on her acting skills to appear more mature.

'Thank you, Ran,' she said cooingly.

He frowned suddenly and picked up his pint. 'Are you all right? Don't feel unwell, or anything?'

'I'm fine. Why shouldn't I be?'

'Nothing, it's just that you've gone all polite on me. Not so long ago you were telling me to shut up, Grandad, more or less.'

'Well, that was very rude. I do apologise.'

'Please don't mention it,' he said. 'So, tell me about this wine tasting with dinner I'm being dragged to?'

Ellie bit back her natural indignation at his attitude; it would do her no good. 'Well, it should be very pleasant. I'm going to think up some lovely little dishes to eat with the wine, so you'll get good food, good wine, and possibly good company.' Without knowing who else was going, she couldn't promise he'd find someone interesting to talk to. 'But you're supposed just to talk about wine, anyway.'

'Hardly my favourite topic. I'm happy to drink it, but I can't be bothered to think up amusing little ways of describing it. To me, if it smells of cabbage water, it smells of cabbage water.'

'Perfect! That's just the type of no-nonsense description that Grace is looking for. You'll be a natural.' She smiled approvingly. 'And at some point during the evening you'll excuse yourself, come into the kitchen' – where I will be looking particularly sexy, she added silently – 'and I will show you the panels and you can have a look at them.'

'Having concealed my magnifying glasses about my person?'

'Exactly. It's going to be easy! Ah, here's the food, I'm starving.'

'So you're not nauseous any more?' he asked as the waitress set down plates heaped with food on the little table in front of them.

'Oh yes, sometimes, but in between times, I could eat a horse.'

'Pity it wasn't on the menu. I would have liked to have seen that.'

Chapter Fourteen

'OK, we've got to do it now,' said Ellie as she and Grace sat together in the kitchen a fortnight later. They had been enjoying a late, leisurely breakfast after Grace had delivered Demi to the bus that went all the way to her college.

Getting Hermia to agree to Grace driving Demi to a bus stop, and not all the way to college, had taken a little firmness on Grace's part, but when Hermia realised that Grace was not going to be bullied into driving Demi all the way and back now an alternative had been found, she had accepted defeat on the matter.

'It does save time, not having to take Demi to the door,' said Grace, putting the last square of toast and marmalade into her mouth.

'Yes, and to be honest we need the time. The food is as ready as it can be at this stage, you've got the wine, the glasses, the marking forms, and enough people are coming. But there's still the drawing room to be decorated, and if we tackle it now we've got time to make it really beautiful.'

'It's already beautiful,' said Grace, trying not to mind that Flynn hadn't responded to her invitation, in fact hadn't spoken to her at all since his return, although she'd driven to his house to feed his cat every day for a fortnight. She wouldn't have known he was back if she hadn't seen his car in the drive yesterday morning. She hadn't gone in to say hello and felt she'd been a bit of a coward.

'In a minimalist sort of way, it is,' agreed Ellie, so as not to hurt Grace's feelings. 'But in a way quite inappropriate for the house. Apart from anything else, we need a table.'

Grace sighed and accepted that the room would have to be faced. Now the day was upon them, she found herself annoyingly edgy. 'OK. Let's go into the stables and find the ping-pong table. It may not have all its legs.'

'It's only half-past eleven. We've got time to mend them. Come to that, we've got time to buy a whole new ping-pong table, if necessary.' Ellie had her own nerves to contend with. Not only had she had to devise six courses for ten people, she had to think of a way to get Ran on his own, in the dining room, without the others noticing. It was with this in mind that she had persuaded Grace into inviting so many – it would be easier to winkle one out from the crowd.

Chairs scraped on the stone floor as they got up. 'It's such a shame that Graham and his magazine friend couldn't come,' said Grace. 'Even when we changed the date for this Friday night. All this work would seem more worthwhile if they were going to be there.'

'This is a dummy run,' Ellie reminded her, not for the first time, aware that if Ran agreed that the panels were valuable, Grace's financial problems would be over.

'And I can't talk you into eating with us? I could do with the support.'

'Really, it would be so much easier for me if I was in the kitchen, cooking the next course, taking away plates.' Sneaking off to the dining room with Ran, she added silently.

'I suppose so. But shouldn't you be there for – what's his name? Ran?'

'No. He's only coming for the free food and wine. He's not interested in me. As a person,' she added hurriedly. Since their day out at the antiques fair, Ellie had gone to visit him three times, and reorganised his kitchen cupboards and his bathroom. Any minute now, she was convinced, he would let her do something in the studio. Not actually touch a painting, of course, but be near them, which would be a start. Her plans to seduce him were no further on, but tonight would be a turning point. She wasn't going to be sitting down and eating and drinking, but when she whisked in and out of the room with plates, she was going to be wearing a very little black dress and he would notice her as a woman if she had to tip boiling soup in his lap!

'It's a pity Demi ducked out of helping and arranged to spend the night with a friend,' said Grace, carrying their breakfast plates to the sink. 'But she has been awfully good and it's nice that she's settled in so well back at college, and has met new people and stuff. It can't have been easy for her.'

'You don't sound quite as happy as you ought to be about it,' said Ellie.

'I'm not. There was something about the way she asked me, something a bit shifty about it. It didn't seem like Demi, somehow.' She dried her hands, still slightly worried. She really hadn't been keen on Demi disappearing off, but couldn't think of a reason to stop her. 'Then again, she has been different since she saw her mother.'

244

'You could ring the mother of the girl she's staying with and check?'

'I could – possibly should – but Demi would never trust me again if she thought I didn't trust her!'

'True.'

'And she was pleased to get all her stuff, to make herself a bedroom,' said Ellie, remembering the fun she and Demi had had, putting it all together.

'I'm sure she's fine,' said Grace. 'Let's go and tackle the spiders.'

'Oh, is that why you've been so reluctant to go into the stables! Scared of spiders, huh!'

'It's quite a common phobia, you know,' said Grace, leading the way out of the back door.

'I know,' replied Ellie. 'I've got it, too.'

Apart from the spiders, of which there were a great number, the stables contained some very useful bits and pieces.

'I love doing this!' said Ellie, hauling out an old wash-stand base. 'It's like creating a stage set. Do you think there's a top to this anywhere?'

'There might be. Allegra and Nicholas only took the good stuff. Anything that was broken ended up in here, but that doesn't mean we can't mend it.'

'Do you mind about Flynn not coming?' asked Ellie, dragging out an old carpet by a corner and disturbing a spider as big as a mouse.

'I suppose I do, really,' said Grace, watching the spider warily. 'Although I wouldn't have thought I would have, if that makes sense.'

'Perfect sense.'

'I mean, he's so not my type, but there is something rather . . .' She paused, looking for the word.

'Nice?' suggested Ellie, who had spotted the ping-pong table and was trying to work out how to get to it.

'No. I don't think that's quite what he is. He's just totally unlike Edward.'

Ellie took a breath to say that this was a good thing – but didn't. Why Grace was still carrying a torch for Edward Ellie couldn't fathom. Rick had stayed in her mind for about five minutes after she had decided he was a waste of space and left him – although maybe that was partly because it had been her choice. Ran, on the other hand, was occupying far too much of her brain, possibly because he had refused to respond to her increasingly blatant advances.

'I think if we get this lot out first, we should be able to get to the table,' she said, deciding against commenting on the man who had left Grace with this pile of junk while he swanned off with his antiques.

'And there might be some quite nice stuff in here, if we just got rid of the cobwebs.' Grace looked up suddenly. 'I've got some gardening gloves. That would help.'

'Will it matter that the china doesn't match?' asked Grace, not for the first time.

'No. It's a harlequin set! Which is a posh way of saying it doesn't match!' Ellie declared.

Preferring not to ask Flynn to lend her china, as she hadn't seen him since his return, Grace had gone to the local junk shop. There she had managed to buy a couple of quite pretty but incomplete dinner services as well as some chairs, some hideous but useful occasional tables and some lovely serving dishes. Grace had spent the afternoon washing them all, while Ellie cooked what she could in advance.

'It is quite fun, this,' said Grace, who had been slower to come to this realisation than Ellie. 'When we did it for Allegra, it was a bit more worrying. Although there are going to be far more people, and we're feeding them and everything, it's potentially more satisfying. Also, they're not going to try and make me sell my house.'

'Although we didn't have to make the drawing room into a dining room for Allegra.'

'Oh, do you think we should have used the dining room? If you think it would be better—'

'No! After all, a room is only a dining room if it's got a table in it,' said Ellie, wishing she'd never mentioned the dining room. It was going to be hard enough to get Ran to see the pictures, without filling the room they were in with people.

'And if these evenings go well, we won't want to have them where you're restoring the paintings. Do you think you know enough about it to start soon? Like tomorrow?'

Ellie took a breath, about to tell Grace the truth; that she would never know enough to start on the paintings, and that she planned for Ran to do it. But she didn't. Grace didn't need the extra anxiety, not now. She'd tell her tomorrow, when the evening had been a fantastic success and Grace would be feeling mellow and relaxed. 'Hmm, tomorrow, probably.'

'It's just we do need to get this dry rot sorted. I rang another company about it and they would have charged more. So we need to sell the pictures.'

'Do you still think Allegra and your brother might want a cut of whatever you get for them, too?'

'As long as I get enough to put the dry rot right, I don't care. They can have everything that's left over.'

'I don't want to be rude about Allegra – I mean, she's your sister and everything, but . . .'

'Go on, don't bother to spare me. Tell me what's on your mind.'

'Will she be happy to let you take out the dry-rot money first? Won't she say that the paintings belonged to her and your brother?'

'How can she? They are definitely fixtures and fittings! They're on the shutters.'

'Well, I know, but you'll have to take them off to sell them and—'

'You think she'll say if they're removable, they're hers and Nick's?'

'Well, what do you think?'

Grace considered for a few moments, suddenly looking rather pale. 'The trouble is that, although she's my sister, I don't really feel I know her very well. I mean, I don't know if she wants me to sell the house because she wants money, or because she doesn't think I should have this house. If it's money, she might try and say they're hers, but if she just feels this house is too grand for her little sister to live in all on her own – I suppose she still might. Because if I've got money I can fix the house and keep it.' Grace sighed deeply. 'I don't know why she's being like this, really. She's very well off herself. Her husband's loaded.'

'I once heard someone say that being rich didn't stop people being greedy. Have you got any more tea towels? I'll help you dry up,' Ellie went on, to disguise the fact that she'd been quite so frank about Grace's siblings.

'Oh no, don't bother!' said Grace, glad to be distracted

from her larger problems. 'They can drain.'

'It's just I need the space,' said Ellie. 'I've got my tartlets to sort out.'

'So, what are we having? I can remember the wines because I chose them, but I've forgotten about the food.'

'Roasted tomato tartlets, gravadlax – makes a change from smoked salmon. And I've got some lovely mushroom pâté. The soufflés, salad, breast of guinea fowl—'

'Ellie, you never managed to buy all that expensive stuff with the money I gave you?'

Ellie had actually subsidised Grace a bit, but didn't want to say so.

'I'm a very good manager! We're finishing up with the most delicious chocolate mousse in the world, but you'll have to tell me what order you want the other dishes served in.'

'Sounds fab.'

'I would have done a chocolate tart but we've already got pastry.'

'Let me know how much I owe you,' said Grace, regarding Ellie very firmly.

'OK,' said Ellie, aware that she'd been caught out. 'When I dig out the receipts.'

At five minutes to eight, the two women hovered in the drawing room, now converted into a dining room, tweaking cutlery, realigning napkins and checking that the candles were all burning safely and evenly.

'It does look lovely,' said Ellie from the doorway, ready to run to the kitchen the moment the doorbell rang.

The room did. They had lit the fire and about fifty candles so it was pleasantly warm. Tea lights occupied every space where there wasn't room for a candle in a bottle.

'Bottles are fine,' Ellie had insisted. 'It's a wine evening, it's only proper that the candles reflect that. And it's not as if the candles in bottles are on the table. People won't get confused and take a swig out of a candle.'

'Ellie! They're all going to behave very well, and in a dignified way.'

'Sounds dead boring. No, only joking! It's all lovely!'

A huge bunch of bare branches were apparently growing from the old chimney pot, and Ellie had entwined them with fairy lights. Grace had agonised for a few moments about this touch, wondering if Edward would think it terribly naff, but then rapidly consoled herself with the thought that a) Edward wasn't going to see the fairy lights, and b) she didn't care what he thought any more. She was not entirely convinced this was true, but as the fairy lights looked extremely pretty, she decided to work on it.

The table was enormous, but by the time each place was set with several sets (although not quite enough) of cutlery, and six glasses at each place, it did not look empty. Grace had discouraged Ellie from doing individual flower arrangements by each place.

'They'll get knocked over. When people are writing things down, and using lots of glasses, they'll be a nuisance. And you have got your viburnum.'

Ellie's favourite bit of decoration was practically a tree. It was a huge branch of *Viburnum x bodnantense* which Grace had almost encouraged Ellie to hack down. Its pale pink blooms looked like blossom and the fragrance was enchanting. Grace was a little concerned that the perfume might interfere with the wine tasting, but decided that only purists would object and that it was unlikely there were any of those coming tonight.

'It is amazing what you can do with enough space and enough candles,' said Ellie now, extremely satisfied with the result. 'The trouble is, my mother says, that most people have far too much clutter to really make their houses beautiful.'

'Well, there I am in with a head start,' said Grace wryly. 'No furniture cuts down on clutter really well.'

'Not many people would be prepared to make the sacrifice for beauty, but you, Grace, are braver than most. You look wonderful, by the way,' said Ellie. 'Is that designer?'

Grace looked down at herself and picked at a bit of fluff. 'Yes. Armani. Edward bought it for me. He likes clothes.'

'Was – is he a dandy, then?'

'No! Well, yes, I suppose he is. But he liked buying me clothes, too. And jewellery.' Grace's eyes widened. 'It's in the bank. I have no idea how much it's worth, but it might be quite a lot! I could sell it!'

'Fantastic,' said Ellie, thinking a little bitterly how much time and effort she and Grace had put into getting money for the dry rot only to have Grace remember there was a fortune's worth of diamonds in some bank vault.

'On the other hand,' said Grace, deflating slightly, 'it might not be worth all that much. It's mostly modern silver. I just put it in the bank when Edward left so I wouldn't . . . Actually, so I wouldn't be reminded of him by it. How sad is that?'

For Ellie, who'd had her hopes raised and then dashed, it was very sad indeed.

They had just managed to convince each other that no one was going to come, and they could relax, clear away the table, drink all the wine and have a private party of their own, which would be so much less stressful and a million times more enjoyable, when the doorbell jangled.

They both jumped and Ellie looked at the door like a captured animal, desperate to escape to the safety of the kitchen.

'I hope it's that young couple who came the first time. The Cavendishes. They were great,' said Grace.

'Well, answer it then. You can't sell evenings of food and wine to people if you don't let them in. Just let me get away first.'

Grace sighed. 'I'm not really cut out for this, you know.' Then she went to the door.

It wasn't the young couple, it was Flynn. He came in and hugged Grace roughly. An odd combination of relief and excitement rushed through her. 'I'm so sorry I haven't been in touch. Family crisis. Can I still come?'

Grace thought of the ten individual tarts that Ellie was probably putting in the oven now, the ten individual soufflé dishes, greased and collared, waiting for their mixture, the ten perfectly arranged plates of salad which would shame most artwork with their mastery.

'I'll have to ask Ellie. And I'd need to set you a place.' Resentment and nerves at her first reaction tugged at her, making her ungenerous.

'I'll ask Ellie,' said Flynn and strode off to the kitchen.

Ellie, Grace knew, would say it was fine and that it was no trouble to make another tartlet, or rustle up another soufflé, cooking it in one of the less precious, more robust, teacups. As she went into the drawing room, now converted to a banqueting hall, to check on the candles, she was aware that somehow the evening loomed less heavily over her now that Flynn was here. She smiled.

Ellie came into the drawing room, bearing plates, their oldest and most bent cutlery and some glasses. 'It's nice that Flynn could come, isn't it? I'll put him in here. We did have far too many women.'

'I'm sure there's some superstition about not having eleven people at the table,' said Grace.

'That's thirteen, and stop being ungracious.'

Grace laughed.

To Ellie's extreme frustration, Ran was the last to arrive. Everyone else had been seated round the table for some time, exclaiming, for the most part, at the attractiveness of the room. Only the double-barrelled couple who had come to Grace's first wine tasting didn't appear to be enjoying themselves, and were making snippy remarks about candles in bottles and the vulgarity of fairy lights. Ellie had asked Grace why, if they'd been so snooty before, she'd allowed them to come again. 'First of all, I forgot who they were when they rang up to book, and then I thought: What the hell, I'll show them.'

'Good for you,' said Ellie. 'Now, are you sure you can carry three plates at a time? You've never been a waitress, have you?'

'Maybe not, but I can still manage these.' Grace hesitated. 'I am sorry about Ran not turning up.'

At that moment, the doorbell rang. 'You go,' said Grace, 'I'll take these in.'

Grace paused before she entered the drawing room and saw Ran's expression when Ellie opened the door. Surprise, admiration and shock pretty much summed

it up. Grace hoped that Ellie found his reaction satisfactory – she would have done.

'. . . now, if you've all finished marking, I'm going to
ask you to pass round the next bottle quite quickly as
the next course is a cheese soufflé and we'll want to get
stuck in as soon as it arrives.'

She happened to catch Flynn's eye and his smile was
a mixture of approval and congratulation. She permitted
herself to smile back. The evening was going well. Ran
was proving a success with the female members of the
party: he didn't say much, but he did look stunning in
his dinner jacket. Grace made a note to tell Ellie that
although the women flirted with Ran, he parried it well
but didn't reciprocate. He could possibly be seduced by
a younger woman yet.

The food had all been superb so far, and the snooty
couple had been forced by peer pressure to join in the
general approval. The man had been particularly compli-
mentary about a South African Sauvignon which he said
had chocolate aromas and was 'drinkability itself', and
Grace was still basking in this compliment when Ellie
came in, plates with individual soufflés balanced up her
arms, her mobile phone clamped in her armpit.

'It's Rick,' she muttered urgently from the corner of
her mouth. 'He's ringing from Demi's phone. Apparently
she's ill or something!'

Grace's heart stuttered as she took the phone and got
up from the table so she could speak. Why on earth was
Rick ringing about Demi?

'Is that Grace?' demanded a slurred voice. 'I've got
Demi. She's a bit wasted. She wanted me to ring you.'
Grace had to take a couple of deep breaths to steady

herself. Rick sounded fairly wasted himself and questions were flying around in her head like moths.

'OK,' she said, her calm voice belying her rising panic and her sudden urge to cry. If anything happened to Demi she'd never forgive herself. 'I'm coming to get her. Where are you?'

'At home,' said Rick.

'Where's home?' demanded Grace, then, aware that she would never be able to get comprehensible instructions from Rick, she said, 'Never mind. I'll ask Ellie. You're at the house in Bath, yes?'

'Yeah.' The phone apparently slipped from Rick's hand because Grace could hear background noise and then a clunk.

For a moment, all the moisture left Grace's mouth and apparently transferred itself to the palms of her hands. She forced herself to breathe, to think, to remain calm. Ellie had already left the room. Grace returned to the table.

She cleared her throat and took a sip of water. What on earth could she say? Keeping it simple and truthful seemed the best way. 'I'm awfully sorry, everyone. I'm going to have to go. My stepdaughter's been taken ill and I have to go to her. But please do carry on – Ellie will look after you, and I do need your feedback. Flynn, perhaps you could take charge for me?' Silently, she tried to convey how much she needed him to help her and yet not betray her anxiety to a roomful of strangers.

Flynn got up. 'No. I'm coming with you.'

'No, Flynn, really, you stay here.' Grace indicated the guests, who were all watching her. 'I can't just abandon everybody.' She tried to sound light-hearted but it came out as shrill.

'You need someone with you,' Flynn said steadily.

'Yes, you do,' said the man who ran the village shop. 'We'll look after ourselves. If you've got an emergency, you have to see to it. We'll be fine. I'll make sure everyone writes down what they think about the wine.'

'Really . . .' Grace felt awful. This was her opportunity to do something for herself, and she was having to leave the job half done. 'Flynn, if you stayed—'

'I'm not letting you go who knows where on your own,' he said firmly. 'There's no point in arguing.'

'Just do what he says, love,' said the wife of the village-shop man. 'It's easier in the end. And we'll manage just fine.'

'If you're sure—'

'We're sure,' chorused several people.

'Now you go off.' The woman from the shop was so motherly that, worry about Demi overriding her embarrassment, Grace succumbed to temptation to give her a hug and a kiss goodbye before she left the room, closely followed by Flynn.

'Is it Demi?' he asked when they were outside.

'Yes! I don't know what can have happened. Why isn't she with her friend?' Aware she was sounding hysterical, she struggled for control. 'I should have checked up on her. I shouldn't have just trusted her!'

'So where is she?'

'That's the weird thing! She's with Rick, Ellie's ex. How did she get there? I'm so confused.'

By this time they were in the kitchen. Grace handed Ellie her phone. 'I didn't know Demi knew Rick that well! Did you?'

'I suppose I did know she fancied him. And she did mention meeting him, but I thought it was just casually.

Don't you remember, she told us about seeing him in the street, on his bike? But I'm amazed she remembered how to get to his house. I'm so sorry! I feel so responsible!'

'It's not your fault! Don't be silly! But can you give me directions to the house? How long will it take us to get there?'

'Grace,' said Flynn. 'Why don't you get some things organised for Demi, just in case . . .' He paused, just long enough for Grace to understand what he was trying not to say. 'Could be useful. I'll help Ellie get the next lot of soufflés in and then get directions.'

'Oh. Yes, of course. I should get some things. Oh, Demi! I do hope you're all right!'

Grace raced upstairs to Demi's room. She paused on the threshold; it looked so innocent and girlish, it was dreadful to think of Demi out of her mind on alcohol or drugs – possibly both – with Ellie's ex-boyfriend. She grabbed the oversized T-shirt which was lying on the bed and some knickers from the drawer. Then she found a jumper which was heaped on a chair and stuffed it all into a carrier bag. Demi's toothbrush was probably in the bathroom.

By the time she got downstairs Flynn was waiting in the hall, jingling his car keys. 'I think I know where we're going.'

Grace was struggling into her coat when the drawing-room door opened and Ran appeared. 'I'll help Ellie. Could you direct me to the kitchen?'

'Oh! That's so kind! She will need someone to give her a hand. It's just down that passage and then right. Do you see?'

'Fine. Yes, I will. And good luck.'

* * *

'I've come to help,' said Ran from the doorway of the kitchen.

Ellie, who was taking a tray out of the oven, put it on top of the Rayburn before turning towards him. 'Have you? That's very kind.'

'And you don't expect me to be kind, do you?'

'Well, no. But I'm glad to see you can be.'

'What would you like me to do?'

Ran was looking incredibly attractive, thought Ellie, who hadn't had an opportunity to study him in a good light before. He was wearing a dinner jacket with the shirt undone at the neck and his bow tie loose. Lots of separate emotions fluttered through Ellie as she looked at him but she knew at least one lot of them had to be pushed firmly out of her mind.

'I can't decide,' she said. 'Should we grab the opportunity to look at the paintings? Will they be all right in there on their own for a bit?'

'I wouldn't leave them too long. There's a woman whose name I forget with a delightful cleavage and, while I don't want to seem conceited, I think she has her eye on me.'

Ellie was quite sure she had her eye on him. In fact, she'd noticed it earlier. She put a hand up to her own cleavage, to check how much of it was on display. She didn't want it to be obvious that she was competing for the attentions of a slim, dark man with a cynical expression.

'OK. I'll get you to help me take in the gravadlax. Then I'll need someone to start the discussion. Who do you think would do it?'

'That older couple, Mr and Mrs Rose? I think they run the village shop. They said they'd be in charge.

They seemed quite knowledgeable.'

'Oh, them! Yes, they know loads, Grace said. That's perfect. So as soon as I can get away, I'll show you where the paintings are. They're not to know you're not doing something in the kitchen.' She frowned. 'It's awful to say it, but in some ways it's easier with Grace not here. Although I am worried about Demi. Rick does a lot of drugs and she's only a kid. I could kill him!'

'Shall we deal with the next course?'

'The trouble is,' Ellie went on, loading him up with beautifully arranged plates of salmon, dill, quails' eggs (from the 'reduced for quick sale' section of the super-market), stuffed cherry tomatoes, and a dribble of balsamic vinegar dressing, 'I can't help feeling it's my fault in some way. After all, if Demi hadn't come with me to fetch my stuff, she wouldn't have met Rick. And then she told me she'd seen him on his motorbike. That wouldn't have helped matters.'

'Is Rick particularly desirable, then?'

'Greek God, definitely,' said Ellie frankly, looking up into Ran's eyes and deciding that she'd grown out of Greek Gods and was now into men with crinkles at the corners of their eyes.

He held her gaze just long enough to make her wonder and then said, 'She'd have met another Rick sooner or later. These foolish creatures always do.'

Ellie looked down at the plates he was holding, hoping that her blushes would look like heat from the kitchen, which was now considerable. 'OK, let's get these in.'

'By the way, have you got a screwdriver handy?' Ran asked, just as Ellie was opening the door with her elbow. 'I might need to take the panels off.'

'What? Take them off? Will you have to?'

259

'Yes, I probably will. I can't get any proper idea of their condition except in good light and I'll need to see both sides.'

'I could get you a torch.'

'Has it an X-ray function?'

'Of course not!'

'Then I'll need a screwdriver.'

'Oh well. Perhaps it's too late to worry about what Grace will say. There's one in the kitchen. I'll get it for you. Here goes.' She gave the door a push with her hip and entered, smiling. 'Here we are, everyone! Mr Rose, did you volunteer to be in charge?'

'Yes, and it'll be no trouble,' said Mr Rose. 'The bottles are numbered quite clearly.'

'And the food is lovely,' added Mrs Rose, with a smile.

'Besides, the other bottles are empty,' said Will Cavendish, who was now getting the benefit of the cleavage as the only presentable man still present.

'Good,' said Ellie. 'I'll get back to the kitchen then. Ran?'

Ran, who had been exchanging 'I'm sorry, I wish I could but I'm being dragged away' looks with the owner of the cleavage, followed Ellie out of the room. She walked ahead rather briskly, cursing her high heels. Why couldn't she have chosen someone who fancied her to have an affaire with? It would have been so much easier.

'I'll get you the screwdriver,' she said, still crisp.

'No need to get snappy,' he said down the back of her neck. 'I'm only flirting to be kind.'

'I thought we agreed you didn't do "kind",' said Ellie, rummaging in a drawer, wishing she didn't sound jealous.

'Oh, but I do. Which is why I'm here now.'

She turned and handed him the screwdriver. 'I'll get you a torch, too. Then I'll take you to the dining room.'

She helped him take down the curtains she and Grace had so carefully pinned in place and then waited for his reaction. And waited – until she realised that if she didn't go back to the kitchen her doll's-house-size portions of pâté, this time with bundles of shredded leeks, would dry up.

She flounced back to the kitchen, cursing all men. They make you pregnant and then they make you wait and won't give you a straight answer about anything.

Chapter Fifteen

❦

Flynn drove awfully fast, even faster than Edward. 'I'm sure you don't need to drive quite so quickly,' Grace said, holding her seatbelt and keeping her right foot free so she could press it to the floor as a virtual brake.

'Sorry.' He slowed down. 'I've done so much driving lately and always with less time than the journey takes.'

Partly to take her mind off Demi, Grace said, 'Any particular reason?'

He nodded. 'My ex-mother-in-law is in a home and has been ill. My ex-wife isn't in the country, and the rest of the family are so . . .' He paused, his lips pursed. '. . . useless.'

Grace sensed the missing expletive and wondered why he didn't swear when she felt sure he would have done if he'd been with Ellie, or even Demi. 'What did you have to do?'

'Find another home. Get her put into it. Sort out her house. Stuff like that.'

'Did you get on particularly well with her when you were married?' The thought of doing such things for Edward's mother, the grandest of dames who managed to make even Edward appear a little gauche, gave her a frisson of pure terror.

'Not particularly, but I couldn't have left her in that hell-hole. It was awful.' He grinned suddenly. 'I thought

262

·

for a while I'd have to have her living with me, but fortunately she rebelled.'

'It does sound as if it would have been a bit of a nightmare,' said Grace, whose palms were still sweating at the thought of Edward's mother.

'You have no idea what an understatement that is.' He laughed softly, giving Grace the impression that, nightmare or not, he would have coped quite well.

'Well, I hope your ex-wife is grateful to you for looking after her mother.'

'I expect she's pleased her mother is settled, but I don't know about the grateful part. I'm not sure it's a concept she's quite got to grips with.'

'I think she ought to be grateful. Why should you deal with it, after all?'

'I couldn't just let the poor woman rot, now could I?' He smiled again. 'Besides, the neighbour who went in to visit her had my number for some reason, probably from when I was still married. She put the hard word on me. I had no choice.'

Grace didn't reply. She was wondering if Edward, who was a kind man, would have done such a thing for her mother, if they hadn't got on. She decided probably not and sighed. She had clung on to the idea that Edward was a kind man in the face of all evidence to the contrary. Although he *had* been kind to her, she insisted to herself, and you can only judge people by how they behave to you. Then she sighed again, knowing this was not true. He had not been particularly sensitive to his daughter's needs.

Her sighs must have been audible because Flynn said, 'Are you worrying about Demi? I shouldn't think it's as bad as your imagining.'

Guilty, because she'd forgotten the state Demi was in for a few seconds, Grace said, 'Rick sounded awful but at least he could speak. Why didn't Demi?'

'She may just be really drunk, didn't want to slur her words and so didn't want to speak to you directly. I'm sure she'll be fine.' He tried to sound soothing.

'I do hope so.'

'It's odd that she rang you and not her parents.'

Grace sighed. 'No, it's not. She lives with me and she knows I won't blast her from here until next week about this. It's perfectly understandable. And for all we know, she did ring her parents but they couldn't come for some reason.'

'I'm sure if they knew they'd have dropped everything and gone. Any parent would.'

'I'm sure you're right,' said Grace, hoping that were indeed the case. She could almost hear Demi's mother saying, 'You got yourself into this, you have to get yourself out.'

'You will have to tell them if it's really bad, you know that,' went on Flynn.

'Yes,' Grace agreed. 'But I'll check it out myself first. It's going to reflect really badly on me, anyway. I should have looked after her better.'

'Oh come on! It's hardly your fault she got involved with this Rick person, is it?'

He changed gear and Grace shut her eyes as he prepared to pass the car in front. She knew she would have to die sometime, but she didn't want to see death coming. When she opened them a few seconds later, they were safely past.

'Hmm?' Flynn prompted her.

'I know it's not really my fault, but I can't help

blaming myself. I should have rung the mother of the girl she said she was staying with, but I didn't want Demi to think I didn't trust her. And I shouldn't have trusted her! God! Children are such a worry, and Demi isn't even mine.'

'Would you like to have children of your own?'

'Oh yes,' she answered, before she could consider whether it was a question Flynn should have asked her. 'Definitely. It was the main reason Edward and I broke up.' She hesitated slightly. It seemed that tonight she was compelled to tell the truth and that Demi was not the only person who'd taken mysterious substances. She seemed to have ingested a truth drug somewhere along the line. 'That and the fact that he found someone else.'

It seemed completely understandable to leave someone because your feelings about children were different. The fact that he'd gone off with a beautiful and sophisticated woman felt somehow less acceptable.

'Those problems combined would probably be beyond the scope of most agony aunts,' said Flynn seriously.

'Are you laughing? My marriage broke up and you think it's funny?' Grace didn't quite know how to react. She was so accustomed to sympathy, to the 'all men are bastards' line, she didn't know how to respond to Flynn, who seemed to take it as a bit of a joke.

'I'm not really laughing,' said Flynn, who was, 'but there is a certain irony in it. You see, I've just spent the last fortnight looking after my ex-mother-in-law, you're making a mercy dash across the country for your ex-stepdaughter, and our marriages both broke up for the same reasons.'

'Oh?'

'Mm. Annette was very into her career. I wanted a

family but there was never a good time. I even offered to be the main carer—'

'Big of you. Why shouldn't you, after all?'

'No reason! But I did offer. I wasn't asking her to give up her career, but she seemed more interested in keeping her figure. And she found someone else, too. They have no children, don't ever intend to, and are very rich and successful.'

'Are you bitter about it?' Grace wanted to know and couldn't tell from the matter-of-fact way he was speaking.

'Not any more. After all, having a baby does have a huge impact on a woman's life. However much the man does, it's still her body that has to go through all the pain and change.'

'You've obviously thought a lot about it.'

'We rowed a lot about it. I learnt all the arguments, on both sides. Didn't you?'

'We didn't actually argue, no. I didn't argue with Edward ever, really. Looking back, I was terribly passive.'

'You don't strike me as passive now. In fact I've found you quite spiky.'

'I think I've grown up a lot recently. About time too.'

Flynn laughed and slowed for the approaching junction. He was, Grace forced herself to acknowledge, not for the first time, really quite attractive. And as they had discovered their marriages had broken up for similar reasons, they should have lots in common. But this was not a Lonely Hearts column, where people matched themselves up: likes and dislikes; non-smokers and smokers; the possessors of good senses of humour and those without (although no one ever advertised themselves as tall, affluent, own car,

266

no sense of humour whatsoever, when it probably applied to so many people). Just because she and Flynn both wanted children did not make them a good match.

'The sad thing for me,' said Flynn, 'was my house. I told you I made my living out of property. Well, in the past I always did up houses, sold them and moved on. But the house I'm in now is the one I did for us, for the family we're never going to have. It has the best quality workmanship, the materials I actually wanted, not a cheaper version, and there I am, living in it all by myself.'

'That's something else we've got in common,' said Grace. 'Beautiful houses, no babies to put in them.'

'And no partners either,' said Flynn.

'Yes, but I don't mind about that,' said Grace firmly, wondering if it was still true.

Flynn laughed. 'Well, it looks as if you'll have Ellie's baby to keep you going until you have babies of your own. And you have got Ellie and Demi to keep you company.'

'Yes,' she said on a sigh. 'I just hope Demi's all right!'

'We're nearly there now,' said Flynn. 'I think I've got quite good directions. Would you like to have a look and keep us on the right road? Have you ever been to Ellie's old house?'

'No. And if I had, I might have seen this coming. Oh, why did Demi have to meet bloody Rick!'

'You don't know that, and at least we know where Rick lives and a bit about him. She could have fallen in love with anyone. They do, at that age.'

Grace took the paper and struggled to read it under the streetlights. 'And you know all about it, I suppose.'

'About falling in love? I've done it a couple of times. Now, where do we go at this roundabout?'

'Where's that nice man gone?' asked the woman with the cleavage when Ellie appeared with the pâté.

'He asked the way to the loo,' said Ellie. 'Perhaps he ate something that upset him.' Then she wished she hadn't said that, as it made everyone look slightly uncomfortable. 'He told me he'd had a burger just before he came, so he wouldn't be drinking on an empty stomach,' she improvised hastily.

'No chance of that,' said Sara Cavendish. 'You're a marvellous cook! I don't suppose you'd come to our house and do it, would you? I'm crap – sorry – hopeless at it.'

'I'm sure we could arrange something,' said Ellie, glad to think there was something she could do successfully.

'Shall we get on?' said Mr Rose. 'We've got a few wines left to go through.'

'I'll get back and fetch the other plates,' said Ellie, wishing that Ran really was helping her in the kitchen, and not taking a screwdriver to a lost art treasure.

Ran joined her in the kitchen while she was boiling kettles for coffee. She had served the rest of the dinner, for all those people, on her own and was not in a good mood. True, she could have accepted help – both Margaret and Sara Cavendish had offered – but she hadn't wanted them in her kitchen to see the mess, the lack of facilities, or the primitive cooking arrangements. Mostly, she admitted, she didn't want Ran coming in and saying something indiscreet if anyone else was there.

'Well?' she demanded, piling gold foil-covered mints on to saucers.

'I've put them in the car. I can't do anything about them in situ, and the condition is really worrying. I found a couple of nails – obviously been there for centuries – so I couldn't tackle them there and then. I cut out the shutters in the end.'

'My God!' For a moment she thought of the devastation but then dismissed this as trivial. 'But are they any good?' She was practically jumping up and down with frustration. Why wouldn't he give her his verdict?

After what seemed to Ellie to be about ten years, he smiled. 'Oh yes. They're very good. But they're very damaged and I need to have a proper look, with decent light, to see how good. Even daylight would be better than what we've got now.'

'Well, yes, it would be.'

'So I've taken them down. Very carefully, of course. We don't want any more damage.'

'Well, give me a hand with the coffees, would you?' She was jumping up and down with excitement. 'And think up an excuse for your absence. I told them you'd had a dodgy burger.'

'You what?'

She shrugged insouciantly. 'Well, I had to tell them something! What other excuse would you have for disappearing for almost the entire meal? I'll tell you what, we'd never have managed it if it weren't for Demi getting into trouble.' Her exhilaration faded. 'I wonder why they haven't rung?'

'I'm sure they will the moment they've got something to say,' said Ran, taking the tray from Ellie and heading for the door. 'Just try and put it out of your mind.'

Ellie was already loading another tray, wishing that having lots and lots of important, serious things to think about, like valuable paintings, sick friends, and a baby, didn't stop you obsessing with something that was both unimportant and totally irrelevant. Bloody men!

Mr Rose handed Ellie the completed forms, all slightly food-and wine-spattered now. 'All present and correct, I think.'

'Thank you so much for taking charge, Mr Rose. Without you the entire evening would have been a complete waste! And I'm sure Grace will want to confer with you when she comes to write her article, as she wasn't actually able to be here.'

Mr Rose was not unmoved by Ellie's gratitude, not to mention her cleavage. 'She's welcome. I just hope her stepdaughter is all right,' he said. 'It's been a grand evening. I think everyone enjoyed it. Grace should try and do it again. And charge next time.'

'And you must give me your details so you can come and cook for me,' said Sara Cavendish. 'You're brilliant!'

'And you,' said the cleavage woman to Ran, who stood beside Ellie in a way that made her feel lovely and coupley even if it didn't mean a thing, 'must give me your card. I've got a lovely old picture which needs restoring. I could bring it down to you.'

'I have got quite a lot of work on at the moment,' he said politely but firmly, 'but I'd be happy to recommend a colleague who might be able to help.'

'I'll wait for you,' said the woman, brushing his cheek with her hand. 'I'm sure you'll get round to me eventually.'

'What was that woman's name?' asked Ellie when she had finally gone.

'Can't remember.'

Ellie found this answer entirely satisfactory.

When everyone else had gone home too, Ran followed Ellie into the kitchen. She had long since given up the idea of him fancying her at all, in spite of the cleavage, the black tights and the specially done hair. It was either her still invisible pregnancy that bothered him, or her. It was easier to think that it was her pregnancy; the 'her' was a permanent condition.

'Ellie—' he began, and then, life being what it is, her phone rang.

It was Grace. She sounded very tired but not completely distraught. After some discussion about Demi she added, 'I don't think we're going to get home tonight. Will you be all right on your own?'

'I think so,' said Ellie, who suddenly felt that she wouldn't. 'As long as Demi's all right. I've been so worried.'

'She will be,' said Grace. 'I'm just plucking up the courage to ring Edward or her mother.'

'Can't you get Flynn to do it?'

'No, that wouldn't be fair. It's my responsibility.'

'Not really, but I suppose you would see it like that.'

'I do, I'm afraid.' Grace paused. 'Well, I'll let you go then. There must be loads of clearing up, but please do leave it for me. It's the least I can do having left you with all that to cope with on your own.'

'No, it's fine. I'd rather do it. You know me. And if it hadn't been for Demi coming with me that time, she would never have met Rick.'

'Ellie! I've wasted enough time beating myself up about it all, don't you start! Now, goodnight, and take

271

care. Sleep in my bed, where the phone is.'

'Oh, I'll be fine! See you tomorrow. And love to Demi when she's conscious.'

'Was that Grace saying she wouldn't be home tonight?' said Ran.

'Yes. Shall we go and put out the candles in the drawing room?'

'Will you be all right?' He followed her down the corridor which now seemed very dark.

'Of course. I'm a grown-up. And Grace lived here on her own for ages.'

'It's different. It's her house.'

Ellie didn't reply as they crossed the shadowy hall to the drawing room, where at least there was light and signs of life. The candles still flickered and, although the table was full of dirty glasses and plates, it still had an air of festivity – the air of a party, over now, but with the ghost of it still present. 'The room does look lovely, doesn't it?' said Ellie. 'Like a painting.'

'You know the French refer to still life as *nature morte*. That sort of applies, doesn't it? There has been life; now it's gone, but its spirit remains.'

'You've got very philosophical all of a sudden,' said Ellie, blowing out candles, understanding and agreeing with him completely.

'Would you like to come back with me and stay the night?'

'What?' Ellie knew she'd heard him perfectly, but she wanted confirmation.

'As my guest, rather than leave you here on your own. I have a spare room with a futon in it.'

Ellie would have liked time to think, time to make a plan, to work out what would be for the best. But Ran was looking at her, waiting for an answer. 'I don't know. I mean, I'm sure I'll be fine.'

'I know you're a very capable young woman, but I think you might be a bit lonely, spending the night here on your own.'

'Well, I'm glad you think I'm capable. I thought you thought I was a child hardly out of school.'

'I promise you, I've never thought that – at least, not after the first five minutes. So are you coming?'

She wrinkled her nose, wishing he'd elaborated a bit on the capable young woman he didn't see as a child. 'I don't suppose you'd like to spend the night here instead?'

'No. Apart from anything else, I don't want those panels spending the night in my car.'

'Because they might get lonely, too?' She put her head on one side, trying rather half-heartedly to flirt.

'No,' he said firmly.

'We could bring them back in.'

'And risk more damage to them? They're very fragile, they should be handled as little as possible.'

Ellie wanted very much to tell Ran that she was not remotely fragile and that handling wouldn't do her any harm at all, but didn't dare. 'If they're so delicate, should you have hacked them about like that?'

'I didn't hack them. I removed them as carefully as possible.'

'If you say so.' She looked up at him challengingly, enjoying this moment of banter. It was time out from her having to make a decision about whether or not to stay with him.

'Ellie! I know you must be tired and it's way past your bedtime, but now you're getting silly.'

'Sorry. I know it's quite hard for older people to stay up past six o'clock,' she teased.

He narrowed his eyes at her. It made him impossibly sexy. 'Go and get your things and come and spend the night with me – on the futon in the spare room,' he growled, in case she hadn't got the message.

'I'll have to take my car. I need to be back really early in the morning.' Ellie felt short of breath and dithery.

'I'll drive you back. I'll want to be up early too.'

'What will Grace think if she comes back and I'm not here?'

'It's unlikely, but you could leave her a note. Now I wish you'd stop making difficulties about doing something you know you're going to do!'

'OK. I'll go and get my stuff.'

'And change out of that dress. It's very distracting.'

Ellie smiled broadly. 'Is it? Oh good.'

Holding that tiny spark of hope to her, Ellie ran upstairs to get some clothes together. She changed out of the dress and hung it on a hanger, sad to think she probably wouldn't have a chance to wear it again before she had the baby. It was already a little tight. And her jeans fitted a little too snugly, too.

'Hell!' she said to herself in the mirror as she flung make-up into a bag. 'If he only fancies me a tiny bit now, what will he think of me when I'm the size of a whale?'

On the way downstairs, with her bag over her arm, she wondered if she was attracted to Ran because she was subconsciously looking for a father for her child.

When she saw him waiting for her in the hall, she knew there was nothing subconscious about it. She just fancied the pants off him.

'I still feel guilty abandoning the house,' said Ellie. 'Not to mention all the clearing up. I always clear up.'

'I know Grace wouldn't expect you to do it all on your own. We locked every door and window that had a lock,' said Ran, 'and you wrote a note. Why don't you ring Grace and tell her, if you're that worried?'

'She hasn't got a mobile. She rang from the hospital phone.'

'Then you've done everything you can. Now get in the car and go to sleep. I'll wake you up when we get there.'

Aware that this was a polite way of telling her to shut up, and that a less polite way would follow if she didn't comply, Ellie closed her eyes. It would be a good opportunity to make a plan of campaign. If she couldn't seduce Ran while she was actually in his house, at night, she didn't deserve to have him. Unfortunately, her condition and her very long day fought her anxiety and her decision to plan for a night of passion and won. She slept.

'Wake up, we're here.'

'Oh,' said Ellie blearily. 'Did I sleep the whole way?'

'Yup. Not surprising, really. You've had a long day.'

'And being pregnant doesn't help,' she said, and then could have kicked herself. Why draw his attention to something he might well have forgotten?

'Can you manage your bag? I want to get the paintings into a stable atmosphere as quickly as possible.'

'Of course.'

He handed her a bunch of keys. 'You get the house unlocked and yourself in it. I'll bring the paintings.'

'I could come back and carry one.'

'No, you couldn't. You have no idea of how to handle such delicate objects.'

'Well, that's your fault for not teaching me anything, only making me clear up stuff.'

'Will you get in the house! I'll be quicker if the door is open and we can get both panels somewhere safe!'

'OK, OK, keep your hair on.'

She juggled with the keys. 'Which one first?'

'Oh, for God's sake!' He took them from her and unlocked the door himself.

'You are a bad-tempered old so-and-so, aren't you?' said Ellie.

'I wonder why it took you so long to come to that conclusion?'

Chapter Sixteen

⚜️

Grace shifted Demi's position a little; her arm felt as if it would drop off through lack of blood. She looked at the clock. The hands seemed to be going backwards. They'd been here three hours.

Flynn had gone off in search of coffee. The drinks machine was only serving tepid water, possibly because it was after office hours and a Friday. Grace closed her eyes and tried to doze, but it was hard with Demi slumped on top of her.

It had been such a shock, finding her like that. They'd known they were at the right house because of the music which seemed to make the building actually throb. They'd been lucky that the front door was ajar or they would never have been able to get anyone to open it. They could have knocked all night before anyone heard them.

As they squeezed themselves past several people talking and smoking in the hallway, Grace gave Rick credit for having rung Ellie. Demi could be anywhere in this lot, but he must have been sufficiently aware of her state to realise she needed help.

Only the kitchen seemed to have any lights on, and it was there that they found Demi. She was sitting on a chair, staring into space, blood pouring down her face. A young man, presumably Rick, was beside her, dabbing at the wound with a filthy tea towel.

'What's happened!' Grace shrieked at him in panic. 'You never said anything about her being injured!'

Rick was making a supreme effort to keep upright and to enunciate clearly. His eyes were in a condition that told even Grace, who'd led a sheltered life, that he was very very high on something. 'She wasn't. Injured. When I rang. She fell down the stairs after.'

'It looks quite a bad cut,' said Flynn. 'I think it needs stitches. We'd better get her to A and E.'

It took Grace a few moments to realise he meant Casualty. 'Demi?' she shouted into her face, almost pleading with her to wake up and not be dead. 'Can you hear me? It's Grace. Demi?' She patted her cheeks until at last Demi turned towards her and blinked.

'Grace?'

'Yes.' Relief that Demi could talk and recognise her made Grace feel a lot calmer, although her breathing was still fast. 'Now, what have you taken?' A moment later Grace realised that Demi was probably not the best person to ask. She turned to Rick, who was at least standing. 'Rick! What has she had?'

'Only some dope. And alcohol, of course.'

'What sort of alcohol?' asked Grace.

'How strong was the dope?' asked Flynn.

Other people, aware their space was being invaded by people who were very uncool, shifted away slightly. 'It was skunk,' said someone who seemed to be working his way through an entire packet of biscuits. 'Well strong.'

'And what alcohol?' Grace repeated, turning her question on to the man who had known about the dope.

'Mate, I have no idea!' He held up his packet of Rich Teas in a gesture of surrender. 'I don't do alcohol.'

'Oh, for God's sake, let's just get her out of here,' said

278

Grace. 'It's no good asking this lot anything.'

'Shame,' said Flynn. 'The hospital is likely to ask us a whole lot of questions we don't know the answers to.'

'We'll just have to tell them we don't know!' snapped Grace. 'Demi!' she shouted in her ear. 'Can you walk? We're taking you to hospital!'

'Don't want to go,' said Demi. 'I just need to lie down.'

'Your head is cut open,' said Grace. 'You need stitches. You're bleeding.'

'Oh,' said Demi, and burst into tears.

No one in the house was in any state to help Grace and Flynn get Demi into the car, but they finally manoeuvred her into the back seat and Grace got in next to her.

'I hope she's not sick,' she said, for the first time conscious of her Armani dress. The blood from Demi's head had become sticky and slow moving; Grace felt able to avoid it.

'There should be a roll of kitchen towel somewhere. See if you can find it before we set off.'

Grace burrowed around in the footwells until she found the kitchen towel. She tore off a couple of sheets, and then struggled to get Demi strapped in. 'OK, all set. We can go.'

'Do you have any notion about which direction I should go in?' Flynn asked.

'Oh shit! No. Just go towards the town centre – there are bound to be signs.'

Grace was beginning to feel sick herself by the time they lurched into the hospital. The back streets of Bath had felt like a maze – just as you felt you were getting out, you found yourself confronted by another one-way street.

'I'll have to drop you off and park the car,' said Flynn, drawing up in front of the hospital. 'They'll clamp me if I stay here more than a second.'

'Surely not! You're getting a patient in!'

'It's how they make their money these days. Can you manage?'

'I'll have to. Come on, Demi! Wake up! You've got to get out of the car now.'

'Want to sleep,' pleaded Demi. 'I'm so tired!'

'You can sleep when you're inside,' said Grace. 'Now move your leg. Please.'

Flynn got out and came round to the back, opened the door and hauled Demi out of the car. Grace scrambled out after her and took her weight when Flynn handed her over. He didn't get back into the car.

'I'll be back as soon as I can. You could just wait here,' said Flynn.

'I think we'll try and get inside,' said Grace. 'Apart from anything else, I'll freeze to death with only this cardigan and Demi should be in the warm too. She hasn't got much on.' Grace wondered if they should have got her something warmer than a jumper to wear and then realised how impossible it would have been to get her into a coat. 'Besides, I feel a bit of a fool out here.'

Flynn seemed to think this was funny, and was definitely laughing when he got back into the car. It was all right for him, thought Grace, as she tried to shift Demi's leg with her own, to kick start her, so to speak. He didn't have to take Demi on the long journey from the pavement, through the double doors, and into the hospital.

They had gone about two paces before Grace realised it would be more sensible just to keep Demi upright, and not try and get her to move. But she'd told Flynn she was going to move her, so move her she would. She'd teach him to laugh at her!

'OK, Demi, we're going to play a game. It's a three-legged race, only no one's tied our legs together. OK? You move your leg at the same time as I move mine. I'm holding you up, you can't fall over.' This was a blatant lie, but Demi wouldn't notice. 'OK? Right – move your leg. That one. Good! You're doing fine.'

Several people passed them as they made their slow progress, but as almost all of them were drunk, and even more of them bleeding worse than Demi, Grace decided it didn't matter.

Flynn appeared in time to open the doors. 'Sorry! Bloody car park is miles away, and then I didn't have the right change and had to ask someone for some.'

'I'll pay you back,' said Grace, for the first time aware of how much Flynn was putting himself out for her and Demi.

'Don't be bloody ridiculous. Now let me take her. You go to the desk and register, or whatever it is you do.'

The woman behind the desk looked very tired. Glancing at the clock on the wall, Grace noticed it had gone eleven. It felt still later, somehow.

'I've come with Demi Ravenglass. She's over there,' said Grace.

'Drunk, is she?' asked the clerk.

'Yes. And I think she's taken some drugs.'

'Are you her mother?'

'No! I'm her stepmother – her friend.'

'OK. Give me the details, then.'

Above the desk was an electronic sign, which presumably altered as patients came and went. 'Waiting time three hours.'

'Have we really got to wait three hours?' asked Grace, when she'd supplied the clerk with all the information she could.

'You're lucky. The night is young. You got in before the rush. Go and sit down now. There's a coffee machine down the hall. Next?'

The 'next' was half a dozen very large young men escorting their friend who seemed to have walked into something tougher than he was and mashed his face.

Grace felt dreadfully vulnerable among all these noisy people who all, without exception, seemed to be drunk. How she would have managed without Flynn, she hadn't a clue. She resolved to thank him at the first opportunity.

Flynn came back with something in a plastic cup. 'It's called Hot Chocolate, though it might be Chicken Soup. But it's hot and liquid.'

Grace rearranged her over-sized baby and took the cup. It was chocolate and very soothing. She became aware of being hungry.

'You must be starving,' she said to Flynn. 'Is there anywhere you could get a sandwich or anything?'

He produced a bar of chocolate from his pocket. 'This will have to do. Have a bit.'

The nurses and doctors, perhaps predictably, were not very patient with Demi. The doctor decreed that her wound didn't need stitches, just a clean-up and some Steri-strips to hold her wound together.

The nurse, who was tired, and quite possibly looked after her own children all day while working at night, made it quite clear how she felt about people who got out of their heads on drink and drugs and then fell over.

'They haven't got the brains they were born with! And look at her, obviously comes from a nice home. What is she doing messing around with chemicals at her age?'

It was a rhetorical question but it made Grace hunt around for an answer. 'Just experimenting, I expect,' she mumbled, not feeling this was the place to go into Demi's parents' difficult divorce, the fact that she wasn't welcome at either parent's home, and had felt obliged to live with someone she wasn't related to at all.

'It's not as if they don't teach them about it in school!' went on the nurse, washing away at Demi's cut, none too gently. 'They know what happens, but still they do it. I suppose they think they're immortal. Well, they aren't! You should see the cases we get in here.'

'Perhaps when Demi's more – together – she should—'

'Listen,' said Flynn. 'We're very sorry Demi is taking up your valuable time. We know you have people in here who have not made themselves ill from choice.' He looked through the gap in the curtain. 'Though I'm not sure I spotted any. But could you just clean her up so we can get her home?' His Irish accent, never very apparent, came out stronger now, and there was just enough anger in his voice to make the nurse purse her lips. She was not accustomed to being stood up to.

'She's very young,' said Grace in a placatory way. 'I'm sure she's never done anything like this before.'

'It's a pity she's done it now.' Then the nurse looked at Grace. 'You're quite young yourself. Are you her sister? You should keep a better eye on her.'

Grace, who inside was dying of guilt for having

allowed this to happen, said, 'I did my best! You can't keep them under lock and key, you know!'

'You could have told your parents you thought your sister was taking drugs, couldn't you?'

'Could we finish with the lecture now?' said Flynn, his anger more evident. 'This young woman' – he indicted Grace – 'has taken this child into her home out of the goodness of her heart. And, as you've noticed, she's hardly more than a child herself. She doesn't need lectures from you about how irresponsible she's been!'

The nurse couldn't actually apologise, but she bent to her work without saying anything else.

'How should I look after her when I get her home?' said Grace.

'We should tell her parents, Grace,' said Flynn. 'You shouldn't have to look after Demi now.'

'No! I can't betray her! Not unless it's really necessary. And if she was that ill, she'd be admitted, wouldn't she?' she asked the nurse.

'If there was a bed available, yes. But she'll be all right as long as she doesn't choke on her own vomit.' The nurse said this as if she felt it would be a just reward for Demi's foolishness. 'Treat the hangover in the morning. If the cut doesn't heal take her to her own GP to see the practice nurse. OK? God! If you knew the waste of time and resources these cases are to the rest of us, you would not allow your . . . whatever she is to you to run around getting drunk and stoned.'

'Do you think I was aware of what she was doing?' demanded Grace, holding back her anger so firmly it made her mouth hurt. 'Do you think, for one second, that I would have allowed any drinking or smoking or whatever to go on, had I known what was likely to happen? I thought she was staying the night with a friend! With parents! Now come along, Demi, we're going home.' Grace was shaking, feeling that if she had to stay in the company of the nurse a second longer, she would do something she'd regret.

Flynn and Grace walked slowly one each side of Demi and got her out of the hospital. Then Grace and Demi waited in the freezing air while Flynn fetched the car. The cold woke Demi up a bit.

'Oh, Grace, I'm so sorry! You won't tell my parents, will you?'

'I won't tell them yet, Dem, but I may have to later.' Grace frowned, wondering how she should deal with this.

'They'll go ape! Mum will make me go and live with her and I couldn't bear it!'

Grace sighed. 'I'm really tired, Demi. I can't make decisions like that now. Let's just get you home and see how you are in the morning.'

'I think I'm going to be sick!'

Before Grace could plan how to get her back inside to the lavatory, Demi deposited a large quantity of red wine and some unidentifiable food items on to the grass verge, just by where they were standing.

Grace sighed. 'I suppose that's a good thing. Better an empty house than a bad tenant, as my father used to say.'

'I think I'm going to die,' said Demi.

'Then I'll definitely have to tell your parents, both of them. What sort of music do you want at your funeral?'

'Don't joke, Grace! It's not funny!' Demi was near tears.

'I know it's not funny! I'm not laughing! I just want

to know what to say to Edward. "So sorry, Demi's died of a hangover and she wants" – well, what? "at her funeral!"'

The corner of Demi's lips twitched. 'I'm so sorry. I never realised what would happen. I thought I could take my drink, but the time came when suddenly I didn't care that I was drinking too much and just went on.'

'And the dope? It was just dope, wasn't it?'

Demi nodded. 'It's cool, really it is. I—'

'No, it's not cool. If it was, you wouldn't be here now. And nor would I.' Grace shivered violently. 'I hope the heater's efficient in Flynn's car. I think I'm suffering from an overdose of coolness right now.' She glanced at Demi, wondering if now was the time for a lecture on how much she'd put Flynn out as well, and decided not. Demi's conscience was coming back with her consciousness, and Grace didn't want to rub her nose in it any more. She'd suffered enough.

To her enormous credit, when Flynn appeared with the car and opened the back door, Demi said, 'I am so sorry, Flynn. I've made a complete arse—idiot of myself, and you've had to drive all the way down here and rescue me. Thank you so much.'

Flynn smiled his rather lopsided smile. 'Get in. And don't vomit on the upholstery. There's a rug there to cover yourself with. Grace, you'd better have my coat.'

It was like a warm embrace around her shoulders. It had been a long time since Edward had made that sort of romantic gesture, although Grace was sure it wasn't meant romantically at all. The coat smelt faintly of Flynn's aftershave.

'Won't you be cold?' she asked him, concerned that

he'd already put himself out so much for her and Demi, and now he was going to freeze as well.

'No. There's a very good heater. Now you get in the back with Demi.'

Both young women slept, sharing the rug, in the dark warmth of the back of the car. When Grace woke up, she realised they were nearly back.

'You must be shattered,' she said.

'I expect you are, too.'

'But I've just had a nap and I haven't driven however many miles it is. And you were probably driving before this.'

'I probably was.'

'I can't thank you enough, really I can't.' Her rush of gratitude literally did make it hard for her to speak. 'I could never have coped with all this alone.'

'I know. That's why I came with you.'

'Well, of course, I could have coped. It would just have been a lot harder.'

'That's what I meant.'

Grace stopped talking. Working out what Flynn meant was not easy.

Demi was able to get herself into the house under her own steam. She was still woozy, but fully conscious and hugely embarrassed. 'Oh, Grace, please don't send me back to Mum's!' she pleaded as Grace unlocked the front door. 'I mean, I wouldn't blame you if you did, but I couldn't bear it!'

Grace wasn't quite sure what the right thing to do was. 'I won't send you back but your mother might insist when she hears what's just happened.'

'You don't have to tell her, do you?'

'Oh, Demi, I don't know! I'll have to think about it!'

She couldn't honestly promise any more than that.

Demi sighed.

There was no sign of Ellie when they got through the front door and into the hall. The light was on, but that was all.

'I expect Ellie's gone to bed,' said Grace. 'You go up, too, Demi. I'll come and look at you before I go myself.'

She waited until Demi had said her goodnights, had kissed her awkwardly, and gone up the stairs, a sadder but a wiser girl. Then she turned to Flynn.

'I don't know what to say,' she said.

'How about: Would you like a cup of coffee or tea, or something, Flynn? Or a sandwich. I'm starving.'

Grace laughed. It was kind of him to take all the awkwardness out of the situation for her. 'There's bound to be some leftovers in the kitchen. Come on. Let's see.'

What they saw was Ellie's note. *Didn't want to be on my own in the house. Sorry! Pathetic, I know. But I've gone to stay in Ran's house.* Grace could picture her, chewing the pen, trying to write something which wouldn't give Grace – or Ran – the wrong impression. *I'll be back early in the morning. Lots of love, Ellie.*

There were only puddings left, so Grace found bacon, eggs and tomatoes, and made Flynn breakfast.

'It's been ages since I've cooked for a man,' she said, pushing the bacon to the side to make room for the eggs. 'It's nice.'

Then she blushed, and stayed with her back to him so he wouldn't see. Did she sound possessive? Could 'a man' be interpreted as 'my man', and would Flynn feel pressured?

'It's a long time since any woman has cooked for me,' said Flynn. 'That's nice, too.'

'Good,' she said cautiously. 'Now would you like fried bread?'

'Yes, please. This is dinner as well as breakfast.'

'What about baked beans? Demi has them with a cooked breakfast, but I'm not sure Edward would approve.'

'I'm not Edward. I like beans.'

Still keeping her face out of his sight, so he couldn't see her colour, she found a tin of beans and opened them.

Eventually, she had to sit down opposite him. 'Where's yours?' demanded Flynn.

'I never have breakfast, at least, hardly ever, and not at four in the morning.'

Flynn didn't reply. He loaded his fork with a sample of everything on his plate except the beans, then he turned it towards her. 'Open wide.'

'No, honestly. I'm fine. You eat it.'

'Pretend you're a baby bird. Open your mouth.'

Giggling, Grace obeyed him. She didn't want to start a quarrel. He placed the forkful carefully in her mouth. 'There.'

She ate it, still laughing. It was delicious. She had had no idea she was hungry. He loaded up another forkful and she ate that, too. There was something silly and sweet and tender about sitting opposite each other, him feeding her. She didn't feel like a baby bird, but like a female one, being fed, on her nest, by her mate.

After three mouthfuls she really had had enough and his plate was emptying. 'That's enough, really it is. But it was nice.'

'Yes, it was,' said Flynn. He was looking into her eyes and didn't seem to be talking about food.

'I'd better make some more tea or something,' said

Grace eventually, thinking she should break the invisible thread between them. Not because she wanted to, but because it felt dangerously intimate.

He put his hand on hers to stop her moving. Then, his hand still there, he got up himself, came round the end of the table and drew her to her feet.

His arms around her were so strong they made her feel weightless. Her eyes closed in spite of her efforts to resist the swimmy feeling, the dizziness, the sensation of being in his arms gave her. His kiss tasted of bacon and beans and made her feel like heaven.

She struggled a little, clinging on to sanity with the last remaining fragment of her mind. This would be so embarrassing in a minute. This might spoil their odd, tenuous relationship. It was too soon after Edward.

He shifted her so she fitted more neatly into the shape of his body and she forgot about Edward, about being embarrassed, and relaxed into his kiss.

Either it went on for a very long time, or she lost all sense of time. When he finally released her mouth, but not, thank goodness, her body, she felt boneless, brainless, and insanely happy.

She forced herself back to reality. It's only a kiss. Nothing to get fussed about. People kiss each other all the time, it doesn't mean a thing.

As if sensing her doubts he pushed his hand into her hair and looked intently at her. She could almost feel his eyes on her face, taking in each freckle, the line of her mouth, the mole on her cheekbone. She lowered her lids, embarrassed by the intensity of his expression.

'Come on,' he said and, keeping his arm tightly round her shoulders, he walked her out of the kitchen, along the passage, into the hall and up the stairs.

'What are you doing?' she laughed, knowing perfectly well what he was doing.

'I'm taking you to bed,' he said, opening the door to Ellie's bedroom and rejecting it. Another few paces and he found her bedroom, recognising it by its simplicity.

'Are you coming with me?' she whispered as he hesitated on the threshold. She knew he wouldn't cross it unless she invited him. And she knew that she didn't want this insane, gooey, sleep-deprived feeling to end.

'Only if you want me to.'

Grace sighed. 'I know I'll regret this in the morning, but yes I do.'

'It is the morning. And I don't want any regrets. I don't want a single unhappy thought about me crossing your mind. Do this with your brain fully engaged. I'm not seducing you when you're tired and vulnerable. Think about this, Grace.'

'Oh, shut up,' she whispered, taking his hand and leading him into her bedroom.

Chapter Seventeen

Ellie turned on to her back to get more comfortable on Ran's futon. It was in his spare room, which was used for a lot of other spare things apart from a bed, and initially she'd slept, but the hardness of the mattress had woken her. Now she lay and thought about the humiliations of the evening.

She'd been so sure she could seduce him! He'd said that thing about her dress being distracting, so he must fancy her a bit. But did the jeans and top take away all her sex appeal? She hadn't had time to go through all her little tops, to find the one that didn't make her arms look fat and showed a bit of cleavage without clinging too much round her stomach, but she'd been moderately content with her look as she pulled her fleece on over the top. Her excitement as she ran down the stairs to Ran, waiting in the hall, was more than she'd felt over anything, seemingly for years.

Once inside the house, after the fiasco of the keys, Ran had been quite host-like. He'd offered Ellie a hot drink, which she'd accepted, not because she yearned for cocoa, but because she wanted to watch him make it, and make him watch her watching him.

This was the moment, she'd decided. It was now or never. If she couldn't make him have an affaire with her now, she'd never make it. She was in his house, ready, willing and eager. Only a monk would turn her down in those conditions.

She'd pulled her top down a bit, so her cleavage showed just a bit more than normal. Flattery, that was the answer with most men. Tell them how clever they are and they think you're gorgeous.

'I'm so glad it was you I got work experience with,' she began, deliberately lowering her voice a little and making it breathy. 'I mean, supposing some charlatan had taken me on? Those panels might have been in the hands of any old amateur. They could have been ruined. With you, I know they'll have the best possible treatment.' She was about to add, 'because you're the best,' but decided it was over the top.

Ran paused in the process of mixing cocoa into a paste with cold milk. 'How do you know I'm not a charlatan?'

Ellie hesitated before replying. Her instinct was to snap, 'I'm not a complete fool, you know!' but she knew this would not help her cause. 'I do know a little bit about you, you know,' she said cooingly, determined not to sound at all acerbic.

'Do you? Well enough to tell, just from the adverts in the *Yellow Pages*, the good picture restorers from the bad ones?'

'Well, not just from that, obviously, but when I met you, I knew the paintings would be in good hands.'

'You were intending to restore them yourself when you first met me. It could have been fatal. They could have disintegrated completely.'

'Oh, surely not.' She lowered her head and looked at him out of the top of her eyes. She'd never actually tried this technique before, but then again, she hadn't tried to seduce anyone before, and although she'd been an avid fan of Marilyn Monroe films when she was in her early teens, she wasn't sure she'd studied them with quite enough concentration.

Ran sighed, and Ellie realised he must be really tired. Being tired had never affected Rick's desire for sex, but Ran was that bit older. It might be different for him. That would be so annoying! Her one chance to get him into bed and he turned out to be too tired! She must try harder.

She wiggled on her stool, put her head on one side and gave a little lopsided smile. It probably made her look like a complete idiot, but it worked for Marilyn.

'How much sugar would you like in your cocoa?' he asked.

Unfortunately he didn't turn round, so he didn't see the smile or the wiggle. Was he aware of what she was up to? Perhaps he wasn't looking so he wouldn't be tempted! Perhaps if she said something really witty he would have to look at her. As long as it didn't make her fall off the stool, she could always wiggle again. She trawled through her memory of Lauren Bacall and Humphrey Bogart films. They were famous for their one-liners. There was bound to be something. Sadly, Ellie couldn't even remember any of the films, let alone the dialogue. Could she make something up? Something about him being enough to sweeten the most bitter drink?

'Well?' he snapped.

'Two, I think,' she said hastily. 'I usually have drinking chocolate.'

He went back to his stirring. How seductive was that little remark? 'I usually have drinking chocolate!'

They'd be using that to lure people on to porn sites on the Internet! Who could resist? Irritated with herself, Ellie decided to postpone her plans until the cocoa was actually in her hands, then she could look over the mug at him and, provided she didn't get a chocolate moustache, that might be quite appealing.

At last – it seemed to have taken hours – he handed her a mug of cocoa. 'Would you like a biscuit?'

'No, thank you.' Then she wondered if that had been a mistake. After all, if he was intent on going straight to bed, being forced to stay up while she ate a digestive would give her some valuable extra time. 'Actually,' she said, 'can I change my mind?'

He gave her the sort of long look that teachers gave to pupils when they'd heard a totally unbelievable story as to why their homework was not going to be handed in. It was considering, contemplative and not encouraging. 'If you take your cocoa and your biscuit to bed with you, you can have the whole packet, but I'm not in the mood to play games.'

'What do you mean?' Her velvet tones developed an edge of acid. 'I asked for a biscuit, not a Scrabble tournament!'

'You know what I mean, Ellie. You're trying to seduce me. And while I am not unattracted to you, far from it – I think you're a lovely, bright, sexy girl – I am not going to take advantage of your wild hormones and let you do something you may regret.'

'What do you mean?' she said again. 'My wild hormones? What's that all about?' She had a vision of her hormones as animals, pacing up and down behind bars, lashing their tails, attacking anyone who came near.

'You're pregnant.'

'Not in my head! It doesn't affect my brain! It's only the size of a peanut, you know!'

'According to my sisters, the brain is one of the first places it does affect.' He frowned. 'And I'm not sure it doesn't stay affected, but that could just be them.'

'I am not out of my mind!' She was furious. 'I know perfectly well what I'm doing!'

'That is as may be, but you'd better content yourself with cocoa and biscuits because I'm not going to take you to bed.'

'But why not?' Ellie felt all the indignation of the ideal candidate being rejected for a job; she wanted feedback and very possibly compensation as well.

'Because I'm not interested in casual sex with a very young woman who may not be emotionally completely stable.'

Ellie only just stopped herself throwing the cocoa at him. She slid off the stool and it slopped over the edge of the mug on to her jeans. She squeaked.

'I don't think you realise the risk you're running with this sort of behaviour. Other men might take advantage of you.'

'I – I am not emotionally unstable!' she spluttered, incensed at his suggestion that she would throw herself at just anyone. 'I'm pregnant! The two things do not necessarily go together!' As the words came out of her mouth she remembered how her first symptom, even before she'd thought of taking a test, had been suffering from what had seemed like very bad PMT.

'Go to bed, Ellie. You'll feel very relieved in the morning that nothing happened.'

Ellie had flounced out, indignation having to do instead of dignity.

She had found her way round the various bits of equipment and on to the futon with very bad grace, and determined to get herself into that bloody man's bed if it killed them both.

Now, awake in the early hours, she considered her situation. Was Ran right? Would relief be her strongest emotion in the morning? Or would she regret a lost opportunity? Mind you, it wasn't *her* lost opportunity – she had done her very best to maximise it – it was Ran's. But while she was still in his house, while that sliver of opportunity was just within her grasp, should she get up and get into his bed? Having taken all her clothes off first, perhaps?

Put like that, her decision was easy. If she did that, he'd just think she was a tart. Perhaps she should have explained her desire to have an affaire before pregnancy and motherhood took over? Then he might have understood, and taken her in his arms, and thence to bed. She felt like crying. It had all gone so horribly wrong, and it seemed extra painful after their lovely day out together. She punched her pillow into a shape less pancake-like, turned on to her side and tried to think about something other than Ran. It was impossible. He filled her brain. Oh, God! She hadn't fallen in love with him, had she? That would be awful! Just put him out of your mind, Ellie. Let go; move on.

It was only after a huge effort of concentration that she managed to wonder about Demi, Grace and Flynn.

Grace woke, but didn't open her eyes, aware that she was naked and that there was someone else in her bed. For a nanosecond she was confused. Was it Edward? Then she realised it couldn't possibly be Edward, not only because he'd left her, over two years ago now, but because there was a hand on her shoulder, and she and Edward had always slept in bed together without touching.

Flynn. It wasn't that Grace's heart sank, exactly, but the feeling of 'what have I done?' flooded over her. He had been so kind, so supportive, so rock-like over Demi. And he'd given them the Rayburn. He'd become a friend. Sleeping with him might have ruined all that, and although he'd unnerved her to begin with she definitely didn't want to lose him.

She knew she ought to get up and check on Demi, but that would involve opening her eyes and opening her eyes would force her to deal with the situation in which she found herself: in bed with Flynn.

Why had she invited him into her bedroom? He would not have crossed the threshold if she hadn't asked him, she knew that. He wouldn't have made her feel obliged to do so out of gratitude. But was that the reason? Was she just grateful for him being her rock when she needed someone to rely on?

She allowed her mind to shift from the philosophical to the physical and realised she was content. Her body, though a little stiff in places, knew it had definitely had a good time. She smiled and then felt foolish, lying in bed smirking while Flynn snored gently beside her. She had had sex. And what sex! With this realisation, and her acceptance of what had happened to her, she discovered why she had invited Flynn into her bed. She had wanted him, and for very good reason.

After Edward left her, Grace had felt for a long time that she would never have sex again, would never want to have sex again. Finding herself in Flynn's arms, wanting to go to bed with him very much, had been a surprise and a relief. It had meant she was normal, she wasn't a heartbroken Ice Queen, destined to lie alone in her double bed for the rest of her empty life.

But now he was still there, in her double bed, with their relationship altered for ever.

What exactly had their relationship been before? It was hard to say. It seemed they hardly even knew each other before he arrived on the doorstep yesterday – aeons ago – for the food and wine evening. But in the hours that followed they'd developed from new friends to lovers, and while they had been long, stress-filled hours, it was still a short time to make the jump from one thing to another. There should, by rights, have been a bit of courting in between.

Flynn stirred, turned over, and pinned her to the bed with his arm just as she'd been contemplating slipping out. She shifted a little, testing to see if she could creep out from under without him noticing.

'Where are you running off to?' he murmured huskily.

'I'm not running! I want to check on Demi, that's all.'

He kissed her. 'I'll check on Demi. You stay here. I have plans.'

'She's my responsibility!'

'I'm perfectly capable of seeing if she's OK. Possibly more capable than you.'

She closed her eyes as he got out of bed and she heard him pulling on his trousers. She didn't want to see him naked, it might confuse her. She shouldn't have let him go, of course, but it seemed pointless to argue. Besides, while he was seeing Demi, she could get up, go downstairs, start washing up. But instead, she stretched and gave her pillow a thump, grateful to Edward who had insisted on their bedding all being the finest cotton and goose down. She tried to feel guilty about making love to Flynn in what had been her and Edward's bed, but she couldn't. It was her bed now, and she could do what she liked in it. Right now it was very pleasant to lie in the slightly rumpled cotton sheets and close her eyes. While in many ways it had been a long night, not much time had been spent in bed, and precious little of that had been spent in sleep.

Flynn came back. 'She's fine. She's had a drink of water, and has gone back to sleep. She's dreadfully embarrassed about what happened.'

'So am I.'

'Well, it was hardly your fault.' He slid off his trousers and got back into bed with a bounce. 'You didn't give her the wretched drugs.'

'I didn't mean that.'

He turned and propped himself up on his elbow. He seemed very tanned and very sexy and she realised she hadn't really seen him last night, and he hadn't really seen her. In a fit of belated modesty, she checked that the duvet covered her breasts.

He noticed her gesture. 'You're embarrassed about what happened between us?'

She nodded.

'Why?'

'Because! Because . . . I don't know you very well. We're not going out or anything . . .'

'Did it seem wrong?' He looked into her eyes intently and spoke softly.

'Not at the time, no.'

'But now it does?'

Grace bit her lip, uncertain how, precisely, she felt. 'Not wrong, exactly, just unexpected. Too soon, possibly.'

'You're not sure you wanted to make love yet?'

She shook her head, still confused. 'At all! If you'd asked me say, yesterday morning, if I had any intention of sleeping with you, I would have laughed.'

'Oh?' He sounded offended.

'Not because there's anything wrong with you! Nothing at all! But I didn't think we were that close, just as friends, even. I was just someone who fed your cat.'

His eyebrow went up a millimetre and his voice was softer and huskier than ever. 'You were never someone who just fed my cat.'

Grace swallowed. He'd just made cat-feeding seem incredibly sexy. 'Well, good.'

'You've been in my mind constantly, almost from the first moment we met.'

Grace frowned. 'Have I? Why?'

'You're such an eejit. Why do you think I asked you to feed the damn cat in the first place?'

'I don't know! So it wouldn't starve to death?'

'No. My cleaning lady is always happy to feed her. I did it to get close to you. It was for the same reason I gave you the Rayburn.' He frowned slightly. 'Although there were humanitarian reasons for that as well.'

'But why?'

'Are you really so unself-aware? You're a very attractive woman and I – like very attractive women.'

'Margaret's a very attractive woman.'

'She is, but in a different way.'

'Sara Cavendish thinks you're attractive, too.'

'Are we going to waste our entire morning in bed together discussing women who think I'm attractive? Because I should warn you, there are lots of them you don't know about, and if I have to tell you about them'

– he kissed her, and brushed her hair back from her face – 'we could be here for hours.'

'You're so vain,' she breathed, as his fingers moved from her naked shoulder to her breast. Then she sighed deeply, and he pulled away the duvet.

'And you're so beautiful.'

She should have argued, but he started kissing her and she forgot.

Grace finally got down into the kitchen at ten-thirty. There had been no point in going down earlier, Flynn had insisted, because there would have been no hot water to do the washing up, as it was past nine before Grace remembered to put the immersion heater on.

'If I can't get the Rayburn plumbed in myself,' said Flynn. 'I'll get a friend to do it. This situation is ridiculous.'

They had both had rather small, chilly, separate baths, and Flynn had obviously wanted something deeper and hotter that involved both of them at once.

'We can boil kettles. What would you like for breakfast? I'm afraid the bacon is all gone, but there are still some eggs. And leftover puddings.'

'Do you want bacon? I could go and get some, and the Saturday papers. Croissants, possibly?'

Grace smiled. It was such a cosy idea: she loved it; but it seemed more appropriate for city life than for people buried deep in the country. 'Where would you go for croissants?'

He named the nearest out-of-town hypermarket, which was twenty miles away.

'You could go if you want, but I'd better stay here for Demi. She was still asleep when I looked last, but I don't want her waking up and finding the house empty.'

'Better a stale loaf where love is, than orange juice and croissants and hatred therewith,' said Flynn, hunting in the bread bin.

'What are you talking about?' Grace was clearing the end of the table of their previous breakfast.

'Just misquoting one of my favourite bits out of the Bible, particularly appropriate for my ex-wife and me, where we always had food of the very highest quality but never an appetite.'

'So what's the quote?'

'Better is a dinner of herbs where love is, than a stalled ox and hatred therewith.'

Grace blushed at the word 'love', so unsure was she of her own feelings. She wiped the table and found two clean plates and mugs, no mean feat in the circumstances, wondering how she felt about Flynn, who was now washing up glasses. Did she love him? She couldn't, it was far too soon, but if she didn't, what the hell had she been doing going to bed with him!

She sighed, hunting out some butter and marmalade. What was love? Was it the obsessive, driven feeling she had had for Edward, that took up every atom of thought, every inch of her body? Or could it be a gentler, kinder emotion, that crept up slowly from behind and embraced you?

Now was definitely not the time to start philosophising. Flynn needed feeding.

'You're always washing up,' she said, after they had enjoyed a companionably inelegant breakfast of toast and marmalade, and Flynn took the plates over to the side. 'You wanted to do it after the wine tasting.' She frowned a little, wondering if perhaps she shouldn't have brought up that sticky first meeting. 'Although

303

you were a bit prickly,' she added, remembering how he hadn't been at all like the stereotyped Irishman, and that she'd thought of him as the Spy.

'Prickly! You should talk! You were a veritable Pear of Prickliness!'

She giggled. 'That is either the most ridiculous thing I've ever heard, or rather poetic. I can't decide.'

'Poetic, definitely. It's nothing more than the truth. You certainly put Mrs Tiggy-winkle into the shade.'

'I just felt a bit unsettled by – everything,' she explained. 'I hadn't had a man in my kitchen who wasn't some sort of workman for years. And you looked at me.'

'You can't blame me for that. You're beautiful.'

She blushed.

'Would you like me to do the washing up now?' he asked, looking at her in exactly the same way that had so thrown her before.

'I think that would be a good idea.'

'Perhaps I should use cold water.'

'Silly! I'll do it.'

He moved her out of the way. 'I don't want to leave it all to you. You'll have Demi to look after. Are you going to tell her parents?'

Grace bit her lip and shook her head. 'I haven't decided! I know I should, but I don't know what's to be gained if I do.' She screwed the lid back on the marmalade jar. 'Her mother will go mad and Edward . . . well, Edward might be very angry, and that is not a pretty sight.' She smiled, to soften her words. 'Not one I'd put Demi through without very good reason.'

'So you won't tell them?'

'It depends on Demi. If she is genuinely remorseful and shows no signs of wanting to do anything like that

304

again, I'll probably slip something into the conversation in a casual way. I can't quite square it not to tell them, but if I rang them now, they'd have Demi out of here before we could squeak, she'd be miserable at home, and the whole thing is much more likely to happen again. What do you think? I'm tired of trying to be Solomon.'

'It's not my business. I'm not a father myself, you're not a mother . . . What is it?'

Grace had suddenly felt slightly sick. 'I've just thought—'

'What! Tell me, woman!'

'We had unprotected sex,' she whispered, hugely embarrassed to talk about what they'd done now they were both dressed and in the kitchen.

'Is that what it was? I thought we were making love.'

Flynn's expression had an edge to it, as if he were hurt in some way, and yet he would surely accept they had been very irresponsible. 'We were – we were doing both.' Grace was still blushing ferociously, partly because she was remembering the conversation she and Ellie had had about asking Flynn to give her a baby. Now it seemed a terrible idea – so exploitative she could hardly bear to think she'd ever made such a flippant remark.

'OK, so what's the worst that can happen because of it? You could get pregnant. You want a baby, so how bad is that?'

'Very bad! Oh, you know what I mean.' She could hardly tell him what she and Ellie had discussed, not when she was agonising over the fact that he might think she'd tricked him into making her pregnant. 'I do want a baby, more than anything, but not – not as a single parent! I'm not brave like Ellie. I couldn't cope with everything – my family, the shock-horror – on my own.'

'And why do you think you'd have to? Why do you assume that I'd run off and never speak to you again if I made you pregnant?'

'I don't know! Perhaps you wouldn't, but perhaps we – I – should do something to stop it happening.'

'Take the morning-after pill? Is that what you want to do?'

'I don't know!' she said again, lying this time. 'I'm all confused. I just don't understand how I got myself into this situation.' She smiled ruefully, trying to lighten the atmosphere. 'It's totally out of character for me.'

He came up to her and put his arms round her. 'So you let yourself get carried away. Is that such a sin?' He ruffled her hair and stroked her neck in a soothing way. He smelt nice, his arms were strong and his voice was low and comforting. And very sexy. She struggled gently.

'Let's not worry about any of that now,' she said briskly. 'I need to get the rest of the stuff out of the drawing room.'

Reluctantly, he allowed her to free herself. 'Tell me: in a house this size, why did you choose to have the meal in the drawing room? There must be a dining room, for goodness' sake.'

'There is. We didn't use it because it hasn't been used for a while and we tidied up the drawing room for Allegra – as you might remember.'

'I'd love to see the dining room. I've always been curious about this house.'

'And you've never had a tour? You should have said. Come and see the dining room.'

306

She took his hand and led him out of the kitchen to the dining room, then opened the door and drew him inside. The curtains which she and Ellie had hung up so carefully had all fallen on to the floor. Hardly surprising, she thought, they'd banged them up with very little care. And then she realised.

'Oh my God,' she said. The spaces where the shutters and the panels had been were vacant. She felt sick. Sweat sprang from her hairline and palms. She felt herself sway slightly.

'What?'

She rubbed her lips together to moisten them, so she could speak. 'The paintings. The paintings are gone! They must have been stolen!'

'What paintings?'

She put her hands up to her face, as if she needed to hold on to herself so she wouldn't collapse. 'There were some painted panels, here, on the shutters. They're gone!'

'Well, who can have taken them?'

'A burglar! Who else?'

'Are you sure? Most burglars only take stuff they can sell easily down the pub for ready cash. Who else but you knew about them?'

'Ellie does.'

'You don't think Ellie took them!'

'No! Of course not.'

'Then calm down. Would there be any reason for Ellie to do anything to them?'

'She was going to restore them. They may be worth millions and I have to sell them to pay for the dry rot. Which is thirty thousand pounds' worth, I should tell you!'

'It is expensive stuff.'

Now her hands were in her hair, clutching at it. 'And how am I going to pay for it if someone's run off with the bloody paintings?'

'I don't suppose they were insured.'

She almost screamed with anxiety and frustration at his inability to understand how awful the situation was. 'Of course they weren't! No one knew they were there except us! I could never have afforded to have them insured!'

He was being maddeningly calm about this major catastrophe. 'Then if no one knew about them, it is terribly unlikely they've been stolen. It will be something to do with Ellie. What did she say in her note?'

'Nothing about stealing the paintings!' Grace wailed, running from the room so she could look at the note again.

'She just says she's spending the night at Ran's house,' she confirmed a few minutes later, when she had gone through the rubbish and found the note.

'Then she'll be back soon. It's nearly twelve, all we have to do is wait for her to come back and ask her.'

'But supposing she knows nothing about them?' Grace sank into a chair. 'What then?'

'Then we make a plan. Why don't you ring Ellie on her mobile?'

'Of course! Where's the bloody phone?'

Chapter Eighteen

Ellie had intended to get up early, but after her disturbed night had not managed to be in the kitchen, making breakfast, when she first encountered Ran. Instead it was him in there, grinding beans, making coffee. Which was unfortunate because the smell of coffee made Ellie so sick she had to leave the room.

When she came back, she said, 'Morning! No coffee for me, please,' and tried to be her usual breezy self, as if he had not practically told her she was a tart the night before and she was not remotely in love with him.

'Sorry. I forgot. What would you like?'

He looked, if such a thing were possible, even more sexy. His cheekbones were enhanced by his stubble, and his hair, all ruffled and 'just got out of bed', begged to be smoothed by sensitive fingers. Bastard! thought Ellie. He might have put a shirt on. For although the little kitchen was not all that warm, Ran had chosen to make breakfast wearing nothing but a pair of torn jeans. His torso was bare and in surprisingly good condition for someone past their twenties.

'Tea. I'll make it!' Ellie cursed herself for sounding like a Girl Guide. If she hadn't felt so miserable, she would probably have had a last crack at seducing him. She probably wouldn't have the time, the location and the desire again. Unfortunately, although those three were enough for her, the desire seemed to be missing on Ran's part, making the first two requirements redundant.

'Would you like me to cook you something?' she asked, when she had found a mug and a tea bag. 'I'm a very good cook.'

'I know,' said Ran, regarding her over his coffee mug. 'I ate your food last night.'

'I'm glad you liked it.' Ellie wrung out a dishcloth, which smelt slightly, and wiped the work surface, then she started running hot water into the sink so she could wash up. What am I doing? she asked herself. Trying to housekeep her way into his heart?

She knew it wouldn't work. Ran was sitting at the kitchen table in a way that told her quite definitely that he was a) not a morning person and b) had quite recently given up smoking. She could almost see the phantom Gauloise between his fingers. Not even a supermodel, who wasn't pregnant, and who hadn't made a complete fool of herself the night before, would have a chance with him right now.

She carried on cleaning up the kitchen but didn't speak. If she couldn't drag him back into bed, and optimistic and determined as she was she accepted that she couldn't, she wanted to get back to Luckenham House. She didn't want Grace facing the mess alone after a night in hospital, and, more importantly, didn't want her wandering into the dining room and finding the paintings gone. She also wanted to be out of this awkward situation as quickly as possible.

Ran, to his credit, seemed to realise this. 'I expect you're in a hurry to go,' he said when Ellie had done all the washing up and was making a start on the cooker.

'I'll just finish this coffee, have a quick shower, and drive you back.'

'It's terribly kind of you—' she began.

He got up from the table and she turned to face him. She was still clutching a cloth covered with creme cleanser. 'I thought we'd established I don't do kind. I expect you to pay me back.'

'But I haven't got any—'

'Shush. I've been thinking. Were you serious when you said you were interested in picture conservation?'

'Yes! I told you—'

'Then you can be my apprentice. I probably won't let you actually touch anything for a while, but you can make yourself useful, watch what I do, and eventually, I might let you do a little scraping off glue from the backs of paintings. Under strict supervision of course.'

A flicker of optimism the size of a birthday candle lit itself in her heart.

'But I thought you didn't want me!' She put down the cloth and wiped her hands on her jeans.

'Oh, I do want you,' he said softly, 'but possibly not in the way you want me.'

Ellie lowered her eyes, which was unfortunate because her gaze landed on the zip of his jeans, which was not what she needed just now when she was trying to hold herself together. She was dumped, she knew that; he'd made it perfectly clear. But she would see him again, and even if she ended up as his cleaning lady, that would be better than not seeing him.

He lifted her face so she had to look at him, his hand tender on her cheek. 'I want you to come over a couple of mornings a week, do what I need doing, and study what I'm doing.'

'Of course. Anything.'

His eyebrow flickered. 'I will pay you the going rate, of course.'

'Oh no! I'll do it for the pictures. You're restoring them.'

'Sweetheart, you could redecorate my house from top to bottom, and clean it with your toothbrush, and you couldn't pay me for restoring the paintings. I'm doing that because they are very beautiful and very precious and possibly a great contribution to the artistic world.' He paused. 'And Grace might be able to pay me if she sells them.'

'So why do you want me – to come and be your apprentice?' she added after only the tiniest hiccup of hesitation.

'Not many people understand how something that can seem mind-numbingly boring is in fact incredibly important. I need someone who is painstaking and careful and pays enormous attention to detail. I've needed someone for some time but haven't got anyone because there aren't many people I can stand being around while I'm working.'

'Oh.'

'Yes, that is a compliment, sort of. Now go and get your stuff sorted out. I won't be long.' Then he leant forward and kissed her nose.

She stood in the kitchen, immobile from every sort of emotional agony. Here is a man, she fumed silently, whom I have practically told in words of one syllable that I will go to bed and have mad passionate sex with, and he kisses my nose! As if I'm a kitten or something!

Indignant as she was, she couldn't help feeling slightly warmed by his gesture. It wasn't what she wanted from him, but it was better than nothing. Even if he did see her as a kitten, needing a saucer of milk, while she saw him as a sex god, at least he responded to her in some way. And if she scraped off glue, or whatever he wanted doing, she would at least see him from time to time.

'You're a fool, Ellie Summers,' she told herself as she stuffed her things into her bag. But the bubble of hope wouldn't be suppressed.

It was only when they were nearly at Luckenham House that Ellie thought it would be nice to ring Grace and tell her she was arriving, so she turned on her mobile phone. 'Six missed calls,' she said. 'Oh, they're from Grace.'

'Beside herself' didn't really describe Grace when she opened the door to Ellie. Flynn was in the background, and Ellie had time to wonder why and how long he'd been there before she realised how Grace was feeling. She almost feared that without a restraining presence, Grace might have flown at her like a feral cat – terrified, but still damaging.

'The paintings! They've been stolen!' she wailed, her hands in her hair, her eyes wild.

'Let them get through the door,' murmured Flynn. 'We can't have this scene on the doorstep. There isn't room.'

'And the paintings haven't been stolen,' said Ran. 'I've got them.'

'What?' Grace turned to him. 'Who are you?'

Shortage of sleep, an emotional rollercoaster worthy of Alton Towers, and the conviction that her only asset had been taken from her, had affected Grace's memory.

'I'm Randolph Frazier. I'm a picture conservator. I'm going to restore the paintings for you.'

'But I can't afford for you to do that! Ellie's going to do it.' Grace was still distraught. It took Flynn's hand on her arm and firm voice to calm her.

'Let's go into the kitchen. We can discuss what's happened or what should happen in there.'

'It's OK,' said Ellie. 'Really it is. I'm sorry about the paintings, but Ran insisted they shouldn't stay here another night.'

'They were deteriorating rapidly,' he said from behind Grace's head as they trooped to the kitchen.

'None of this is anything like as bad as you've been fearing, Grace,' said Flynn. 'Trust me.'

In a very confusing, frightening world, Grace realised that she did do that.

Ellie went to make hot drinks, as the situation seemed to demand the rituals. Flynn sat Grace down at the table. Ran sat next to her.

'I realise it must have been a dreadful shock to find the paintings gone,' he said.

'I should cocoa,' muttered Flynn, who was hovering.

'But I felt I had to get them out of here as soon as possible,' went on Ran. 'They've already got dry rot in the top and it spreads, rapidly.'

'Tell me about it,' said Grace, putting her elbows on the table and hiding behind her hands. 'Thirty thousand pounds is what I'm going to have to pay to have it put right. It's as much as a house.'

'No,' said Flynn, 'but it's quite a good car.'

Grace opened her eyes and regarded him. He seemed to be being flippant again.

'Anyway,' said Flynn. 'Much as I would like to discuss fine art, now that your pictures have turned up safely I have got to go.' He leant over the table, ruffled the back of Grace's head and kissed her cheek. 'I'll give you a ring later, my love.' He raised his hand to the others. 'See you!' Then he left the kitchen.

Grace knew she was blushing. She could feel it, and even if she couldn't, she could tell by the way the other two were looking at her. She missed Flynn and cursed him in the same thought. If he'd wanted to inform the world that they had slept together it might have been less embarrassing if he'd just said, 'By the way, in case you're wondering, Grace and I have done it.' What he'd done instead was so much more intimate. And the endearment melted her heart.

Grace took a breath. 'The paintings . . .' she said at random, with no idea what she was going to say about them.

Fortunately for Grace, Demi appeared. She looked as ruffled and sleepy as a toddler picked up out of a cot. 'What's going on?' she said.

As Grace had a very confused expression, Ellie took over. 'Demi! What happened to you? Are you all right? Your face!'

'I cut it when I fell over,' said Demi.

'Yes,' said Grace, pulling herself together. 'How are you? Have you got a headache?'

'A bit.' Demi frowned at Ran, confused. 'Sorry, should I know you?'

'No,' said Ran firmly. 'I am not generally considered someone that young women in oversized T-shirts should know.'

'Don't tease her, Ran! She's been ill!' said Ellie, jealous of this flirtatious remark. 'Let me make you something, Dem.'

'There's no bacon,' said Grace. 'But there are some eggs.'

315

'There is bacon,' said Ellie. 'I got some a couple of days ago.'

'We ate it,' said Grace, trying not to blush all over again.

'Oh.' Ellie continued to rummage in the refrigerator. 'We've got lots of milk, you could have cereal.'

'Mrs Ravenglass . . .' began Ran, not wanting to be party to a conversation about Coco Pops.

'Grace, please,' said Grace.

'The paintings. I think I should tell you, I consider them to be very fine. I'm not an expert about value, of course, but they should definitely go to an auction house or something to be properly valued.'

'Was it really necessary to take them away?' asked Grace. 'It was a bit of a shock to see them missing like that.' She frowned; she'd suffered so many shocks in such a short time she seemed to have lost her ability to form proper sentences.

'It must have been, and I'm terribly sorry, but I could do very little with them in situ, and the dry rot situation can't be ignored. Until that's fixed, you couldn't really put them back again.'

'I'm going to have to sell them anyway, I think.'

'It seems a shame. After all, they've obviously been in the house a very long time, and were possibly painted here. That's where they should stay.'

'But I need money to pay for the dry rot,' said Grace.

'And the insurance would be astronomical,' agreed Ran. 'What sort of security system do you have here?'

'Minimalist?' suggested Demi, who, after a few spoons of sugar-coated puffed rice, seemed to have perked up quite a lot.

'Which isn't a problem if the paintings aren't in the

house,' said Ellie, wondering about Ran's own locks and bolts.

'The thing is, I can't pay you,' said Grace. 'At least, not until I sell the paintings.'

'I'd do them for nothing—' began Ran.

'I'm going to be his apprentice,' announced Ellie.

'So I'm perfectly happy to wait for a bit for any money,' Ran continued. 'Now, if you're quite happy for me to have the paintings and to do what I can to preserve them, I'll go.'

Grace was finding it hard to think straight. She didn't know if she was happy or not. Supposing he left the country with them and she never saw them again? Unable to express these fears, she said, 'As you've already got them, and I know nothing about picture restoration, I suppose I am happy.' She gave him a rueful smile. 'But I don't know very much about you, either.'

'I could give you some references, if it would make you happier. I have worked for some quite major museums and stately homes. These places can't afford their own conservation studios in the way they once could.'

Grace's earlier doubts faded to nothing. 'I don't need references. I trust you.'

'That's good,' said Ran. 'Without being too modest, I am the best.' He smiled, and Grace realised why Ellie had chosen this man to have a last fling with: he was gorgeous.

Ellie got up. 'I'll see you out.'

'There's no need.'

'But I must!'

'No, you mustn't. I'll give you a ring in a couple of days and arrange about you coming.'

317

Then he was gone. The three women who lived in Luckenham House watched the space he had left by the door for a few seconds, each drawing breath to question the others about what had happened to all of them since they were last together, but before any of them could say a word they heard voices and footsteps coming along the corridor.

'Oh fuck!' breathed Demi as the kitchen door opened. 'It's Mum!'

Grace would have said the same, only it wasn't Demi's mother who would have inspired such an expletive, but the additional presence of her own sister, Allegra. They both hovered on the threshold observing the detritus of several breakfasts.

'We more or less met on the doorstep and that man let us in,' said Allegra disapprovingly.

'Demeter!' said Hermia, 'what has happened to your face? And you're not even dressed!'

Grace dragged her last atom of good manners up from somewhere and got to her feet. 'How nice to see you both. Coffee? Tea?'

'I'll make it!' said Ellie quickly, forcing Grace to sit down again, deprived of her escape route.

'Personally, I'm not here for social reasons,' said Hermia, 'but if you've got a herb tea I'd be grateful. Demeter, I don't suppose you're aware of this, but a very drunk-sounding man used your phone to ring me last night. Fortunately it didn't wake me, but he left a very garbled message. Something about you not being well? A headache, possibly? I know the word "head" came into it somewhere.'

Ellie, from her refuge behind the process of boiling the kettle, knew what the message had said and was grateful that Demi's mother had not understood it. 'Off her head' was the phrase Rick would have used.

Grace didn't dare look at Demi. She couldn't possibly conspire with her against her mother. But on the other hand, nor could she bring herself to tell Hermia what had happened, especially not in front of a room full of people. 'Demi did have a bit of a fall at her friend's house, which is how she got the cut on her forehead. We took her to casualty and they put the Steri-strips on. They also advised us that she would have a bit of a headache and it would be best if she didn't go to college for a couple of days so she could be kept an eye on.'

'But why did that boy ring me up if it was only a headache?' demanded Hermia. 'If I'd got the message last night, I'd have been furious! In fact, getting it this morning would have been a bloody nuisance only they've closed the pool at the gym for repairs or something, so I had a free morning.'

'That's good!' Grace got up on the pretext of looking for biscuits and took the opportunity to scoop a few things off the table. 'Allegra, you'd like coffee?'

'Not instant, no thank you.'

'Not instant!' corrected Grace. 'We've got some fresh, left over from last night.'

'Hardly fresh, then, is it?' muttered Allegra.

'What happened last night?' asked Hermia.

'Well,' said Grace, before anyone else could speak, 'we had a wine tasting with food. People came and tried wine with food.'

'The expression "wine tasting with food" does seem to be pretty self-explanatory,' said Allegra silkily. 'And I don't want last night's coffee heated up.'

'We've got ground coffee which I had blended

319

specially,' said Ellie, who had by now cleared the kitchen table with the efficiency of a practised waitress. 'I'll make it.'

'I still don't know why that boy had your phone, Demeter,' said Hermia, sitting at the table, having first wiped her chair free of crumbs. 'Have you got it now? You're so careless!'

Demi looked horribly vague, which made Grace realise she had no idea where her phone was. As Grace hadn't either, she said, 'Demi said she didn't want to be around for the wine tasting, and that she'd rather spend the night with a friend. But then she had the fall and we collected her. Someone she was with before then must have got her phone. Isn't that right, Demi?'

Demi gave a sort of affirmative whimper.

'So you had to go and collect her while you were having a wine tasting? Typical of you, Demi. You have no consideration for others.'

'Oh, it was no trouble,' Grace assured Hermia, aware that this was her first actual lie, and that, technically, it would qualify as a white one. 'And if Demi wasn't well—'

'Is that coffee nearly ready?' asked Allegra. 'I don't want to seem rude, but I haven't got long. I'm meeting people for lunch.'

'It was very nice of you to pop in, then,' said Grace, wondering how or why Allegra had driven over a hundred miles to Luckenham House without notice. Popping in didn't really describe it.

'I didn't really do that, dear,' said Allegra, 'but I wanted to see you about something, and it was so nice to meet up with Hermia again.'

'When did you two last meet?' asked Grace, hoping

to divert Allegra from her terrifying 'something'. 'At my and Edward's wedding, perhaps?'

'I didn't go to your bloody wedding,' snapped Hermia, causing Grace to blush with embarrassment at having forgotten Hermia's connection to Edward for a moment. 'No, we met at mutual friends', in France.'

'Such a small world,' said Allegra. 'We were getting on like a house on fire and then discovered who the other was. We decided it was much better to be civilised about these things, and we just carried on.'

'But you didn't plan to come here together?' asked Grace, who wouldn't put anything past her sister.

'Good God, no!' said Allegra. 'That was pure coincidence. I just came to see what you'd done about the dry rot.' She looked around quickly as if checking who was present. 'I suppose I should say this in private, really, but as we're all friends, I might as well say I came to ask you if you'd sorted out the money to pay for it yet.'

Wondering why her sister would class the ex-wife of her ex-husband as a friend, Grace's heart sank. What on earth could she say to Allegra? She couldn't confess to the paintings, or say that she planned to earn her fortune doing wine and food evenings. She could only pray that something would come to her.

'And I came to check on Demi. We met on the doorstep. Who was that man?' asked Hermia.

'A friend of Ellie's,' said Grace, hoping firstly that she didn't let slip what he did for a living and secondly that he didn't ship great works of art to dodgy foreign collectors on the side.

'Did he stay the night?' demanded Hermia, scowling at Ellie. 'It would be a very bad example for Demeter.'

'Of course not!' said Grace, not sure if Demi knew

321

who had actually stayed the night but if she did, trusting that she wouldn't say anything about it. 'I know you must be concerned about her, but do please be assured that we look after Demi very well.'

'I wish you wouldn't keep calling her that. It's so common.'

'It's dreadful when people abbreviate your name,' agreed Allegra. 'My siblings insist on calling me Legs. Frightful!'

'I like being called Demi,' said Demi in a small voice.

'Never mind about that now,' said Hermia. 'Tell me how that boy managed to get hold of your phone?'

Demi drew breath, possibly to spill the beans. Ellie couldn't bear to watch and jumped in. 'It might have happened while Demi went to the loo. You know? At the pub? Someone might have just picked up her phone and looked up Mum in the phone book and pressed dial, just for fun! Demi probably didn't know anything about it.'

Well, that was true enough, thought Grace.

'Here's the coffee,' went on Ellie. 'And that's your herb tea. Peppermint.' She couldn't bring herself to say Hermia's name, it was too weird, but she smiled.

'But what were you doing in a pub anyway! You're not old enough to drink!' said Hermia, having sipped her tea approvingly.

'Oh, but all young people go to pubs under age!' said Grace. 'Didn't you, Hermia? I bet you were terrifically social.'

'I didn't go to the sort of pub where people would use your mobile phone without asking,' said Hermia sniffily, obviously not wanting to appear as if she had had no friends when a teenager, but not wanting to associate herself with riff-raff either.

'But they didn't have mobile phones in those days!' said Demi, not helping her case. Aware of this, she said, 'Actually, my headache's got worse again. I think I'll go back to bed.'

'Well, as long as you don't make a habit of going to pubs, I won't make you come home with me now,' said Hermia.

'You wouldn't want me to,' said Demi, biting her bottom lip. 'My room's a gym and my bed's here!'

'Go to bed, Demi!' ordered Grace, before Demi burst into tears or could say anything else damaging. As her stepdaughter left the room, she went on, 'I do assure you, Hermia, Demi won't be going to any pubs for a while. Certainly not during termtime.'

'I didn't know you could be so responsible, Grace,' said Allegra, reluctantly impressed. 'I hope you're being equally sensible about the dry rot.'

'Dry rot?' said Hermia. 'In this lovely house?'

'I'm afraid so,' said Allegra. 'It is a shame, isn't it?'

'I've got the matter well in hand, Allegra,' said Grace. 'Besides, we don't want to bore Hermia with my maintenance problems.'

Hermia grunted bitterly. 'I didn't think you had any of those, Grace. I'm sure Edward left you much better off than he did me!'

'I didn't mean that sort of maintenance!' insisted Grace, who wanted to bang her fists on the table in a very unladylike way, 'I meant house maintenance!'

'Of course,' said Hermia. She drained her peppermint tea. 'Well, as long as Demeter is all right, and you're not letting her run wild, I'll go now. I just had to check. That telephone call, it was quite worrying. The boy who made the call must have been really drunk.' She stood up. 'Allegra, I'll give you a call? Perhaps if we're both in the Dordogne in the same month, we could meet up for a meal?'

'That would be lovely,' said Allegra, rising to receive Hermia's peck on the cheek. 'One always eats so well in France.'

'Lots of people, not just one, eat well in England,' muttered Ellie, having a childish moment.

'Oh, God!' said Allegra, ignoring this comment because she didn't really understand it. 'Is that the time? I must shoot off. Grace—'

'I'll see you out,' said Grace, trying not to show how eager she was to get her sister off the premises.

'Don't bother. I've got to talk to you before I go. I'll just see Hermia out. I want a quick word with her.'

Grace grimaced in horror as Hermia and Allegra left the room. 'I'm exhausted!' she said in a stage whisper. 'I feel as if I've been through hell and back, what with Demi and now those two! Why do you think she wants to come back?'

'I don't know!' Ellie paused in her washing up. She was more interested in what had gone on between Grace and Flynn the previous night. She hadn't been able to help noticing the way Flynn had kissed her goodbye, and called her 'my love' – and not without a pang of envy. It was possible that they'd got this close in the A and E room of the hospital, but it was a bit unlikely. She needed to find out as much as she could before Allegra came back, but she spoke as casually as she could. 'There wasn't a little trip to heaven as well as to Casualty, then?'

What Grace had been through over the past few hours amounted to a sort of emotional heptathlon: the depths

324

of worry and despair over Demi; the peaks of love and passion with Flynn; and several smaller mountain ranges of doubt, guilt and simple physical enjoyment in between. And shortly afterwards, she'd had to cope with two of the most difficult women on the planet. Perhaps it would be good to confide in Ellie. Besides, Ellie would then have to confide in her.

'Well, perhaps it wasn't all bad,' she said, trying not to sound smug as some of the pleasanter memories came back to her and she thought back to what she'd been doing in the early hours of the morning.

Ellie abandoned the sink, dried her hands on her jeans, glanced at the door to check that Allegra hadn't crept up on them and joined her at the table. 'So, you and Flynn? Are you . . . an item?'

For a moment Grace had felt fantastically happy when she thought about Flynn. It had all seemed so right at the time. But now, suddenly, her spirits plummeted, bypassing reality, taking her straight to depression. Tiredness, uncertainty and the stress of lying to Demi's mother conspired to swamp all positive feelings. 'I don't know! We might.' She wasn't actually sure.

'Well, did you do it?'

'Do what?'

'Don't mess me about! You know perfectly well what I mean!'

'Did we make love? Yes, we did.'

'And was it all right? I mean, it worked OK?'

'Yes! You're so nosy,' she added without rancour.

'Well, it doesn't always, the first time,' said Ellie.

Aware that Ellie had much more experience than she did, Grace said, 'It was better the second time, of course.' And then laughed at the look on Ellie's face.

'So tell me, before your sister comes back! Are you and Flynn àn item?'

Grace pushed her fingers into her scalp and rubbed, as if trying to pummel her brain into being logical. 'The trouble is, Ellie, I had a rather overprotected childhood, and then I was married very young. I don't know all the signals. I never learnt how to do "dating". Does going to bed together mean you're an item? When I was a girl you didn't go to bed with someone until you were an item. I seem to have done it backwards. And . . .' She groaned, laid her head on her arms and closed her eyes.

'What?' Ellie was beside herself with frustration. Grace kept beginning to confide in her and then stopping. It was driving her mad.

'We had unprotected sex,' Grace mumbled into her arms.

'Did you?' Ellie didn't know quite what to say. Was she expected to tell Grace off? Or tell her that it was fine? She didn't feel qualified to do either.

'What happens if I get pregnant?' Grace was still talking to the table and Ellie had to struggle to hear.

'Well, you do,' said Ellie, a little bitterly, because she had not had unprotected sex and she had still got pregnant.

Grace raised her head. 'He'll think I did it to trap him. He knows I want a baby.'

Ellie sat down opposite Grace. Perhaps if they were face to face, Grace would stop flinging herself about. 'Then it's all right if you get pregnant. He won't think you were trying to trap him, and, after all, presumably he had unprotected sex, too.'

'What?' This was a bit complicated for one who had had so little sleep.

326

'I mean,' explained Ellie, 'he didn't produce a condom and you didn't say you didn't need one because you were on the pill, or something?'

'Of course not.' It was Grace who looked over her shoulder for Allegra this time, but fortunately she and Hermia apparently had a lot to discuss.

'Well then. You're both adults, you both did it, you'll both take the consequences – which, I might add, are not that bad!'

'I'm sorry, Ellie, that must have sounded dreadfully tactless. I just don't want Flynn to think I tried to manip-ulate him into something he doesn't want.'

'He won't! He's a nice guy! A very nice guy, and he knows what you did as well as you do. And . . .' Ellie paused, wondering if she should stray into such sensi-tive territory and then deciding that she had to. 'I think he's really fond of you.'

Grace gave Ellie her full attention. 'Do you? Why?'

'I've been telling you for ages that he cares about you. The way he was with you. The way he called you "my love". It's all proof.' Ellie had been unreasonably touched by this endearment, possibly because it was one she'd have given anything to hear from Ran.

'You think that's significant? It isn't how all men talk to the women they've just had sex with?'

'No! Oh, Grace, you're so lucky.' Ellie laughed. She had had a trying night, too, and now it was her turn to prostrate herself on the kitchen table, to smell its woody, bleachy, old-knife smell, and observe a smear of rasp-berry coulis at close quarters.

'So tell me what happened between you and . . . Thingy? Allegra will be back at any moment.'

'God, Grace, I made such a fool of myself! He told

me quite clearly that he's not remotely interested, and obviously thinks I'm a complete slapper.' She sighed gustily. 'I did everything except get into bed with him, and he kissed my nose!' Ellie suddenly began to cry. 'Sorry,' she sobbed. 'It's my hormones.'

Grace found some kitchen towel and handed it to Ellie, who was crying quite noisily now. She patted her shoulder. 'That sounds ... quite sweet, kissing your nose,' she said.

'I didn't want sweet!' wailed Ellie. 'I wanted sex!'

'Did you really not want a relationship, too?'

Ellie straightened up, blew her nose and pushed her hair out of her eyes. 'We've been over this. I'm pregnant, Grace! What sort of man would take on another man's child?'

'A nice one?'

'Exactly, and Ran isn't nice!'

'Nice enough to give my paintings to, though.'

Ellie smiled, as she was supposed to. 'Oh, he's definitely the best person to have them. He said they were dreadfully unstable—'

'I know how they feel.'

'But that they should be worth a lot of money.'

Grace looked guiltily in the direction of the door to check Allegra wasn't in earshot. 'But he doesn't know how much?'

Ellie shook her head. 'Not his thing. I expect he'll know how to find out, though.'

'And you're going to be his apprentice? Won't that be a bit difficult? After he's turned you down?'

'Yes. No. I don't know. Not sure I care.' Ellie felt it was time to put her cards on the table. 'The thing is, I think I've gone and fallen in love with him. And if I'm

328

sweeping his studio floor, or whatever it is apprentices do, I'm at least seeing him.'

'You love him? How can you tell?'

'You loved Edward. How did you tell?'

Grace sighed the sigh of painful years. 'I couldn't think about anything else but him. He took up every atom of my existence. There was not part of my head that wasn't filled with him.'

'Exactly,' said Ellie softly. 'That's how I feel about Ran.'

Grace sighed again. 'The trouble is, I was hardly aware of Flynn before we – had sex. He's always made me a bit nervous – maybe because I realised he liked me, and then he asked me out after the first wine tasting, but I've been so used to being in love with Edward that I didn't really think much about it. Then I was really pleased to see him when he turned up last night.'

'And you were miffed when he didn't reply to your invitation.'

'Was I?'

'Yes!'

'But I wasn't – I'm not – in love with him in the same way I was with Edward.'

'But you do really like him?'

'I don't know! Flynn is like a warm blanket, wrapped round you, protecting you from the cold. Edward was like the sun. The source of all life, but too bright to look at. I knew he wouldn't – couldn't – love me for ever. But Flynn is . . . different.'

'I think there are lots of sorts of love,' said Ellie. 'And that's one of them.'

'The thing is . . .' Grace paused, trying to put her feelings into something at least faintly comprehensible.

'What I feel for Flynn is so unfamiliar. And if I don't recognise it, how can I trust it?'

'You don't have to decide. No one's going to rig you up to a lie detector and ask you if you love Flynn. You're not on *Trisha*.'

'But I ought to know, oughtn't I? You shouldn't sleep with someone you feel ambivalent about.'

'But you don't feel ambivalent – whatever that means – about him, do you? I mean, you'd be upset if anything bad happened to him?'

'Of course I would, but I'd feel upset if anything bad happened to Mr and Mrs Rose, or any of the people who came last night. But is that enough?'

'It's enough for now. You're allowed to have a relationship for a bit before you decide where it's going and all that. You don't have to decide if this is for ever instantly, just because you've slept together.'

'Are you sure? It seems a bit . . . I don't know, really. Wrong?'

'Well, it isn't. Join the twenty-first century, Grace! You may live in a seventeenth-century house but you don't have to live by seventeenth-century rules!'

'I'm not sure people were all that moral then, either.'

'So stop worrying about it! Now let's get cleared up. What on earth has happened to your sister? Do you think you should go and look?'

But just then Allegra appeared, looking a little windblown. 'We went for a little walk. Hermia wanted to see the garden.'

'What?' Grace was furious. 'If Hermia wanted to see my garden, she could have asked me to show it to her!'

'No need to get all worked up. You were busy and

she only wanted to see a bit of it. Let's sit down. I've got something I want to tell you.'

Ellie hovered, wanting an excuse to leave. Seeing this, Grace said, 'You couldn't just run up and have a look at Demi, could you? Just check she's all right?'

'Certainly. And would you like me to dismantle the ping-pong table, or shall we leave it up for a bit?'

'I don't know,' said Grace. 'What do you think?'

'I'll have a look and decide.' Ellie left the room, trying not to look as if she was running.

'Well now, Grace, I've got some really good news!' said Allegra keenly.

'Have you? Did the man make a mistake and find out I haven't got dry rot after all?'

'No! Don't be silly! But they are willing to knock five thousand pounds off the price. That's jolly good, isn't it?'

'Yes, it is.' There was still twenty-five thousand to find, but it was an improvement on thirty thousand.

'They'll want to come and photograph the results, of course, so they can use it in their brochure. Oh, and you'll have to write a testimonial. Do you think you could do that?'

'I do write wine articles, I think I could probably manage a few words saying what lovely boys they were, and what a good job they'd done.'

'Fine!' said Allegra, getting to her feet, completely missing Grace's sarcasm. 'Now, I must be off.'

Grace followed her to the door, hardly daring to believe that she really was going this time. She had the door open and was almost counting the minutes before Allegra would be out of sight when her sister paused. 'Oh, and did I tell you? They're starting on Monday.'

'No, you did not tell me!' Grace was furious. 'And you know you didn't!'

'Sorry, darling. It slipped my mind for a moment.'

Grace took a calming breath. Nothing ever slipped Allegra's mind that wasn't pushed.

'You will be able to pay them promptly, won't you? You've got enough left from your divorce settlement? It's one of the reasons they're reducing the price: I told them they wouldn't have to wait for their money.'

Allegra's expression hardened very slightly and Grace realised she was waiting for her to say that she couldn't pay. Then Allegra would offer to lend her the money and have the hold over her she craved. Grace just nodded, not wishing to lie out loud.

'And just one more little thing: you've all got to move out while they do it. Won't be a problem, will it? Demeter and that other girl have presumably got homes to go to. And you could stay with someone locally, couldn't you?'

Grace stared at her sister for a few moments, debating whether she should tell Allegra to cancel the whole thing, but then decided it wasn't worth the row. 'I think you'd better just go, Allegra, before you say something that really makes me lose my temper! And in future,' she called from the front door, as Allegra got into her car, 'could you ask your precious dry-rot people to communicate with me directly?'

Allegra waggled a hand out of her car window, and shot off, spraying stones into the air as she went.

Ellie appeared at the foot of the stairs before Grace had got the door shut.

'Well?' she said.

'Do you want the good news, or the bad news?'

'The bad news.'

332

'The dry-rot people are coming on Monday.'

'Oh. What's the good news?'

'They're knocking five thousand pounds off the price if they can use me for a testimonial. Which means' – she smiled brightly and artificially – 'we only have to find twenty-five thousand pounds by the week after next!'

'You don't have to pay before they've done the work, surely?'

'No, but it's only going to be a few days, isn't it? Not long enough to earn any money!'

'Oh, I don't know,' said Ellie. 'We're a couple of fit-looking girls, we could go up West and see what we could pick up.'

Grace smiled in spite of herself. As always, they gravitated to the kitchen. 'And we've got to move out while they do it!' she managed eventually. 'Would you fucking believe it!'

'Grace,' said Ellie, impressed. 'You swore!'

Chapter Nineteen

❧❧❧

Flynn found Grace later that afternoon at the far end of the garden, pulling at dead brambles with the fierce determination of one intent on demolishing Sleeping Beauty's magic forest armed only with a pair of blunt secateurs. She was wearing gardening gloves, a thick coat and enough undergrowth to support a small bird's nest. 'I tried to phone you, but I couldn't get an answer.'

'Sorry. I just had to get out of the house for a bit.'

'Aren't you cold out here? And it's nearly dark.'

'I know. And yes, I am cold, but I don't care.'

'Darling! What's wrong?'

'Nothing.' Grace felt herself blush at his endearment and tugged at a particularly stubborn bramble. She tore her gardening glove and then her palm. 'Oh, shit,' she muttered, aware that she was very near tears, and not wanting Flynn to precipitate them.

'Are you hurt?' He moved forward to look, but she snatched her hand away. She was going to keep herself together if it meant she bled to death.

'I'm fine! No need to fuss!'

'Then let's go in. I want to talk, and unlike you, I'm not dressed for the Arctic. We can light a fire and I'll make you tea.'

'I've drunk so much tea I'm awash with it,' Grace grumbled.

'I'll find something stronger then. Demi's up, and Ellie's making her scrambled eggs.'

Her hand was hurting, and her nose was beginning to run. The thought of a fire, friendly people and alcohol was very tempting.

'They sent me out to get you in.'

'OK.' Being near him made Grace feel calmer, and she was proud of herself for not flinging herself into his arms when he first asked her what was wrong. If she could keep her troubles off the agenda, she'd be fine. What she didn't want was for him to get her to tell him her troubles, because he would feel obliged to invite them all to stay at his house. After all, it was enormous and practically empty, it would be the logical thing to do – and she didn't want that either. Not because staying with him would be particularly unpleasant, but because she didn't want him thinking he had to look after her just because they'd slept together. She had fought very hard to become independent after Edward left. She didn't want to lose what had been so hard won in the first five minutes of a new relationship.

'So why were you gardening on a cold winter's night?' he asked conversationally as they walked in together.

'Well, these things pile up if you don't get round to them.'

'Most people do these things in daylight.'

She allowed her mouth to twitch. It *was* a strange time of day to be pulling up brambles. 'I've been busy. This was my only opportunity.'

He smiled back. 'Right. But Demi's obviously fine now.'

'Yes, thank goodness. Did they tell you her mother

turned up? She'd had a call from Rick, too. I didn't mean to lie to her, but when the time came I found I just couldn't drop Demi in it. It was probably terribly irresponsible.'

'I don't think anyone could accuse you of being that, Grace.' He paused and looked down at her, flicking her nose with his finger. 'A little odd in some ways, possibly, but not irresponsible.'

'What do you mean?' she said indignantly. 'I'm not remotely odd!'

'It may be news to you, but usually when people have spent a very pleasant night in bed together, they're a bit more friendly when they see each other again. Of course, things may be different in England.'

Grace stopped and turned to him, overcome with remorse. 'Oh, Flynn, I'm sorry! Was I being unfriendly?'

'A little chilly. What's the problem?'

Having walked a little way in his strong, comforting presence, and feeling soothed by it, Grace was able to make herself sound unconcerned. 'Oh, nothing much. Did Ellie and Dem tell you that my sister arrived at the same time as Demi's mother?'

'I think they did.'

'Well, she always manages to rattle me. That's all.'

'Are you sure? She didn't bring you bad news?'

For a moment she considered denying it, but decided it wouldn't work. 'Just boring stuff about the dry rot. They're coming to do it on Monday, and you know how tiresome it is having people in the house.'

He regarded her intently. 'I do indeed. And I also know that they probably want you out of the house while they do it.'

'Do you? How do you know that, then?'

'I had a house once which was quite badly affected. It's easier for them if they can just take all the plaster off and get on with it.'

'Hmm.' Grace opened the little gate which led to the path to the back door.

'So would you all like to come and stay with me? I've got plenty of room.'

'Oh no! There's no need for that! In fact, I'm not at all sure it's necessary for us to move out at all!'

He paused, stopping her with a hand on his arm. 'Grace, what's the matter? Why aren't you telling me anything? Why are you being so stubborn? Was it something I did? Or are you just regretting going to bed with me?'

In many ways she was. Life would have been simpler if she hadn't. She could have happily gone to stay with him, accepting the help of a neighbour. Making love to him had made things different: more complicated. She moved to go into the house, to avoid his question, but he wouldn't let her. Instead he stood in front of her and took her face in his hands. 'Well?'

Grace looked up at him, into his kind brown eyes with the curly eyelashes. She let her gaze slide over his firm, curved mouth and strong chin, and wondered why she hadn't realised how attractive he was when they first met. 'I loved making love to you,' she said, 'I loved everything we did together. But life has suddenly become rather complicated.'

'It's been complicated ever since we met,' he said dryly. 'What's different?'

She didn't want to tell him. She didn't want his sympathy, she didn't want him to sweep her into his arms and hold her while she sobbed out her troubles.

'Come on, Grace.' He gave her a little shake. 'Spit it out.'

'It's nothing. Just a money thing.'

'And you can't tell me? Grace, my darling, after what we've been through together with Demi, and then afterwards, surely you could tell me if it was "just a money thing"?'

'No! I couldn't! Don't you see? If we were just friends, perhaps I could have told you, although I probably wouldn't have. But now . . .'

'But now?' he prompted when she didn't speak for several seconds.

'Now you'll feel obliged to help me, and I don't want to be helped! I want to sort things out for myself. I was too dependent on Edward, and it was so hard getting myself back together again after he left. I feel as if I've climbed a long, high hill, and I'm teetering at the top. If I'm not careful, I'll fall back all the way I've come.'

'Carrying on your analogy to its logical conclusion, if you take a step forward, you'll fall down just as far. It's going to be uncomfortable, teetering on that peak, unable to move. Standing first on one foot, and then on the other.'

She smiled at him. 'It does sound rather precarious.'

'And lonely.'

She sighed very deeply. 'But I'm used to that.'

'There's no need for you to be used to it now. You've got Ellie, and Demi and—' He paused only for the tiniest second. 'Me.'

'I know. But none of you are really mine. I mean, Ellie won't live here for ever. Demi will probably go back home eventually, and if not, she'll go to university—'

'And me? I know we haven't known each other that

long, but surely you don't need to assume that I'm going to wander off sometime in the future?'

'Don't I?' Grace was angry now. 'You said it yourself, we hardly know each other. I have no idea what you're likely to do! I certainly shouldn't have slept with you!'

'I thought you said you loved it!'

'I did! But it's complicated. We don't know how we feel about each other really, and you shouldn't go to bed with people just because you want to!'

'Why not? We're both single.'

'Just look at the trouble it's caused!'

He sighed. 'The only trouble it's caused is in your mind, Grace. Now let's go in. You're getting cold.'

'I can take responsibility for my own temperature, thank you! And I've got a thick coat on.'

'Oh, shut up and come on.'

As arguing didn't seem an appealing option just then, Grace went.

Ellie could tell straightaway that things weren't quite right between Flynn and Grace. What was wrong with the woman? she wondered as she offered tea and put more bread in the toaster. Flynn was so lovely. Attractive, sexy and kind. Why couldn't Grace see what a jewel she had in him? Was she still hankering after Horrible Edward? If so, why?

'Hi, guys. Scrambled egg? We've just about got enough eggs.'

'Actually, we've decided to go out for dinner, if you two won't miss us too much,' said Flynn.

'No, we haven't!' said Grace. 'You didn't even ask me!'

'I wouldn't have got an answer if I had. Now go and

339

get the brambles out of your hair and hurry up. You don't need to change.'

Grace frowned at him for a moment and then decided that being told what to do was rather restful sometimes. Obediently, she left the room.

When they had both gone, ten minutes later, Demi sighed deeply. 'For an older man, Flynn is definitely attractive.'

Chapter Twenty

Ellie and Demi didn't mean to wait up for Grace, but Demi, having been asleep all day, wasn't tired, and there'd been a film they wanted to watch on telly. Ellie had slept through it all, but woke up with the closing credits.

'Well, I do hope Grace asks Flynn if we can stay with him,' said Demi, stretching. They were curled up together on Demi's bed, covered with a duvet. 'If you say we've all got to get out of the house on Monday, I'm not going home.'

'I suppose I could go home, if I had to.' Ellie considered her parents magazine-standard house and shuddered, although it was far warmer than Luckenham House.

'But what about Grace? I shouldn't think she'd want to stay with her sister or anything.'

'Good God, no! She lives far too far away, for one thing. And I wouldn't want to stay with her.'

'Nor me. It's mad her being friends with my mother. What sort of coincidence is that?'

'A bit like the sort of coincidence that you were at a party at Rick's house,' said Ellie, who felt it was time to ask Demi a few questions.

'Oh,' she mumbled. 'That wasn't a coincidence, actually.'

341

'No?'

'I knew where he lived because I'd been there with you, and he's so gorgeous!' Demi pleaded. 'Although of course, a complete dopehead.' Demi tried to give the impression that this cancelled out all his attractiveness.

'And a bit older than you?'

'Well, that doesn't matter. My father was ages older than Grace—'

'And it didn't work out!' Then Ellie frowned, aware she was interested in an older man herself. Just as well Demi didn't know about it.

'No, but not because of that. It didn't work out because he found someone else.' She looked down and fiddled with the duvet. 'He always does. He's such a tosser sometimes.'

'Demi! You're talking about your father!' said Ellie, who'd muttered similar things about her parents in her time. 'But anyway, you still haven't told me how you got yourself to a party at Rick's house.'

Demi sighed, not particularly looking forward to this confessional, but aware she might feel better afterwards. 'I told you I saw him on his motorbike? He actually bought me and my friend a drink in the café and we had a chat. Well, he was really friendly, and said to come over any time, and so one day I went round there, with my friend, after college. He was really nice.'

'I bet he was,' said Ellie. Suddenly it all made sense. 'You're a pretty girl, Dem.'

'Am I?'

'Yes, and you've got a great figure.'

'I'm too fat.'

'Rubbish. And men don't like really skinny girls, anyway.'

'Don't they?'

'Well, Rick invited you to his party, didn't he?'

'No, actually, he didn't. We sort of invited ourselves, and then my friend couldn't come, so I went on my own.'

'That was brave!'

'Yeah. Too brave, really. I was so scared I got another friend to buy me some vodka and I drank quite a lot of it before I got there. Then when I arrived I drank quite a lot of other stuff as well.'

'What stuff?'

'Can't remember.'

'And what about the dope?' Ellie was becoming insistent. She and Rick had had plenty of arguments about how much of it he smoked, and how Ellie was fed up with him being in a semi-permanent daze.

'It was only weed, for God's sake! I wasn't mainlining heroin or taking ketamine!'

'I'm glad to hear it!' Ellie knew she was sounding a bit prim, but forged on. 'And you didn't take anything else? God knows what rubbish there is at Rick's parties now I'm not there.'

'There was other stuff, but I was too scared to take it.' Demi smoothed out the duvet over her knees. 'I only smoked one joint. I didn't really like it. It made me feel sick.'

'From what I hear it made you actually *be* sick, several times.'

'Yeah. I don't think I'll take it again. And you know, it's really quite expensive!'

'I do know. I used to get livid with Rick spending so much money on it, when we had so little, and what we did have, I was earning.'

'That's so unfair!'

343

'Yeah. Oh—' The sound of a key in the front door made Ellie sit up. 'That's Grace! Let's go and see how her evening went.'

It was hard to tell in the very dim light of the hall, but Grace appeared to be blushing. 'Oh, hello. I hope you didn't wait up for me.'

'No,' said Demi. 'We were watching a film, or at least I was. Ellie snored her way through it.'

'I don't snore!'

'No, not really. So, how did you get on?'

Grace sighed for a moment, deeply happy, and determined to hold on to the feeling before her worries started to batter away at it. 'We had a lovely meal.'

'And?' demanded Demi.

'And – well, he persuaded me that we should all go and stay with him while the dry rot is fixed. But we're having our own bedrooms.'

'So I should think!' said Demi. 'He lives in a bloody great mansion. He surely wouldn't expect us to huddle together in one bedroom.'

'In the attic,' said Ellie, fanning Demi's indignation. 'Using just the cold tap in the yard for washing in.'

'What are you two going on about? I mean Flynn and I are going to have separate bedrooms. And two of us will share the twin room. But there's another perfectly nice spare room with its own bathroom.'

'You're not sharing with Flynn?' said Demi. 'Why not? He's so cool!'

'Well, yes, he is. But I don't think – I mean . . . Anyway, it's none of your business, and I'm really tired.'

She went up to bed, holding close to her heart the sound of Flynn's voice, the little things he had said to her – not declarations of love, but casual endearments which reminded her of the intimacy they had shared the previous night. How she had held out for separate bedrooms she didn't know, but although she was beginning to feel that the warm feelings, the tenderness, and, she had to admit it, her desire for him might amount to something like love, she wasn't ready to submit to the fire that had so nearly consumed her the last time she tried it.

Ellie went to her own room feeling lonely, and envious of Grace for having Flynn so obviously devoted to her. Not that she begrudged Grace her happiness, or more accurately her potential happiness, but she so wanted some for herself.

She knew she wouldn't get what Flynn gave Grace from Ran. He was such a different sort of person. But she did want what she felt he could give her if only he weren't so stubborn. By its nature any fling would have to be short, but it could be very, very sweet. And she wanted something she could remember and hold close during the long months – years possibly – before she could have a proper, full-time relationship. It wasn't that she didn't want that from Ran, she did, but would he ever want the same from her? Sometimes he seemed to like her, fancy her, even, but then he would go back to treating her as a child and strictly off limits. There was probably no hope she could change him. Even if she did ever manage to seduce him, a quick affaire was all she could hope for. Anything deeper and more permanent was out of the question. There was no point in her even thinking about that: crying for the moon never got you anything except a sore throat and angry phone calls from the neighbours.

She chuckled to herself as she thought of Flynn, as

their nearest neighbour, ringing up to demand to know what was going on at Luckenham House. And then a thought occurred to her. Why shouldn't she stay with Ran while Grace and Demi stayed with Flynn? It would make perfect sense, or at least, it would by the time she'd framed her argument. She was seeing Ran tomorrow. She smiled as she put toothpaste on her brush. She still had a chance of a fling, even if it was a bit flimsy.

Ellie was determined that she would be very cool today. She was not going to tear off her clothes, tear off Ran's clothes, or generally behave in an undignified way. But she couldn't stop her heart racing at the thought of seeing him, couldn't help taking great pains with her appearance – unnecessary pains given that she was going to be doing dirty work, and might well end up just sweeping the studio floor. She liked him a great deal. If she was honest, she knew she might be in love with him, but he wasn't in love with her. It was sad, but there was a certain relief in admitting how she felt. And at least she got to see the object of her adoration. She thought of Grace, abandoned by Edward, whom she went on loving for a tiresomely long time after he had proved he was totally unworthy.

Ran let her in almost as soon as she rang the bell. 'I'll give you a key,' he said. 'So you can come and go as you need to.'

'Thank you,' said Ellie, feeling this was progress.

'After all,' he went on, spoiling the effect of his previous statement, 'I may not always be in when you come.'

'No. Actually . . .' She bit her lip as he stared at her. She hadn't actually formed a plan on how to ask Ran if she could stay. Perhaps the direct approach was best.

'What?'

'I was wondering . . . The thing is . . . I need somewhere to stay for a few days. Luckenham House is being treated for dry rot and we've all got to move out.

'Also,' she went on when he didn't answer, 'I haven't seen a doctor or anyone since I discovered I was pregnant because I'm signed on in Bath. It would give me an opportunity to go to her.' She smiled, hoping he wouldn't point out that as she was planning to commute to his house every day, why couldn't she just visit her doctor and go back to Luckenham House when the dry rot was dealt with?

'Where are the others going?'

'Grace is going to stay with Flynn.' She didn't mention Demi, because Ran might correctly assume that if Flynn had room for Grace and Demi, he might also have room for Ellie.

'So you want to stay here?' His expression was maddeningly inscrutable.

'If that's all right. Of course, I don't have to, it's just . . . my parents live miles away, and—'

'Well, I suppose that's OK,' he interrupted her, looking at her rather sternly, as if warning her against any funny business. 'When do you want to come?'

'They're starting on Monday.'

'So you could just bring your stuff when you come anyway?'

'Yes, I could.' Somehow, everything had worked out all right. Perhaps it was a good omen.

'Do you want to make us both something to drink before we start work? Bring it in when it's ready, but for God's sake don't spill anything!'

*   *   *

347

The panels were lying on their backs on an old sheet.

'I haven't done anything to them yet. I wanted to think how best to proceed.'

'How will *you* deal with the dry rot? Will you have to flood them with toxic chemicals? I think that's what they're planning to do at Luckenham House.'

'No, nothing like that. I'll make up a fume tent and fill it with nitrogen. That should kill anything else that's alive in there.'

Ellie shuddered. 'What do you mean?'

'Woodworm, mainly.'

Ellie studied the beautiful brushwork, admired the delicacy of the tiny flowers and birds which were scattered at the feet of the figures. 'Do you think they're very valuable?'

'They could be priceless. Although they're in quite bad condition in places, at least they haven't been braced or cradled – with a framework of wood, I mean, so the wood can't move.'

'That's bad, then?'

'Very bad. Wood has to be able to move,' he said solemnly, but with that underlying layer of wit which was what made him so sexy, in Ellie's opinion. 'There isn't a signature, unfortunately,' he went on. 'There were a couple of initials, but one has been virtually eaten away.'

'Where is it? Perhaps I could make it out.'

'Not being as old and grizzled as I am, you mean?'

She smiled, glad to be back on familiar ground. 'You said it! And I just want to see.'

He showed her the place. There was a clear letter R and the second letter looked a bit like a C but could equally be fly droppings. 'Does that mean we can't find out who did them?'

'Not at all. It'll just take a while, that's all.'

'But it would add to their value if we knew who did them?'

'Hugely. And if we could also find some provenance, how they came to be in the house, stuff like that, it would help enormously.'

'So how are you going to find out all that?'

'I'm not. You are.' He said it very coolly, as if it were perfectly simple.

'I am? But I don't know anything about things like that. Don't you need a specialist?'

'No. I'll point you in the right direction, but you'll have to do the spadework. It'll be good training for you, if you're really interested in conservation work.'

'So where will I have to go?'

'The Witt Library. It's part of the Courtauld Institute, in Somerset House.'

'Then what?'

'Most of the records of English artists are there. You'll have to go through all the ones with first names beginning with R, and see if anything fits with what we know.'

'But we know nothing!'

He shook his head. 'We've got a rough date – within a century or two – we have a locale, and we have a subject.'

'But I don't feel remotely qualified to do anything like that! I'm an artist, not a historian!'

'Look, do you want to do the best for these panels or don't you?' He was looking stern again, which Ellie found very distracting. 'I don't have time to do the research – I'm working on the panels for nothing, when I've got my own clients stacking up. I can't take days off in London to do research.'

'No, sorry. I wasn't thinking . . .' about his work, anyway. She lowered her eyes contritely.

'Well then, start! And then get the hoover out.'

'But I'm an apprentice, not a cleaner!'

'Apprentice means dogsbody, for at least seven years! Oh, and make an appointment with your doctor.'

'Yes, sir,' said Ellie, trying not to laugh.

By the time Ellie went back to Luckenham House that night she had not only cleaned Ran's house, and had her first go at scraping off glue with a scalpel, which was very nerve-racking for both her and Ran, but she had a sheaf of notes about the panels. She was longing to tell Grace all about them, about how all the panels of that period came from the same firm of brothers who imported Polish oak, which meant that the artist hadn't just started painting the window shutters, but had probably put them up there himself. The nail holes were visible.

She was very glad that Grace was in the kitchen so she could spill out her enthusiasm. 'I've had the most amazing day!' she said. 'Ran is absolutely fascinating.'

Grace smiled as she put the kettle on. 'I know that, you've made your feelings quite clear.'

'I don't mean like that! I mean as a conservator! All the stuff he's told me, it's brilliant!'

'I thought he was a picture restorer.'

Ellie shook her head. 'What Ran does is much more about conserving what's there, making it stable, so it doesn't deteriorate any further. He does do restoration, but they don't like to be called picture restorers.'

'Those sound like words from the master!'

'You'd better believe it! He's so gorgeous when he's

350

strict! If only he'd cave in and take me,' she ended rather wistfully.

'I thought you wanted a bit more than that from him,' said Grace more seriously.

'Well, yes, but if I can't have that, and I can work with him, I might get a proper career out of it.'

'But I thought you had to go to university and do a course?'

'Well, probably, but it would be so wonderful just to watch him work.' She looked up at Grace. 'I know you just think I'm totally in love with him, but I'm also in love with what he does. It's so important! You remember all that row about restoring Michelangelo's David?'

'No.'

'Well, the conservator resigned her job, the best job in the entire world, because they – some authority or other – wanted her to do something to it that she felt was wrong, and would possibly damage it.'

'Dreadful.' Grace tried to summon up the right degree of outrage and didn't think she'd quite managed it.

'It's so fascinating. Did you know that Indian Yellow was apparently made out of the urine of cows fed entirely on mangoes?' She frowned, her brain addled with information overload. 'Or was that a myth? Anyway, it's gripping stuff. I can't wait to go back the day after tomorrow.' She frowned. 'It's so odd how things turn out. It never occurred to me that conserving pictures might be remotely interesting. If we hadn't found the panels I wouldn't have given it a thought. But meeting Ran has shown me how utterly fascinating it is. I could get quite obsessional.'

'I am glad. Otherwise you're devoting hours and hours of time just for me and the panels.'

'I'd do that anyway, Grace. But I wasn't expecting to be so interested. And if I did persuade him to let me work for him, I could probably fit it in round the baby.'

'I could look after the baby while you work,' offered Grace. 'I love babies.'

'But you might have one of your own soon,' Ellie reminded her with a mischievous grin.

Grace rolled her eyes in horror. 'I hope not! How soon can you tell if you're pregnant?'

'I didn't mean that! Although of course it is possible. I meant you and Flynn, might . . . get together.' She had been about to say 'get married', but held back.

Grace sighed. 'I don't know. Really, I don't. I don't really want to talk about it. It might all go away.'

'Fine. I do understand.' But Ellie didn't really understand. Being a very confiding person herself, she'd have wanted to dissect every sentence she and Flynn had exchanged if she'd been Grace, to extract every atom of meaning out of it. 'By the way,' she added. 'I've arranged to stay with Ran while the dry rot is being done. Is that all right?'

'Oh! Yes, of course it is. I'll have Demi as a chaperone.'

'Do you need a chaperone?'

'No!' Grace sounded startled. 'No, of course I don't. I just . . .'

'What?' demanded Ellie, unable to be tactful any longer. 'What's going on with you and Flynn?'

'Nothing. We're just . . .'

'What? He's a lovely man, Grace, and there aren't many like that around!'

Grace looked confused. 'I just don't want to rush things. And if I was staying with him, in his house, on my own, I'd feel I was pushing him into something. He had a very bad marriage and a messy divorce. He's not going to want commitment, stuff like that. And after Edward—'

'In my opinion, "after Edward" has gone on far too long. And what makes you think Flynn won't want commitment? He seems very keen to me.'

'Well, perhaps it's me who's not ready. Anyway, it'll be fine. Demi will be there with me.'

'I see,' said Ellie, deciding that Demi wouldn't. Perhaps she'd benefit from a little spell with her mother while the house was full of toxic chemicals. Grace definitely needed pushing, and if she wouldn't be pushed with Demi there, Demi would not be there. Demi loved Grace, and she owed her. And so, after she had had the facts explained to her, Ellie was sure she would go back to her mother's, if not happily, at least with resignation.

Chapter Twenty-one

✧❀✧

The following Monday morning, they assembled in the hall of Luckenham House.

'Right, Demi. That's the bag you want for tonight?'

Demi nodded. She and Ellie hadn't actually told Grace that Demi was going to stay with her mother yet. They didn't want to panic her.

'OK. We'd better get in the car. I'll come back after dropping you at the bus, let the men in, and then move out.' She frowned. 'I really don't want to go! It seems cruel to leave the house to have a major operation and not even be with it.'

'It's not a pet, Grace,' said Ellie, who had butterflies in her stomach at the prospect of staying with Ran. 'It's a house.'

'It's like a human to me,' said Grace. 'Well, sort of,' she added, when she realised how sentimental she had sounded. 'Anyway, we must dash or you'll miss the bus.'

'Goodbye, house!' said Demi. 'See you soon!'

It was only when they were nearly at the bus stop that Demi said casually, 'Oh, by the way, Grace. I thought I'd spend a couple of nights at Mum's. She's picking me up after college.'

'What? Demi! Why didn't you tell me? Anyway, I thought your room had been turned into a gym!' Grace slowed the car so she could concentrate on this new crisis. Apart from not wanting to stay at Flynn's on her own, an awful doubt occurred to her: was Demi really going to stay with her mother, or was she thinking of sneaking back to Rick's? And how could she find out without looking as if she didn't trust her? 'I didn't think you'd want to go home!'

'She's got a spare room, and I thought I should go and check in with her, just for a little while. So she can see that I'm doing my college work and stuff.'

'Demi—'

'It's all right, Grace. Mum really is collecting me. You can phone her if you like. I rang her the other day. Ellie suggested it. She said if I volunteered to go home for a couple of nights, Mum would be impressed and worry less.'

A twinkle of light flickered in Grace's brain. Ellie suggested it, did she? Hmm. And not just so Demi and Hermia could have some quality mother-daughter time, either.

'You and Ellie aren't throwing me together with Flynn, are you?'

Demi managed a look of pure innocence. 'Grace! Now would we do a thing like that?'

'Yes! Now hurry. There's the bus coming down the road.'

Grace drove back towards the centre of town slowly and thoughtfully. Could she still stay with Flynn when the others weren't going to be there? Or, a more difficult question, how could she tell Flynn that she wasn't going to stay with him because the others weren't going to be there? He had been quite forceful when she'd initially refused to accept his hospitality, when he'd taken her out to dinner. She wasn't frightened of him, she could never be that, but there was something a little awe-inspiring about the thought of explaining that she was finding bed and breakfast accommodation rather than spend a few nights under his roof.

'Sometimes I wish I lived in Victorian times,' she muttered, scanning the rows of cars in the car park, looking for a space. 'There'd be none of this nonsense then! We'd just live with the dry rot. Ah! A space!'

As she locked up the car she wondered whether talking to yourself was a sign of madness if no one caught you at it.

Her first errand was at the bank, where she had arranged to get her jewellery out of the vault. She then had an appointment with a jeweller, who was going to value and then sell it for her. She thought it might be worth about five thousand pounds.

Then her plan ran out, and she didn't have another one. How was she going to raise twenty thousand pounds in a week? It didn't seem possible. The thought of loan sharks, which she had always rejected out of hand, suddenly seemed a real option.

Two hours later she drove back to her house, having discovered that nothing was worth quite what it should be, because it was too modern, or too old, or in an unfashionable style, but that five thousand pounds was a fairly accurate estimate. As to the rest of the money, she wondered if there was a little bit of garden she could sell. Someone might want space for a few chickens, or a goat? But who would pay thousands of pounds for a few square yards? No one.

When she got to the house, she found the woodwork-treatment men already there, getting stuff out of their van. They had protective clothing and masks with them. It all looked extremely sinister. And, strangely, Flynn's friend, Pete, was also there.

'Flynn asked me to come along and plumb in the Rayburn while all this lot's going on,' he said.

'That was nice of him,' said Grace, wondering how she could possibly pay for Pete on top of everything else.

'He's waiting for you back at his house,' Pete continued.

'Is he? I'll be along as soon as I've sorted out these people.' She tried to smile as the foreman approached her, but it was the vain attempt of someone trying to appear pleased as the dentist asks them to open wide, drill in hand.

Chapter Twenty-two

Grace sat in the car for a few moments, psyching herself up to knocking on Flynn's door. She would have stayed there longer, only he came out of the house and round to her side of the car. Feeling that he might physically wrench her from it, she got out of her own accord.

'Hello, Flynn,' she said, overcome with shyness.

'Hello, you. How lovely to see you!' He wrapped his arms around her and hugged her tightly. 'Come in.'

There was something extremely nice about being welcomed in this way, Grace acknowledged as she picked up her handbag and her post while Flynn got her bag out of the boot.

'But I mustn't get used to it,' she said aloud.

'What's that?' Flynn called from the doorstep.

'This personal service,' called Grace. 'I mustn't get used to it.' It was a convincing sounding lie and she smiled.

'I don't see why you shouldn't,' said Flynn as Grace joined him on the doorstep. He seemed to be replying to what she'd really said, and not what she'd pretended to say.

'Do you think I should employ a butler at Luckenham House, then?' she said.

He ushered her into the kitchen. 'Not necessarily. But

someone to carry your bags for you, from time to time, would be no bad thing. Now, coffee?'

'Yes, please. I saw Pete, by the way.'

'Oh, good.'

'He said you'd sent him to plumb in the Rayburn. You must let me have a bill when he's finished.'

'It's a present.'

'No,' she said firmly. 'It can't be. I can pay him myself. You gave me the Rayburn in the first place, and made it cook. You don't need to plumb it in for me. Not literally, of course.' She laughed, hoping to give the impression that the whole matter of who paid for the plumbing was on a par with who paid for lunch at the pub.

'I could have done it myself. I've done similar jobs many times. In fact,' he said, pouring coffee beans into a grinder, 'there are very few jobs I can't or haven't done myself. Electrics, plumbing, building, joinery, I've done it all in my time.'

'You're a useful man.'

'Yes, I am.' He regarded her intently, as if there was a subtext he was willing her to understand.

'Shame you don't do dry-rot treatment.'

'I have done that, but not on the scale that you've got it in Luckenham House. I had a word with Pete. He's seen it and he agreed you'd always have to get professionals in to do that, especially in an historic building.' He ground the beans and Grace sat down, idly sorting her post, wondering if there was anything except junk mail in it.

'I suppose so.'

'But, of course, it is fantastically expensive,' he went on.

Grace looked up. 'Well, there for once my sister did some good! They're going to use Luckenham House in their brochure – because it's so beautiful and the dry rot is so bad, I suppose – and she negotiated five grand off the price! Imagine that! I could never have done it. I'm hopeless with things like that. Although it did mean we had to have them when they were free to come. They'd had a cancellation.'

'So how are you going to pay for it?' he asked casually, as if this had been the topic of conversation.

Startled, Grace looked at him. 'It's all right! I've just sold all my jewellery.'

'What, all of it?'

'I didn't wear it. It was in the bank. I put it there when Edward left.' She glanced down at her fingers, remembering how she hadn't wanted the things he had given her with love reminding her how he didn't love her any more.

'Thirty grand's worth? Good for Edward.'

Grace laughed. 'No! Not thirty grand's worth! But five grand's worth. I think that's a lot.'

'So do I.' Flynn appeared impressed for an instant before he went on, 'So how will you pay for the rest of it?'

'I just will! Besides, it's none of your business.' Grace found herself blushing, wondering if she'd sounded rude, wishing this conversation would go away.

'But you're my business, Grace,' he said softly.

'Am I?'

He nodded, bringing the tray of coffee to the table. 'What happens to you matters to me.'

'Oh.'

'So I'd be very happy to lend you – give you, in fact,

360

but I know you wouldn't accept that – the money for the dry rot. I know you don't want to borrow it from your sister.'

'And how do you know I haven't got the money in my current account?' Grace tried to hide her confusion behind false indignation.

'Because you wouldn't be giving wine-tasting evenings, sitting on tea chests and selling your jewellery if you had. Do you want milk?'

'Black with sugar, please.' A cup of strong coffee might be just what she needed to help her cope with Flynn. This whole situation would have been so much easier if they hadn't slept together. Although, when she glanced up at him, sipping his coffee, she realised that he was perfectly relaxed. It was only she who felt awkward, unsure of the etiquette. Would he usher her to a spare room, as she hoped? Or would he take it for granted that she would share with him?

'I've got to pop out for a short time,' he said. 'Why don't I show you where I've put you, let you sort yourself out, and then take you out for lunch?'

'You're always taking me out for meals. I should cook you something,' said Grace, relieved at the implication that she was being given a room of her own.

'Can you cook?'

'No.' She laughed. 'Cheese on toast suit you?'

'Admirably, it's just my colour, but I fancy something a bit more substantial and there's a new restaurant I want to try. It's a bit of a drive, but it should be worth it.'

'You're spoiling me. If we go out I insist on paying. It's my turn.'

He put his hand on her cheek and kissed her. 'No,' he said firmly, making her blush again. 'Now come

361

upstairs. Let me show you the guest suite.'

The guest suite was gorgeous and Flynn's pride in it was obvious. It consisted of a bedroom containing a double bed the size of a patio and a bathroom with a walk-in shower and free-standing bath. There was a little dressing room next to it, which didn't seem to have much purpose, but was divinely pretty. A little balloon-backed chair covered in toile de Jouy fabric stood in the corner.

'This is delightful! Did you choose all the colours and materials yourself?'

He shook his head. 'I employed a very talented, very expensive, interior designer. She did a good job.'

'She certainly did,' said Grace, aware of a shadow of jealousy. 'She has excellent taste.'

'So have I. And I do appreciate the good things in life.'

This time he put his arms round her and kissed her on the lips, long and hard. When he let her go, Grace was breathless, and (she admitted reluctantly to herself), perfectly ready to sully the pure white bedspread with a little impure passion.

When she was alone in the house, she went back downstairs. Now Flynn was gone, her anxiety about how to pay for the dry-rot treatment came flooding back. Distracted, she sorted through her post without really seeing it, until something caught her eye. And so, to her surprise, and immense satisfaction, Grace had solved the problem before Flynn came back to take her out to lunch. Freedom from this worry, even if it was only for a short time, made her quite skittish.

'I do love being spoilt,' she said when he opened the car door for her and she got in.

'If I wasn't so hungry I'd spoil you properly,' he growled, before sublimating his desires by firing the engine of his powerful car and setting off far too fast.

In Bath things were going quite well for Ellie. She had dumped her bag in the room she had slept in before, shook out the duvet and made it look as comfortable as possible. Then she washed up and hoovered all the rooms except the studio. It took a bit of courage to knock at the door and go and speak to Ran, but she managed it.

'Anything I can do for you in here?' She looked across at the view, wondering when the windows had last been cleaned. 'Run round with the vac? Do the windows? Give the painting on the easel a good scrub with bleach and soda crystals?'

He completely ignored this pleasantry. 'Have you made an appointment to see your doctor?'

'No – I . . .' she began. Her flippancy evaporated, leaving her feeling caught out and guilty, although she had no reason to.

'Do it now. One of the reasons you came to stay was so you could see your doctor. Then I'll let you see what I'm doing here,' he added, as if she needed a reward.

Ellie grinned. She did like Ran. She knew she fancied him rotten, but the liking part was a pleasant surprise. In the time it took her to go to the telephone and haul out the directory she wondered if she'd fallen for him because, deep down and well hidden, he was a nice guy, but reluctantly decided not. She was probably perfectly capable of falling in love with a toad if he was as sexy and attractive as Ran. Perhaps her hormones were in a funny state. But how did he feel about her? Was he just being kind, or did he fancy her just a bit?

The receptionist told her that if she could get to the surgery in fifteen minutes, her doctor could see her then. She'd had a cancellation. 'Oh, and if you think you're pregnant, bring a urine sample,' she added.

As Ellie knew she was pregnant, she was in the kitchen, going through a cupboard looking for a nearly empty jam jar when Ran came in. 'I've got to go immediately. She's had a cancellation. Are you ever going to eat the rest of this Apricot Conserve with Brandy and Almonds? I need the jar and it's gone off anyway. I must clear your cupboards out. They're in a terrible state.'

'Help yourself.'

'And would you like me to do a bit of shopping after I've been to the doctor's? You've got no bread, hardly any milk and no Marmite.'

'I don't like Marmite.'

'But I do. And the washing-up liquid's nearly all gone.' She tipped the remaining jam into the bin and started washing the jar. 'God, I'm going to be late!'

'What do you need the jam jar for?'

'Don't ask, or use your imagination.' She flapped an irritated hand at him.

'So, when do you think you conceived?' said the doctor, when she'd finished putting cold hands on Ellie's stomach.

'I'm not exactly sure. It wasn't planned. Before Christmas?' she said, blushing, although she wasn't remotely ashamed.

'I think you'd better have a scan, to find out exactly

how pregnant you are. But on the whole you're very well, your blood pressure's fine. You did well to bring a sample.'

'Your receptionist told me I should when I said I was pregnant, making the appointment.'

The doctor laughed. 'She's well trained. And you've answered all the questions correctly: you don't smoke or drink too much.'

'And I don't eat soft cheese or empty cat-litter trays.'

'Well done. You've been reading the books, too.'

'Well, I haven't,' Ellie confessed, 'but I will now.'

'And I'll arrange a scan for you as soon as possible and an appointment to see the midwife. Where would you like to have the baby?'

Ellie was shocked. She hadn't actually thought about having the baby; being pregnant seemed enough to cope with.

'Well, here, I suppose. Or perhaps a home birth?' Would Luckenham House still be full of toxic chemicals by the autumn?

'Well, I can't prevent you from having that, but I would advise against it. There's an awful lot of blood, and although it wouldn't amount to much in quantity, it can seem a bit shocking for the onlookers and it's much harder for us if anything goes wrong. Lighting's always a bit of a problem too, unless your house has arc lights, of course. Will you want your partner with you?'

'Um. I haven't got a partner or arc lights. Perhaps I'd better have the baby in hospital after all.'

The doctor patted her hand. 'That would be sensible. Now, have I got all your details down correctly? Address? Telephone number? Things like that? We'll get in touch as soon as an appointment for a scan comes through.'

'Well, I'm not still at my old address. In fact, I've sort of got two addresses . . .'

The doctor could not have been kinder. Nothing she said or did should have made Ellie feel uncomfortable, and yet somehow, she did. It was, she decided as she walked back to the car, because of her feelings for Ran. She wanted to say she was living at his address, and, for a few days, she was. But it was a very temporary partnership and they were linked only by very ephemeral things like Marmite and washing-up liquid. She sighed deeply as she negotiated her car out of the parking space and headed for the supermarket. What should she cook for him tonight? she wondered. What would make him fall head over heels in love with her? Nothing that came out of an oven, she accepted sadly, but it wouldn't stop her trying.

'How did you get on?' asked Ran as Ellie hauled bags of shopping into the house. He took the bags from her as she did so.

'Fine. I'm well. I'm going to have a scan, and I've bought some lovely steak for supper. It was on offer,' she added.

'Good. I'm sure you should eat red meat when you're pregnant.'

'You seem to know a lot about it.'

'Sisters,' he said, as if that explained everything. 'And I'm glad you're well, because I want you to go to London tomorrow, to do a little research.'

Ellie cooked steak, sauté potatoes and wilted spinach. It was, she was forced to confess, extremely good. She had taken immense pains with it, as it was their first supper together, and she was privately very smug about the outcome. For pudding she'd stewed some apricots and prunes, added rum to the syrup and was going to serve it hot, with mascarpone cheese mixed with crème fraîche.

She wasn't quite sure if mascarpone counted as soft cheese or not with regard to its undesirability for pregnant women, so she wasn't planning to eat very much of it herself, but she hoped Ran liked it. He had opened a bottle of wine to eat with the steak, but she had refused it.

'I haven't eaten a steak as good as this since I was last in France,' said Ran, spearing a piece of meat which was perfectly pink in the middle and slightly charred on the outside.

Ellie blushed and awarded herself a point. 'I learnt to cook steak while I was an au pair in France. And I suppose that's when I learnt to like food, really. I'm glad you approve. Have some potatoes.'

Ran picked up the dish and shovelled half of them on to his plate. 'You must make sure you take the money for all this out of the petty cash box.'

'No! This is on me, to thank you for having me.'

'Ellie, you're already doing quite a lot to thank me for having you, you don't have to pay for the food as well. It would defeat the object of me paying you to be my apprentice.'

'My parents gave me some money when I told them I was pregnant.' Quite why Ellie felt obliged to tell him this, she didn't know. Maybe so he'd know she wasn't entirely dependent on his largesse.

'Why? Did they want you to have an abortion?' He frowned.

'Oh no. At least, they didn't say so. They just didn't want to offer to have me at home. My mother can't face the thought of being a grandmother just yet and the thought of a baby, or worse a toddler, in that house, was enough to give all of us nightmares.'

'Oh. So Grace took you in?'

'It wasn't quite like that. She wanted the company. It's been very lonely for her since her husband left.'

'It must have been, in that great big house all on her own.'

'And then there's Demi, the one Grace and Flynn had to go and rescue the other night.'

'Where does she fit in?'

'She's Grace's ex-stepdaughter.'

'Ah.'

'She doesn't get on with her mother.'

'So where is she now? Staying with Grace and Flynn?'

'No.' Ellie grinned a little sheepishly. 'With her mother. I told her she had to. Grace and Flynn need space to be on their own.' She frowned and looked at her watch. 'I wonder what they're doing?'

'Eating a meal, possibly. Do Grace and Flynn know they're being manipulated?'

'I shouldn't think so. I didn't say anything to them, only to Demi.'

'And you don't think that Flynn and Grace can sort their own lives out without help from you?'

He obviously disapproved of her matchmaking, probably because he'd hate it himself. 'I'm not helping them, or manipulating them, I'm just making the circumstances more . . .'

'Propitious?'

'Probably. Grace is very shy. She'd find it hard to get

it on with someone if her stepdaughter was around. Not that Demi's not lovely, but you know, two's company.' Worried that he might think she was implying that anything should go on between them by her comments about Grace and Flynn, Ellie stopped talking. After her initial attempts to seduce Ran had failed so spectacularly, she wanted him to believe she'd completely given up anything in that line.

'You're not eating much.'

'I'm not all that hungry.'

'Why not?'

'Tired, probably, being pregnant and all.' It sounded like a good enough reason to her. In fact, she wasn't hungry because she wanted him so much and he was sitting opposite her, friendly and often flirtatious, but apparently not interested. It was enough to put any girl off her food.

'You'll manage a trip up to London tomorrow?'

'Of course. I'll be fine after a good night's sleep.'

There was a pause as they both got on with their steaks, then Ran broke the companionable silence. 'So how long do you think you'll go on living with Grace?'

Ellie frowned. This didn't seem a fair question. 'I don't know. As long as she'll have me, I suppose. She was very keen on the idea of me having the baby there. She wanted children, it was one of the reasons she and her husband broke up – she wanted them and he didn't. He already had Demi and there's a son, too.'

'He must have been quite a lot older than Grace, then.'

'Oh, he was. I can't remember what the age gap was now, but it was huge.'

'How old are you, Ellie?'

'Twenty-five. Why? What's it to do with you?'

'I'm thirty-five. Ten years is quite a large gap.'

'So it is,' said Ellie. 'Just as well I'm not planning to marry you, isn't it?' Then she blushed the colour of the piece of steak on her fork. A moment later, she forced herself to meet Ran's gaze and realised that she had been right; he was warning her off, explaining why he wouldn't let her seduce him. 'On the other hand,' she went on, willing herself to stop but somehow unable to, 'lots of people don't get married these days. They just have a relationship.'

Ran sighed. 'Ellie, I should tell you, although you may well have guessed, that I have had quite a lot of relationships, long-term and short-term, mostly the latter, and they have always been with sophisticated women, either older or the same age as me. I like you a great deal, but you are far too young and sweet to be part of that string of women.'

'Sweet!' She dropped her knife and fork loudly on to her plate. 'Sweet! If you really wanted to insult me, you couldn't have done better than that!'

'Sorry. Insulting you really wasn't my intention.'

'Well, it was the effect! I may be young, but I've been around. I've had my own failed relationship, you may remember, which is why I am now carrying a child! I'm quite capable of deciding for myself if I want a relationship, thank you!'

'So am I, and I don't, in this particular instance.' He spoke very gently, and that somehow gave Ellie confidence.

'Fair enough.' She regarded him, not shy any more, but challenging. 'That's your choice. Don't blame me if you live to regret it.'

He returned her look and they confronted each other,

the sexual tension between them almost palpable. Ellie knew he wouldn't give in and sweep her off to bed, but more importantly for her, she knew he wanted to, very much.

'I don't suppose you'd like to eat my steak?' she said demurely, changing the mood while she was still in control. 'I really can't eat it and it would be a shame to waste it.'

'You must have a few more mouthfuls,' he said firmly, holding her gaze. 'You need the iron.'

He put down his own knife and fork and picked up hers. Then he cut off a small portion of steak and held it to her mouth. She took it, still looking at him, still defying him not to want her. This, she realised, as she chewed, not lowering her eyes, was flirting on a grand scale and it was enormous fun. Playing with fire can give you a really warm feeling.

'Ellie,' he said, when he had fed her three bits of steak which she had dutifully eaten. 'I do want to take you to bed, as you very well know, but I am not going to do it, which you know very well, too. So you might as well stop sending me smouldering looks.'

'But if you're not going to respond to them, there's no harm in my sending them, is there?'

'Not if you don't mind giving me a sleepless night, no.'

Jubilant, Ellie lay down her knife and fork. 'Have some spinach, why don't you?'

'I hate spinach,' he said.

'I'll eat it then. That's got iron in it, too.'

'You really are the most maddening child.'

'Child? I don't think so. After all, I don't suppose you've ever wanted to go to bed with anyone below the age of consent, have you?'

'No.'

'Then stop sulking and I'll go and fetch the pudding.' He continued to glower at her. She grinned, and because she couldn't help herself, she got up from her chair and kissed the top of his head. 'Serves you right for being so bossy,' she said, and left the room, wondering if perhaps she'd gone a bit too far.

Chapter Twenty-three

❧

Over lunch, Grace had lost her awkwardness with Flynn. By the time he had fed her, bought her several large drinks, and made her laugh so much she wondered if she could ever be serious again, she no longer had any anxieties about their sleeping arrangements; she would let things run their course. If they ended up in bed together, they did, and if they didn't, well, that was all right too.

'Would you like some tea?' asked Flynn as they got back through the front door.

'I'll make it. Do let me. You've looked after me so well all day, it's the least I can do.' She turned and smiled as they entered the kitchen. 'Well, actually, it's probably the most I can do.'

'I don't know how you can know so much about wine and not care about food.' He regarded her with an intentness which both scared and intrigued her.

'Oh, I do care,' she insisted. 'I just can't cook. I never learnt. Edward always did it and he was such a foodie—' she broke off. She'd made it a rule never to say anything negative about Edward. She even tried not to think anything negative about him.

'Yes?'

She glanced up, accepting the blame for this herself. 'I was scared to try, I suppose, in case it went wrong.'

She smiled, trying to get him off the subject. 'I'm very good at washing up, though.'

'Loading the dishwasher can be tricky,' he said seriously.

'Oh, shut up!' She threw a tea towel at him, wondering if she was a bit drunk. 'I'll make the tea.'

'Let's have it in the sitting room. I've spent enough time looking at you across a table, usually a kitchen one. I'd like to try another setting.'

'It might be an improvement.'

'I doubt it, but I do like variety.'

'Then go away and leave me to it.'

While she was in the kitchen, Flynn's cat appeared and rubbed itself against her legs, asking for food.

'I'm just a trigger for you now,' she said, cuddling him. 'You feel hungry whenever you see me.' Then she found the cat biscuits and put some in a bowl and watched as he crunched into them. 'Perhaps I'll get a cat,' she said aloud, and then filled the kettle.

She carried the tray into the sitting room, which was beautiful. It had elm boards on the floor with a few very worn old rugs. The furniture was a mixture of antique and modern but it blended so well together, she only noticed it wasn't all the same period when she put the tray down. Set against a wall was something very similar to Edward's favourite Dutch table, with cabriole legs. The room felt elegant and yet still comfortable, somewhere to relax.

'Biscuits?' asked Flynn, who had been lying on one of the pair of sofas with his feet up and had swung them down as she entered the room.

'You can't want biscuits. You ate a huge lunch. Besides, I've no idea where they are.'

'I'll get them. You sit down and pour the tea.' He rose,

374

but stayed, looking at her as she sank into the welcoming embrace of feather cushions and silk velvet and fiddled with the cups. She glanced up and was surprised to see him looking at her with an expression which caused her heart to flutter in an unnerving way. Then the corner of his mouth twitched to indicate he was only teasing her and made everything all right again.

He came back with a packet of the sort of biscuits her sister Allegra would serve: organic, with Royal connections. Grace was just about to comment on his excellent taste when she noticed that he was also carrying her post, and that his expression had changed.

'What's this?' he asked, handing her a flyer with her handwriting all over it.

'Oh, just something,' she said, trying to sound unconcerned. 'Rubbish, really.'

'So why have you made notes on it?'

'Doodling.'

'It doesn't look like doodling to me, Grace.' He sat down on the sofa next to her and made her look at it. 'It looks like calculations for borrowing money from loan sharks. Tell me you haven't. Please,' he added, his tone horridly reminiscent of Edward's when she'd done something wrong.

But he was not Edward and she was not afraid to stick up for herself. She'd arranged the loan while Flynn was out and now realised she should never have left the evidence lying around. 'It's nothing to do with you!' she said defensively.

'Tell me,' he said, biting out each word, 'that you haven't borrowed money at such an extortionate rate of interest that you will have paid double the amount you borrowed by the time you've finished.'

'But it's only until I sell the paintings!' She was partly angry with herself for leaving the evidence where he could find it, but also horribly aware that she'd done something she'd told Demi that no one should ever, ever do.

'When will that be? You'll owe them thousands in interest alone. And there's likely to be a huge penalty charge if you pay them back early. Give me that paper. I'm going to stop this.'

Grace snatched it away from him. 'Flynn, you have no right to behave like this. It's my money, my loan, my house and my business!' Some part of her noted that it was satisfying being able to argue with Flynn. Edward could silence her with a look, a raised eyebrow, and a withdrawal of his favour which felt like a total eclipse. 'Who are you to say who I can borrow money from or not?'

Flynn snatched the paper back. 'I'm someone who cares about you, and will not stand by and let you be fleeced by these sharks!'

He left the room and Grace struggled out of the sofa and followed him, running to keep up with his long strides. 'Give that back! It's mine!'

He took no notice, he only walked faster and crossed the hall to his study. He went in and shut the door, practically in her face. She tried to follow him but found herself the wrong side of the door, hearing the key being turned in the lock.

She was incensed: an anger fuelled by guilt and an awareness that she'd done something very ill advised. But she hadn't been able to see an alternative. It was only a short-term loan and without it she couldn't pay for the dry rot to be fixed. Surely, in the circumstances, it wasn't quite as lunatic as Flynn seemed to think? He obviously didn't understand how much the house meant to her and how desparate she was not to lose it.

She fumed impotently, and when the cat emerged from the kitchen, she muttered into its sleek fur about its owner. The cat seemed immune to the insults and just purred and rubbed its face against her. Grace was just wondering if taking a knife to Flynn's study door would be effective, or whether she should just cut all the left-hand sleeves off his suits, distribute his wine cellar to the neighbours with the milk, leave a kipper in the central-heating system, or whatever else it was that women did when they were so furious they were vibrating with it, when he came back out.

'I'm sorry, Grace.' He didn't sound sorry. He sounded angry. 'I didn't mean to shout, but it's all right now. I've told them where to get off, and they shouldn't bother you again.'

She put the cat down so she could shout. 'How dare you do that? It's none of your business! It's my loan! My responsibility! How many times have I got to tell you?'

'You can tell me until you're blue in the face, but you're not borrowing money from loan sharks! Not while there's breath in my body to prevent you!'

'Flynn—'

'I love you, Grace!' It was a statement he felt explained everything, but when it obviously didn't, he elaborated. 'I'm sorry. I didn't mean to say it like this, when I'm mad as a Kilkenny cat, but it's the truth. And it's why I'm not going to let you do this bloody stupid thing. If you need money you can borrow it from me!'

'But I don't want to borrow it from you,' said Grace, hanging on to her rage and trying to ignore what he'd said about loving her. 'I want to borrow it from someone who has nothing to do with me, who'll treat me like a normal human being who can make her own decisions!'

'No one in their right mind borrows money from those people. Come into the study and we'll talk about it sensibly.'

'No! This is my fight, I'll choose where to have it!'

'No, you won't! You'll fight somewhere more comfortable. Come in here.' He opened the door, took her wrist and encouraged her into the study.

The change of scene threatened to evaporate Grace's diminishing anger completely. He drew her over to the window and sat her down on the window seat. She refused to look at him, turning her attention instead to the way the last beams of winter sun shone on the remnants of last summer: achillea, with flat, plate-like flowers given back some of their summer goldness by the fading light; stems of cornus, bright crimson, glowed against the stalks of grass behind. It reminded Grace of the one time she had visited her godmother at Luckenham House and she resolved to get into gardening properly when things were back to normal, instead of just pottering about. It was a relationship she had at least a chance of making work.

'Grace, I'm sorry. I've been bossy and overbearing,' Flynn said. This time he did sound contrite, but for his manner, not for his actions.

'Yes.'

'But I can't let you borrow money like that. However much the paintings are worth you don't want to be giving those rogues thousands more than you borrowed.'

'How did you get them to agree to cancel the loan?' she asked flatly.

'I just did.'

'What did you do? Did you threaten them with the heavy mob?'

A reluctant smile tugged at the corner of his mouth. 'You won't like this.'

'I don't like it already. You may as well tell me the worst.'

He still hesitated for a few seconds before saying, 'I told them you were under age and had no possible chance of paying back any of the money.'

'That was a lie,' she said after a moment.

'I know.'

She sighed. 'The thing is, I do need to borrow the money for the dry rot. It would take for ever to arrange a mortgage in the normal way, or a bank loan. I did make some enquiries. They'd both need surveys, valuations, stuff like that, and I don't want people crawling over my house. I want to keep the paintings a secret as long as I possibly can.'

'Then I'll lend you the money,' he insisted, impressively patient, she realised.

'No! Don't you understand? I can't borrow money from – from you.' She baulked at giving him a title, like boyfriend, or lover. And friend didn't seem to quite cover it. 'It wouldn't be right. It would be like selling a car to a friend. It could ruin the relationship.'

He made a sound between a grunt and a chuckle. 'At least you acknowledge we have a relationship.'

'No, I don't! That sounds awful!'

'Only to you, Grace. To me it sounds just fine.'

'Well, it may do, but I'm not borrowing money from you.' Doing that would make her dependent on him, something she swore she would never be again.

'Borrow it from your sister, then.'

'I'm not borrowing it from her, either. I don't want her knowing about the paintings any more than I want the bank knowing.'

'They'll all find out eventually.'

'But not before they absolutely have to.'

'Then I'm your only option. You can't or won't borrow it from normal lenders, or your family, so it's me or go without.'

It was all so simple, the way he put it. But still . . . she sighed again. 'You must see my point! If I borrow it from you—'

'You're afraid it will put you under some sort of obligation to me. That it will make you feel obliged to sleep with me, even if you don't want to. Hell, you may even have to marry me to square it with your conscience!'

She laughed. 'The first part is true, although not the sleeping with you bit and certainly not marrying you. But I would feel under an obligation and you must see why. You'd be the same, if I tried to lend you money.'

'I don't think I would, actually. But it probably is different for me.'

'Yes.'

He chewed his lower lip for a few moments and she noted how white and even his teeth were. She must have noticed before, she realised, but not really taken it in. 'I tell you what,' he said. 'I'll lend you the money, but I'll charge you interest. That way you can't possibly feel obliged to me because I'd be earning money from you.'

'OK,' she said slowly. 'That sounds good. But it'll be the same rate of interest I would have paid the loan sharks.'

'Don't be ridiculous! I'll charge you the same as the mortgage rate.'

'Now you're being ridiculous!'

'Then what the bank charge for an overdraft.'

'No.' Grace felt quite exhilarated with her determination. 'It's the sharks' rate, or there's no deal. You can give the extra money to charity, if it bothers you so much.'

'It's usury.'

'It's the deal.'

'You're a tough woman, Grace Soudley.'

Grace suddenly smiled. 'I know! It's good, isn't it?'

'I still don't understand why you did it,' he said. 'It seems so irrational. So unlike you.'

'I know. And it was irrational, but it was a quick fix. Getting a loan any other way would have taken so long and I felt panicked by the people arriving so soon, and Allegra nagging me and everything.' She hesitated, feeling she should confess everything. 'And it was also something I could do on my own. My independence is quite new and fragile. Turning to loan sharks may be barking, but it didn't involve anyone else, like Allegra.'

'Or me.'

'Or you. And now you are involved.'

'Because I want to be.' He came towards her and drew her to her feet. 'I do love you. I know you don't love me, or if you do, you don't recognise it, but that's OK. I just want you to know there's no ulterior motive in anything I do for you. I want to do things because of my feelings for you. I don't want or need anything back – or at least nothing you don't want to give me, not out of gratitude, but out of . . .' His eloquence deserted him.

'What about passion?' whispered Grace, putting her arms round him and pressing her ear against his heart.

'Can we do things because of passion?'

'I think that would be fine,' he whispered back. 'Do we have to have dinner first?'

'Oh no. We've only just had lunch.'

'Come on.' He put his arm round her to usher her out of the study when the phone rang. He paused. 'I'll ignore it. They'll ring back.'

'I think you should answer it,' said Grace. 'It might be important.'

He reached for the phone, laughing into her eyes, unconsciously reminding her how very sexy he could be. 'If it's a double-glazing salesman, I'll be very annoyed. Hello? Demi? Grace, it's for you.'

Grace came back into the room and took hold of the telephone, prepared for disaster.

'Demi? Are you all right?'

'I'm fine,' said Demi in a small voice, 'but I think I should tell you . . .'

'What? What's happened? Your mother did pick you up? You're not at Rick's or anything?'

'No, I'm at home – where used to be home, anyway. It doesn't feel much like it now.'

'Then what's the problem?'

'There may not be one,' she hedged.

'Demi, love, you're driving me mad! Can you please tell me why you rang?'

'You sound in a hurry to go and do something. What can you be finding to do at Flynn's?'

Grace took a breath. 'Look, if you just want a chat, that's fine. I'll find somewhere to sit. I'm leaning over the desk at the moment.' She caught Flynn's eye and interpreted his look, which said he had been enjoying the view. 'OK, tell me all.'

'Mum knows about the paintings.'

'You mean – my paintings?'

'Yeah. I'm afraid I told her, by mistake. It just slipped out.'

Grace licked her lips and swallowed. There was no point in being cross. It wouldn't change anything.

'I'm terribly sorry,' said Demi. 'She was asking about the house and everything and the dry rot and I said we had to get the paintings out because of it. She said, "What paintings?"'

'Well, she would, but never mind. She might not tell anyone else.'

There was a silence which indicated that Demi did not agree with this statement.

'So whom will she tell? Your stepfather?'

'Your sister.'

'Oh,' said Grace after a moment. 'Are you absolutely sure? I mean, they don't know each other that well—'

'I've only just managed to get the phone – Rick's still got my mobile. They've been talking for hours. Mum was on to her like shit off a shovel. Oh, sorry.'

'It's all right. Do you know what Allegra said?'

'Not exactly, but going on how Mum was, I imagine she was livid.'

'Why? It's not my fault I found valuable paintings in my house!'

'But you didn't tell her about them. She thinks that's deceitful.'

'Figures, I suppose.' Grace sighed deeply.

'But she doesn't know where Flynn lives,' went on Demi, sounding pleased with herself. 'I refused to give them his address.'

'Oh well done, Dem! That was good. How did you

manage it?' Grace tried to sound congratulatory but this wasn't quite the coup Demi obviously thought it was as it would only give Grace a few days before she was descended on by Allegra, and quite possibly by her brother as well.

'It wasn't that hard,' Demi mumbled. 'I didn't know it.'

'Oh. And I suppose Allegra now knows the telephone number?' Grace picked up a pen and began to draw flowers down the margin of a newspaper.

'Yup. I'm so sorry, Grace! I didn't mean to say anything.' Demi sounded really contrite, and Grace could imagine how hard it would be to resist all the questioning Hermia would put her through.

'I know you didn't. It's all right. I'd better go and think about what to do.'

'I'd better go now, too. Mum will kill me if she finds out I've warned you.'

'Don't worry, I'm sure it will all be all right,' said Grace, with an assurance she didn't feel.

'So that's it,' she went on when she had replaced the receiver. 'That's the cat well and truly out of the bag.' Grace subsided into Flynn's office chair.

'And is the cat on her way round to scratch your eyes out?' asked Flynn.

Grace laughed in spite of herself. 'No, not yet. We're spared that because Demi didn't know your address. Poor little thing. She was riddled with guilt.'

'And I expect her mother pounced on the news and tortured every scrap of information out of her, to keep on with the cat analogy.'

'Yes. Don't know why.'

'Well, think about it! She has an opportunity to get

back at the woman who took her husband! Of course she's going to grab it!'

'But I didn't take Edward! I mean, well, not on purpose. They were separated before he met me.'

'I hate to say this – to admit it even – but men always say that, even when it's not true.'

'But it was true! Oh, never mind. It's all a long time ago now. What should I do about Allegra?'

'Do you have to do anything?'

'Eventually I will. I'm only safe for a few days, while I'm here. After that, she can attack at any time.' She smiled, trying to make light of what was, in fact, making her feel sick with anxiety. It was hard to believe that less than five minutes ago she and Flynn had been on their way upstairs. Now she could no more have indulged in lovemaking than she could have flown.

Flynn moved around behind her and drew her to her feet. 'Let's go and sit down in comfort and talk about this. I'm sure it's not as bad as it seems.'

'People always say that when it's not their problem.' She smiled, trying to tease him, and not quite managing it.

'I know. But we can sort something out together.'

Ensconced in Flynn's comfortable sofa, a glass of very nice wine in her hand, Grace did feel a bit better, but she knew it was only temporary.

'The thing is this,' she explained to Flynn, who was sitting opposite her with his legs crossed. Why hadn't she noticed before just how good-looking he was? she wondered, with a part of her brain which refused to concentrate on the matter in hand. 'Allegra and Nicholas are quite likely to say that the pictures are theirs, because they're not fixtures and fittings.'

'But that's ridiculous, they are. I thought you said Ran – whatever his name is, the conservator – had to cut them out or unscrew them or something?'

'Well, yes, but if they'd been painted on the shutters, they'd have been part of the house. As it is, they're not.'

'I think the fact that they were nailed or screwed down means that they are.'

'You'd think that because you want the paintings to belong to me – so I can pay back the money you're going to lend me – but Allegra and Nicholas might think differently.'

'I'm sure they're not going to be that unreasonable.'

'People are always unreasonable where money is concerned.'

'True.'

Grace curled her feet under her and closed her eyes for a moment.

'I'm going to light the fire,' said Flynn. 'Then I'm going to make us a cosy supper, which we'll eat in front of it. Then we'll watch television or something before I run you a hot bubble bath. Everything will seem better in the morning.'

Grace closed her eyes and sighed. 'No, it won't. I'll just be able to worry more because I'll have more energy.'

'You really do believe Allegra and your brother will try and make you give them the paintings?'

'I don't know for sure. But Allegra was putting a lot of pressure on me to sell the house. If she could try and take away my home, she wouldn't baulk at a couple of pictures, surely?'

'I don't know Allegra, what she's capable of, but I don't *think* she's a monster.'

386

'I really hope she's not, but Nicholas is very into money; he might encourage her.'

Flynn regarded Grace for what felt like a long time. 'I tell you what, darling. I'm going to take one of your worries away from you.'

'You've already done that, by offering to lend me the money.'

'Another one. I'm not going to try and lure you into bed with me until this whole picture thing is sorted out. Unless you decide you want to sleep with me, we'll sleep apart.' He hesitated. 'Am I right in thinking you were worrying about that, too?'

She looked up at him and nodded, surprised and touched by his perceptiveness. 'It would make everything more complicated for me. I know most people can walk down the street and chew gum at the same time, but I would find having . . . a relationship' – they exchanged glances and he smiled – 'distracting, while everything else in my life is confused.'

'Then that's just fine. I won't lay a finger on you unless you want me to. I would hate you to be distracted.'

It was only after he'd said this that Grace wondered if it was what she'd wanted after all. A little distraction might be a very good thing, and maybe a night of unrestrained passion was what she needed. Still, she could hardly ask for it now.

'Now you go up and have a long, hot bath, and when you come down I'll make you something nice on toast.'

She sighed, annoyed with herself for turning down the chance of more than 'something nice on toast'.

Chapter Twenty-four

❧

'I'll give you a lift to the station,' said Ran firmly next morning.

'You don't have to. I can drive myself.' Ellie, feeling anxious, was determined to be independent.

'But you'll be coming back in the dark. Finding your car on your own, at night, in a car park, is never pleasant.'

'Honestly, I'm fine. You're busy—'

'Oh, shut up. I'll get my keys.'

He is quite bossy, she thought as she made her way to the ticket office and bought a ticket. Why don't I object? Was it because in this particular instance, his bossiness worked in her favour? With Rick she would be nagging for a lift, giving him statistics about women being attacked in car parks at night. She was always the adult, the one who initiated things, made decisions.

Once on the train Ellie settled back into her seat and tried to concentrate on the tasks before her, not the man who had set her to them. Being in love was terribly distracting. She got out the *A–Z* and plotted her route yet again. Ran had given her directions, but Ellie liked to see for herself where she was to go. Luckily it didn't seem a difficult journey, and Somerset House would be hard to miss, even for someone not familiar with London. Once there, she had to find the Courtauld

Institute and then the Witt Library. That was when her task really began.

It took her a little thought to work out which bit of the Courtauld Institute she wanted, but eventually she found the right door and bravely asked for the Witt Library. Before she arrived, she was convinced that no one would let her in looking so studenty. Surely you had to look like a serious academic to be allowed in to handle the contents of a place Ellie had never even heard of? But Ran had told her it was the most comprehensive library of all the artists on the planet, practically, and it was where they would find their artist.

It seemed very small when she first went in, but then she realised she was only in the first room. It was lined with shelves, on which sat file after green file, with either letters or artists' names on them.

'Can I help you?' A respectable, middle-aged woman, of the kind likely to be put off by a nose stud and several earrings, spoke to Ellie.

Ellie cleared her throat. Her question seemed so silly, but then she realised that the woman was smiling, not disapproving, and that there were a couple of other obvious students around. So she smiled back.

'It's rather an odd thing, but I'm trying to research an artist . . .'

'Who?'

'That's the thing – I only have his initials. And we're not quite sure if we've got those right, exactly. Only the first one is quite clear.'

The woman didn't snort derisively, or laugh, but nodded, as if situations like this were not all that unusual. 'English?'

Ellie nodded. 'Most probably.'

'And you know his dates, roughly?'

'Very roughly.'

'Well, over there you'll find an index of all the artists we have records for. If you plough through all of them, you should eventually find artists with the right initials, and then you can narrow it down by date. But then you'd have to be able to recognise their work to make sure it's the right one.'

'That's all right. I think I could do that.' She had some Polaroids which Ran had taken in her bag, if her memory failed her.

The woman smiled. 'Good luck. And let me know if there's anything else I can do for you.'

There were lots of desks with lights over them where a couple of people were cutting photographs out of catalogues and pasting them on to card. As Ellie pushed past them to get to the index, she realised they were updating the records of who owned various pictures now, and how much they had been sold for.

The index boxes reminded Ellie of the school library system, before it had gone on to computer. She loved their old-fashioned woodenness. Very happy now, she dumped her bag at her feet, and began to go through each card in the 'C' section, looking for artists with the initial 'R'. She soon began to feel at home, resting her elbows on the open drawers, searching through, feeling soothed by the atmosphere. The arched window behind her looked out on to a huge rectangular space, which might at one time have been a parade ground. Now there were fountains, and Ran had told her that sometimes in winter they flooded the entire space and turned it into an ice rink.

Time passed slowly and quickly at the same time. She was absorbed in her task, recognising so few of the names she read, regretting her ignorance and yet inspired to improve her knowledge of painting.

It was a good thing she'd brought sandwiches; she was starving before she'd got through the first box. 'Remember people don't always use all their initials. Don't disregard the middle initial,' Ran had told her. 'Or sometimes people are called by their second initial, so if our artist was in a hurry, he might have used an initial which isn't in his proper name at all.'

'You mean D. T. for Dick Turpin, when usually he'd be Richard Turpin,' said Ellie, taking the point but feeling slightly patronised, all the same.

'You've got it.'

He had smiled at her, and remembering the smile made her feel warm and optimistic. Just thinking about him working away in his studio was enough, sometimes. At other times, it was tantalising.

At last she got a good match, and went to hunt out the file. There had been a couple of matches which hadn't been the right date, but this one was of the period and Ellie felt reasonably positive. There were several files: he was obviously a very prolific painter but was Richard Coatbridge also the painter of the panels?

Ellie was optimistic. His dates were right, but when she opened his file, and saw the photographs of what he'd painted, she realised the subject matter was totally different. This artist painted portraits, landscapes, tasteful subjects – nothing like the rioting foliage, the profusion of animals and the erotic figures of the panels. And yet his work did seem familiar.

Ellie spent some time searching through the file of

images, wondering if she'd seen other, more famous work by this artist, perhaps on a greetings card or something, which is why it looked familiar. Or possibly the panels were something he'd painted for a whim; not commissioned, just for his pleasure and amusement.

She went outside and telephoned Ran. 'I've found this artist, right initials, right period but he's done nothing else remotely like the panels.'

'Check all the other artists of the right period with the same initials, but don't panic. They could still be by him. I wonder if Grace has any written provenance.'

'Considering she didn't know the panels existed, it seems unlikely she'd know if she had. And there's very little stuff in that house, considering how big it is.'

'What about the attics?'

'I don't know about them.'

'Go back and see if you can find another artist. If you can't, make a note of the whereabouts of this guy's most prominent works. I could tell a lot by looking at his other stuff.'

Back went Ellie to her quiet, green-lined space and continued her research, getting more and more excited by the prospect of discovering the creator of the panels that had caused so much havoc and potentially so much happiness for her, and relief from anxiety for Grace.

It didn't matter personally to Ellie if the panels were old and valuable or not – through them she'd not only met Ran, she'd also found something she might want to do with her life. But it mattered to Grace that they were precious. She needed them to be by an old master, or at least a painter of some repute, and although Ellie checked all the other possibilities, none of the artists gave her the breath of hope that her first one had.

One of his paintings was in the National Portrait Gallery. A little look at her *A–Z* told Ellie she could walk there easily.

She put back the file, said thank you to the kind woman in charge, who now seemed like an old friend, and left the building, phoning Ran as she walked.

'There's something at the National Portrait Gallery,' she told him. 'I'm going there now to see if I can decide if it's him or not.'

'Are you sure you'll be able to tell?'

'Well, are you offering to come to London and look?'

'Don't get all worked up. I'm sure you'll manage just fine.'

'You're so patronising sometimes, Ran,' she said, and disconnected. But she was smiling.

Seeing an actual painting, in its full, enormous, glowing glory, made Ellie gasp. The subject was of some great man or other leaning up against the horse his wife was sitting on, side-saddle. They were under an enormous tree, and there was an equally magnificent mansion in the background. The wife was looking down at her husband, who was looking into the middle distance, possibly telling her about something she wasn't really interested in. The horse was objecting to the dog, which looked up at it, unsure whether to bark or run away. Obviously a commissioned work, it was a beautiful painting of real people, and real animals, even if it was unlikely they had posed in the sylvan setting. She stared at it for some time, thinking she should make more time to look at paintings – there was so much joy to be had from it.

Unfortunately, this stately masterpiece was so unlike the panels she felt it was unlikely to be by the same artist. She glanced at her watch; it was time to go for her train, but something drew her back to the painting. She could not stop looking at it. The colours were all as light and vivid as a colour-slide; she felt she could climb into it and walk through the trees, scattering the birds and animals as she did so.

Then she spotted it: a tiny rabbit, so small it was hardly noticeable among the painted grasses. But she recognised it! She definitely recognised it. There was one very similar on the panels. And once she'd spotted the rabbit, she realised there were birds which, if not identical, were very similar to those which frolicked by the feet of Adam and Eve.

She got the photographs out of her pocket to check, but, frustratingly, they were nowhere near good enough to be of any help. She looked back to the painting before her. Now she'd spotted the rabbit it seemed obvious it was the same artist. It was in the detail of the landscape behind the figures, in his use of light – things you'd never pick up from a photograph. This was their artist, she was sure.

She rushed back out into the bustle of London and telephoned Ran again. 'It's him, it's him, I'm sure it is! The panels must be worth a fortune!'

'Calm down,' he murmured, but she could hear a definite note of excitement beneath his caution. 'You could easily be wrong.'

'I am an artist, you know! And I'm not a complete fool! I can recognise brushstrokes, colours, stuff like that.'

'OK, OK, I'm sure you're very clever, but don't get too worked up. You may be doomed to disappointment.' He was maddeningly sensible. At any moment he would warn her about 'tears before bedtime'.

'Would you like to come up here and tell me I'm wrong?' she raged. 'If you won't take my word for it, that's what you'll have to do! There's an identical rabbit!'

'It is hard to tell one rabbit from another you know. They're all brown with white tails.' He was teasing her now.

Ellie just stopped herself calling him something very rude. 'Not in art, they're not!' she said, not daring to open her jaws again in case something more escaped.

'No need to get all worked up. I'll see if there's some of his work nearer here. In the meantime, you need to get on to Grace to see if there's the remotest possibility she's got any papers. Richard Coatbridge is a famous artist. If she's to get full value for the paintings, we need to be a hundred and ten per cent sure it is him.'

She sighed deeply, disappointed that he didn't share her optimism. 'OK. But I'm coming home now. I'm exhausted.'

On the tube journey to the station Ellie lost some of her enthusiasm. It was so crowded for one thing, and she found herself nervously protecting her stomach from her fellow commuters. Supposing she'd just thought the rabbits were the same because she wanted them to be? Perhaps she'd transferred what she saw in the portrait into her memory of the panels, because she wanted them to be by the same artist? Perhaps it was all a figment of her pregnant, addled-by-lust imagination? By the time she slumped into her seat on the train at Paddington, she had lost all hope, and was not at all pleased when the ticket inspector told her that her cheap ticket was not valid on that train. Fortunately it had already moved off and, perhaps seeing her fatigue, he didn't make too much fuss, just made her pay the excess.

'It's an omen!' she thought. 'Having the wrong ticket is an omen. They're not by him, after all!'

But before she closed her eyes she decided that the fact that she hadn't been forced out of the train at Reading meant it was a *good* omen, and slept soundly for nearly the entire journey.

Her mobile phone battery lasted just long enough for her to tell Ran which train she was on, which was another good omen. As the train pulled into the station she asked herself why it was so important to her that it was Richard Coatbridge who had painted those panels. She put it down to omens again.

'I think being pregnant has made me terribly superstitious,' she said to Ran, kissing him on the cheek and ignoring the fact that this greeting came as a surprise to him. 'I was wondering why I care who the artist is – they'll be valuable, whatever. But somehow I do care. If the baby's a boy, I'm going to call it Richard.'

'It's terribly unlikely it is him, you know. I mean, he's very famous.'

'I haven't heard of him.'

'As I said, he's very famous, or he wouldn't have work in the National Portrait Gallery.'

'There were loads of artists in there I'd never heard of.'

'Doesn't mean a thing. I don't want you to get your hopes up.'

'But I'm completely certain it is him. I can feel it in my water. Which, as you may have noticed, is very free flowing at the moment.'

'I'm afraid that doesn't mean a thing either.' He unlocked the car and she got in. 'Did you get me a *Standard*?'

'Yup.'

'Now that is good news.'

'Ooh,' said Ellie suddenly, just before Ran switched on the ignition. 'I think the baby moved!' She stared at him in wonderment, trying to connect the fluttering in her stomach with all that had gone before that moment; she was not just pregnant, she was having a baby.

Ran didn't speak, he just returned her solemn gaze. Then he lightly kissed her slightly open mouth.

Ellie didn't telephone Grace until the following day. She just ate most of the supper that Ran had cooked for her, had a bath and fell into bed. When she awoke the next morning, she tried to put Ran's kiss behind her. Don't read anything into it, she told herself firmly. It was just a response to the baby moving. It didn't mean anything.

Grace answered the telephone nervously, expecting it to be her sister. She had spent all yesterday on tenterhooks, but Allegra, astonishingly, had not rung. Flynn had gone out somewhere and she was very tempted just to let it ring. On the other hand, if it was her sister, about to give her hell, she was a grown-up, she could cope. Since she'd met Flynn, confrontation did seem less terrible; not pleasant, but sometimes necessary.

It was a pleasure to hear Ellie's enthusiastic voice.

'I think I've found him! Our artist! I went to London yesterday and did research. It's Richard Coatbridge!'

'Um . . .'

'I hadn't heard of him either, but according to Ran he's really important and famous! Those panels could be worth millions!'

Grace was more cautious. 'I'm not sure that's a good thing! Think how much trouble it's going to cause everyone!'

'Now don't be silly, Grace. If they're worth millions, it means you can pay for the dry rot and give loads to your sister and brother. And put in some central heating,' she added.

'Hmm. I must say, central heating is rather wonderful, when you're used to it. And ad lib hot water.' In fact, as she looked around Flynn's comfortable, well-appointed house, the advantages of money did present themselves to her quite forcibly.

'But . . .' Ellie paused for dramatic effect, and Grace felt her rising spirits descend a notch.

'There's always a but.'

'There is, isn't there? And this is quite a big one. One you may not have.'

'What are you talking about?'

'Have you got provenance for the panels? I mean, are there any old letters or papers or anything which might refer to them? Oh, I know you didn't know anything about them,' Ellie hurried on, 'but are there any papers, of any kind, in your house?'

'Apart from those waiting to be recycled?'

'Grace! It's not like you to make jokes! Now think. What about in your attic, anything up there?'

'I don't think so. I had the roof done and I don't remember finding a treasure chest up there.'

'But are you sure? In that television programme where they go up into people's attics they always find valuable antiques and things.'

'I have no idea what you're talking about.'

'Sorry, I forgot you didn't have television for years. Well, the people are trying to make money, the antiques people come and find broken pots and things and they sell them for a fortune at auction.'

'I think you might have mentioned this before. How do the antiques get there? Do the television people put them in the attic first?'

'Now you come to mention it, perhaps that is what happens. Anyway, I'm coming up. We're going to have a look.'

'The dry-rot people are still there. But on the other hand,' – Grace became more enthusiastic – 'if I'm out, my sister can't ring me.'

Ellie didn't try to make sense of this and arranged to see Grace in just over an hour.

Grace wrote Flynn a note: *I am going home to search in the attics for valuable papers I know are not there, but Ellie thinks might be. I think that girl watches too much television.*

Then came the hard bit. If she wrote 'love, Grace' like she would at the end of any other note she might write, except perhaps to the milkman (whom she no longer had, and so hadn't written to for years), would Flynn read anything into it?

She put 'love, Grace' anyway. It didn't matter if he read anything into it; she was beginning to think it was possibly true.

The two women met outside Luckenham House. Ellie was full of enthusiasm and bounce, and Grace was full of amused scepticism, but glad to get out of Flynn's house and away from his telephone.

'I'm sure there's nothing there, because I cleared it all out when I had the roof repaired,' said Grace, as they climbed the stairs having had a scary look at the devastation caused by the dry-rot people.

'So did you throw everything away?' asked Ellie, following Grace up the final flight.

'It was mostly rubbish. There were a couple of boxes I put in one of the stables.'

Ellie hesitated. 'You mean, the attics really are empty? Anything we might find will be in one of the stables?'

Grace nodded. 'The one with the table-tennis table, remember?'

'Spiders?'

'That's the one. It's the driest.'

'Let's go back down and look there then.'

'But, Ellie, it's raining! It's cold and dark and I really don't think we're going to find anything.'

'Maybe,' said Ellie, leading the way back downstairs, 'but we are going to look! We can take the boxes into the kitchen, and look through them in the warm.'

'Except it's not warm. The Rayburn isn't lit. Although it is plumbed in,' she added. 'Flynn had it done for me. Isn't that kind?'

Ellie shook her head in despair. 'And you're still doubtful that he has feelings for you?'

Grace blushed, remembering their recent argument when he'd made his feelings quite clear. 'No.'

Ellie paused, her hand on the back door. 'So are you and he . . . you know?'

'An item?'

'I meant sleeping together, but the item thing will do.'

Grace stopped. 'I rather blew the other bit. He said he's not going to come near me until my life is in order and I'm not so stressed.'

'But that's very considerate! He's lovely, Grace, really he is!'

'I know! But I want to go to bed with him now, not wait until this is all sorted out!'

Ellie giggled. 'I'd offer to give you some tips except I'm so crap at seduction.'

Both women smiled vapidly at the man in the boiler suit who walked by at that particular moment, and then shrugged.

'Come on. Let's face the spiders,' said Ellie.

Eventually they found the two boxes Grace was fairly sure she had put in the stable, but then Ellie spotted something else.

'Look! That box is wooden and says Ulster Apples on it. Did you put it there?'

While Grace contemplated the box in question, a large spider clambered out of it. 'No, I don't think so. That must have been here before.'

'It looks like it's got some old files in it. Let's take that inside as well.'

Grace regarded Ellie. 'Do you fancy picking it up?'

Ellie sighed. 'Where are the gardening gloves?' She found them, gave them a good shake, and put them on. 'And at least the spider got out!'

'But he left his wife and children behind.'

'Grace! It's really important we leave no stone—'

'It's not stones, it's spiders.'

'Spiders then. It's really important we leave no spider unturned, looking for provenance. You're not taking this seriously!'

'I am, really I am,' Grace insisted.

'OK, you take those nice clean cardboard boxes, which you put here.'

'And have nothing useful in them.'

'They must have, or you'd have thrown them away. And I'll take the Den of the Killer Spider family.'

They retreated to the house, gingerly carrying their separate burdens, equally anxious to dump them on the kitchen table.

'You go first,' said Grace, indicating the Ulster Apples box. 'There are cobwebs there you could make dog beds with.'

'Why me?'

'Because you're the one who wants the provenance. I just want the money.'

'Ah, but how much money? Here goes.' Still wearing the gloves, Ellie got out the first manila file. It had an illegible label on it, and the corners had all been eaten by something. 'Have you no idea what any of these papers are?'

'Nope. Let's see.'

They were love letters, probably dating from the war, all bound up with blue ribbons. 'Oh, it's so sad!' said Grace as she looked at them. 'They're to my aunt! Her lover must have been killed!'

'Now don't get all sentimental. We're not looking for love letters. What else is in there?'

'Nothing in that file. Let's have a look at another.'

They found an awful lot of ancient household bills which were fascinating, but, Ellie insisted, not relevant, and therefore not to be pored over. There were also some dress patterns and a sheet of paper which told you how to make knickers out of parachute silk. They searched through every file, and Ellie even went through the love letters, just in case.

'Oh. That's a bit disappointing,' said Ellie.

'Sorry.' Grace felt disappointed for Ellie, but hadn't been expecting anything else. 'Do you mind if I just have a look through this stuff?' she said, referring to a pile they hadn't bothered with. 'I know it's probably just bills but there's no point in taking it all back to the stables if I really should have thrown it away. I was in a bit of a state when I stuffed it all in here.'

'No, go ahead. Shall I help you? Quicker if we both do it.'

At first they amused themselves by trying to decipher the disintegrating scraps of paper which described strange items of haberdashery; ribbons and trimmings for giving old hats a new look, but soon they just gave each one a quick glance. Near the bottom of the box Ellie found some letters, tucked into the same bundle as a bill for rebuilding the stable wall, and another, very ancient bill for repairing the panelling in the dining room. It caught Ellie's attention because unlike the others, it didn't have 'paid' written on it.

'Grace,' she said, holding a scrap of paper. 'Could that be anything, do you think? It looks very old.'

Carefully, Grace took the paper. It was brittle and yellow with age and covered in elegant sloping writing, which was pale and almost illegible. 'I don't know. It's very ancient, but it could say almost anything.'

'And it's in with all those old bills – it's probably nothing.'

'Let's take it to the drawing room and look at it under a lamp.'

Both women flew down the passage and across the hall, trying not to get too excited, knowing disappointment was bound to follow.

Grace switched on one of the table lamps.

'I feel sick,' said Ellie.

'You often do. You're pregnant.'

'Read it then.'

Grace put the paper under the light. 'I can't. I need a magnifying glass.'

'Haven't you got one? This is so frustrating!'

'Flynn has. There's one on his desk. Let's go.'

Chapter Twenty-five

Flynn's drive was full of cars, or so it seemed.

'Flynn's back, and he's got guests,' said Grace, nudging her car into a space next to the wall. 'I wonder who?'

'Perhaps I shouldn't come in,' said Ellie, suddenly aware of her clothes, 'I'm filthy.'

Grace looked down at her own long skirt and matching sweater and cardigan, which had looked quite smart when she'd put them on that morning. 'I'm covered in cobwebs too,' she said. 'Never mind. We can sneak in and go into the study. They may not see us, whoever they are.'

'They', or at least one of them, was hanging about in the hall, waiting for Grace and Ellie. It was Demi.

'Oh, hi, Dems!' said Ellie, holding the envelope with the scrap of paper to her as they hugged.

'Is your mother here?' asked Grace, when she too had kissed Demi.

Demi nodded. 'In there. With Flynn.'

'I'll go and say hello,' said Grace with a sinking feeling that good manners should take precedence over her desire to inspect the paper. Flynn had probably been entertaining Hermia for hours, waiting for her return.

Her hand had depressed the handle before she heard Demi say, 'Your sister's there, too!'

'Oh, God,' muttered Grace, and carried on into the room. 'Come with me, Ellie!'

Ellie slid the envelope with the paper under her jumper, and then prepared to follow Grace.

There were three people in the room, and they all looked round as Grace and Ellie entered. Flynn seemed relaxed but his expression warned Grace that she was in for trouble. Allegra was wearing an expression of exasperation which was very familiar. And Demi's mother, Hermia, was looking at her with a strange combination of respect and resentment, which Grace didn't have time to work out.

'Hello, everyone,' said Grace, wondering how Allegra and Hermia had discovered where Flynn lived from just a telephone number.

'Darling, you're horribly dirty,' said Flynn, making this seem like a good thing to be. He walked across the room to kiss Grace's cheek. 'Hi, Ellie.'

'We've been to Luckenham House,' said Ellie. 'Checking on the men doing the dry-rot treatment.'

'Yes . . .' How to explain the dirt? Grace thought frantically. 'I thought I'd left something important in one of the old stables.' Grace hoped no one could see she was blushing. Her heart had leapt so at the warmth of Flynn's welcome that her ability to lie and deceive, which had sharpened up so much lately, had disloyally abandoned her.

Ellie, seeing Grace's reaction, tried frantically to cover for her. 'We were looking for an old bill,' she said, her head full of what they'd found, only aware how odd she'd sounded when she saw everyone looking suspiciously at her.

'Where's Demi disappeared to?' asked Grace, looking round rather desperately.

'I expect she's playing on my computer,' said Flynn. 'Would you two like a drink? We're trying some Madeira. I think you might like it. It's very dry and smooth. Quite unusual, I think. Hermia's brought Demi back to us.'

'She wouldn't stay with me,' said Hermia. 'She's been in a terrible strop. Said she couldn't cope without her computer and got all moody because I wouldn't let her use mine. God, I find teenagers difficult!'

Ellie silently cursed Hermia for being unable to be pleasant to her daughter even for a few days; she'd gone to a lot of trouble to arrange for Flynn and Grace to be alone, and now they wouldn't be any more. But then, Grace had told her that Flynn had said he wouldn't touch her until everything was sorted out, so perhaps it wasn't a total calamity.

'And I'm sure you know why I'm here,' said Allegra crisply. 'I've been talking to Hermia. Grace, you've been lying to me.'

'No, I haven't! What on earth are you talking about?' Grace's indignation was more from guilt than anything, but she thought it sounded quite convincing.

'Sit down, both of you,' said Flynn calmly. 'Ellie, can I get you something soft?'

'No, an ordinary chair will be fine.' The tension had made Ellie flippant.

'I meant to drink!' said Flynn, probably grateful for the light relief. 'I'm not sure what I've got, but there will be something.'

'I'll come with you and choose,' said Ellie. 'Then I want to see what Demi is up to.'

Knowing Flynn would be back as soon as he could, Grace faced the two women who now confronted her.

'Why didn't you tell me about these panels?' demanded Allegra. 'Really, it almost borders on deceit.'

'No, it doesn't! We found some old painted panels, which might be worth something or nothing, and I didn't tell you! For goodness' sake, do you tell me every time you find something you didn't know you had?' Then she realised that this would never happen to Allegra. There was nothing, in any corner of her house, that she didn't know about.

'It's not the same, and you know it,' snapped Allegra, obviously well bolstered up by Hermia in her indignation about Grace's inheritance. 'By rights, those pictures belong to me and Nicholas.'

'No, they don't!' said Grace. 'Or if they do, so do all the doors and windows and skirting boards! They were nailed down!'

'*Were* nailed down? So where are they now?'

To Grace's enormous relief, Flynn and Ellie came back into the room, with a reluctant-looking Demi. 'I'm having them restored. They were nearly attacked by the dry rot.'

'So how are you going to pay for that?' demanded Allegra.

'Allegra! I'm surprised at you, asking me to discuss my personal finances in front of . . .' She indicated Hermia and the others, but realised that however she felt about some of them, she couldn't quite refer to Demi, her mother, Flynn and Ellie as strangers. '. . . non-family members,' she managed eventually.

'I think we practically are family,' said Hermia, enjoying the opportunity to see Grace put on the spot.

'After all, we were married to the same man.'

'But not at the same time,' said Ellie, trying to draw Hermia's fire.

'Whatever the relationships,' said Allegra, dismissing this as a detail, 'we're all adults. I'm sure we can be frank with each other.' She swept the room with the look that controlled every committee she ever sat on, demanding agreement.

Not long ago, Grace would have sighed and complied with her sister's demands, but no longer. 'Oh, come on, Allegra!' she said. 'You were always telling me off about discussing money in public. You said it was vulgar. You can't expect me to disregard all those years of training and do it now.'

'I'm not that much older than you,' said Allegra, glancing at Flynn.

'The ten years did seem a lot when I was a child,' said Grace, feeling cruel, but pleased that she seemed to have managed to shut her sister up for a few minutes.

'Let's all have another drink,' said Flynn.

Ellie glanced at her watch. It was one o'clock. She was starving and she desperately wanted to look at the paper which crackled occasionally from its place under her jumper. 'I really should be getting back—'

'No!' Grace jumped to her feet. 'I promised you lunch! Flynn?' She met his eyes across the room and blushed again. 'Is it all right if I get Ellie something to eat? She's pregnant—'

'I think we know that.' Hermia yawned. 'There's no stigma attached to being an unmarried mother these days.' Her expression revealed that she personally rather regretted the current laxity of society's morals.

'—which means she has to eat regularly.' Grace took

Ellie by the arm and almost dragged her from the room. Once in the kitchen they flopped down at the table.

'My God!' Grace was shaking with rage and frustration. 'I don't believe it! My sister is the giddy limit! She'll claim those pictures if she can!'

'She can't. They were nailed down. Now come on, we need a magnifying glass. Could you go and get one out of the study?'

Grace shook her head. 'Not with them in there! Will Ran have a magnifying glass, do you think?'

'God yes! He's got special glasses with lights in them. You have to have that if you're conserving paintings,' she added, pleased with her new knowledge.

'Then you take it to him,' said Grace, glad to pass the responsibility to someone else. 'Get him to read it. And ring me immediately. I have to know if they are by this Richard Coat-thingy.'

Ellie was affronted. 'I know they are, Grace. I told you about the rabbit.'

'No, you didn't!' Grace was confused. 'What rabbit?'

'Oh.' Ellie dismissed this oversight. 'It's one in the painting in the National Portrait Gallery that is a dead ringer for one in the panels. I told Ran about it, but he's not convinced I could tell one rabbit from another. It's why he's insisting on some sort of proof.'

'Which that bit of paper may not provide!'

'It might! But you're right, it might not.'

'And in a way it would be a good thing if they're not all that valuable,' said Grace, trying to look on the bright side, although Ellie's enthusiasm was infectious and she'd found herself starting to believe the panels might be important. 'I mean, think of the trouble if they really are by this . . .'

'Richard Coatbridge,' helped Ellie.

'Richard Coatbridge!' came a voice from the door that could have reached the back of the stalls, no problem. 'Did you say Richard Coatbridge?' Allegra marched into the kitchen, her high heels pounding threateningly on to the tiled floor.

'It's terribly unlikely,' said Grace.

'Yes, terribly. In fact, Ran – the picture restorer – doesn't think they are for a minute,' said Ellie. 'And now I've got to go.' She looked longingly at the biscuit tin on the side, and then opened it and helped herself to a couple of them which, handily, were already wrapped in cellophane.

Grace shot to her feet. 'Fine! You go. And ring me, if there's any news. About the baby!' she added desperately, wondering what news there could possibly be considering it wasn't due for months.

'I'm having a scan!' said Ellie helpfully.

'I'll come to the hospital with you,' said Grace. 'No, I insist! Is it now?' It was rather grasping at straws, but she really didn't want to be left with her sister.

'No!' Ellie frowned and shook her head as if Grace had gone completely mad. 'But I'll tell you as soon as I know when it is, I promise.'

Grace exhaled as her window of opportunity for escape closed. 'OK. Good. I'll see you out.'

Flynn arrived in the kitchen, possibly in pursuit of Allegra.

'Ellie's just going,' said Grace.

'Oh,' said Flynn.

'Yes. Is it all right if I take these?' Ellie indicated the biscuits.

Flynn seemed confused. 'Yes, yes, of course. But do

you have to rush off? I was going to suggest we all went out for lunch.'

'No, no.' The thought of having lunch in the company of Grace's sister, and Demi's mother, was grisly, even if she hadn't been pregnant; but it was the thought of the bit of paper, as yet unexamined, which made going out to eat really impossible.

'Ellie's got things to do,' said Grace, who was just as anxious to have Ran inspect the scrap through his magnifying glasses with lights in them.

'Right,' said Flynn. 'But, Allegra, you can come out to lunch with us? You and Hermia?' By leaving the kitchen himself, he lured everyone else out.

'Yes. Yes, I think I could.' Allegra smiled, oddly girlish in the presence of Flynn's charm.

Demi, who had come into the hall, looked pained, as if invited to go on a cross-country run in the middle of winter. 'Can I stay here? You've got some really good games.'

'Of course,' said Flynn.

'Perhaps you should ask your mother,' said Allegra.

'Do what you like. There's no pleasure in taking sulky young women out for meals,' snapped Hermia.

Grace sighed, wondering whether if she put on a really good pout, she could ally herself with Demi and not go either.

Ellie felt mean abandoning Grace, but she knew that Grace wanted the paper read as much as she did. Besides, Grace had Flynn to support her. Ellie sighed. Flynn was so lovely. She did hope Grace would realise that he wasn't just someone to have as a short-term boyfriend, but as a partner for ever.

Ran, on the other hand, was specifically designed to be short term, which, if only he'd gone for her original plan of a quick affaire, would have been fine by her. In all likelihood, she'd have been over him by now. But he'd held out, and now she'd gone and fallen in love with him. It was probably because she was pregnant – it had put him on some sort of moral alert. She was sure he wouldn't have turned her down in normal circumstances. She didn't have an exaggerated idea of her own attractiveness, but whenever he forgot his determination to keep his distance he didn't seem able to help flirting with her. It was so confusing. The whole situation was completely pants; she hadn't had a lovely affaire, and was completely preoccupied with Ran, which would mean she wouldn't want to have an affaire with anyone else, and she was running out of time. Men were so selfish sometimes!

Ran took the paper carefully. 'Why is it warm?'

'It's been up my jumper. I was hiding it from Grace's sister. She's heard of Richard Coatbridge.'

'Most people have. It's only you who hasn't. Now, let's get this where we can see it.'

'Mm,' he said later. 'It's part of a letter.'

'But what does it say?' Ellie had been jumping from foot to foot, beside herself with frustration. It was like having your teacher mark a piece of work in your presence.

'Obviously, most of it is missing . . .'

'Yes!'

'But what there is left says: *called away*, then there's a splodge, but there's quite a clear bit. . . . *not to embarrass your servants, I have concealed two panels behind the*

413

curtains. I will collect them on my next visit . . . Then it just goes on about the weather and something about paying for something.'

'But is there a signature?'

'No. Not on this scrap of paper, there isn't. Are you sure you've got it all?'

'Yes. We were very thorough. We were quite pleased to get that bit.' Ellie felt deflated. All that work, all that searching, the reward of actually finding something, and now the 'something' wasn't enough.

'It's still useful. What we need is someone to tell us whether Richard Coatbridge was known to visit Luckenham House.'

'He says "on my next visit".'

'The person who painted the panels did. It's just checking who that is.'

'I wish you'd look at the painting. If you could just see the rabbit . . .'

'Ellie, I do believe you. It's just getting a bit of proof.'

'But surely an expert could tell if the panels were by Richard Coatbridge?'

'Experts have been known to make mistakes, but yes, I'm sure an expert could.'

'And you can't be our expert?'

'No.'

Ellie felt very tired. 'More research? Finding the expert we need?'

'I'm afraid so.' He looked at her. 'Have you had lunch?'

'I've had biscuits. With bits of ginger in them. Very nice.'

'But not lunch. Let's go and eat.'

'I must ring Grace first.'

'Ring her mobile while we're waiting to be served.'

'I told you, Grace hasn't got a mobile. And they were going out to eat, too, and won't be back for hours. Damn! I know, I'll ring Flynn's mobile.'

Grace took Flynn's mobile into the Ladies to talk to Ellie. It was too cold to stand outside.

'So there's nothing on it that says who did the panels?'

'No, I'm afraid not. But it does mention hiding the panels behind the curtains, and coming to collect them next time he visited.'

'So it definitely links whoever wrote that letter with the panels?'

'Yes.'

'So we need a graphologist. To check whose handwriting it is.'

'Oh, Grace, don't you think everyone's handwriting looked the same back then?'

'Well, I do, but I'm not a handwriting expert.'

'Ran thinks we need a Richard Coatbridge expert.'

'And how do you find one of them? Oh. Hello, Hermia,' said Grace. 'Ellie, I must go. I'll ring you when we get back.'

'Was that about your friend's scan?' asked Hermia, obviously sure that it wasn't.

'No.' Grace swallowed.

'Grace, I really do think you're behaving badly over this painting. You got far more from your aunt than your brother and sister, and Edward left you very well provided for. Not to mention the money he's giving you for looking after Demeter.'

'Hermia, this is none of your business and anyway, I refuse to discuss it in the Ladies' lavatory!'

Grace stalked out, feeling that perhaps all Allegra's

415

indoctrination about how to behave hadn't been wasted after all.

But Allegra herself would be harder to deal with. Back at the table, she looked ready for battle. All through the meal Flynn and Grace had managed to keep the conversation away from the subject of the paintings, but now, with Allegra and Hermia deeply into the coffee, Grace knew she would have to talk about them.

She took a sip of the prophylactic brandy that Flynn had ordered her in case things got really sticky.

'Well,' demanded Allegra. 'Are you going to come clean?'

'Allegra! I have not been deceiving you!'

'Haven't you? Then how come I had to hear about the paintings from Hermia, because Demeter told her?

'Did Edward know about the panels?' Allegra went on. 'He lived here for some years!'

'I know, but we never drew the curtains. He liked the fact that the curtains were so old, and therefore very fragile.'

'I find that very hard to believe!'

'The truth often is,' said Grace quietly, taking another sip of the brandy.

'Because there was nothing to say about them. They could have been nothing. You wouldn't expect me to tell you if I found graffiti on the walls of the privy!'

'That's not at all the same,' said Allegra crisply. 'And you know it.'

Grace did know it, but wasn't going to concede totally at this stage. 'OK.' She nodded calmly. 'So it's not exactly the same, but how would you have reacted if I rang you up and told you I'd found some panels, falling apart, behind the curtains in the dining room?'

'If you thought they were totally unimportant why were you so secretive about them?' asked Hermia.

'Secretive?' Grace was playing for time.

'Yes. Demeter was really upset when she realised she'd mentioned them to me.'

'So you immediately mentioned them to Allegra?'

'Yes! She's my friend!'

Grace sighed.

'I think what Grace is trying to say' – Flynn's calm, deep tones came down like a blanket over a parrot's cage of shrillness – 'is that until she knew what she was telling you about, Allegra' – he put slight emphasis on her name for a second, in a way Grace knew Allegra would find very attractive – 'there was no point in telling you anything. I know she planned to tell you the moment she had a bit more information.'

'And have you got more information now?' Allegra might not have been lulled completely, but she was a bit less strident.

'A little, yes,' said Grace. 'But not much.'

'Well, share it. I promised Nicholas I'd get all the information I could out of you.'

Flynn's eyebrow rose in a way that reminded Grace of Edward when he was displeased. 'Allegra, I'm sure you didn't mean to express yourself in quite such a haranguing way. Grace hasn't done anything wrong, you know.'

'She has been devious, Flynn. I'm sorry to say it, but she has.' Now Allegra sounded sulky, and it gave Grace courage.

'Very well, Allegra, I'll tell you everything we've discovered to date. OK? I found the panels, but had no clue about them, which is why I asked Ellie to ask her friend who is a picture conservator—'

'A what?'

'Restorer' – nothing about Ellie's hunt through the *Yellow Pages* and her frantic tales about wanting to do a work placement – 'to give his opinion. He had to take them away to look at them properly, and to stop them being attacked by the dry rot.'

'I thought they were nailed down,' said Allegra.

'They were.'

'So how did he get them out?' asked Hermia. 'If they're movable, they belong to Allegra.'

'I don't know how he got them out,' said Grace. 'I wasn't there. I imagine he used some sort of tool.'

'Don't you think you should have been supervising this procedure?' said Hermia.

'I dare say she would have done if she hadn't been spending the night in hospital with your daughter,' said Flynn.

'Flynn!'

'What?' Any cup less robust would have shattered as Hermia dropped it into its saucer. 'You said you just went to have a cut treated!'

Flynn ignored Grace's protest and continued calmly, 'I know Grace promised Demi she wouldn't say anything as long as Demi never did anything remotely like that ever again, but the night Demi's friend rang you she was actually very ill. We took her to hospital and stayed with her in A and E most of the night.'

'Grace! That's appalling! Keeping something like that from Hermia! It almost amounts to child abuse!' Allegra was incandescent with outrage on her friend's behalf.

As Grace did feel extremely guilty, she didn't prevaricate. 'I am sorry, Hermia. I know it was very wrong of me. And I'll quite understand if you think you should take Demi back home with you.'

'You certainly don't deserve to have her, deceiving Hermia like that!' Allegra managed to make Demi sound like an unruly puppy allowed to wreak havoc and then sent back.

'I didn't actually ask to have her, you know,' Grace pointed out gently.

A look of horror passed across Hermia's face as she contemplated having Demi home on a permanent basis. 'I think that might be overreacting, Allegra. After all, there was no permanent damage. And, quite honestly, life is very much easier without her.'

Relieved, but still wounded on Demi's behalf, Grace said rather acidly, 'It's a good thing I don't feel like that, isn't it?'

'It's so much easier for you. You're not her mother.' At which Hermia, whom Grace had always seen as a health fanatic, took out a packet of cigarettes and proceeded to light one.

While Allegra appeared to be wondering how to react to her friend's sudden departure from her normal behaviour, Flynn put a hand on Grace's shoulder. 'Drink your brandy, darling,' he murmured, 'and leave these appalling women to me.'

Grace was very tempted, but she'd always let Edward protect her and, ultimately, it hadn't done her any good. 'No,' she murmured back. 'I must fight my own battles.'

'Well, I'm here for you if you need back-up.'

Hermia inhaled deeply. 'Look at what the wretched girl's done to me! I haven't had a cigarette for years!'

'Well, I hope you haven't had the same effect on Demi,' said Grace. 'I made her swear not to smoke anything, and only drink under supervision.' She couldn't remember exactly what she had made Demi promise, but as no one could contradict her, she felt fairly safe.

'We're getting off the point,' said Allegra. 'I think we should have a family meeting. Get Nicholas down.'

'What for?' asked Grace.

'To discuss these paintings. To decide who owns them.'

'Oh, Grace owns them,' said Flynn firmly. 'There's absolutely no doubt about that. I used to be a solicitor, and I know that for a fact. They were nailed down, you see.'

'Oh,' said Allegra after a moment's consideration.

'But, of course, if they do turn out to be valuable . . .' said Grace, not sure how she meant to go on.

'Well, why can't we find out?' demanded Allegra, still keen, even if she had accepted they weren't half hers.

'We've done some research, found a bit of paper, but we're still not certain who painted them.'

'But you think they might be by Richard Coatbridge?'

'Goodness!' said Hermia, impressed.

'We've only got initials. And Ellie is convinced that a rabbit she saw in a painting in London is almost identical to one in the panels.'

'Oh,' said Allegra, not impressed.

'So we need a Richard Coatbridge expert, who knows his movements, and who can recognise his handwriting. We've got a scrap of paper. We found it in the stables.'

Allegra looked at her watch and took charge. 'Right. I'll see to that. Give me the telephone number of this picture restorer. I'll get decent slides and a copy of the letter. Leave this to me! We're going to get the proper amount for those panels, or I shall die in the attempt.'

While Hermia and Allegra went to the Ladies, probably to discuss Grace and Flynn, Grace said, 'At least she said "we", so perhaps she is including me.'

Flynn chuckled.

'And were you really a solicitor? I didn't know that.'

'God, no, I made that up. But I'm sure it's true about you owning the paintings. Part of the fabric of the house.' Then he kissed the top of her head. The feel of his breath so near her ear gave her delicious shivers.

'But I'm going to sell them, they can't be part of the fabric of the house.' Then she sighed as he put his hand on her knee.

'Don't worry, the house won't fall down without them.'

Chapter Twenty-six

⚜

Later that afternoon, Ran received a telephone call from Allegra. The moment she realised who it was, Ellie went and made herself useful in the kitchen by knocking up a batch of cheese straws, having read somewhere that they were the fast track to a man's heart. She felt embarrassed that it was indirectly because of her that he had to deal with such an annoying woman.

Fortunately Ran was accustomed to dealing with annoying women and came into the kitchen a little later appearing his usual calm, cynical self.

'I'm so sorry about that,' said Ellie, rolling pastry. 'She's a nightmare.'

'She had some very good ideas and is prepared to go to quite a lot of trouble to find out all she can about the panels,' said Ran, being irritatingly reasonable.

'Only so they'll be worth more!' Ellie refused to give Allegra credit for anything. 'I'm sure she's trying to claim them as hers.'

'She said not, that Flynn had told her they definitely belong to Grace, because they were nailed down.'

'Pity it didn't occur to Grace to nail down some of the furniture, although I'm not sure exactly how you'd do that. Can you pass me the big knife?'

'You're always cooking. If I lived with you permanently I'd get as fat as a pig.'

Ellie concentrated on scoring straight lines in the cheese pastry. Was he telling her, yet again, to give up hope with regard to him? Just as well he didn't realise that she'd surrendered her free will with regard to him ages ago. 'I don't think so,' she said. 'You're a thin type.'

'And I'm unlikely to live with you permanently.'

Now he was definitely telling her something, but not anything she didn't know – in her head, at least. She looked up. 'So is she going to come here and look at the panels? If so, I'll arrange to be out.'

'There's no point in her doing that. I'm going to send her slides and a copy of the letter, such as it is. I've given her a few names which might be helpful, then she's going to find out who the expert on Richard Coatbridge is, and he'll come and look at them.'

'Or she. It could be a woman, you know.' Ran had sexist tendencies that had to be suppressed.

'Or she,' he agreed without argument. 'What are you going to do with those strips of pastry?'

'You'll see. The telephone's ringing.'

She had the cheese straws in the oven by the time he came back to say the phone call was for her.

It was the doctor's surgery. 'They've had a cancellation,' said Ellie as she came back into the kitchen after taking the call. 'They can do my scan tomorrow. Isn't that good?' she added to disguise the fact that she felt a bit scared. 'I must ring Grace.'

'Why?'

'Because she's going to come with me. For support, you know. So I don't feel so much like a single mother.'

Ran frowned. 'Do you mind being a single mother?'

Ellie shrugged. 'I don't suppose it's ideal, but it's the

only sort of mother I've had any experience of being.'

'And you're OK about it?'

'I think so. There's no point in being anything different, is there?'

'But you still want support?'

'Yes.' She frowned. 'Does that make me seem very pathetic?'

'Of course not. Ring Grace. And when will those things be edible?'

'When the pinger goes. Can you take them out of the oven for me, in case I get held up?'

Grace was excited about the thought of Ellie's scan being so soon.

'I've been lucky. They've fitted me in because they need to find out when I'm due,' said Ellie. 'Can you be here for eleven?'

'Of course. It'll give me time to take Demi to the bus, and then I've got to nip home to see the dry-rot people off and then I'll come straight down.'

'I'm quite annoyed with Demi for coming back,' said Ellie cautiously. 'I told her why she should go and stay with her mother.'

'And she did go, but we've had a long chat and it really is miserable for her there. She tried to stick it out but she just couldn't. She burst into tears when she apologised.'

'You're too soft for your own good,' said Ellie.

'So are you,' countered Grace.

Ellie laughed. 'So you'll be down in good time? We need plenty of time to park and I've got to drink lots of fluid so I have a full bladder.'

'You always seem to have a full bladder.'

'Not really. I just need to wee a lot – not quite the

same. How are you and Flynn getting on?'

'Fine. He's so easy to be with . . .' She paused.

'Not like Edward, you mean?'

'Mm. I was always on edge with Edward, trying to please him, trying to live up to his expectations. With Flynn it's, well, easy.'

'Like the comfortable old slippers you put on after the killer heels?' Ellie thought lovingly of the Snoopy slippers she had gone on wearing long after the toes were worn through.

'Not sure about that. He's a lot more exciting than slippers.'

Ellie would have liked to prod more, but decided the telephone was not ideal for such intimacies. She was still annoyed that her plan for them to be alone had been messed up by Hermia. It was more than likely that Grace didn't feel she could sleep with Flynn while Demi was staying. Ellie wouldn't have felt like that herself, but she was fairly sure that Grace was more sensitive.

That evening Grace and Flynn ate supper at the kitchen table. Demi had taken a tray up to her room so she could watch a video, although Grace suspected it was an excuse to leave her and Flynn alone together.

Grace had cooked spaghetti and tomato sauce and insisted on putting candles on the table. 'If I had a Chianti bottle, in a nice raffia coat, I'd have used that, but I've managed to make do with this old candelabra,' she said.

'Which, being Georgian silver, is quite pretty.'

'Quite pretty,' she agreed.

'Unlike you, who are very pretty.'

Grace straightened the mat by way of reply, not meeting his gaze.

'It looks very appetising,' Flynn went on bracingly. 'Good thing I ate a lot of lunch.'

That made Grace look at him. 'Thank you for that vote of confidence in my culinary skills.'

'A pleasure,' he said calmly, looking into her eyes in a way that made Grace look away again.

'Ellie rang,' she said brightly, trying to change the mood. 'Her scan's tomorrow. I'm going to go to it with her. Just for moral support.'

Flynn smiled, his eyes crinkling at the corners so that his curly eyelashes mingled, but somehow managed not to tangle. Grace wondered why she hadn't noticed the way they did this before.

'That'll be interesting for you. Will you go and have something to eat afterwards?'

'I expect so. I'll take Demi to the bus, then pop over to Luckenham House to say goodbye to the men and then go down to Bath.' She paused. 'When the men have gone I can move back in.'

There was a moment of something: it could have been hurt; and then he said, 'You don't have to. You could stay here.'

'I can't stay here indefinitely,' she said awkwardly. 'I've trespassed on your hospitality long enough.'

Flynn laughed. 'I bet you've never trespassed in your life. I bet if you see a notice by a wood saying "Private", you move right on, and don't put even your little toe across the boundary.'

'Well, yes. I am very law-abiding.'

'And you're no trouble to have to stay. You clear up after yourself, the cat likes you, and you even cook.' He

426

indicated the pasta and tomato sauce and made a perfect coil of spaghetti. 'After all, if I've got Demi here, you might as well be, too.'

'I would take Demi with me! That's one of the reasons I should go, Demi coming back.' She laughed. 'Honestly, we can't both stay here for ever.'

He was quite serious. 'But you can both stay as long as you like – until Luckenham House is properly habitable, anyway.'

'It'll be properly habitable tomorrow,' Grace insisted gently. 'The moment the men have gone.'

'I don't mean by your standards of habitability' – he made a dismissive gesture – 'but by the rest of the world's. Central heating, furniture, perhaps the odd carpet?'

'Carpets?' Grace was shocked. 'On my beautiful wide elm boards?'

'The odd rug, then. But seriously, wouldn't it be much easier to decorate, to set it to rights, if it was empty?'

'As you've so often pointed out, it is empty – enough to make slapping on a couple of coats of emulsion easy, anyway.'

'Is that all you want to do to it?'

Grace considered. 'Well, no. Since staying here I've realised that a few home comforts are, well, comfortable, but I've managed without them so long, and I've never had any money—'

'You might soon be going to have quite a lot of money.'

'I doubt it. Once I've paid for the dry rot and given Allegra and Nicholas a cut—'

'You're going to do that?'

'Oh yes. Money's not that important to me and it is

427

to them. As long as those panels earn me enough to pay my debts and my siblings, I can manage without under-floor heating in the kitchen.'

'Hmm. Not sure that I can.'

'What do you mean?'

'Nothing. I was just thinking that if I was going to live there, I'd need a bit more background warmth.'

Grace nodded. 'I know what you mean. I might put a wood-burner in the hall, if I can find a chimney.'

Flynn sighed. 'You're not very good at taking hints, are you?'

'Aren't I? What are you talking about? You don't want to live in Luckenham House! You've made this house perfect and you love it. You're not going to want to up sticks and live in my draughty old barn even if . . .'

He only let her flounder for a moment before he said, 'Shall we change the subject?'

'Oh, please let's!' She smiled and thought again how easy he was to be with, even when things were difficult.

The next morning Grace made Demi breakfast, and she ate it very tidily and politely, on her best behaviour in front of Flynn.

'I don't know why Hermia finds you so difficult,' he said to her. 'You're a dream child.'

The dream child broke her vow of good manners sufficiently to poke her tongue out at him and said, 'Thank you, Grace, that was great. I'll just run up and get my stuff.'

'She likes it here,' said Flynn. 'Look how well she behaves.'

'She won't be able to keep it up, and being the parent of teenagers is very hard. Much better to start on babies and work your way up.' Grace, thinking of Ellie's scan, suffered a sudden pang of broodiness.

'You're managing OK with a teenager.'

'Yes, but I'm not old. I can still remember what it was like and empathise.'

'Cheek!' he said as she scooped up the dirty dishes and carried them to the dishwasher.

'You see, you're getting impatient already.'

He came up behind her at the sink and put his arms round her. 'Yes, I am, actually,' he murmured into her ear, causing her to catch her breath with sudden longing.

The thought of Flynn's strong arms and sexy voice warmed Grace as she drove Demi to the bus and then went on to Luckenham House.

It looked wonderful in the bright spring sunshine, and the garden was just stirring into life with early primroses spangling the banks with yellow stars. 'I know why I want to live here,' said Grace to herself. 'It's a beautiful house.'

But latterly, though its beauty remained constant, its suitability as a home had been challenged. Possibly it lacked certain things she had become accustomed to very quickly since living at Flynn's house.

The men seemed satisfied with what they'd done, and proudly showed Grace where they had made good the walls. When she had seen them safely off in their van, she went into the kitchen to see the newly plumbed-in Rayburn.

But something was wrong. It took her a moment to work out what, and then she realised: there was a puddle of water on the floor, yards away from the sink.

At first she didn't think much about it and was about

to get a mop when it occurred to her to wonder where the puddle was coming from. She looked up and saw the sort of bulge made famous in advertisements for the *Yellow Pages*. She knew, without any experience or technical know-how, that the ceiling would come down at any moment unless she did something.

She ignored her instinct to ring Flynn. She was going to be independent and sort it out herself. If it went wrong she could ring him, but he mustn't be her first line of defence. No man must ever be that again.

If she wanted the ceiling to stay up she had to let the water out. She found a broom, stood on a chair, and very gingerly prodded the swelling. Water and what seemed like half a ton of plaster poured on to the kitchen floor, drenching her. But she did notice that the water was warm.

It took her a few moments to stop spluttering and gasping. 'That was a mistake,' she noted aloud. 'Perhaps I'd better go and see why all that water was there. Or should I go and change first?'

Then she remembered Ellie. Could she abandon the house for the sake of her friend? Of course she could. The house didn't have feelings, and Ellie did. She would ring Ellie and tell her that she might be a little bit late, but that she would be there, just as soon as she had changed, found out where the leak was coming from and turned off the water.

'Ellie? It's me. I'm at the house.' She was starting to shiver. 'There's a bit of a problem. But don't worry!' she hurried on. 'I'm still coming. I've just got to change my clothes and may have to get a plumber first.' A hot bath would have been nice, but there wouldn't be time for that.

'What's happened? It sounds dreadful!'

'Well, I came into the kitchen to find a puddle on the floor and a big balloon of plaster hanging from the ceiling. I poked it with a broom and it all came down.'

'Oh dear. You probably shouldn't have done that. At least, not without an umbrella.'

'That's the conclusion I've come to now, but it seemed the best thing to do at the time. Anyway, I'm just ringing to warn you I might be a bit late.'

'I don't think you should leave the house in that condition.'

Grace laughed. 'It's not pregnant, you are.'

'No,' Ellie agreed. 'But unlike the kitchen ceiling, my waters haven't broken, which sounds like what's happened.'

'I know, but—'

'Look, don't worry, Grace, it's only a scan,' said Ellie calmly. 'I'll be fine on my own. As long as you promise to be with me when I have the baby.'

'Ellie! I'm not sure I'm up to that!'

Now it was Ellie who chuckled. 'It's OK, you can read all the books beforehand so you'll know what to do. But, seriously, you don't need to come with me. You sort out the ceiling. Let me know how you get on.'

'Are you sure?'

'Positive. It's no big deal, really it isn't. You can come with me next time I have one.'

Eventually, Ellie convinced Grace that her presence wasn't necessary. Ran came in as she was finishing the conversation.

'That was Grace. The kitchen ceiling's come down and soaked her to the skin. I've told her not to come. I'll be fine on my own, and she's got to sort out plumbers and

431

things.' She concentrated very hard on making her voice matter-of-fact, hiding her disappointment and anxiety.

'Right.' Ran's voice was just as bland. 'Well, that's OK. I'll come with you.'

'Sorry?'

'I'll come with you for the scan. For support.'

She was horribly embarrassed, and cross with herself for not hiding her anxiety better. 'But, Ran—'

'To stop you feeling so much like a single parent? Remember?'

Why had she ever told him all that? It was all coming back to haunt her. 'Really, it's not necessary,' she said firmly. 'I can go by myself. It's no big deal.'

'Unless you'd prefer a woman, of course.'

Ellie suddenly wanted to cry. It was her hormones, of course. Ran was only being kind, offering to fill in for Grace, but her heart had leapt, even hearing him make the offer. And did she want him there? Did she want Ran sitting by her while they put KY jelly on her stomach and swooped about on it with a sort of iron, or would it be terribly embarrassing? She closed her eyes. Yes, she decided, she always wanted Ran with her.

'It's really not necessary,' she repeated, hoping he'd ignore her.

'That's decided then. Tell me when we need to be there. And do you have to bring anything?'

'Thank you—' she began, but he cut her off.

'Oh shut up.' He smiled, just slightly, and very lop-sidedly, but it made Ellie sigh.

Why did she like him so much? He was bossy, very bossy. Old – well, ten years older than her, and look what had happened to Grace when she married an older man! He broke her heart! Not that that was an option for her, of course. Ran was the man who'd turned down the offer of a fling; he would probably never get married, just glide from sophisticated woman to sophisticated woman, with no upset, no unpleasant scenes and, probably, no babies. No wonder he didn't want her. But he was kind to her, very kind.

She picked up a leftover cheese straw and her hormones had their usual, lachrymose effect. As she sniffed, reached for the kitchen towel and buried her nose in it, she allowed a flicker of reality to penetrate: of course she was thinking of marriage; why else was she baking for him, cleaning for him, generally making herself indispensable, quite apart from doing the things she was there to do, if not to convince him that having her around was a good thing? She shook her head hard, like a wet dog, and then did the washing up.

Ellie fought off the feeling of being protected and looked after that walking from the car to the hospital with Ran beside her gave her. She couldn't afford feelings like that. They were only temporary; she mustn't get used to them.

In her effort to keep a distance from him, she kept bumping into him, as if she couldn't walk straight. By the time they had found the right department, walking several miles in the process, she was desperate to go to the loo. She had found one and sat down before she remembered about the full bladder. But nothing could stop her now, and she only remembered about bringing a urine sample when the last drops had descended.

She washed her hands, feeling a fool on many levels. At least they were early, and there might be time to make reparation.

'I'm so sorry,' she said to the woman at the desk, hoping Ran had gone suddenly deaf, 'I've just been to the loo. And I forgot to bring a sample. My appointment's at quarter past.'

The woman sighed and produced a paper cup and a sample tube. 'Go to the cafeteria and drink as much as you can. But do the sample before you're desperate, and then drink some more. It's really important that you have a full bladder.'

Ran's expression – amusement, bafflement and, strangely, sympathy – made Ellie smile. 'To the cafeteria then?' he said.

'Be back in half an hour. Otherwise you'll miss your appointment. You're lucky we're running a bit late.'

Ellie fought back a childish desire to giggle. 'Yes,' she said, narrowly avoiding adding 'miss'.

'It was silly of me to forget about the full bladder thing,' she went on as they negotiated the many corridors to the cafeteria.

'Well, never mind. I'm sure we can soon fill it up again. Goodness me, look at those people out there.'

He indicated a couple of people sitting in wheelchairs, buried in blankets, hooked up to all sorts of drips and machines, smoking.

'Did you used to smoke, Ran?'

'Uh huh. Still do, in my dreams.'

'It's awfully silly to smoke, especially when you're ill, but I did always suspect that smokers have more fun.'

'It may seem like that, but it isn't really. Ah, it's down here. Now, what do you fancy drinking? Not coffee, obviously. Tea? Something cold and fizzy?'

Ellie settled for tea and got through two cups of the

not-quite-hot-enough brew before she retreated to the Ladies with her cup and her bottle.

'So, is your bladder still full?' asked Ran in what seemed to be a very loud voice.

'No! Of course not! I can't just do a sample and then stop! I'm sure I should be able to, but you'd need to train for it, and I haven't.'

'Have another cup of tea, then.'

'Lager always makes me want to pee very quickly after I've drunk it.'

'Let's sneak off to the pub, then.'

'Good idea! I've done my sample, so they shouldn't be able to tell.'

They hurried out of the building, through the miles of corridors, Ellie feeling horribly furtive, as if she was escaping from something. The woman at the desk had obviously triggered ideas about prison warders, compulsory cold showers and enemas. Fortunately there was a pub right opposite the hospital.

'A pint of lager and a half a Guinness,' said Ran. 'And a packet of crisps.'

'I'll never drink a whole pint! Not in ten minutes! And I really shouldn't be drinking alcohol while I'm pregnant.'

'I'm sure it can't do you that much harm. Now drink up.'

'It's hard to drink when you're not thirsty.'

'Not for lots of people, it isn't. It's depressingly easy. Have a crisp. It'll inspire you.'

Ellie took a couple of large gulps, paused, and then took another couple. 'It's silly, but I really feel I'm drowning.' She concealed a belch behind her hand. 'Oh no. That's all I need. Wind!'

'Come on, drink up.'

Manfully, she got about half a pint of lager down.
'Is your bladder full?'

Ellie shrugged. 'It doesn't feel it, but I'm sure it will by the time I get back to the unit. You know how it is, you go to the loo before you leave the pub, but you're still bursting to go by the time you get home.' She frowned. 'Oh. That's not what we're talking about, is it?'

'Not quite. But I'm not taking any chances. Have another go at finishing your drink.'

'Ran,' she suggested, 'you're not trying to get me drunk so you can have your evil way with me?'

'In your dreams, sweetheart. Now drink up.'

Ellie was not only bursting to go to the loo, but also felt distinctly tipsy by the time she got back to the fierce woman at the desk. She handed over her sample, relieved it would be mostly caffeine and not lager.

'We're running even later, I'm afraid,' said the woman. 'Just sit down over there. Won't be long.'

Ellie sat down, grateful the chairs were made of plastic. 'I hope I don't have to wait long, I'm bursting!'

'Well, cross your legs or something. I'm not taking you to the pub again.'

'I'm not supposed to cross my legs. The doctor told me it would give me varicose veins or thrombosis or something.'

Ran sighed. 'Press your knees together then. It would be good practice for you.' His dry tone belied the twinkle in his eye.

'Ran! You are so unfair!' she squeaked. 'Does it show that I'm drunk,' she added, in a stage whisper that wasn't as quiet as she'd intended it to be.

'Not if you don't tell everyone, it doesn't.'

'Have you got a mint, or something? I don't want them to smell it on my breath. They'll take the baby away at birth and put it in rehab.'

'What are you talking about?'

'I may be getting muddled up with the babies of heroin addicts. Not alcoholics.'

'You are not an alcoholic! Haven't you got anything in your bag? Girls always have sweets in their bags.'

'I am not a girl,' said Ellie solemnly, 'I'm a pregnant woman. But I might have something minty in there.' She opened her bag and rummaged about for a few moments. 'I can't seem to see anything. You look.'

He took hold of her bag. 'Ah, here we are,' he said, triumphantly producing an indigestion tablet. 'It was behind the hot tap.'

'What? Don't confuse me. It's not fair.'

'Behind the hot tap of the kitchen sink you've got in there.'

Ellie took the tablet and her bag back sulkily. 'It's all useful stuff.'

'Well, I'm sure there is a use for till receipts, but I've never found one.'

'Ah ha!' she said triumphantly. 'I keep those so you can pay me back for the groceries I buy.'

'But I do pay you back.'

'But you only take my word for it. You should have the receipt.'

'You don't lie to me, do you?'

'No,' she said, almost on a sob. 'Ran, if I don't go to the loo soon, I'm going to die.'

He put his arm round her and held her to him. 'Not long now, poppet. You just clench yourself together and think of England.'

'But England's awfully wet,' she muttered into his coat.

When her name was finally called, she didn't think she could walk without Ran's support. Somehow she got to the desk.

'You wait here, Ran. I don't suppose I'll be long,' she said.

'Nonsense,' said the nice, smiley woman in the white coat who had appeared to collect her. 'I'm sure he wants to see the baby. Don't you?' she asked Ran.

'Yes, I do. I've done all the boring part,' he said firmly. 'I don't want to miss out on the main event.'

'But he's not the father . . .'

The woman paused. 'Who are you then?'

'I'm a close friend and a responsible adult. Come along, Ellie.'

Chapter Twenty-seven

❧❧❧

Relieved of scan duty by Ellie, Grace contemplated her situation. She was beginning to get extremely cold. She had clothes upstairs, but not many as most of her things were at Flynn's. Besides, she couldn't find where she should turn the water off. And Flynn would know of a plumber who wouldn't rip her off. She decided to go home.

The thought alone shocked her. She'd thought of Flynn's house as home! She paused in turning her car round. No, it wasn't the house that was home, it was Flynn.

He happened to be in the hall when she opened the front door. The moment he had taken in what she looked like, he laughed.

'It's not funny! I'm soaked to the skin and freezing to death!'

'It is funny. You've got plaster all over you. What happened?'

'It's all your fault!' said Grace. 'Or Pete's.'

'What is? Shall we continue this conversation in the bathroom?'

She allowed herself to be led upstairs while she related her grievances. 'I just went into the kitchen to see the Rayburn – which was alight – and noticed a puddle on the kitchen floor. It was coming from the ceiling!'

'What was? Come into my bathroom, it's bigger.'

'The water! There was a huge bulge in the ceiling, dripping. I had to do something.'

'And you poked it with a broom? Here, I'll turn on the taps. And you might like some bubbles or something.'

'How did you guess about the broom? Anyway, it all came down on top of me.'

'That's awful.' He was unbuttoning her cardigan and pulling off her jumper, murmuring, as if he were grooming a horse.

'And I didn't know where to turn the water off, so it's still dripping on to the kitchen floor.'

'That's so dreadful.' He lifted her feet so she could step out of her skirt.

'Just as well it's got good honest tiles on it, and no poncy under-floor heating!'

'That is a good thing.' He eased off her shoes, one by one.

'I'll have to get the ceiling replastered now.'

'Mm. You will.' He slid her tights and pants easily down over her hips.

Without really noticing how it happened, Grace found herself naked, in his arms. 'It'll be an awful job painting it,' she said, trying for insouciance.

'It will,' he agreed politely 'Now, what would you like in your bath, bubbles or bath oil?'

'Flynn, why do you have these things in your bathroom? Is there something you haven't told me?'

'Well, yes. I bought them specially, in the hope I might lure you in here someday soon. So which do you want?'

'Bubbles, please.'

'OK.' He poured in a generous amount and then

440

dipped his hand into the bath and agitated the water. 'Is that too hot for you?'

She sighed and allowed him to hand her into the bath. 'That's lovely. Don't you think you should give me some privacy?'

'No, actually. I think I should get you something to drink.'

She slid down into the water and felt its blissful water work its magic on her chilly limbs. 'A drink would be too decadent. It's only about ten.'

'Eleven actually. Darling, I'm just going to pop downstairs and make a phone call, put my life on hold. I'll be right back.'

'OK.' She slid further down the bath, revelling in the wonderful heat of the water, aware that it was much bigger than the bath in the spare room. She closed her eyes, thinking that she mustn't be tempted to doze off. The last few days had been quite stressful and she hadn't been sleeping all that well.

'Hey, don't go to sleep.' She opened her eyes again and saw Flynn, naked, holding a bottle and two glasses.

'What's all this?' She tried to sit up and protest, but couldn't quite manage it. He had joined her in the bath and handed her a glass of champagne before she'd thought out what to say. By then, there seemed no point in protesting. She took a sip. 'Oh, that's quite nice.'

'It ought to be. It was very expensive.'

'Doesn't mean a thing,' she said. 'What are we celebrating?'

'Oh, I don't know. What would you like to celebrate?'

'Well, my kitchen ceiling is on the floor, making my house unlivable in—'

'I'll drink to that!'

'That's not fair. It's my kitchen. I'll have to redecorate it.'

'I'll drink to that, too.'

'And my house! I can't stay in it!'

'No. You'll have to go on staying with me. Have some more champagne.'

She took another sip. 'Are you trying to get me drunk?'

'Not drunk, just relaxed.'

'I am relaxed.'

'Good.' He took her glass away and put the bottle and both glasses out of the way. 'Then close your eyes.'

Up to her neck in warm water, Grace shut her eyes as bidden. She knew she couldn't slip under the water now Flynn was there to prevent it and it was nice, feeling his warm limbs entangled with hers. Nice, and quite sexy.

Flynn took hold of one of Grace's feet. 'Hey! What are you doing? That tickles!'

'I'm kissing your toes,' he said, and then kissed each one. 'It's the only part of you I can reach just now.'

'Oh,' she said. 'No one's ever kissed my toes before. Oh,' she said again as he took one into his mouth. 'That's very— Oh, my goodness . . .'

'I think we'd better get out,' he said a few moments later. 'I'd hate to drown you.'

It was an easy transition as the floor was thickly carpeted and there were lots of very large towels to hand so it wasn't too hard. Flynn was, Grace decided when her brain was connected again, a very imaginative lover.

The champagne was less cold now, but still delicious. 'Did you plan this?' asked Grace.

'Plan what? Making love to you on my bathroom floor? Plan is putting it a bit strong, but fantasise, definitely.'

She giggled. 'Strange!'

'Not at all. I've thought about making love to you in every room in this house. Except the larder. Oh, and the downstairs cloakroom.'

'Honestly! Do you think about nothing else?'

'Only enough to get by. I'm very much in love with you.'

Grace pulled a corner of towel over her and buried her face in her champagne for a moment. 'It's probably just a sexual attraction.'

'Don't knock it! Besides, it isn't.'

'What?'

'Just a sexual attraction. I fell in love with you when making love to you was about as likely and as comfortable as making love to a thorn bush.'

'I wasn't that prickly, surely.'

'No, but you had a protective hedge about you which would have defied leprechauns. Invisible to everyone but me, naturally.'

'Naturally.'

'So . . .' He paused. 'I know I'm risking getting an answer I don't like, but . . . how do you feel about me?'

She closed her eyes and thought about it. She wanted to tell him exactly, and accurately, how she felt. It had taken her some time to work out in her head. She didn't want to make a mistake translating it into words. 'It's hard to say, and I'm not always very good at expressing myself, but when I was all soaking wet and miserable in the kitchen, I wanted to come home. Then I thought: But this is my home. And although it is, definitely, I realised that what I meant was, home is where you are.'

'Oh. Right. I think that qualifies as a satisfactory answer.' They didn't speak again for some time.

'So if you think I should sell Luckenham House,' she said later, when she'd sat up and finished her champagne, 'I will.'

He tucked a strand of hair behind her ear and made himself more comfortable on the muddle of towels. 'No. No, I'd never ask you to do that. It's a lovely house and it's yours. You – we – should live there.'

'But you want to live here! It's so much more comfortable here.'

He nodded. 'Yes it is, but we don't want to keep up separate establishments do we? I know it's an idea which works for lots of people, but I don't think we need a seven-bedroom mansion each.' He became thoughtful. 'Although that would be fourteen locations for making love. At least.'

Grace ignored this frivolity. 'But you've put your heart and soul into this house. I remember you saying how all the other houses were for other people, and you made compromises over materials, and that for this one, you had the best of everything.'

'I've put my heart and soul somewhere else now.'

'What do you mean?'

'You know what I mean. Or you should. They're with you. Where you want to be, where you are, is where I want to be. Besides,' he went on briskly, 'Luckenham House is beautiful, well worth doing up.'

'I know, I just don't know if I'll have the money.'

'If I sell this house we'll have shedloads of the stuff.'

Grace shook her head. 'No. I'll sell it, if you want me to, but if I'm going to do it up, I'll pay for it myself. Or not do it up.' She raised herself on her elbow and studied him earnestly. 'Does that seem mean? Or silly?' He didn't reply, and she felt obliged to explain. 'I've fought very hard to be independent and while I love you and trust you totally, for me, I have to keep something. If you paid to have Luckenham House done up, I know it would be beautiful, but it wouldn't be all mine. And while I'll want your advice every step of the way, colour schemes, everything . . .' she indicated the opulent, comfortable bathroom where they were having this intimate conversation. 'Although I did think that no one had carpet in their bathrooms any more and had tiles instead.'

'It rather depends on what you want to do in your bathroom,' he said soberly.

Grace giggled but wouldn't be distracted. 'I just need to pay for my house to be done up. I hope you understand, and don't think I'm being prickly.'

He sighed. 'No. I do understand. I just hope those bloody panels turn out to be worth something. Come on, let's get up.'

'We should. I've got to organise a plumber.'

'So you have.' But he led her into the bedroom, and they didn't get round to organising a plumber until it was nearly time to collect Demi from the bus.

While Grace and Flynn were otherwise occupied, Ellie was shown into a room containing a low examination table and a lot of equipment she preferred not to see.

'Here goes,' she said.

'And I'm right behind you,' said Ran.

'Just hop on to the table. It's not high,' said the woman. 'I'm Suzanne, by the way.'

Ellie smiled, trying to look relaxed, still so desperate to pee she was aching all over her lower body.

'Now, just pull up your jumper and pull your trousers down under your bump.' Ellie's eyes met Ran's. He smiled reassuringly. She gave a little sigh. She wouldn't have guessed that Ran had 'reassuring' in his repertoire of smiles, but he did it very well.

Suzanne spread jelly over Ellie's stomach.

'Oh, it's warm. I was expecting it to be cold,' said Ellie.

'Not these days,' said Suzanne. 'Now, I'm going to pass this instrument backwards and forwards over your tummy, and you can see what your baby's up to on those screens.'

Ellie looked and tried to make out a baby from the wavy, black and white picture which looked like a very badly tuned television. Suzanne moved her instrument forwards and backwards, until suddenly she stopped.

'Hang on,' she said, after peering into the screen for a few seconds. 'I'm just going to get someone else.'

Sweat immediately broke out all over Ellie's body. She suddenly felt so frightened she couldn't move or speak as she registered the implications of what the nurse had just said: her baby, which until recently had only been a reason for a lot of strange symptoms, might have something wrong with it. Why else would she need a second opinion? This was supposed to be a straightforward check-up but now . . . Ellie fought to stay calm. She had felt the baby move a couple of times since the first time, and it was just beginning to feel it was real. What if . . . ? She raised her eyes and caught Ran looking down at her. He took hold of her hand and squeezed it. Ellie closed her eyes and started breathing deeply, repeating silently, like a mantra, 'It'll be fine, it'll be fine.'

Ran didn't speak either. He just held her hand, very tightly, so tightly it hurt. Ellie opened her eyes to remonstrate but saw that he'd gone deathly pale. He must be squeamish about hospitals, she thought, which makes it extra kind of him to come with me. Having Ran's support didn't stop her anxiety for the baby, but it moved her, hugely.

Suzanne came back with an older woman. 'Now, let's see what's going on here!' she said briskly, and took Suzanne's seat, and her instrument.

'No, no. It's all fine.' Ellie relaxed, and only then realised quite how scared she had been. 'It's just a shadow. There's nothing wrong with the baby's heart,' the woman said. 'In fact there's nothing wrong with any of him.'

'Is it a boy?' asked Ellie, eager to know.

'Oh, sorry. No. I mean, I don't know. I just said "he" for convenience; you can't tell reliably at this stage. You'll have to wait a bit longer for that information, I'm afraid.' She smiled at Ran. 'Don't buy the train set just yet.'

'I don't think we mind what sort of baby it is,' he said. 'As long as it's healthy. Isn't that right, Ellie?'

Ellie nodded. She couldn't speak and she didn't think she could move. She was glad to stay where she was while the scan was finished and the pictures taken, so she could sort out her emotions a little.

At last, Ellie was allowed off the couch so she could totter to the loo. When she came out, Ran was holding a grainy picture of what was obviously a baby.

'Do you need to sit down or anything? You don't look terribly well.' He put his hand on Ellie's shoulder.

'I'm fine.' She tried to think of something flippant to say, but couldn't. 'I just want to go.'

'Come on, then.' He put his arm round her shoulder and walked her to the door.

Once in the car, Ellie felt better. There wasn't anything wrong with the baby, and they had pictures to prove it. Now she should thank Ran for being so supportive.

'Ran.' She wanted to put her hand on his sleeve but felt suddenly shy and she found her hand patting the air. 'I just want to say . . .' She faltered. At that moment the words 'thank you' seemed incredibly difficult to pronounce.

'What is it?' He was very gentle and it made her even more shy. She needed him to be acerbic and sarcastic, then she'd be fine.

'Nothing. I just wanted to say, thanks for being there.' She didn't comment on his squeamishness – he might not want to admit to it, but it made her even more grateful.

He didn't answer immediately, then he said, 'That's OK. You needed someone around to look after you, make you drunk . . .'

Ellie laughed, all the tension of the past hour dissipated. Somehow, she wasn't exactly sure how, Ran had made everything fine.

'Now come on,' he said. 'It's lunchtime.'

'I can't believe that's my baby,' said Ellie, when they were settled in a pub half an hour later, inspecting the photograph instead of the menu.

'Could you just concentrate on what you might like to eat?'

'Oh, I don't know!' It didn't seem important compared to everything that had happened that morning.

'Just think, or I'll decide for you.'

Ellie looked up at him. 'Really, Ran. Thank you. I don't know what I'd have done when – when Suzanne had to go for re-enforcements – if I'd been there on my own.'

'I couldn't have let you go through that on your own.' He stated it as a fact, yet there was a tenderness in his eyes which moved her.

'But you didn't know beforehand that there was going to be a problem. It all might have been perfectly straightforward, and without you—'

'I wouldn't have taken the chance. I'd never have let you go alone. Now, what would you like to drink?' He obviously didn't want her to thank him any more. He had shown a side of him she wouldn't have predicted – tender, paternal, protective – and she smiled, tentatively. She didn't want to spoil the moment; it would be a fleeting thing and there was no point in trying to catch butterflies.

'Tomato juice,' she said eventually, 'it's practically a solid food.'

'And then I think you should have a steak, something body building. You're eating for two, you know.'

'Yes, and one of them's the size of a hamster. A fact you've seen for yourself.'

'Nonsense. You need to eat properly. You can have a baked potato instead of chips.'

Something stirred in Ellie that was not the baby. It was a little hamster-sized feeling of hope. 'Yes, Ran,' she said meekly, not feeling meek at all.

He got up and looked at her for a few seconds before he went to the bar.

'I'd better ring Grace later and see when the house will be habitable again,' Ellie said when he'd come back to the table with the drinks.

'Well, make sure it's really habitable. It can't be good for you living in a house that's freezing cold and has no furniture.'

'Ran, people were pregnant and had babies before there were houses, on wagon trains, in tents. I'm a fit young woman, I'll be fine.' Although she was protesting, inside she loved the fact he was fussing.

'But there's no point in suffering unnecessarily. Are you finding the futon comfortable?'

'Sort of,' said Ellie, after a moment's thought. It could have been an opportunity, but she didn't know how to make the most of it.

'Only sort of? I'll see what I can do to improve things when we get back.'

'Fine.' Ellie thought that she would see what she could do to improve things, too.

'Shall we go, then?'

'I'll just pop to the loo.'

Ran made Ellie lie down on the sofa when they got back. 'But I've got to ring Grace,' she protested as he covered her with a rug.

'I'll do it. I think you should rest. Then we'll have a look at the futon.'

Ellie sighed and closed her eyes. Surely there would be an opportunity later to redirect Ran's caring for her as a pregnant woman into something a little less Madonna like while they were fiddling about with what amounted to a double bed.

'I spoke to Flynn,' said Ran, just as Ellie had dropped off. 'He says Luckenham House won't be habitable for at least a week. In fact, he's going to try and keep Grace with him until the house is properly done up.'

'Oh. That's a bit of a surprise. I mean Grace – I can't see Grace being willing—'

'What?'

'Well, I can't imagine her staying with Flynn until Luckenham House is decorated unless—' She cleared her throat, embarrassed. 'Well, you know, she and Flynn are – close.'

'Well, close or not, you're not going to want to be there by yourself, and even if you did, I wouldn't be happy about it.'

This snippet made Ellie very happy, but she didn't let on. 'Well, I won't be there by myself. Demi will be there too.'

'I wouldn't consider Demi, who I am sure is a lovely girl, a fit person to keep an eye on you while you're pregnant.'

'Wouldn't you?' It was music to her ears. 'But I don't need anyone to keep an eye—'

'Anyway, Demi's staying with Flynn and Grace.'

'Oh. Then I'd better go to my parents. Or there's the friend I was going to stay with before I went to stay with Grace,' she added, more enthusiastically.

'No. You'd better stay here. It's more convenient for doctors' appointments and things, anyway.' He looked away. 'Honestly, Ellie, I only realised today how fragile a pregnancy can be. You can't expect to just carry on as normal.'

'Can't I?' Ran was being incredibly bossy, but Ellie somehow didn't mind. She couldn't let him have his own way though.

'No. You need someone to look after you.'

'I'd better go to my parents, then,' said Ellie, sad, but firm.

451

'Why? I got the impression you didn't want to do that.'

She didn't, but there didn't seem to be much choice. 'I know, but I ought to see them, and it would only be for a short time.'

Ran sat down on the end of the sofa and looked at Ellie.

'It would be much more convenient for you to stay here.'

'But I haven't got another doctor's appointment for ages,' she said, slightly thrown. 'Besides—'

'You could have my bed. I'll sleep on the futon.'

For a moment Ellie was tempted – a week more with Ran – but then something pulled her back down to earth. Yes, it was a lovely thought, but it was playing with fire. She already liked Ran far more than was good for her, when he clearly had no intention of thinking of her as anything more than a friend, and in a week's time it would only be harder to leave him. She thought of the baby inside her: he or she needed a proper, grown-up mother, not an emotional wreck of a woman hung up on someone who'd never want her. She took a deep breath, and decided to be sensible.

'No. Sorry, but you don't understand. I can't stay with you, Ran.'

'Why not?'

'Because it's too hard for me.' She saw his confusion and forced herself to continue. 'Being here with you. I want something that you don't, and I thought I could hack it, but I can't. I think that scan made me grow up somehow, made me see things a bit clearer. Thank you so much for everything, but I have to go.'

Ran looked stunned. 'But I don't want you to leave.'

'You've been incredibly kind—'

452

'I'm not being kind!' he said irritably. 'I just don't want you to leave!'

Ellie stared at him, hoping for some indication of what he really meant. Why didn't he want her to leave? And why didn't he say? 'I don't understand,' she breathed eventually.

Ran exhaled deeply. 'Nor did I, until you had the scan.'

'What?' Ellie was more confused than ever.

'I didn't realise, until that woman had to go and get someone else, how much I cared that you were all right. It was such a shock, all of it, but the biggest shock was that I was terrified that something would happen to you. Your panic was all about the baby. But I was worrying about you. Ellie, I couldn't bear to lose you.'

'There was never any question about there being anything wrong with me—'

'I know, but it didn't feel like it at the time. You were coping so well, breathing, keeping calm in a crisis—'

'I didn't feel calm—'

'You were being so adult, and it made me realise how mature you are in some ways.' He gave a little rueful smile. 'Quite old enough to be a mother.'

'Just as well!'

'So if you're old enough for that, I suppose you're not too young for me. Or at least, you don't think so, do you?'

It took a few moments for his words to sink in properly. When they did, she got up from the sofa and shook off the rug. 'Certainly not.' She put her arms round Ran's neck and then, when she felt she had hugged him long enough, she kissed him. A proper, adult, x-rated kiss he could not possibly misunderstand.

'Are you sure you really want me to stay?' Ellie asked

a few minutes later. 'I can easily go home to my parents.'

'I'm quite sure,' he said definitely and kissed her again in a way that left no doubt that he'd stopped thinking of her as a child.

'I expect it's just because I can cook,' Ellie commented later with a contented little sigh.

'Oh no,' he contradicted her. 'You're good, but not that good.' And he kissed away her indignant protest.

Ellie smiled, blissfully happy. 'I'll tell you one thing, this feels right,' she said, snuggling up to him and pulling his face down so she could kiss him again.

'But, Ran, are you really sure you want to have a relationship with someone like me? You didn't seem to before.'

'I know, and now I'm not even sure why. It's just that, somehow, you made me feel like a wicked old roué.'

'That's my favourite kind of roué. What's a roué?'

'French for a dirty old man.'

'So what made you change your mind?'

'I just finally saw you for who you are. Thinking you might be in danger put it all into perspective, and I realised how much I care about you. And I also realised that although you're more grown up than I thought, you need someone, whatever you say.'

'I would have been fine on my own, really. I don't want you to be with me out of pity.'

'I know. But perhaps I need someone too.'

Ellie sighed with happiness and the kissing started again.

Grace rang Ellie at lunchtime the following day. She sounded dreamy and giggly and thoroughly silly. 'Don't tell me,' said Ellie. 'You've done it!'

'I'm certainly not going to tell you anything. Yes.'

'Oh, Grace! I'm so pleased! It's so lovely! Are you going to get married?'

'We haven't discussed marriage yet.'

'No, nor have we, but I think maybe—'

'Ellie? What's this? Are you talking about you and Ran?'

Ellie sighed deeply and nodded before remembering Grace couldn't see her. 'When we went for the scan – did I tell you he came with me?'

'Tell me!'

'Well, in the middle of it the woman who was doing it stopped, and had to get someone else to check everything was all right. Those moments while she was out of the room were about the worst in my entire life, but then afterwards Ran was really different. And finally, when I told him I was going to move out, he said he wanted me to stay, and . . . well . . . you can imagine the rest!'

'That's so wonderful! We could have a double wedding!' Grace was practically squeaking with excitement.

'With Demi and Allegra as bridesmaids. What shall we make them wear? Purple? Turquoise blue? Shiny satin, obviously, so they look really fat.'

'Poor Demi, she doesn't deserve that.'

'And I wouldn't start planning the double wedding yet, either. I think Ran and I have got a way to go before we start discussing marriage!'

'No, OK,' Grace agreed. 'But the reason I rang is Allegra wants to have a meeting of all the relevant parties, at Luckenham House, next week. Tuesday. Is that OK for you?'

'What do you mean "relevant parties"?'

'Everyone involved with the panels. She says she's got hot news and wants an audience to hear it. Can you and Ran come?'

'I'll have to ask him, but I expect so. Is the Richard Coatbridge expert going to be there?'

'I don't think so, though she did find one. She's terribly excited.'

'I can imagine. And so am I, actually. Never mind, it'll be fun finding out about the panels after all this time.'

'I know, as long as they are worth something. It'll be such a disappointment if they're not.'

'Should Ran bring the panels?'

'Has he finished them?'

'No. He's had to fit them round other work.'

'Then they may as well stay where they are, in safety. I'm not putting them back up, after all.'

'That's a shame, really.'

'No, actually, it's not. If they are valuable think of the insurance! Besides,' she added shyly, 'they may not fit in with Flynn's colour scheme.'

'Flynn's colour scheme!'

'Yes. He has got a good eye – and a good interior designer. He's made this house lovely.'

'So, are you going to live in his house?'

'Nope. We're going to sell it. He says he doesn't mind.'

'That's so romantic!'

'What, selling his house and living in mine, thus making a fairly large fortune?' said Grace crisply. 'Nothing very romantic about that. It's called property speculation.'

'No! Idiot! Giving up his dream home so you can have yours.'

'Yes. It is, isn't it?' Grace subsided into dreaminess again. 'He's so lovely.'

Chapter Twenty-eight

When Ran and Ellie drove up to Luckenham House four days later, they saw by the cars in front that Grace, Flynn and Allegra were there already. There was another car, long, low and expensive-looking, as well.

'That probably belongs to Nicholas, Grace's brother,' said Ellie. 'I hope they don't try and bully Grace.'

'They won't have a chance with Flynn there.'

'Although Grace has been very determined to fight her own battles lately, I've noticed.'

'Come on. Let's go.'

The front door was unlocked and Ellie and Ran went in unannounced. They could hear voices from the dining room and followed them.

Grace was standing by the window looking flushed and extremely pretty. Flynn was standing by a tea chest covered with a cloth, and on the cloth, were a couple of bottles of champagne and several glasses.

Allegra, in a black jacket with a hound's-tooth skirt, stood by the fireplace with a man Ellie didn't know. She assumed he was Grace's brother Nicholas. Next to him was a tall, slim, elegant woman inspecting the panelling. She looked part of Nicholas, and Ellie wondered if she was inspecting the panels for paint, and therefore more money.

Demi, who'd been texting someone on her mobile

phone, was the first to see Ellie and came up to greet them. 'Hi!' She hugged Ellie and nodded to Ran. 'This is all so exciting!'

'Not at college, then?' asked Ellie.

'No! I can't miss this.' She frowned. 'And I don't think Mum's coming, is she?'

'No reason why she should,' said Ellie. 'But would that stop her?'

Grace noticed that Ellie and Ran had arrived and danced across the room to greet them. 'Allegra is being terribly coy about what she's discovered, but Flynn and I thought we ought to celebrate anyway. After all' – she gave Ellie a meaningful look – 'lots of good things have happened lately.'

Ellie smiled in agreement; an awful lot of good things had happened to her lately, too.

The doorbell jangled and Grace went to answer it. 'Oh,' she said. 'It's you, Edward. And Hermia.' Grace waited for her emotions to come rushing in to swamp her, but nothing happened, and the certainty that she was now over Edward for good added to Grace's store of happiness, which was already pretty full.

'We didn't come together,' snapped Hermia.

'But why did you come at all? Not that you're not always welcome,' she added, opening the door, wondering what they would say when they saw that their daughter wasn't at college, and not really caring.

'I came to look after your interests, Grace,' said Edward. 'You're such a child in these matters.'

'What matters?'

'Money matters. Hermia told me about the panels.'

Did Edward and Hermia want a cut? Grace wondered as she followed them into the dining room. Well, not

Hermia: there was no way she could justify it. But Edward? No. He'd never been mean about money. He was presumably here just out of interest, or to protect her. She hoped there wouldn't be any awkwardness between him and Flynn. She absolved Edward of having any feelings for her, but she didn't want Flynn becoming all Irish and quarrelsome on her.

'Is everybody here?' asked Allegra, after greetings between parents and daughter had been exchanged, and murmured admonishments for bunking off college administered. She was obviously impatient to deliver her bombshell.

'I'll just make sure everyone knows each other,' said Grace. 'Edward, come and meet Flynn.' She made the introductions warily.

'So are you and Flynn together?' said Edward with a mixture of concern and amusement.

'We are,' said Flynn firmly.

Edward nodded. 'I thought Grace was looking even more lovely than usual.'

Grace looked away so she couldn't see Flynn's reaction to Edward's statement. It was odd: once she'd have opened a vein for a remark like that. Now, it was just a compliment – a nice compliment, but no more than that – from a man she'd once loved. When she was confident a fight wasn't going to break out, she added, 'Edward, you know Nicholas, of course. And that's his girlfriend, Erica.' Erica nodded at Edward across the room.

'Right, *now* we're all here,' said Allegra firmly. She glared at Hermia, who was still telling Demi off for not being at college. 'Can you all stop talking, please?'

'What have you found out, Legs?' drawled Nicholas from his pitch by the fireplace.

'If you keep quiet, I'll tell you!' Allegra was getting annoyed. It didn't usually take her this long to bring meetings to order. Finally satisfied she had everyone's full attention, she began.

'As most of you know, it was thought that these panels were by Richard Coatbridge.'

'Who?' interrupted Erica, earning herself an unexpected place in the hearts of Ellie and Grace.

'He's very famous, darling,' said Nicholas.

Erica shrugged.

'And, fantastic as it may seem, it appears they are indeed by him!' Allegra smiled as if she were personally responsible for this.

'It's not fantastic,' said Ellie indignantly. 'I knew they were!'

Ran put his arm round her. 'Don't heckle, it'll only hold things up.'

Allegra glared in Ellie's direction, and she was quite glad of Ran's protective arm.

'Apparently it was known that he spent time in this part of the world as he had a sister in Devon and he used to break his journey here, often for several weeks, and—'

'So what are they worth, Legs?'

Allegra gave her brother a withering look. 'My expert wouldn't say. He said it wasn't his business. He could only verify that it was ninety per cent likely the panels are by Richard Coatbridge.'

'All this for nothing?' said Erica.

'No!' snapped Allegra. 'I went to Sotheby's and asked them.'

'And what did they say?' asked Edward.

'They said they couldn't possibly judge without

actually seeing the panels, but looking at the slides, and having documentary evidence—'

'That scrap of paper?' asked Grace, surprised.

'They would probably fetch around the two million mark, and if more than one person was really interested, it could go through the roof.'

There was a silence; at last Allegra had the attention that she wanted. Grace was feeling sick and Ellie supremely smug.

'So, what happens next?' asked Nicholas. 'Do we take the panels to Sotheby's?'

'The publicity will be enormous. Something like this, hidden for centuries,' murmured Edward.

'And the more attention they get, the more money they'll make,' said Nicholas. 'We may need to hire a PR firm to make sure every reputable museum and buyer in the world knows they're on the market.'

'Who would you recommend?' asked Allegra.

'Ask Erica. It's more her field than mine—'

'No,' said Grace loudly and firmly. 'I don't want any publicity.'

'But you have to have publicity – I mean, lost old masters and publicity go together,' explained Nicholas. 'You can't have one without the other.'

'I'm afraid they're going to have to. I'm not having the place swarming with press and photographers and all that nonsense. I'm trying to get my life together. I don't want any of that.'

'I'd be there to support you,' said Flynn.

'I know, but I'm still not having it. Can you imagine it? The place full of people, the phone ringing all the time; it would be ghastly.'

'Oh, Grace! You're such a wimp sometimes,' said

Allegra. 'Not to mention ungrateful. I've gone to all this trouble to find out about those bloody panels, and now you say you're not going to sell them.'

'I didn't say that. I just said I wasn't going to have a whole lot of publicity.'

'You won't be able to avoid it,' said Nicholas. 'Not if you do want to sell them.'

'She doesn't have a choice about selling them.' Allegra snapped. 'She needs the money! How else is she going to pay for the dry rot?'

'I didn't know you had to buy it, I thought it just came with the territory,' said Erica dryly.

Grace regarded her with more interest than she had done previously; she had a sense of humour.

'Perhaps now would be the time to tell people, darling,' said Flynn and then addressed the room. 'We're going to get married. If Grace doesn't want to sell the panels she doesn't have to. I'll pay for the dry rot.'

'You never said anything about getting married!' Allegra was furious.

'No, you didn't,' said Grace, turning to Flynn, her face a mixture of surprise and delight.

'Didn't I? Sorry! I'm so forgetful. Grace, will you marry me?'

Grace collapsed into giggles. It was so ridiculous, being proposed to in a room full of people that included her ex-husband. Behind her laughter she felt giddy with happiness.

'Well?' demanded Flynn.

'Ask me again later,' she said, teasing him, her eyes giving him his answer. 'I can't think about that now. But I'm definitely going to sell the panels. I'm not having my – husband – paying for my dry rot.'

'Hm,' said Edward. 'You didn't seem to mind me paying to fix the roof.'

'That was my divorce settlement. You weren't my husband at the time.'

'I see, a subtle but important difference.'

'I don't suppose we could open the champagne, could we?' said Erica. 'I've been staring at it for ages, and I am dying for a drink.'

'Yes of course,' said Grace. 'Where are my manners? Flynn, be a love and—'

'Of course, darling, on the small condition that you answer my previous question in the affirmative.'

She flapped her hand at him merrily. 'I said I'll speak to you later, but do open the champagne.'

'OK,' said Flynn, putting a cloth round a bottle and adjusting glasses. 'Just as long as we're definitely celebrating.'

'It seems to me there's loads to celebrate,' said Erica eager to get to the champagne.

'Oh, this is so exciting,' said Demi, jumping up and down and clapping. Then she stopped. 'Will this mean you won't want me to live with you any more?'

'Not at all, Demi!' said Grace. 'You can live with us as long as you like.'

'Until you go travelling, anyway,' said Flynn, possibly less enthusiastic than his fiancée about this arrangement.

'She's not going travelling! She's going straight to university!' snapped Hermia.

'I wish you'd all concentrate!' said Allegra. 'Some valuable old masters have been discovered, and Grace is refusing all publicity!'

'And yet she does want to sell them,' agreed Nicholas.

464

'There must be another way,' said Ellie, handing round glasses.

'There is,' said Ran.

'What?' demanded everyone.

'Sell them to a private buyer.'

'But how can you find a private buyer if Grace doesn't want anyone to know they exist?' demanded Allegra.

'Sorry to interrupt, everyone,' said Flynn. 'But could we just have a small toast to our engagement? I know it's not important in the present scheme of things, but I wouldn't like the moment to go unmarked.'

'Oh for goodness' sake,' hissed Allegra.

Grace caught sight of Ran putting his arm round Ellie again and wondered if they had an announcement too, but decided it was too soon for them just yet.

'What is it about men, having to do everything in public?' asked Erica. 'Why can't they even ask a woman to marry them while they're alone?'

'You have to absolve *me* of that,' said Edward. 'I never proposed to a woman in public. We were always entirely alone.'

'What, every time?' asked Grace.

'Yes, cheeky!' He looked down at Grace, a speculative expression in his eyes. 'You really have got extremely attractive lately. Why did I leave you, I wonder?'

'You got bored, Edward.' She glanced at Ellie, hoping that Ran wouldn't turn out to be like Edward. She couldn't help feeling protective towards Ellie, and knew that Ellie felt the same about her. Grace and Ellie's eyes met across the room, both were rivalling the champagne for sparkle. Ellie gave Grace a happy, reassuring little nod, and Grace relaxed. Ellie had Ran well in hand.

Allegra, fed up with sentiment and lovers, raised her glass. 'OK, to the happy couple! Hooray! Congratulations, all that stuff. Now! Can we please get back to the point!'

'Which is?' asked Edward.

'How are we—'

'Is Grace,' corrected Flynn firmly.

'—going to go about selling the panels, even to a private buyer, if she doesn't want anyone to know they exist!' Allegra took a big gulp of champagne, obviously relieved to have finished her sentence at last.

There was a silence.

'Grace, darling, I think you might have to put up with a bit of publicity,' said Flynn. 'But I'll be there to protect you.'

'I don't think she should do anything she doesn't want to,' said Ellie. 'She's been through so much lately, and she's taken me and Demi into her home. I think she should just do what she wants.'

'Demi wasn't exactly homeless,' said Hermia.

'No, but neither of you wanted her living with you.' Ellie looked at both of Demi's parents, and was forced to acknowledge that Edward was very attractive, if you liked that sort of thing.

'None of this is relevant,' said Nicholas. 'Do you want to sell the panels or not, Grace? If you do, you have to cope with what goes with becoming a millionaire overnight.'

'No, she doesn't,' said Ran. 'As I said, there is another way.'

He had spoken quietly, in his usual slightly drawling way, but he got the attention of the room in an instant.

'What?' demanded at least three people at once.

'Don't you lot listen? Sell them to a private buyer.'

'Well, that's obvious,' said Allegra. 'But how the hell do we find a private buyer?'

'You can hardly advertise in the small ads,' agreed Nicholas. 'Millionaire wanted to buy old masters, with a box number.'

'What you all seem to be overlooking,' went on Ran calmly, 'is the fact that I am a picture conservator.'

'Oh, what's that?' asked Erica.

'He restores pictures,' muttered Nicholas.

'But what's that got to do with anything?' said Allegra.

'I'm in contact with private collectors all the time, when I'm not dealing with museums and art galleries.'

'So?' prompted Ellie.

'So, I've been making a few enquiries, and I happen to know a private collector who would be very happy to buy these panels.'

'That's fantastic!' said Grace.

'But I should warn you that you won't get anything like as much as if you had a big auction, with buyers from all over the world with millions to spend.'

'I don't want millions,' said Grace. 'Just enough to pay to have the dry rot fixed.' She frowned slightly. 'And to give some people a bit of money.'

'I think he'd pay the basic two million,' said Ran. 'But he won't go much above that.'

Grace suddenly felt faint. 'That would be more than enough for my needs,' she said weakly, after a few moments.

'But, Grace, you could get so much more!' insisted Allegra. 'Are you sure you want to throw away this opportunity to become rich?'

'I'm already rich,' said Grace. 'I've got this lovely

house and a lovely, lovely Irishman to live in it with.'
She looked at the lovely Irishman and smiled.

'Can you get in touch with this private buyer, then?'
asked Nicholas, impatient with all this sentiment.

'He's waiting to hear from me,' said Ran.

'I do think you might have said something before,'
Ellie complained.

He sent her a lazy, loving, sensuous glance. 'I didn't
want to say anything to anyone until we were sure they
were by Coatbridge.' He was almost the only person in
the room not jumping and down with excitement. 'I
told him it was definitely possible.' He looked at Ellie.
'Practically certain, in fact, and he's always very keen
on anything early English. I've done quite a bit of work
for him. I didn't say anything because I knew you'd all
be on me like a pack of jackals.'

'Ring him up!' demanded Allegra, not pleased to be
likened to a jackal. 'And put us all out of our misery!'

'Are you sure he'll pay two million?' said Grace, as
Ran fished out his mobile phone and began to search
through the phone book. 'It seems an awful lot of money.'

'He said he'd pay what a major auction house thought
was the lowest they'd get.'

'Is that fair?' asked Edward.

'It is if Grace wants to keep it all private. He'll also
pay for the restoration. Now, if you'd all be quiet for a
moment . . .'

'Ooh,' Demi squeaked, 'It's like *Location, Location,
Location*.'

'You watch far too much television,' muttered
Hermia.

'Will you please all shut up!' said Ran. 'I think I'll
take this outside.'

Although many were tempted, no one dared follow him. Flynn refilled everyone's glasses, including Demi's, until he got to Ellie. 'Oh, Ellie, we forgot all about you. I'll get you something soft.'

'I'll get it! I want to see the kitchen.'

'You don't,' said Grace. 'It's a mess. But it's going to be gorgeous! We've got such plans. If only Ran's collector—'

'Ah, here he is!' said Flynn.

'Right,' Ran announced, still very cool. 'It's as I said, he's prepared to offer you two million pounds for the panels, private sale, no publicity. He doesn't want any either.'

'He's getting a bargain,' muttered Allegra.

'I think that's fantastic!' said Grace. 'Can you tell him I'm very happy to accept his offer?'

'I already have.'

'Two million pounds,' said Demi. 'That's an awful lot of money.'

Hearing Demi say the amount somehow brought it home to Grace all over again. She put the back of her hand up to her face to cool her cheeks, which were suddenly flushed. 'Yes, it is, isn't it? An awful lot of money. Thank you so much for organising all that, Ran.'

'A pleasure,' said Ran going to stand by Ellie. 'I'm sorry I had to be so secretive about it.'

'So what are you going to do with all that money?' asked Edward.

Grace took a sip of champagne. 'I've thought about this already. I'm going to divide it into four parts. One part, I'm going to keep for myself, to pay for the dry rot, and do up this house. Another part I'm going to give to Ellie, to help—' she hesitated for an instant,

469

wondering if she dared make any assumptions about Ellie and Ran, but decided not although they seemed welded together just then, '—her with her new life, and the baby, and everything.'

'God, I knew babies were expensive,' said Edward, 'but I didn't realise they cost that much.'

'That always was the trouble,' muttered Hermia.

'And the other two quarters I'm going to give to Allegra and Nicholas, in case they feel they were treated unfairly by my aunt's will.'

There was a silence. Allegra blushed and even Nicholas looked abashed.

'That's awfully good of you, sis,' said Nicholas, 'but are you sure you don't want to get even more money for them? They're obviously worth a real fortune.'

Grace frowned at her brother. 'Two million is a real fortune, and I'm quite happy with it.'

'I was only thinking,' her brother persisted, 'now you've got a man to sort things out for you—'

Grace interrupted. 'Listen, everyone, I've made my decision and I'm sticking by it. I don't need a man to sort things out for me. I love my man' – she gave him a look which confirmed this more than adequately – 'but I can look after myself.'

'And there's no need for you to give me money—' started Ellie, but Grace cut her off.

'I'm not going to discuss it any more!' she said firmly. 'Is that clear?'

The room fell silent. It seemed it was indeed clear.

'Well, I don't know about the panels,' said Ellie, 'but it seems to me that Grace is definitely restored.'

'Yes, I am!' Grace confirmed. 'And now could I please have some more champagne?'

If you enjoyed Restoring Grace, *why not try*
Katie Fforde's irresistible new novel . . .

Flora's Lot

Flora Stanza has sub-let her London life in a bid to join the
family antiques business. Her knowledge of antiques extends
only to the relics of information she has crammed from
daytime TV, but what she lacks in experience she makes up
for in blind enthusiasm. So she is more than a little put off
when she doesn't receive the warm country welcome she
expected. Her curt, conservative cousin Charles and his
fiancée Annabelle are determined to send Flora packing, and
their offer to buy her out is tempting . . . until a strange
warning makes her think twice.

Stuck with a cat about to burst with kittens, Flora has little
choice but to accept the offer to stay in an abandoned holiday
cottage miles from any neighbours, let alone a trendy wine bar.
And between fighting off dinner invitations from the devas-
tatingly handsome Henry, and hiding her secret eco-friendly
lodger William, Flora soon discovers country life is far from
dull as she sets about rebuilding the crumbling business . . .

Read on for an extract . . .

Chapter One

A yowl from the plastic box at her feet made Flora look down anxiously. Was Imelda actually having kittens, or was she still just complaining about being shut up in a pet carrier on a hot summer day?

'Not now, sweetie, please!' Flora implored through gritted teeth. 'Just hang on until I've got this meeting over. Then I'll find you a nice bed and breakfast where they like cats.'

Aware that her pleadings were really a displacement activity, Flora picked up the yowling Imelda, hooked her handbag over her shoulder, hitched her overnight bag over her arm and went up the steps. She was slightly regretting her new shoes. They were divinely pretty with a heavenly fake peony between the toes, but not worn in and therefore killingly uncomfortable. Not one to sacrifice prettiness for comfort, Flora ignored the incipient blisters and pressed the bell. Seeing her own surname on the brass plate above it gave her a strange thrill. The family firm, and she was joining it.

The door was opened by a tall woman wearing a lot of navy blue. She was a little older than Flora, and had a no-nonsense look about her which inevitably made Flora think of Girl Guides. My shoes may be not quite suitable, thought Flora, to give herself confidence, but nor is that colour in this heat. In other circumstances, Flora thought, she would yearn to do a Trinny and Susannah on her.

'Hello,' said the woman, smiling professionally, 'you must be Flora. Do come in. We're so looking forward to meeting you. Especially Charles.'

Flora smiled too. 'I hope you won't mind, but I've got my

cat with me. I can't leave her in the car in this heat. Apart from anything else, she's very pregnant.'

A little frown appeared between the woman's eyebrows as she looked down at the box. 'Oh, well, no, I'm sure it will be fine for a short time. Although I'm terribly allergic, I'm afraid.'

'Oh dear. I suppose I could leave her outside the door . . .' Flora bit her lip to indicate that, in fact, she couldn't leave Imelda anywhere except at her feet. 'But she might have her kittens at any moment.'

'You'd better come in,' said the woman, her professional manner beginning to fray. 'We're in here.' She opened the door of a room which was mostly filled with a table, around which were several empty chairs.

The room's sole occupant, a tall, conventionally handsome man wearing a dark suit and a very conservative tie, got up. Obviously Charles, her cousin fifteen million times removed.

Not promising. Flora depended on her charm to ease her way through life and had learnt to spot the few with whom this wouldn't work. He was a classic example, she could tell; he didn't like girls with pretty shoes, strappy dresses and amusing jewellery. He liked sensible girls who wore driving shoes, or plain leather courts with medium heels. His idea of good taste was a single row of real pearls with matching earrings, and possibly a bangle on special occasions.

When the woman who had brought her in (displaying all these signs of proper dress sense) touched his arm and said, 'Darling, this is Flora,' Flora wasn't at all surprised to see the sapphire and diamond engagement ring on her left hand. They made the perfect County Couple.

'Flora,' said Charles, holding out his hand. 'How nice to meet you after all these years.' He didn't sound all that pleased.

'Mm.' Flora shook the hand, smiled and nodded; she wasn't that pleased, either. She had totally reorganised her life to take a part in the family business with, she realised now, desperately inadequate research. Charles and his worthy, conventionally dressed fiancée didn't want her, wouldn't make her

473

welcome, and her spell in the country could turn out to be horribly dull. Still, she'd made her bed, and she'd have to lie on it – at least until the sub-let on her London flat expired. 'It's very nice to meet you, too. I can't think why we haven't met before.'

'You spent quite a lot of your early life out of the country,' he said soberly, as if she might have forgotten.

'I suppose that explains it. We did miss out on quite a lot of family weddings.' She smiled. 'Though perhaps I won't miss out on the next one?'

'Oh yes, haven't you two introduced yourselves? This is Annabelle, Annabelle Stapleton. My fiancée and possible future partner in the business.' His smile, though conventional, did at least prove he brushed his teeth, which was something.

'How nice,' said Flora, wishing she'd made more enquiries about the business before telling that nice man of course he could have her flat for at least six months, she wouldn't be needing it.

'Yes,' agreed Charles. 'Now, let's sit down and discuss your part in Stanza and Stanza.'

'Would anyone like a glass of water, first?' suggested Annabelle.

'Oh yes please,' said Flora. 'And could I post a little to Imelda? In the box? I need to check on her anyway.' Flora delivered one of her most appealing smiles to her distant cousin, a last-ditch attempt to get him on her side. 'I wouldn't have brought her if there'd been any alternative, I assure you.'

'That's fine,' said Charles smoothly, almost, but not quite, concealing his impatience. Then, when the water had been dispensed and the cat seen to, he said, 'Tell me, Flora, I hope this isn't a rude question, but how much do you actually know about antiques and the auction business?'

Flora took another sip of water. 'Ah well, you pick up things like that as you go along, don't you?'

'Do you?' asked Charles, who had, she now noticed, rather

474

strange grey-blue eyes which, beneath his sceptical eyebrows, had the look of the North Sea in winter.

'Well, yes.' Flora tried to think of a suitable phrase, to indicate she knew more than what she had gleaned from a lot of recent, frantic watching of various afternoon television programmes on the subject. 'Cheap as chips' didn't seem to apply. 'Of course,' she said airily, 'having spent so much of my youth in Europe, I'm not so up on English furniture.'

'But you must be au fait with all those glorious ceramics,' said Annabelle. 'I adore ceramics.'

Just for a moment, Flora felt unsure what ceramics were. 'Oh, you mean china and stuff? Yes, I love it too. I collect teapots, funny ones, you know?'

Charles winced visibly. 'I think we'd better get on.'

'Well, yes, we'd better,' said Flora rashly. 'But I do wonder if we will.'

'What on earth are you talking about?' said Charles. 'Now . . .' He opened a file and drew out a sheaf of papers. He was not a man who would get behind with his paperwork. He had that look about him. He was a filer and a putter-into-alphabetical-order-er. It was painfully clear.

'Now,' he began, 'our mutual great-uncle left things slightly awkwardly.'

'Did he?' asked Flora. 'I thought it was all quite straightforward. You'd already inherited forty-nine per cent from your father, and I got fifty-one per cent when Uncle Clodio died a couple of years ago. Clear as sixteenth-century window glass, or something. Although I realise I wouldn't normally have been expected to inherit,' she added as consolation.

'Yes,' explained Charles, openly irritable now. 'But it is awkward. You own more than me. And you know nothing about the business and I've been running this auction house all my life, more or less.'

'Well, obviously I'm not going to sweep in here and make huge changes!' Flora made an extravagant gesture with her arms, observing at the same time that a good sweep, on the

475

floor at least, would be in order. 'I want to learn about the business I'm going to be part of.'

Charles and Annabelle exchanged questioning glances. 'That's encouraging,' said Charles warily, 'but it still doesn't quite settle the matter. I can't have you having more shares than I have. It doesn't make sense, on any level.'

The cat yowled, possibly showing solidarity with Charles.

'Sorry, I must have a peek. In case this is it.'

'It?'

'The moment when she really is going to give birth. It's her first litter, you see, and the kittens can come in about thirty minutes from when she starts. I've read all about it.'

While Flora fussed with the cat she thought about her own situation. She was obviously totally unwelcome and Charles was horrible. Which was a shame – she hardly ever disliked people. She'd probably better make an alternative plan. Staying in the depths of the country with a couple who deeply resented her presence was not going to be a lot of fun. 'If it wasn't for you, Imelda,' she breathed inaudibly, 'I'd hightail it out of town right now.'

'Tell me,' said Charles, when Flora was again upright, sitting back in her uncomfortable chair. 'What exactly do you hope to get out of your trip down here?' The grey-blue eyes were penetrating and cold – they really were just like the North Sea. Flora felt she was being interviewed for a job for which she had no qualifications – which, in a way, she was. She struggled to remind herself that, technically at least, she was more powerful than Charles.

She took a breath and didn't let herself be distracted by Imelda's yowl. 'I haven't been brought up in the business like you have, but I have known about it. I didn't expect to inherit, as I said. It was such a shock to everyone when Niccolò was killed in that car accident and even then, I never thought Uncle Clodio – did you know him, by the way? He was lovely – would leave it to me.'

'No. I didn't know him.'

'It broke his heart when Nicki died, obviously.'

'It must have been terrible,' murmured Annabelle.

'But really, we – my parents and I – were totally surprised when we heard about how he'd left things.'

'Then I absolve you of forcing him to change his will on his death-bed,' said Charles dryly. 'But it still leaves us in a difficult position. In theory you could come in here and upset everything.'

Flora smiled. 'Yes I could, couldn't I?'

'Of course you won't,' Charles informed her firmly. 'But it would be much better if we could arrange things differently.'

'And how would you do that?' asked Flora, sensing they had the perfect plan all worked out.

'Annabelle could buy three per cent of your shares, so I would have one per cent more than you. Which, considering I am the senior partner, is only right and proper.'

'And Annabelle would have three per cent?'

'Yes.'

'And you're going to get married, so between you, you could do what you liked?'

'Yes, but you'd still have forty-eight per cent which would bring you in a nice amount of money, when we make a profit.'

'Which you're not doing now?' Actually, Flora knew they weren't doing that well. She and her father had discussed it at length, but Charles was so prim and bossy that she wanted to make him say it.

'Not at the moment, no,' Charles admitted, 'but we do have plans to improve things.'

'Oh good. And now you've got me! I don't know all that much about the business, obviously, but I can learn. And two heads are better than one – or should that be three heads are better than two?' She glanced at Annabelle, who did not seem to be enjoying herself.

Charles frowned. '*Have* we got you, Flora? I was under the impression' – he glanced questioningly at Annabelle again – 'that you were only down here for a visit.'

'Well, yes, but I was planning to stay for quite a long time. Six months, at least. To see if I can stand – like – country life.'

'Six months!' said Annabelle. 'But where are you going to stay?'

Flora had been faintly hoping for an offer of someone's spare room, for at least a couple of days. As this was obviously not going to be forthcoming, she said, 'I thought a nice little bed and breakfast? Where they like cats?'

'Flora, before we get into the ins and outs of where you can stay, and I'm sure we put you up for a short time—'

'No, Charles!' interrupted Annabelle. 'I'm terribly allergic to cats. You must have forgotten.'

'Sorry, yes I had.' He looked pained for a moment. 'But anyway, putting all that aside for one moment, I think I should make myself perfectly clear. There's really nothing for you to do in this business. It'll be better for us – I mean Stanza and Stanza – and ultimately you, if you just sell three per cent of your shares—' Imelda yowled again. 'Have a short holiday if you must, and then take yourself and your cat back to London.'

'Ah – well,' began Flora, not willing to admit to being temporarily homeless.

'Your parents still own that nice little flat in Lancaster Gate?'

'Yes.'

'And you live there?'

'When I'm in London, yes.' And I'm not in London now, you prig, and I've sub-let it for slightly more than I pay in rent to my parents so I can pay off my credit cards, she added silently, knowing not even thumbscrews would make her admit any of that to Charles.

'So you could go back?' asked Annabelle.

'I thought I was coming down here to live. For the time being, anyway. Downsizing!' she added glibly, not feeling remotely glib. 'It's terribly fashionable!'

'But if you sold me the shares, you'd have quite a lot of money. You could rent another flat, pay off your overdraft,' said Annabelle, who also had blue eyes and an irritatingly patient tone of voice.

Bitch! thought Flora, she knows I'm short of money. She and Charles deserve each other. 'Well, put like that, your offer does sound quite tempting. Of course I will have to consult my father. Although I'm over twenty-one – obviously—'

'Not that obviously, actually,' murmured Charles, and earned himself a flicker of a frown from Annabelle.

'I do usually discuss things like this with him. My parents aren't in the country right now, but we talk on the phone and email all the time.'

'Good,' said Charles. 'I'm sure he'd advise you to accept Annabelle's offer.'

'He might if he knew how much that was,' said Flora and smiled. 'Have you got a figure in mind?'

'Ten thousand pounds,' said Charles. 'Quite a lot more than three per cent is worth, of course, but we want to be generous.'

'That does sound generous,' said Flora, who had no idea if it was or wasn't. 'Do you mind if I think about it?'

'How long do you need? To get in touch with your father, discuss it, etc.?' asked Charles.

'A trip to the loo would be a good start.' Flora not only needed the loo, but to rinse her wrists in cold water, to clear her head a little. It was hot and she was tired. She didn't want to find herself bullied into something against her wishes by this *Country Life* couple with colour coordinated eyes.

'Of course,' said Annabelle. 'Sorry, I should have offered when you first arrived. Stupid of me.'

'No, that's fine,' Flora replied graciously.

'Follow me,' said Annabelle.

'If you could just keep an eye on the cat?' Flora smiled endearingly at Charles, knowing it would annoy him.

Flora dried her hands on the roller towel in the dingy lavatory. Horrid soap, bad light and cheap loo paper, all things she would have changed if she'd been allowed. But although she was very disappointed at the thought that all her plans for country living had been thwarted, ten thousand pounds would sort out her remaining credit-card bills, put a deposit down, and pay quite a few weeks' rent on a new flat. Or she could pay off the tenant in her parents' flat.

She should have felt excited about these new options, but somehow, as she emerged from the converted corridor that was now the Ladies, she felt flat and deflated. Her skills might not have been directly relevant to an auction house, but she did have them.

An elderly man in a brown warehouse coat stopped her before she'd turned into the main passage. 'Excuse me, are you Miss Stanza?'

'Yes.' He was silver-haired and well spoken and yet the shirt and tie, visible beneath the long coat, looked rather worn.

'I'm Geoffrey Whiteread. I knew your great-uncle, years ago. I'm the head porter.'

Flora struggled for a moment. 'The man who holds things up at the sales?'

The man smiled. 'Well, yes, but there is a bit more to it than that.' He looked about him, strangely furtive. 'Things are a bit difficult. I wanted to speak to you.'

Never one to refuse to share a trouble, Flora smiled, even if it did all seem a bit Gothic. 'Speak away.' The man looked kindly and a little troubled.

Just then they heard the office door open and both jumped. The Gothicness was obviously getting to them.

'This will improve the air circulation, at least,' they heard Charles say.

The old man frowned. 'We obviously can't talk here,' he whispered. 'But perhaps we could arrange to meet later? It's very important you don't let that Annabelle woman get her hands on this business.'

'Why not?' Flora whispered back.

He made a gesture to indicate he couldn't go into it just then. 'Because she's a . . .' He paused, clearly on the verge of saying something very rude about Annabelle, and then changed his mind. 'We can't talk here,' he repeated.

With the door open, Imelda's next protest was clearly audible. 'I'd better go back,' Flora nodded. 'Isn't there anything you can tell me now?'

The man shook his head. 'Not now. Just don't let her take control of the business. She's a holy terror.'

Scared lest her words be heard, Flora nodded again and set off slowly towards the door. She had obviously strayed into some sort of mystery novel, and she, Flora, would have to rescue this poor old man from the exploitative fiancée.

'She's a complete airhead,' she heard the exploitative fiancée say. 'But I expect she'll take the money. A fashion victim like her will jump at it.'

Fashion victim? Flora exchanged outraged glances with Geoffrey, who was listening with equal horror. She liked clothes, but fashion victim? Huh!

A chuckle, presumably from Charles, greeted this. 'Yes, she's obviously a natural blonde.'

Flora narrowed her eyes. 'Not as natural as all that,' she mouthed to Geoffrey.

'I never dreamt she'd want to stay,' said Annabelle.

Flora was confused. She knew she'd sent an email stating firmly she was going to take some time to learn what was what. She thought she'd been perfectly clear about it.

'I must say I would have thought even someone like her would have mentioned it. It's rude, not to mention inconvenient.'

'Actually' – it was Annabelle speaking – 'I think she may have said something about it in an email. I just assumed she'd take one look and run back to London.'

There was a small silence while Flora held her breath, terrified in case she made a noise and they discovered she was eavesdropping. 'oh'. This was Charles. 'We'll just have to hope you're right.'

'No need to go on about it, Charles,' said his fiancée.

Even Flora, who wasn't exactly warming to Charles thought this was a little unfair. He'd only said 'oh'.

'We'll have to try and convince her that staying is a bad idea and hope she takes the hint,' he said.

And before Annabelle could say anything more about her, Flora pulled back her shoulders and marched back into the room. Up until the 'natural blonde' comment she'd been in two minds, but that did it. No way was she going to let herself be chased back to London with a cheque for ten thousand pounds! Even without that sweet old man's Ancient Mariner-type mutterings, she was going to give this a go.

'Well,' she said, having made sure both Charles and Annabelle were looking at her. 'I've had a little think, and at the moment, I don't feel I want to take up your generous offer, Annabelle.'

'What? Why not?' said Charles, indignant and surprised.

'Because I really want to find out about my family business, to work here, to learn about furniture and things.' She was aware that the 'and things' rather detracted from her grand statement, but she hadn't had long to prepare and hoped they wouldn't notice.

'My dear Flora,' said Charles, unwittingly using a phrase calculated to turn his cousin into a bra-burning shrew, 'you know nothing about the business. You have absolutely nothing to offer us. There's no room for you. There would be nothing for you to do.'

'Is that so?' Flora replied tartly. 'Then why are you advertising for a "general assistant" in the local paper?'

'When did you see the local paper?' demanded Charles, as if her buying it had been somehow illegal.

'Before I arrived. I was looking for bed and breakfast accommodation.' She was actually looking for somewhere she might rent, for when the kittens were born.

'The local paper is not the best place to look for that,' said Annabelle. 'And I'm afraid there's absolutely none available at the moment.'

'What do you mean? There must be. This is a very pretty little town. Someone must do bed and breakfast.'

'Lots of people do,' said Charles. 'But there's the music festival on at the moment. The town is seething with violinists.'

'Oh. I wonder what the collective noun for those is,' said Flora. A sound emerged from Imelda's box. 'Perhaps that about covers it.'

A tiny crinkle at the corner of his eyes told Flora that Charles found this quite funny but was not going to allow himself to laugh. Well, at least he had a sense of humour, even if he didn't ever use it.

'I had thought of renting, eventually.' In spite of her brave resolutions she was aware that her voice betrayed her misgivings.

Charles sighed impatiently, as if dealing with a toddler he wanted to smack but had to placate. 'We seem to have got off on the wrong foot somehow. We're not trying to stop you being part of the business, it just never occurred to us you'd *want* to.'

This was sufficiently annoying to give Flora another shot of courage. 'No?' Her brown eyes were limpid with disbelief as they met his cold, blue ones. 'But I sent an email. I thought I was quite clear about my intentions. Or didn't you get it?'

Annabelle cleared her throat. 'It, er, it only half downloaded, so we didn't, quite. But I'm sure you can understand that Charles doesn't want you coming in here and messing about with things you don't understand,' she went on more briskly. 'Of course you will want to talk things over with your father, but I'm sure he'll advise you to be sensible and accept my offer.'

'Possibly,' said Flora. 'But I should point out that although he does advise me, I am old enough to make my own decisions.' Aware she was in a position of power, Flora's tones became low and gentle. Let them rant and rave if they felt like it.

'It will take a couple of days to get the legal stuff sorted,' said Charles. 'Perhaps if you had a few days' holiday down here, you might realise that a small market town really isn't the place for a metropolitan girl like you.'

'But where's she going to stay?' demanded Annabelle. 'I can't have her – she's got a cat!'

'And because I've got a cat, who might have kittens at any minute, I can't just go back to London. I might cause an accident. Imagine the News! "*Ambulance called to help deliver kittens after pile up on the M4. The RSPCA investigate.*"'

'Let's not get too worked up about this,' said Charles, not finding Flora's melodrama remotely amusing.

'No, let's not,' agreed Flora, disappointed that he couldn't crack a smile, even to be polite.

'Flora can stay in the holiday cottage,' he went on.

'Don't be ridiculous!' Annabelle dismissed this immediately. 'It's not fit for habitation. Otherwise we would have let it.'

'It's perfectly fit for habitation,' Charles contradicted. 'It's just not quite up to the standard required by the agency.'

'It's in the middle of nowhere!' protested Annabelle.

Charles didn't see this as a problem, in fact, it was probably an advantage. 'Flora has a car.'

'Yes, I have.' Flora smiled, not wanting this lovers' tiff to continue in her presence. 'The holiday cottage sounds wonderful.'

'Honestly, you won't want to stay there,' said Annabelle. 'It's right out in the country, near some woods. You'll be terrified of the owls.'

'You think?'

'I don't want you ringing Charles at all hours of the night because you're frightened of the dark,' Annabelle explained.

'Of course not,' agreed Flora pleasantly. 'Just as well I'm not frightened of it. And owls don't bother me, either.'

'Sorry!' said Annabelle in a rather patronising tone of voice. 'It's just that most people from London seem quite incapable of coping with country sounds – mating foxes, owls, cat fights, stuff like that.'

'When you've heard lions roar and elephants trumpet and there's only a thin bit of canvas between you and them, you don't worry about anything that can't eat you,' said Flora, believing this statement to be true, even if she had no experience of anything like that herself.

'Oh. Right,' said Annabelle, wrong-footed. 'I suppose not.'

'Does the holiday cottage have sheets? Saucepans, a corkscrew?' Flora enquired tentatively, not wanting to cause more annoyance than necessary.

'I'll pop home and fetch some things. I've got plenty of bed linen,' said Annabelle. She unhitched a serviceable leather bag from a chair and extracted a large bunch of keys. 'All right if I take the Landy, sweetie?'

'Of course,' said Sweetie.

When she was alone with her cousin, Flora said carefully, 'I think I should warn you, I do want to work here. I'll apply for the job as a general assistant, if you want.'

'I really don't think you'd like it.'

'You can't possibly know me well enough to say what I'd like and what I wouldn't! We've only just met.'

'I know but . . .'

'But what?'

'Did you used to go out with someone called Justin Mateland?'

Flora became wary. 'Yes. Do you know him?'

'We were at school together.'

'Oh, right.'

'Yes.' Charles's hard blue eyes drilled into Flora long enough to inform her that he considered she had behaved very badly to Justin. He didn't say it out loud, so Flora could defend herself, he just let her know that that was his opinion of the matter.

'Now we've discussed our mutual acquaintance perhaps we could go back to the matter in hand?' she said sharply.

'Which was?'

'The job? I was about to apply for it. If you could just give me a form I could fill it in.'

Charles sighed deeply. 'Oh, it's all right, you don't have to do that.'

'But if you've got other candidates to see . . .'

'No. There are no other candidates. We've been advertising for the post for weeks, and no one remotely suitable has applied.'

'Why not?' This was a bit worrying. Had Charles got a reputation locally for being mean-minded with no sense of humour and a horrible employer? It seemed perfectly possible.

'Because no one with anything about them wants to work here.'

'But why not?' She wasn't expecting him necessarily to admit to the reason, but she might get some clue.

'The wages, dear cousin, are crap.'

Flora bit her lip. Not good news, but not as bad as it could have been. 'I see.'

When he was quite sure that Flora was sufficiently subdued by the prospect of working for practically nothing, in a firm who didn't want her, while living in a remote cottage in the woods, Charles said, 'I must ring the solicitor. Will you be all right here for a few moments? There are a few magazines . . .'

'I'll be fine. You go and do your thing.' She smiled again, from habit, but he didn't notice.